Prais

"I want to walk alongside the canals, my carrello loaded with wine and forget-me-nots, and lounge on my balcony, sipping a cappuccino and munching on a sweet cornetto in the mornings. What a charming journey."
ALKA JOSHI, AUTHOR OF THE NYT BESTSELLING *THE HENNA ARTIST*

"A literary gem that immediately seized my heart... I laughed, cried, and rooted for this extraordinary woman as she courageously embarked on a new chapter in her life."
CAROLINE JAMES AUTHOR OF *THE CRUISE*

"Vibrant as a glass of prosecco... sparkles with wit, wisdom, and warmth."
JANET NEWMAN, AUTHOR OF *LETTERS FROM CLARA:ONE INTREPID WOMAN'S TRAVELS ON THE EVE OF WAR- 1936-1939*

"Both a refuge and a delight... compelling, honest and ultimately uplifting story of love and loss, friendship and community, joy and self-discovery."
SUZANNE LEAL, AUTHOR OF *THE WATCHFUL WIFE*

"With a deft touch, she explores the complexities of grief, love, and the courage to begin anew in one's sixties... radiates with gentle humor and profound hope, transforming the deeply human experience of losing a loved one into a page-turning journey across the globe."
TANA JENKINS, AWARD-WINNING AUTHOR OF *SAILING INTO THE HEART*

About the Author

A transient life has seen Anglo-Australian Apple Gidley live in countries as diverse as Trinidad and Thailand, Nigeria, and the Netherlands, and another eight in between. Her nomadic tendencies saw the first draft of *Finding Serenissima* take place on St. Croix, in the US Virgin Islands, and the last in South Cambridgeshire, England, where she currently lives.

Her roles have been varied—editor, intercultural trainer for multi-national corporations, British Honorary Consul to Equatorial Guinea, among others.

Gidley began writing in 2010, and this, her sixth book, will be followed by a return to historical fiction with the publication of *Annie's Day* in November 2025. She has written for magazines, has short stories in anthologies, leads the Ickleton Jotters in their search for the perfect story, and writes an irregular blog, A Broad View. Research has started on her next historical novel, once again set amidst the turmoil of war.

www.applegidley.com

Finding Serenissima

Apple Gidley

www.vineleavespress.com

For my sister, Val

"Whenever the jetty fountains splash into the marble basins, they seem to me to be telling the story of the floating city. Yes, the spouting water may tell of her, the waves of the sea may sing of her fame! On the surface of the ocean a mist often rests, and that is her widow's veil. The bridegroom of the sea is dead, his palace and his city are his mausoleum! Dost thou know this city? She has never heard the rolling of wheels or the hoof-tread of horses in her streets, through which the fish swim, while the black gondola glides spectrally over the green water. I will show you the place," continued the Moon, "the largest square in it, and you will fancy yourself transported into the city of a fairy tale."

Hans Christian Andersen, *What the Moon Saw*
1805–1875

Chapter 1

Something woke Amelia. A sigh. A shimmer.

Palm shadows danced through the open shutters as a glow heralded a new day. That speck of time when the world was quiet, between the frog chorale of night and the birdsong of dawn. She lay still, breathing in the hush. She wriggled her toes and stretched, cutting it short when her calf threatened to cramp.

The pillow sank as she rolled her head toward Leo. She smiled. Those few moments every morning kept her going throughout each long day. Amelia wanted to lean across and smooth his tangled peppered hair, longer than style dictated, but that would disturb the peace of sleep; those perfect moments when his features were calm. No bewilderment, no belch of anger. No pain.

Then her world stopped.

✝

People came from America. From Australia. Some flew in chartered planes not wishing to chance the vagaries of the local airline. Those of a less risk-averse disposition gambled on scheduled flights with Air Niugini from Port Moresby, the capital of Papua New Guinea. However they landed at Hoskins

9

Airport, they all had to follow the road that skirted the sparkling Bismarck Sea to Patanga, Amelia's home. The car rental company in Kimbe did a roaring trade, as did the fleet of rundown taxis.

Whatever mode of transport, mourners found a way to the haven she and Leo had created on the island of New Britain. Back where it all began, back before independence in the mid-1970s The same people who insisted, ten years earlier in 2005, that she and Leo had been mad to leave the hustle of New York. The fêting, the openings, the parties. But people hadn't known.

Local dignitaries had come too. Their cars, windows blackened, lined the track outside the gates where their henchmen waited, idly smoking. Leo and Amelia had known some of the worthies, like Jonathan Pohai, in the early days, when heady nights had been spent drinking South Pacific lager and talking politics with the idealistic fervor of those eager to build a new country about to be freed from the mantle of Australian paternalism. Or, Amelia grimaced, just call it what it was. Colonialism.

"How are you holding up?" Tom Richardson, a friend from her Sydney days, handed her a glass. "You still on the gin and tonic?"

"Too right, thanks." She poked the slice of lime and took a sip, her eyes wandering over the milling people. "You know what, Tom? When letters began to arrive saying so-and-so would be coming to Leo's funeral, I had to scramble to put faces to names. Now I'm struggling to put names to faces. Most of whom I couldn't care less about, you and Delia excepted."

"Don't be too hard on them, love."

"You, and the girls, have been the only people to see us here, before Leo died."

"You two weren't exactly welcoming. Not," Tom hurried on, "that I blame you."

"Yeah, I know." Amelia raised her glass. "Thanks for this. I'm going to disappear for a few moments."

Avoiding eye contact and dodging reaching hands, Amelia eased along the verandah filled with the sound of clinking glasses, the occasional spurt of laughter bursting through muted voices as a Leo story was told, or retold. There were so many. The hubbub blurred as memories took shape.

Leo teaching English and social history at the high school in Rabaul, she home for a holiday from her job at an art gallery in Sydney, where she earned little but learned lots. A time before temptation and badges of office blurred the integrity of some. A time when they were all carefree.

Twenty years later, their return to Papua New Guinea hadn't been as tension free as either Leo or Amelia had hoped. Law and order could be a problem, even on New Britain. Sporadic rumblings over the production of palm oil bubbled like magma. Unlike before independence, when inter-tribal warfare involved bows, arrows, and spears, guns now exchanged shots. And rather than tribal rivalries, gangs now led the violence against other gangs, and expatriates. Port Moresby had always been mired in strife, but the ugliness had spread to Lae and the Highlands, and then to the outer islands.

In spite of this, the Paigntons had been fortunate on their patch of New Britain. They had few electronics and Amelia's jewelry—what she called her New York glitterazzi—remained locked in the bank. Their house meri, the Tolai woman who helped keep the place clean and tidy and relatively dust-free, had proved honest and reliable. Her husband had helped Leo with the boat and garden, eventually taking over the maintenance of both.

Carefree. The word floated back. Barefoot, Amelia grasped it and slipped down the steps to the jetty. Usually empty except for their little run-around, launches and dinghies now nudged each other in the idling tide. A couple of catamarans bobbed at anchor. She shrugged. Why not? It was a long way to come for a funeral. Ten years had been an age to wait for an invitation from Leo Paignton, although technically it had been an announcement in the *New York Times*, the *Sydney Morning Herald* and the local *Post-Courier* rather than a summons. Why not make a holiday of it? Amelia jumped down to the curving beach and splashed through ripples that sent silvery fish darting like memories.

Her dress, one of Leo's favorites from when he still had an opinion, billowed in mauve and green swirls like a ripe avocado as she sat on a palm trunk that reached over the glistening sea, striations of blue leading to the horizon and above. Voices but not words reached her from the bungalow, open three sides as an invitation to nature. Laughter trickled along the sand. That was good. Leo had loved to laugh. Back when the world had been colored. Before the invidious plaque jangled his brain and reduced both their palettes to black and white.

Carefree. She polished the word in her mouth.

"Mum?"

Amelia turned to her daughters, her lashes trembling with unshed tears. "Hello, my darlings. I'm fine. Just needed a moment. Everything all right back there?" She nodded toward the house but didn't wait for an answer. "Here," she said, patting the tree as she shimmied further along the trunk, her feet dangling over the water, "join me."

They sat, silent with their thoughts. Wind in the coconut grove rustled a psalm around them before it drifted out to sea.

A flash of emerald green, electric blue, and crimson disappeared into the encroaching jungle, a fig parrot on a mission. "He loved you. Deeply, proudly." Amelia broke the silence and reached for Moira's hand. "You must remember that. Not the last five years. They were nothing. A blip in all our lives." Moira, her eyes down, her voice tremulous, asked. "You didn't do anything, did you, Mum?" "No, darling." Amelia's words sounded hoarse, sad, before her head jerked around. "Oh, my God! You mean, did I kill him?" Tears held at bay coursed down her cheeks. She swiped her face. "Moira, no. God, how could you think that?" "Because it's been hell. We know that," Moira looked down, avoiding her sister's glare. "I just wanted to know. And for you to know we wouldn't have blamed you."

"Oh, my darlings, what a lot of things Dad and I left unsaid to you girls. Maybe we were wrong but we thought for the right reasons. You must believe that." Amelia leaned across Moira and took Lucy's hand. "We talked about the 'what ifs' before we left New York. Alzheimer's is often called 'the long goodbye.' And it really is." Amelia squeezed their hands. "Dad hated taking the pills, you know? He said they made him fuzzy. So he stopped and we agreed. No treatments. No rushing back to New York, or down to Sydney. Then the cancer. And we were lucky. It was quite quick."

"You should've told us, though," Lucy said, her voice catching. "Told us it was close."

"Why?"

"So we could say goodbye."

"Oh, darling, we all said goodbye years ago," Amelia paused, "I think it was his spirit leaving that woke me. A whisper of love." She watched their tears merge in the sea. "Huh," she said, "you can forget ashes to ashes. How about salt to salt? All we need is lime and tequila!"

"Mum, for God's sake!"

"Don't be silly, Moira. Dad would've thrown his head back and bellowed!" She saw a smile forming on Lucy's charming face and squeezed her hand again.

"Death is wonderful sometimes, girls. A release. Would you really want him to be locked wherever his mind was, or wasn't, any longer? And in pain he didn't understand. Cancer hurts." Amelia continued, ignoring their shaking heads, "You know, one word keeps coming back to me. Carefree. When he guessed what was happening, and after Alzheimer's was confirmed, that was when we decided to come here." Amelia looked out at the sea, which had been her solace. "Back where we started. Dad was too proud to suffer pity. That his slide into dementia would be recorded by journos, buyers, and friends. Here, we could just be. Not have to worry about what people thought. And those first years were wonderful, when we were building the house and when he could still paint. Look out there," Amelia flung her arm to where the sun had begun to dip into the Bismarck Sea, "how could we not be happy?" She sniffed, wiped her cheeks, and smiled. "Now, come on, we'd better go and toss people back on their boats or shuffle them off to their hotels. Thank God we never built the guest house!" Her eyes gleamed. "How's Liam doing in the hammock, Lucy?"

"Okay, I guess. This is so far out of his comfort zone, he's not sure what to do."

"Why are you with him?" Moira asked.

"Really?" Lucy sent her sister a filthy look. "You ask that today, of all days."

"Dad would've hated him," Amelia said, hugging her younger daughter. "He would have been oh so polite, and we all know what that meant. Moira's right. You don't need Liam."

"I cannot believe we are talking about this now."

"Why not?" Moira kicked sand in a damp arc, scattering tiny translucent crabs. "He is a hunk, in a gym-kind of way, but is it lust or love?"

"I don't know. He can be fun, you know, in his environment. This is just too far beyond his milieu."

"His milieu? Really?"

"Oh, shut up, Moira!" Lucy's push sent her sister into the shallows.

Amelia lifted her long skirts and joined her daughter. "If anyone is watching, they will think we've lost our minds as well."

"I wish you wouldn't say things like that, Mum," said Lucy.

"Lighten up, darling." Amelia stopped and shushed Moira as she opened her mouth. "Lucy, my darling girl, if you loved Liam, you would know. That's all I'm going to say."

"Thank God for that," her daughter replied. "Come on, people are looking." She hauled her sister and mother out of the water and, hand in hand, they went back along the bay, wet hems slapping their legs. "It's nice the Richardsons came, isn't it?"

"Very," Amelia agreed. "Tom was the first bloke Dad met in Sydney. And I've known him forever." She squared her shoulders as they approached the house, then stopped and turned to Moira. "I didn't really thank you for stopping in Lae to collect Dad's ashes, darling." Her voice quavered. "It was bad enough flying over with his body but the thought of bringing him home in a canister was too much."

"Oh, Mum, what a time you've had."

Mourners, drawn to Patanga for Leo, threw off their sackcloths and enjoyed the shimmering clear waters off the northern coast of New Britain before heading home, wherever that was. Much as Amelia enjoyed seeing some of the people she hadn't seen since she and Leo had run away, freedom enveloped her as she waved the last launch off. To be with the girls for a few short days before they flew back to their own lives. Lucy to Sydney, and Moira to New York. Liam's brooding departure three days earlier had also been a relief and, watching Lucy say goodbye, Amelia knew he would not be back.

She smiled. She wouldn't be either. That was today's task. She walked along the verandah surrounding the bungalow, each vista framed by roughhewn columns that held up the woven palm-leaf roof. She stopped in front of a portrait of the girls Leo painted when they had first visited Patanga, when he could still make magic with oils. Each had a hibiscus tucked in her dark hair, one white with a red stamen, one a frilled pink—the girls on the brink of life, not yet aware of their father's decline and thrilled to be on the Melanesian island they had heard so much about. The backdrop could have been sea or sky. Amelia loved it.

She turned to see them dawdling along the jetty, snorkels and masks in hand. They stopped to gaze at something in the crystalline water. She smiled. They hadn't been born island girls but switched gears the moment they arrived.

The coffee machine gurgled its readiness and Amelia poured mugfuls and put a platter of chopped pineapple, mango, and papaya on a tin tray, which she took to the top of the steps guarded by red ginger in huge Terracotta pots.

"Morning, my darlings! A good swim?"

"Lovely. You should've come," Moira wrapped herself in a towel then sat on the grass.

"I saw a spotted ray. Gorgeous. It stayed still long enough for me to see the pattern—lots of little dots around the wings, then bigger splodges spread across the main part. It will be no surprise to either of you," Lucy said with a laugh, "that my next design is going to be a sheer gray silk with polka dots!"

"You love it here, don't you?"

"Yup. Just wish it wasn't so far from New York," Moira said, eyeing the tray. "That looks like a sunset. Too good to eat."

"It's far from anywhere. Still takes a day from Sydney." Droplets fell from Lucy's long hair as she twisted it up.

"I shall miss it." Amelia gazed out to sea. "Some of it."

"What?" the girls asked in unison.

"I'm leaving Patanga."

"Why?" Moira asked. "This is home."

"Not really, my darling. You've swanned in every now and then for a holiday. That doesn't constitute a family home. Your homes are in Australia and the US, where you've made your own lives. And," Amelia smiled at her daughters, "that is exactly how it should be."

"Mum, it's way too soon to make decisions. It's only been a month." Lucy smoothed the lines on her mother's hand. "I read somewhere that no major decision should be made for a year after a death."

"That's pretty arbitrary," Amelia said, stroking Lucy's cheek.

"Not really," Moira chimed in. "It's so all the anniversaries are out of the way."

"Nicely put, Mo," Lucy scowled at her sister.

"You know what I mean! But, Mum, really, it's way too soon to say you're leaving."

"What you fail to realize, girls, is that I have had five years to think about it. More. Sometimes the thought of leaving is all that got me through a bad day. Not because I wanted to desert your father, but because I wanted his misery to end. And mine. So, no, I don't have to wait twelve months."

Moira picked at a slice of papaya then asked, "What about Patanga?"

"I'm going to sell it to NBPOL." Amelia spelled the acronym out for the girls. "New Britain Palm Oil Limited. They're interested. They'd like to turn it into a conference center. There's space over there to build some chalets." She waved to an area between the house and the coconut grove. "Or whatever they want. Where we talked about putting the guest house." She paused. "I'm sorry you won't get to play here anymore, but really, with the security situation, it is not an ideal place to live. We've been lucky. Others haven't. And honestly, I won't feel safe here on my own." She sighed. "Even with a guard on the gate."

"I get it, but you'll miss this, Mum. The water, the birds, the jungle. The solitude."

"Yes, all of those... bar the solitude. That's fine when you have someone to share it."

"Will you come to New York? Or go to Sydney, really back to your roots?" Moira asked.

Amelia looked at her daughters, doubt and concern clouding their eyes, and smiled again.

"Don't worry, my darlings, I'm not going to cramp either of your styles."

"Mum, that is not what Mo meant." Lucy rushed to her sister's defense. "Where are you going then?"

"Italy!"

Chapter 2

The motoscafo nudged the narrow wooden dock then jerked back as the driver slung a rope over a brightly painted post in the small canal. The Rio della Sensa, like most Venetian canals, had a narrow street on one side, while the other had walls rising directly from the water. The driver turned with a smile and held out his hand to help Amelia onto the steps, then heaved her luggage up. Next, he shouted to a youth lounging nearby to carry the signora's suitcase, and whose arms told a story of long hours in an ink parlor.

The fare, Amelia knew, was double that of a water taxi but exhaustion had swayed her. By the time the airport boat had dropped her off at Fondamente Nove, she had long given up counting time zones since she'd boarded the little Air Niugini plane at Hoskins. She longed to collapse into bed and sleep until the last three months of crying jags and packing cases became a distant memory.

"Prego, signora," the young man said, indicating she should follow.

Tattoos rippled on his arm as it flexed with the weight of her case. A few clothes, some photos, and novels, a guidebook to Venice, an Italian dictionary, and two large jars of Vegemite made up the contents. She carried her laptop, her camera, and important papers in her rucksack. The few trunks she'd packed would arrive eventually.

"Eccoci qui," he said, "here it is," pointing to an entrance hidden by large black urns filled with pink and purple hydrangeas.

Amelia scrabbled in her purse for some euros, but the youth covered her hand and shook his head. She smiled her thanks and tried out her Italian for the first time, "Grazie mille."

"Prego," he said again and, with an insouciant grin, went back the way they'd come.

The tall narrow building behind the urns rose three stories, interspersed with barely visible black wrought-iron railings. Baskets hung from them, brimful with geraniums that cascaded in a waterfall of soft blue and mauve down stucco walls aged a dusky pink. The brass handle shone against a heavy forest green door. Stairs led straight to a minuscule reception desk behind which sat a woman of indeterminate age, her bearing regal, her silver hair coiled in a chignon. She raised mascaraed eyes, the blue almost violet, beneath dark brows.

"Signora Paignton? Benvenuta!"

"Good morning," Amelia said, "I'm sorry. I'm so tired I can hardly think in English, let alone Italian. Your website said you spoke English." It was a question.

"Sì, sì. I am Bria Valentina Scutari. After today, only Italian. Then you will learn, eh?"

Amelia nodded.

"Come, sign the book. I must see your passport. It is the rules." The castellana grimaced. "Ecco. I take you to your room. It overlooks the canal but we are not noisy. Your case will follow later. Come."

Amelia's legs shook as they climbed another flight of stairs. She didn't know if she wanted to cry or lie down.

Signora Scutari pulled a huge black key from her pocket and waved it at her guest. "You will not forget to leave it at reception, eh?"

Amelia nodded again. A tired smile slipped across her face as she took in the four-poster bed; covered in a white counterpane, it dominated the room. An armchair with an ottoman promised long afternoons with a book, and a tray holding bottled water and a bottle of white wine in an ice bucket invited evenings of quiet contemplation gazing over the canal.

"The wine, it is from my family's vineyard. Your bathroom. It is small but has everything. Even somewhere to wash your feet!" Signora Scutari's laugh trickled like mercury at Amelia's confused look. "It is what the Americans and English do." She pointed to the bidet.

"And probably Australians," Amelia said, joining in the laughter.

✝

Exhaustion prickled Amelia like the scalding water as she stood under the shower and washed off the travel grime. Wrapping a towel around her chest, she stepped over to the window and looked out at people sauntering along the canal. Snatches of Italian drifted up, adding to her disorientation, her sense of displacement. Untethered.

"Well, that's what you wanted." Her words jarred loud in the calm of the room. "But Italy? You don't speak the language. You don't know anyone?" She could almost hear the words coming out of Leo's mouth, see the petulant tilt of his lips.

She shook her head, and clutching the towel, replied. "No, Leo, I don't, but I can learn. And, Leo, who was it that had to make a life for us while you painted? I can do this." The threat of tears dispersed as anger replaced rootless. Swapping the towel for a sarong, she lay down on the bed. Sleep. That would help. But not too long.

The ping of her phone alarm woke Amelia and, prizing her eyes open, it took her a moment to remember her surroundings.

"Oh, my God, I'm in Italy!" Laughter followed her pronouncement. Shadows playing a different dance to earlier in the day told her hours had passed. And the grumble in her tummy. She had to go out. Take the plunge. And her dictionary.

Pulling on a pair of jeans, she stuck her feet into ankle boots and tucked a green shirt into the waistband. A slash of eyeliner and mascara, a jacket and scarf, and she felt ready.

"I can do this." She repeated her new mantra.

Stepping out of the lift, Amelia saw that a young woman had replaced Signora Scutari at the reception desk. She wondered if the proprietress lived on the premises.

"Buonasera, signora, I am Martina." The woman looked up with a smile. "You go for dinner, yes?"

Amelia nodded, tightening the scarf as a blast of cool air came up the stairs. "Is there somewhere near?"

Laughter followed her question. "Always in Italy there is food nearby, signora. You turn left from the door, go to the next canal, turn right, and you will find a nice, small place. Tell them Martina sent you."

"Grazie, Martina."

"Prego, signora."

True to her word, Amelia found the trattoria. Almost too easily. The walk not long enough to gee herself up. She hesitated. Her stomach growled again. "Get on with it, Paignton." Leo's voice niggled in her head again.

"Buonasera, signora," the hostess welcomed her, saw the dictionary clutched in Amelia's hand and said, "Martina, she send you?" She smiled and urged Amelia further into the cramped restaurant. "You speak a little Italian?"

"No, not yet. I'm sorry."

"No problem. I practice English, eh?" She pulled the square table away from the banquette to allow Amelia room to squeeze in. "Is okay?"

"It's great, grazie."

Taking the menu, panic seized Amelia again as the print merged in a melange of unknown words. She blinked hard. Pasta. Fettuccine. Pomodoro. Okay. And vino. Not so difficult. Amelia looked around. The place seemed to be filled with Italians rather than tourists like her. She shook her head. Not a tourist. Soon to be a resident. She hoped. A woman, her hair permed into submission and sitting across from a grizzled man, smiled at her from the next table. A coterie of young women tottered in on high heels and made for a long table at the back, giggles and gaiety lingering as they passed.

Two men chatted as they lounged against the bar, their hands wrapped around glasses of red wine. People with other people. Amelia pulled out her phone. Who was she kidding? She wasn't checking for messages. Didn't want to see the headlines. But neither did she want to look alone. She should have brought a book, not just a dictionary. So she could look as if she hadn't a care in all of Venice. But she did. Doubts swathed her just as much as the chatter around her. What had she done?

"Get with it, Amelia."

"Prego?" The voice, a quaver, came from beside her. "You say something?"

"No, no, I'm sorry." Amelia felt her face reddening. "Just talking out loud."

"Va bene, okay." The man's grin showed sepia teeth.

She ordered her pasta pomodoro and a glass of house wine and as her stomach filled, and the wine eased her nerves, Amelia relaxed. She would have to get used to eating out alone. Tonight was the first step.

†

"Buongiorno, Luca." Amelia settled at her regular table with the local paper, Il Gazzettino. She pulled out her dictionary, more dog-eared each day, a notebook, and her red pen. "The usual," she called to the waiter's back as he flustered, flatfooted, into the dark interior to get her cappuccino and cornetto— though she still considered the latter a croissant. She smiled. He was a fussy man with a big heart, a white apron dwarfing his slight frame, his glasses fought a constant battle to stay at the bridge of his nose. It was Luca who had borne the brunt of her early attempts at Italian. He and Signora Scutari, she by far the harder task master.

Six weeks. She could hardly believe how much life had changed. Almost five months since Leo died. She rolled her neck and watched a couple clamber up from a vaporetto, the water taxi laden with suitcases. They looked dazed and disheveled. Perhaps they'd had a similar journey to hers. They didn't look Italian. Hours spent wandering the canals and alleyways of Venice, going into whatever place tempted her, then sitting at outdoor tables watching the world pass by, had honed her nationality-guessing game.

Loneliness was not a companion, although it took her a few weeks to realize. Life with Leo had been lonely. Now, she enjoyed the freedom to do as she wanted, when she wanted—a selfish existence that rejuvenated her. Amelia smiled. Forty-two years of togetherness. Heady, exciting years at the beginning. Following Leo and his dreams. Dreams that had become hers. Funny really. In those early days, he had seemed much more than eight years older. Papua New Guinea had been where he decided art and not teaching would be his life. And hers. At twenty, she'd had no real direction. Working in an art gallery had been fun, but she had the honesty to recognize she would never be a great artist. Instinctively she had known Leo could be. Instead, she picked up a camera and recorded their travels, their lives through a lens.

Every now and then, over the years, she had felt her eye the truer. But she had kept the thought to herself. Yes, she could manipulate color in the dark room, later on the computer, but the essence of a shot was always faithful to the subject. How many times had she seen Leo throw a paintbrush across his studio floor when a line did not convey his image of a subject? Painting, more than photography, always at the mercy of the artist. His interpretation.

In her newfound state of self, Amelia had, a couple of times, even ignored the insistent ring tone of either of her daughters. If it was urgent, one or the other would immediately try again, even taking time zones into account. She knew her decision had concerned them but how could this not be an uplifting way to start the day? She looked along the canal to where galvanized pails of fresh-cut flowers lined the worn stone of an arched doorway leading to the florist—blooms and foliage delivered every morning by what she called the petal pedalo. The new apartment in the Palazzo Ambrosio, off the next canal, would enable the continuation of her breakfast ritual. Amelia sighed. She would miss the luxury of a hotel, no matter how small, but it was time to step away from the comfort and protection it gave. Time to set up a home. She had been anxious about broaching the subject with Signora Scutari, then delighted when the hotelier had told her of an apartment that would be perfect. It belonged to Beatrice Bianchi, a friend who had moved to Rome to be near her children.

"Uffa! We Italians do not let our sons go easily," Signora Scutari had said with a sniff.

Amelia had learned that many of her hostess's pronouncements needed no response.

As she waited for her coffee, her phone conversation with Lucy a couple of weeks before intruded.

"But, Mum, does this mean you're staying in Italy, in Venice? I mean, not just having a lovely long holiday?"

"I hardly think even I, Lucy, would have packed up my home, then sold my home, on the thought of a lovely long holiday."

"There's no need to be snippy, Mum. We're just worried about you."

"Why? Because I'm doing something for me, not anyone else?"

"You know that's not what I mean." Silence prickled along the airwaves.

"I'm sorry, darling, but you both seem to think I am incapable of managing." Amelia paused. "It's not always easy. I have been lost." Her soft chuckle eased the tension. "Both physically and metaphysically, and yes, I've cried, but I'm also happy. Now, instead of worrying, start planning a visit."

The apartment on the Rio della Misericordia—a canal that saw more tourists but still far enough away from the Grand Canal for Amelia to feel a part of Venice—was unfurnished. She looked forward to scouring antique shops for the perfect pieces. If she could walk out of the hotel with her bed, she would. She couldn't remember sleeping so soundly for years.

In the meantime, she would camp on an air bed. She had doubts about the tiny and dated stove but it would do for now. As would the gurgling fridge. The best part was the old claw-foot tub, the ubiquitous bidet, her bedroom, and the high-ceilinged reception room opening onto the canal, with a balcony just wide enough for two little chairs and a table. And the flowers. She had to have pots of flowers, and herbs.

She smiled her thanks as Luca dusted imaginary motes off the table before offloading his tray.

"Today you move, sì?"

"Yes," she agreed, "but tomorrow I shall be here for breakfast."

"Bene!"

Amelia blew on her steaming coffee, then sipped and licked fluffs of foam from her top lip before starting her morning routine of reading the paper. A smile flickered. Cartoons had been the easiest things to understand at first, but now it took less time, and fewer cups of coffee each day to plow through the print, and fewer red marks.

Leo floated in. Funny. He appeared more real to her in Italy than at Patanga. Comforting in a way. Amelia remembered telling him a few years earlier that she would leave Papua New Guinea when the time came, but she had never been sure he understood, or even heard. Now, squeezed behind a minuscule table at an outdoor café on a narrow, back-water Venetian canal, she felt sure he'd known. The knowledge alleviated any guilt she might have had at leaving the sanctuary they had created. But sanctuaries are for those wanting to hide from life. She wanted to live it.

She waved at Stefano, the tattooed youth, as he passed with the couple from the vaporetto. He grinned and called, "Buongiorno, signora. Today, eh? I 'elp you. One hour?"

"Grazie, Stefano. Ciao!"

Carefree. One of the first words she'd looked up in her dictionary. Spensierata was one of the few words she preferred in English. Spensierata sounded like she was waiting for something. In a state of suspense. She wasn't. Each day brought new experiences, new people, new words. It wasn't always easy. Tears had, at times, overtaken her determination. Like the time she'd become so horribly confused criss-crossing canals that she'd ended up at the hospital, where she would rather have stayed than ask, yet again, for directions she didn't understand. On occasions, she had returned to the hotel a blotchy mess. Magically, another bottle of Signora Scutari's family wine would appear in the ice bucket in her room.

Amelia thanked her intuition daily for choosing the Cannaregio area as her base. Quite by chance, she had found the perfect place to recalibrate. Even the many names for Venice enchanted her—Serenissima, La Dominante, the City of Masks, of Mirrors, of Canals, and more. Each name etched another facet of the city she was coming to love. Perhaps she'd add another word to her daily meditation—serenissima rolled off the tongue. She grinned, her titter quiet. She could do with some serenity but would give the dominante a miss.

She tucked euros under the saucer, waved to Luca, and sauntered down to the hole-in-the-wall grocery store at the end of the canal. Every couple of days she bought flowers. Today she added a bottle of vino bianco, some crackers, and a wheel of Fontina, a loaf of ciabatta, some Gorgonzola, bacon, and walnuts. And just because she liked saying the word, she asked for a bag of radiatori for the pasta. Lunch and dinner in one fell swoop. Carefree.

Chapter 3

Two months later, Amelia stood on the balcony off her bedroom, the canal glinting below as traffic on the waterways slowed and residents ventured out for cicchetti, the delicious morsels that accompanied an apéritif. "Oh, Leo, I do wish you were here. Why didn't we ever come to Italy?" She turned and raised her glass of Campari and soda to the apartment, the slap of water from the canal the music of the moment.

Her air bed lay on the floor. The perfect bed had not yet materialized but, apart from an inelegant start to the day as she clambered upright to the sound of creaking joints and a groan, sleeping on the floor had not presented a problem, although she knew the girls would not approve.

Like many buildings in Venice, Palazzo Ambrosio took up the width between two canals, rising from the water on one side with a cobbled pavement in front of the other. Signora Scutari had told Amelia it had been built in the fifteenth century, but it had the appearance of reasonable maintenance. She was yet to experience an acqua alta, the high water that engulfed the city periodically, but Amelia felt confident it would not unduly concern her up on the piano nobile, the main floor. She had been relieved to learn the building had its own septic tank, and even more relieved to know her little area of the city did not seem encumbered by sewage finding its way to the lagoon through adjacent canals.

The more she learned about Venice, the more grateful she was to Bria Scutari's friend, Signora Bianchi, living la bella vita in Rome with her sons. And long she would remain there, Amelia hoped as she wandered, barefoot, through to the kitchen. If she owned the place, she would punch out the wall and extend the kitchen into the dining area but, she shook her head, that was a pipe dream. Although she didn't know how long she could manage with the recalcitrant oven. She tweaked pink lilies in a straw-covered Chianti bottle that served as a vase and continued her conversation with Leo.

"I'm not sure how they managed it, but the girls are arriving at the same time in the morning. I'll meet them at Fondamente Nove. It's only one stop from the airport so they can manage on their own. Riccardo—you know, my friendly boatman—is going to bring us home in his motorboat." Amelia picked up her glass and continued past Leo's painting of their daughters to the second bedroom. The room was large enough for the two single iron beds she'd found in the flea market held on the last Sunday of each month. "I'm glad Signora Scutari came with me. She bargained on my behalf," Amelia explained, smoothing a sprigged coverlet. An orange box served as a bedside table, upon which an antique brass goose-neck lamp with a fluted Murano shade sat in all its refined splendor. That had been Amelia's first purchase at the market on her own. The next had been scatter rugs to hide the hideous floor, an ugly swirl of modern tiles wholly at odds with the high ceilings and general style of the apartment. "What I could do with this place if it were mine, Leo?"

†

"Benvenuti, miei cari." Amelia hugged her daughters close, tears not far away. "Oh, I've missed you girls."

"G'day, Mum. Wow, you look fantastic! Your hair's so short. It suits you," Lucy said, ruffling the curls. "You've changed my image of the blue rinse brigade."

"You do look great," Moira agreed. "Italy suits you. You look different. Younger."

"Carefree?" Amelia asked, laughing.

"Yeah, carefree! Oh, God, have you got a lover?"

"Moira! Really! No, I do not."

"Well, whatever it is, I want some. You're glowing."

Delighted, Amelia turned to the man holding the line to the motoscafo, its decks shined to a honey glow in the morning light. "Come on, let's get home. Girls, this is Riccardo. The first man I met in Italy. And I met him right here!"

"Riccardo, le mie figlie, Moira e Lucy."

"Piacere di conoscerti." Riccardo bowed to the young women, his smile welcoming. "Welcome to Venice. Come, I take you to your mother's home."

Stefano waved as they approached, idling the day away at one of his usual spots, waiting for odd jobs that would fund his next tattoo. Today it happened to be just along from the palazzo. Amelia felt certain he would have turned down any job in order to be the first to see her daughters, then report to the various people who had taken her under their collective wings. His eyes gleamed, and Amelia laughed at his eagerness to carry the girls' backpacks, his disappointment at their refusal palpable.

"Stefano, you and your father will join us for apéritifs later, yes, at Luca's?" Amelia's invitation mollified him. "Come on, you two, this way," she said, leading them along the narrow cobblestone pavement.

"How do people not fall in?" Moira asked.

"Muscle memory," Amelia replied with a laugh. "You'd only do it once, but they're not very deep. About a meter and a half, mostly." She stopped and looked into the brackish water. "Way back, in the dark ages of the 1950s, Venice began a massive project to drain and clean the canals, for the very first time."

Lucy looked down. "That must have been smelly."

"But imagine what must have been found in the silt."

"To your point, Moira, all sorts of artifacts, boats, even centuries-old structures surfaced. I guess they're in one of the museums. I must remember to ask Riccardo," Amelia said, moving the girls along.

"Not sure I'd want a swim, though. A bit different to Kimbe," said Lucy.

"Just a bit," her mother agreed, stopping at a double door. "Righto, here we are." Terracotta and white tiles led to an arched, inner courtyard at the far end of which an elevator had been added, sometime in the eighties. "Only one of you can go up at a time with your pack. Or you can put the stuff in, shut the gates and run like hell up the stairs, and catch it before it descends."

Moira swung her pack down, her face flushed. "Oof, that's heavy. Is that how you get your groceries home?"

Amelia looked at her eldest daughter, her eyes quizzical. Something felt off. "If I'm carrying wine, then yes. I bundle in my carrello, then leg it up."

"Your what?" Lucy asked.

"Carrello, a cart on two wheels," Amelia explained. "Nice and easy to get up and down all the bridges."

"A granny cart! No wonder you look so fit," Lucy said.

"Or I bribe Stefano."

"What's with his dad?" Moira asked. "What's his name?"

"Riccardo. He's a sweetheart. He, Stefano, and Signora Scutari are wonderful. They've paved the way for me with all the tradespeople in the area and have been kindness itself. And they have all taken responsibility for my Italian." Amelia touched Moira's cheek and smiled. "I've certainly mangled their language. Sadly, I don't have your gift."

"Of the gab?" Lucy called back down the stairs.

"Ha, ha!"

"Good grief, you've only been together a few hours and you've started." Amelia swatted Moira's arm.

"Actually, Mum, Moira's been in Sydney with me for the last few weeks. Then hours side by side on a plane. We're probably ready for a ding dong."

"What? Why? What's wrong?"

"God, Mum, nothing's wrong. I just needed a break from New York. And it's a slow time in the art world this time of year. Come on, hurry up and open the door, we've been longing to see your fantastico apartamento." Moira deflected any more questions.

"Wow! Okay, you win. It's fabulous, Ma. Wow," Lucy repeated. "It's bigger than I imagined."

"Not your room, I'm afraid." Laughter trailed behind her. "But you do have beds!"

"Don't you?" Moira asked, following her mother through the living room to her bedroom. "Really? You're sleeping on the floor?"

"I'm waiting for the perfect find. Come on, it's almost lunchtime. Let's celebrate and open some Prosecco. It's warm enough to sit on the gallery. I've hardly closed the doors since I moved in. I'm sure winter and rising damp will take some luster off living here but, for now, I love it."

"Actually, Mum, do you mind if I stick to fizzy water?" Moira said. "I'm feeling a bit spacey. Jet lag, I guess."

A slight frown furrowed Amelia's brow and she nodded, her back to the girls as she opened the fridge. "When's the baby due, darling?"

"How the hell can you know that?" Moira rounded on Lucy. "You bloody told her."

"No, she didn't," Amelia said, "I'm your mother. We can tell these things."

"I told you she'd sense something was up."

"Well, I thought I'd have time to choose my moment. Not the minute we walked in the damn door."

"I am here, girls." Amelia poured Moira a glass of water. "I didn't realize there was someone on the scene. You never mentioned anyone." She looked at her firstborn. "So, who is the he?"

"Not part of the equation, Mum."

Amelia bit off a tart reply, instead taking a sip of Prosecco. "Righto, I'm not sure what to say to that, darling. Unless this is an immaculate conception, or anonymous sperm donor, someone has very much been part of the equation."

Lucy swallowed a snigger as Moira glowered at her.

"It wasn't a one-night stand, if that's what you mean. There was someone, now there isn't."

"Does he know?"

"Nope. And he's not going to." Moira held up her hand. "No more, Mum. Decision made. That's it. Let's have lunch. Please."

Lucy jumped in to save her sister. "Good idea. I'm starving."

✝

Amelia worked hard to drop the matter over a lunch of prosciutto and melon, and summer tomatoes drizzled with olive oil on ciabatta, after which they strolled along the canal to Campo Ghetto Nuovo, the old Jewish Quarter and the heart of Cannaregio.

"I think this is where Shylock lived," Moira said, gazing at the muted colors of the buildings.

Lucy smothered a yawn. "Who's Shylock?"

"*Merchant of Venice*, oh philistine sister!" Moira sighed. "Shakespeare."

"I know!"

Too tired to sightsee for long, they returned to the apartment, the girls for a siesta and Amelia for a mug of tea. Her thoughts jumbled, she settled on the Lloyd Loom chair she had found, and which just fitted on her end of the gallery. A grandchild.

"Oh Leo, what the hell do I do now?"

She sighed. Of either of her girls more likely to have a baby before a ring, she would have put money on Lucy. She twisted her wedding band. Not that it mattered. Moira wanted the baby, even if she didn't want the father. But she had to tell him. Of that, Amelia was sure, although she sensed neither of the girls agreed with her.

"She should tell him, right, darling?"

A chuckle escaped on a wisp of steam rising from her mug. She'd get a hell of a shock if Leo ever answered. An image of Moira's previous boyfriend drifted in. An investment banker. A serious man intent on making a great deal of money from other people's money. But he'd cared about her daughter even if he had seemed to parade her rather than partner her.

Perhaps they'd got back together.

"I'm getting cranky," Amelia muttered. No one would be perfect for either of her girls. What was it her mother had said, when she'd first introduced Leo? Something about it didn't matter what she thought of him, no mother should allow a son or daughter-in-law to come between her and her children. Amelia had still been disappointed not to get a rapturous report card and had put it down to Leo being a schoolteacher and not something more prepossessing, in profession if not in looks. He had been gorgeous. Right until the last year, when his frame had shrunk and cheeks caved in. Dementia robbing him of his presence, cancer of his attractiveness.

Funny. Even when Leo had become the toast of New York, shown in London galleries, celebrated in Sydney, her mother had never warmed to him. And he had known but hadn't cared. A polite relationship had developed, friendly though formal.

"But, possum, what are you doing?" Her mother would ask.

A wry smile curled around the rim of her mug. If Moira didn't want the father in the picture, would that be such a bad thing? Plenty of women did it nowadays. Brought up children alone. Successfully. It wasn't as if Moira needed financial help. She had great friends, a job she loved—most of the time—an inheritance from Leo, not to mention some of his paintings which, if push came to shove, she could sell. Amelia snorted. Really? As if she'd let Moira sell her father's paintings. That was for a very dank day. And that wouldn't happen while she was alive. A baby. A chubble of delight! But it wouldn't be easy. No matter what her daughter felt now, emotions would come in to play.

Leo had been a good, if distant father. Spending days in his studio, and nights sometimes. But he was always there for high days and holidays. On show, making everything just a little brighter, a little funnier, whirling them and her in the air in his exuberance.

New York had been difficult, at first. 1984, a lifetime ago. A six-year-old and a three-year-old in a second-floor Harlem brownstone apartment. Amelia remembered the arguments. Leo determined to be on the edge, to live in the heart of life, while she worried about life. But he'd been right. They arrived in Harlem as the area began to lose its less salubrious image and she came to love the vibrancy, day and night.

That's what had taken him to Papua New Guinea in the first place. Wanting a life on the edge. Joining the Peace Corps had been his way out of the monotony of the Mid-West. Away from the plains of west Kansas. He'd told Amelia he never wanted to see another spike of corn. And yet one of his most successful series of paintings were of those very corn and wheat fields. But from a perspective twenty years after he left. Amelia thought of her favorite, one she had been sad to see go. A wide expanse of golden wheat ready for the combine harvester, fringed by wild-flowers in the foreground, and a bruised sky lowering above. That painting had paid Moira's university fees at The Courtauld Institute in London.

Kansas. Amelia smiled at the memory. Her preconceived images all fed by Leo's disdain for the state of his birth. She, though, had loved the vastness of the open plains. The colors, but not the tornadoes. His father, killed by flying debris while Leo was on the other side of the world, before Amelia had been a part of his life. And his mother. A woman, grown stout but still attractive, proud of her Germanic stock and who looked at her only son with adoration, tinged with surprise. So different from his elder siblings. Amelia wondered if they had sold the paintings Leo left them. Or hung them on the walls of their ranch style-homes, proud of the artist their brother had become despite his sometimes aloof manner. It had always been Amelia who smoothed their ready-to-be-ruffled feathers whenever Leo made a disparaging comment. She owed them a letter. Would she ever see them again? Probably not, but that didn't mean she didn't think fondly of them.

Family. Always complicated. But always family. Not something Leo had ever got his head around, instead choosing to play the role without committing the energy required to say "no" or to listen to playground woes of taunting, teenage tales of heartbreak, college inequities. That was her job. But it hadn't been a job, or a role. It had been her joy.

Amelia heard Lucy humming. Had Leo known she hummed when she drew? He had taken pride in her innate talent but had given little guidance, only disappointment when she had chosen design over pure art. Maybe now her daughter would paint. Now his censure, rarely voiced but evident, was gone. Amelia shook her head. That had been gone a long time. Maybe it would be that, time, that would lead Lucy to paint.

She dropped her feet from their perch on the balcony rail, waved and smiled to Signor Malvestio, her neighbor next door who would escape from his haranguing wife to his minuscule terrace to smoke his pipe in peace. His mustache was nicotine yellow, his eyes crinkled from a lifetime of squinting through smoke but they gleamed with humor and goodwill. Another Venetian who made it his business to help the canal's adopted Australian. Amelia picked up her mug and ambled to the kitchen.

"This place is heaven, Mum."

"I thought you'd like it." Amelia peered over Lucy's shoulder. "What are you working on?" she asked, looking at the swirls and dots dancing across the sketchbook page.

"Qantas will be a hundred in four years—2020. They're running a competition for designs for new uniforms. I thought I might enter."

"That's brilliant, darling. The fabric or the actual uniform?"

"Both." Lucy looked up at her mother. "I know it's not what Dad hoped for me, Mum, but I love it."

"Oh, Lucy," Amelia hugged her daughter, "that's not true. Dad was very proud of your work."

"Come on, Mum. He wanted me to paint."

About to refute the bald statement, Amelia was distracted by Moira rubbing her eyes and opening cupboards, looking for a glass.

"Huh, these are gorgeous, Mum," she said, taking the blue tumbler from Amelia's hand. "Did you get everything new?"

"Pretty much. I didn't see the point in packing up dinner services and glasses. I left everything in the house. But not much is new. I'm having fun finding things in the markets." Amelia took down another tumbler and held the pink glass up to the light. "It's funny, isn't it? For a man who considered himself Bohemian, your father liked things to match, be in sets. I don't think I've got more than three plates or glasses that match these days. If something breaks, well, ho-hum, I go in search for another mismatch."

"He wasn't always so straight." Moira defended her father. "Just when he got sick."

"Yes, he was, darling. He was great fun, but actually a pretty conservative kind of bloke. Those Kansas roots went deep despite his denial of them."

"Were you happy, Mum?" Lucy glanced up from her sketch pad.

"Of course I was, my darling. Until the last five years. That was hellish. But Patanga saved me. Saved us. And I do miss swimming. Now, enough of that. Don't forget we are meeting Riccardo and Stefano for drinks at seven. And the signora. Luca promised to save me an outside table."

"Thank God for Luca! Most Italian men's names seem to end in 'o'! I can see me getting horribly confused." Lucy smudged a line. Her focus back on her sketchbook.

Amelia laughed and poured herself a glass of wine. "Righto, I'm off for a bath."

"With wine?" Moira asked.

"Yup! My evening ritual. Pure decadence. La mia serenità!"

Chapter 4

The Paignton women sauntered three abreast along the canal. Their light-hearted laughter brought smiles from Venetians and tourists alike.

"I wonder what people think we are?"

"What do you mean?" Moira peered through a beaded curtain at the darkened interior of an enoteca. "These shops are tiny. How on earth do they make any money?"

"Which question do you want answered?" Amelia asked, smiling at her curious daughter.

"Both!"

"She means what nationality are we?" Lucy chimed in. "I play that game too, Mum."

"Frivolous minds, both of you." Moira dodged Lucy's jab.

"Yours, of course, is on a higher plane."

"Sure is. Like, how do they make money, Mum?" Moira asked again.

"Don't forget, we don't have supermarkets. Well," Amelia corrected herself, "there are some bigger shops but not like American superstores. Not in Venice. Shopping here is a daily adventure."

"I'd hate that."

"No, you wouldn't. You get used to it. And, to answer your question, people—locals—are loyal to their enoteca. The storeowners are the keepers not only of goods but of secrets."

"More likely gossip." Lucy grinned.

"Well, yes, that too!" Amelia admitted. "Remind me to take you to the vegetable barge near the Ponte dei Pugni. It's great fun."

"Pugni?" Moira asked. "Sounds like a boxer."

"Good guess, kiddo. It's the Bridge of Fists. The owner of the barge, can't remember his name, is a sweetie—he explained it to me. He's like a monk, bald but for a fluffy white coronet. And it doesn't matter what the weather, he wears woolen trousers, a long-sleeved flannel shirt, and a waistcoat."

"The story, Mum?" Lucy prompted.

"Oh yes! Well, apparently, back in the 1500s," Amelia chortled, "rival clans would have fisticuffs on the bridges, which didn't have rails or parapets back then, and they'd try and knock each other into the canals."

"God, can you imagine? Venice might not have been as populated but the sewage would be enough incentive to land the best punch, or duck." Moira sniggered. "Puts a whole new spin on shit-out-of-luck!"

"Why do you have to make it so lavatorial?" Amelia asked.

"She's right though," Lucy added. "I bet a few lire exchanged hands."

"Anyway, the Ponte dei Pugni was the most famous."

"I wonder when they added sides." Lucy trailed her hand along a low wall as they crossed another arched bridge.

"There's one that still doesn't. The Ponte Chiodo. Riccardo showed me. Can't remember why not. You can ask him in a minute. We're almost at Luca's."

"Speaking of Riccardo, where's his wife?" Moira asked.

"She died, a few years ago I believe."

"That would make him a widower." Lucy smirked. "Quite a tasty one!"

"Really, Lucy? If you want to continue that vein of thought, consider this, oh devious daughter, that could make tat-covered Stefano your brother!"

"Bloody hell, Mum, you win."

"Okay, both of you, behave, please. Signora Scutari and the others have been so kind to me. I don't want them to think I've raised ruffians."

Their laughter followed them to the café whose few tables and chairs, tucked into the restricted space on the pavement, provided little room for error for those either seated or walking past.

"Good, we're first here."

"Why?"

"I want to make sure Luca knows the tab is mine," Amelia answered.

"Er, Mum," Moira said. "I don't think you should do that."

"Why not?"

"Well, Venice is their city. They might want to treat you. Welcome us. Why don't you play it by ear? Or we just split it."

"Oh, I didn't think of that. But I invited them, Moira."

"Mo's right, Mum. Just see how it pans out. Keep it casual! Here come Riccardo and Stefano."

"Buonasera, ragazze." Riccardo's grin was broad under his waxed, handlebar mustache.

With drinks and cicchetti on the table and banter flowing, Amelia heard Lucy ask about the bridge with no railing.

"Ponte Chiodo. Chiodo means," Riccardo made a hammering motion, "nail. The name of the noble family who owned it. It remains private, so no need for walls. Uffa, in Venezia, we have many bridges." His mustache quivered. "You know of Ponte delle Tette?"

Lucy shook her head.

"You know, Amelia?"

"No, haven't heard of that one."

Stefano, his face red, protested, "Papa, no!"

Riccardo ignored his son. "It is the Bridge of Tits!" He guffawed.

"Let me guess?" Moira joined the conversation. "Brothels."

Straggling home later after a cheerful evening, Amelia watched her daughters ambling in front of her, and smiled. Moira would figure it out, but it didn't ease her concern.

†

"We'll have to come back in September." Lucy slouched on the sofa, her feet on the coffee table.

"Why?" Moira asked from her position at the other end of the sofa, her feet on her sister's lap.

"Because," Lucy thought a moment, "I think Stefano said the first Sunday of the month is when a gondola procession takes place. Can you imagine?"

"Yeah, I've read about that," Amelia said, sipping her tea, the smell of mint sharp and cleansing. "It's called the Corteo Storico—a historical procession."

"That sounds right," Lucy agreed. "And something to do with the Queen of Cyprus, and her abdication in the 1400s—Stefano's English, by the way, is bloody good. Abdication is a pretty impressive word to know."

"That's because it's a cognate—abdicazione."

"How do you know?" Lucy asked.

"Because cognates are the easiest words to learn in a new language."

"Smart arse!" Lucy threw a scatter cushion at her sister. Moira ducked. "No, just a linguist, something you're not."

"Enough, girls! I want to drink my tea in peace."

"Anyway," Lucy continued, "it's a big deal. Most of Venice comes out to watch from the canals and special floating platforms. The gondolas compete, and the gondoliers all wear costumes. Did you know Stefano comes from a long line of gondola builders? That's pretty cool."

"It's a pity gondolas are really only used by tourists now. Especially when you think they've been around since the eleventh century. Puts Australia in perspective," Amelia said.

"Only *white* Australia," Moira said.

"True," her mother agreed, then jumped back to Italy. "Apparently there's one gondola builder left, over on Dorsoduro. Might be fun to go, if there's time while you're here."

The girls nodded. Lucy winked at her mother as they both saw Moira's hand go to her tummy, instinctively protecting her baby.

"I liked Signora Scutari, Bria," Moira said. "What's her story?"

"I don't know it all. She's a widow. Has been for years. Comes from a wine-growing family. And she's been wonderful to me."

"How long's she had the hotel?" Lucy asked.

"I don't know." Amelia repeated. "It's quaint. No bar or restaurant, so I suppose more like a top-end hostel—without the shared bathrooms!"

"Or the bunkbeds and someone else's laundry strung everywhere." Lucy said. "I'm done with hostels."

"And you don't need a bar with one on every canal," Moira added with a grin.

Amelia stood and stretched. "Righto! I'm off to bed. I don't bother closing the balcony doors. Good luck to anyone trying to break in from the street!" She dropped a kiss on each forehead. "Night, night, my darlings. I do love having you here."

"Night, Mum," Lucy said. "I'm staying up, my internal clock is haywire."

"Me too, thanks, Mum, don't let us sleep in too late tomorrow," Moira added.

Lying in bed, the sound of her daughters' muffled laughter drifting through her door, Amelia smiled. The evening had been fun. That was something she loved about Italy. It didn't seem to matter if a hotelier rubbed shoulders with a boatman, or a contessa with a commoner... or maybe that was a superficial observation. Maybe she provided the common ground. The odd Australian searching for something—apart from the correct Italian word—even if she wasn't entirely sure what.

Chapter 5

Joy, and a few tears, punctuated their days. Wanting to see some of the countryside, the girls shouted down all Amelia's reasons not to join them on a bicycle tour from Venice to Florence.

"Come on, Mum, what a perfect way to see Italy. It's not too hot. And I'll be either too rotund or have a sprog in tow the next time I'm here." Moira's comment proved the decision maker.

"Fine," Amelia agreed, "but I want luxury at night."

Moira, ever efficient, found the ideal combination, even promising her mother she could have an electric bike if she so desired.

"Are you having one?" Amelia asked.

"No. We're young and fit." Lucy's grin sparkled up from under her floppy hat.

A challenge Amelia could not resist even if she loathed the thought of wearing a helmet.

"Fine." She looked at her daughters. "And not so young, kiddo. You'll be thirty-five soon. And you, Moira, at thirty-eight, will be considered an 'elderly' primigravida."

Lucy giggled. "Oh God, I love that. Elderly!"

"Shut up," Moira said. "You're not so far behind. And from what I saw, the only man on your horizon is Just Mike, and he knows you too well to be shackled."

"You got that right," Lucy replied, "but he's a good mate. I bet I could persuade him to fertilize me."

"Will you both stop?" Amelia said. "Babies are not to be taken lightly. Either having them or rearing them. Look at you two. A full-time job. And I wasn't a single mum."

"You were in some ways," Lucy said. "Dad wasn't always around."

"He was. For the important things." Moira defended her father.

"Actually," Amelia said, "the really important things are the day-to-day parts of life. The humdrum." She leaned over Moira's shoulder to peer at the website. "Now, show me. I don't want to see a picture of the bicycle. I want to see where I'm sleeping."

✝

Sitting at a tiny fish restaurant on the edge of a canal in Choggia, thirty-five kilometers south of Venice, Amelia wondered why she had agreed to join the girls. It was only day one and her legs ached and her bottom felt as if a thousand thumb tacks were playing pin the tail on the donkey. She groaned. She added a sore shoulder to the list as she picked up her glass. She'd never survive a week.

"I hate you, both," she said to her pain-free daughters. "And tomorrow is longer."

"It's flat though, Mum," Lucy said. "Until the last couple of days. That does look a bit hilly." She jabbed a finger at the map.

"You'll be used to it by then." Moira chimed in. At least we don't have to carry our own luggage and, because we're almost out of season, we don't have hordes cycling with us." She checked their itinerary. "Tomorrow we go to Adria." She read, "'A small, friendly city with lots of charm. Founded by the

Etruscans because of its proximity to the rivers Adige and Po.'
Yadda, yadda, yadda, I bet they're all small friendly places."

Amelia laughed and said, "Pregnancy is turning you into a
cynic."

"She's always been one," Lucy said, smiling at the others from
their tour. She took the itinerary from Moira. "The next day we
get to Comacchio. That's a bigger place. Lots of churches and
bridges. That's different. Huh," she read on, "used to be famous
for salt. Maybe tequila instead of wine." Lucy picked up her
drink. "I'm going to be sociable," she said, and joined the group.

"Darling," Amelia started, taking Moira's hand.

"No, Mum," her elder daughter said, shaking her head and
pulling her hand away. "Is this a setup? I'm not changing my
mind."

"No setup, but an opportunity I am going to take." Amelia
paused. "My darling, I know you want to do this your way, and
I get that. I really do. But this little being has a father. And he
deserves to know he is going to be a father. It's not just about
you. No matter what you think of him."

Moira's face took on the stubbornness of her teenage years.
"That's not it, Mum. He's a nice man. But would not want to be
in the picture."

Amelia buried her nose in her glass. "He's married."

"Got it in one."

"So, not that nice. Did you know?"

"He is, actually. Charming. And, no. Not at first. They were
living apart. A trial separation."

"So what happened?" Amelia's voice turned grim. "I'm sorry,
darling, but he doesn't sound that nice."

"You'd like him, Mum. He's fun. Anyway, I'm not going to tell
him. So that's it. We'd parted ways before I knew I was pregnant."

"Parted ways?" Amelia frowned. "If he was so charming, why did you split up?"

"Oh, Mum, life isn't always black and white, you know?"

"Now that, Moira, is one thing of which I am well aware." Amelia looked at her daughter, searching. "He went back to his wife?"

"Yup. She was pregnant."

"For God's sake, Moira. So the trial included benefits?"

"They were married, Mum. It's not like I had any claims on him. All very casual."

"Did you love him?"

Moira looked down at her sparkling water. "I could have."

"Oh, darling, I'm sorry." Amelia reached across the table. "Okay, I won't go on but I still think he deserves to know. And, Moira, there will come a time when this little baby will want to know. Might need to know. For health reasons."

"Then I'll cross that bridge when I get to it."

Amelia watched Moira's hand go to her stomach. She sighed. It wouldn't be too long before her daughter felt a butterfly flutter—that moment of realization that the growing baby was no longer an abstract event. That moment when every protective instinct was lit and would remain so for the rest of her life. "Okay," she said again, her eyes moist, "here's to my granddaughter."

"Might be a boy, Mum."

"Nope, it's a girl."

✝

The cycle path stretched across the dam dotted with white flamingos, their nests of twigs and branches visible meters away. The birds made Amelia laugh. Their pink legs seemed extra long as they picked their way across the water, knees on backward, as Lucy used to say. Amelia's legs reminded her today was the longest day, and she spent much of it wondering why the birds were white and not pink. She would ask once they got to Ravenna, their stop for the night. Now she just had to keep pedaling, training for tomorrow when the Apennines would loom. Her reward would be a piece of maiolica, the tin-glazed pottery from Faenza, a promised stop on their route. Visiting the ceramic artisans would be a change from churches. Plenty of which she knew would greet her in Florence the day after.

Her mind drifted as her legs pumped. Amelia was glad she'd agreed to join the girls even if aches accompanied her to bed each night, and a helmet-head hairdo. She enjoyed the taste of Veneto and Emilia-Romagna and knew both provinces deserved a less hurried return visit. She looked ahead to where Lucy cycled and chatted to one of the men in the only other group on the tour. Moira was cycling single-mindedly, in defiance, it seemed to her mother. Amelia could ditch neither her anger at the baby's father nor her worry at her daughter's adamant refusal to tell him.

Lucy's words from the previous evening reverberated to the rumble of bike tires over cobblestones.

"Let it go, Mum. She's happy with her decision."

"Not that happy if she flew to see you in Sydney," Amelia retorted.

"She's exploring options."

"What a ridiculous expression, Lucy. She's running from New York. Looking for a job."

"She's not actually, Mum. Come on, you know she's the smart one, she'll be fine."

"Moira is not like you. She needs, likes, structure to her days."

"Well, maybe being pregnant is giving her a chance to re-evaluate."

"That's another silly thing to say. When did you start speaking like a life coach? I'm her mother, and yours," Amelia's tone was acerbic. "It is my job to worry." Her bag over her throbbing shoulder, she had gone to the hotel pool to lie on a sun lounger and survey the stars. Not that they helped.

Maybe that's why today's ride was a struggle. She lifted her gaze from the monotonous rotation of the front wheel and shook her head. The bike wobbled and her legs reached down to stop a fall. She took the opportunity to take another photo.

"You okay, Mum?" Moira's voice floated back. "Isn't this just gorgeous?"

Amelia nodded. A giggle escaped her dry lips. What was it on the woven bracelets the girls used to wear? The ones with beads. That's right. WWDD. Their take on the more reverent question WWJD: they'd replaced Jesus with Dad.

"Well, Leo?" Amelia tugged the bottle of water wedged into the bike frame and took a gulp. "What would you do? Or say?"

There was no response. She shrugged. There hadn't been for years.

✝

Delighted to learn the final day would start with a train ride through the Apennines to Borgo San Lorenzo where they would, sadly, be reunited with their bikes, Amelia reveled in seeing the Tuscan countryside from the comfort of a padded seat. Her daughters had promised her the last cycle path would take them downhill all the way through the affluent suburb of Fiesole to Florence itself.

"I'm having a glass of Chianti," she said, looking across the piazza to where, ready for the final push, the bicycles, like malevolent broomsticks, lined the stuccoed wall of a palazzo. "I will never again take a train for granted."

"Well, make sure it's a decent one," Moira said. "Try the Rufina. It's about seventy percent Sangiovese mixed with I can't remember what. It's nice and fruity."

"When did you become a wine snob?" asked Lucy. "It must be mixing with all those rich New Yorkers. Oh God, do you remember, Moira, when we got legless on Chianti in a straw bottle?"

"We were teenagers," Moira excused their choice.

"Why, might I ask, were you drinking anyway? We were in the US. Where was I?"

"At some fancy-shmantzy opening, I expect."

"Anyway, you can't cry foul now. We were always allowed wine with dinner," Lucy reminded her mother.

"Not always. And watered down."

"Yeah, Dad said we should learn to drink responsibly."

"That obviously worked if you both got drunk the minute we turned our backs."

"Hardly the minute, Mum. You were out a lot," Moira said.

"Yes, I suppose we were. I never asked. Did it upset you?"

"No, we just got drunk!" The girls collapsed in laughter.

"Well, now you can't drink," Amelia said to Moira, "and I have no sympathy for you."

She grinned at Lucy. "Would you join me in a glass of Chianti Rufina, darling?"

"Did you know," Moira asked, changing the subject with a sniff and leafing through a brochure, "that Frank Lloyd Wright lived here? In 1910. He came with his mistress, Mamah Borthwick, to escape scandal. What a strange name?"

"Perhaps you could move here, Moira," Lucy said, her grin stretching wide, "you know, to escape your scandal!"

Moira shot daggers at her sister and continued reading. "Wow, she was murdered?"

"Here?" asked Amelia.

"No, in Wisconsin. She was fifty-four."

"Well, on that happy note, let's eat before we have to bike up." Amelia sipped her wine. "Mmm, you're right, this was a perfect choice. Thanks."

Moira laughed. "There's no need to enjoy it quite so much, Mum."

Amelia listened to her daughters—jousting, laughing, caring— and smiled into her glass. Families. Happy families. She would miss them. She shrugged. Enjoy them while they're here. She finished her lunch, her mind wandering idly from thought to thought when she caught a movement across the square and saw the guide checking bicycle tires.

"Come on," Amelia said. With a sigh, she paid the hovering waiter. "I'm looking forward to never getting on a bicycle again."

✝

The route took them to the center of Florence, and by the time Amelia clambered off her bike, her nerves jangled in time with the car horns and bells. Despite some bike paths, the traffic overwhelmed her. More so, she comforted herself, because there were no cars in Venice. She had got used to the slower pace of life. Cars had become smoke-belching dragons with flashing eyes.

"Never again am I doing that," she said to the tour guide, others in the group, and her daughters, as she handed off her bike.

"Oh, come on, Mum, it wasn't that bad," Moira said. She linked arms with her mother as they entered their hotel, close to the Boboli Gardens and where they strolled the following morning, admiring statues and grottos but steering clear of the Pitti Palace. Once owned by the Medici family, it now had lines of tourists stretching around the art gallery. Florence, even late in the season, remained busy. They had agreed to forego museums and galleries to just wander the city, though Lucy was disappointed to miss the Uffizi.

"The birthplace of the Renaissance and, when I get home, I'll have to admit that I didn't get to one of the world's most famous museums."

"Well, darling, you'll just have to come back." Amelia looked at her daughters. "I want to make a pact. No more than six months between visits, okay? Nine months was too long."

"Certainly long enough to make a baby," Lucy said, patting her sister's slight mound.

"Oh, shut up!" Moira said, swatting Lucy's hand away. "Okay, Mum, it's a pact. Though I won't mind if Lucy can't always make it."

"Yes, you would," her sister answered. "I'm the only one who won't let you get away with anything."

"What about me?" Amelia asked.

"Nah, you're too soft!"

Amelia wondered if indeed she should be more strident about Moira informing the baby's father of her pregnancy. Her internal conversation with Leo continued. Perhaps she had taken the path of least resistance but, she looked at her daughters sitting opposite her, the thought of animosity and tension hanging over her time with them tethered her tongue. Moira was an adult, for God's sake. And Lucy would side with her sister.

The two-and-a-half-hour train ride was infinitely more comfortable than the six-day bicycle tour but, despite her protestations, Amelia had enjoyed spending time with her girls. A time that was fast coming to an end.

Chapter 6

Moira and Lucy's visit had, in some ways, unsettled her. Despite their promise to meet up every six months, Amelia knew it would be impossible. Lucy's comment that she could visit them tickled the edges of her consciousness. Of course she could, but something was holding her in La Serenissima. Perhaps the need to establish herself without well-meant suggestions from friends. Buried in the serpentine canals and alleys was a good, actually a better place than most, in which to figure out what she wanted.

Blue gray wings tinged with pink fluttered in resigned indignation as she shooed a couple of pigeons on the scrounge for a breakfast crumb from her table at Luca's, then nudged the table leg to dislodge the birds from their continued scavenge. Pigeons, the bane of the Venice Municipality. Many laws, like dog leashes, speeding vaporetti, and even the arcane issuance of visas being connected to property rental agreements, were often ignored but the pigeon laws had become inviolate. Certainly, so Luca told her, since vendors had been banned from selling bird feed to massing tourists in Piazza San Marco seven years earlier. Amelia could find little appeal in anyone's desire to be covered in pecking, pooping pigeons.

Luca stood behind the narrow counter lined with Italians standing to gulp down coffee on their way to work or play. It had taken Amelia a while to remember that sitting at a table for breakfast automatically incurred a price hike. One she willingly paid for the pleasure of watching Venice come awake. But as a *cliente abituale* she now received the local discount. She left her euros with a nod to Carmella. Luca's mother, a woman never known to smile and whose sole manner of communication was a grunt, manned the till with steely determination and, disconcertingly, a crossed eye.

Amelia glanced at her watch and quickened her pace to see Signora Scutari—Bria. Though honored to have been invited to call the decorous *castellana* by her Christian name, it was difficult to remember. Amelia wondered about the seriousness of the hotelier's voice on the phone.

"Buongiorno, Amelia," Bria said, drawing her into the office tucked behind the reception. "Stai bene?"

"Yes, thank you. And you?" She took a seat in front of the desk, the only other one in the room little more than a box. "Something is wrong?"

"No, no. Well, maybe."

Amelia had not seen the signora so agitated.

"You like Venice, sì?" she asked. "You want to stay?"

"Of course. You know that." Amelia's heart sank. "Oh God, it's the apartment. Your friend, Signora Bianchi, she wants it back."

"No, no," Bria repeated. "She likes to stay in Rome. But she no longer wants to rent. And to buy she must sell her apartment here. Bah! She has money. Plenty. It is her son's."

The rest of the signora's words blurred as Amelia's mind scrabbled. Dismay. Then the flickering question, why not? Why not buy it? Would she even be able to buy it? A foreigner in Venice. She shook her head. Idiot. Lots of foreigners owned property in Italy. Peggy Guggenheim had, and now her place housed a modern art gallery. Why shouldn't Amelia Paignton? Let's start with an apartment. She grimaced and her head bowed at the thought of the bureaucracy that would be involved. Amelia looked up to see the signora watching, her gaze intent.

"One son, Andrea, in particular. Or maybe his wife." Signora Scutari's melodious voice harnessed her dancing thoughts.

Her last comment eased Amelia's consternation a moment, made her smile. Hell, she already knew what she'd do to the apartment if it was hers. The first thing to go would be the oven. Then the bloody fridge.

"Signora, Bria," Amelia corrected herself. "Do you think Signora Bianchi would sell to me?"

"You like it too much? It is old. Much work."

"I know. But I love it. I love living in Cannaregio."

"Your daughters. They will say what? Maybe they hope you live by them. And Moira. She soon will have a baby. You do not want to be near her?"

"No. I mean, I do. Of course I want to be part of the baby's life, but I don't need to live next door to do that. Do I?" Hesitancy crept in. Amelia could feel her Italian slipping away with her disquiet. She shook her head. "No. My parents, and Leo's mother, all had a good relationship with their grandchildren, and we didn't live on top of one another. And the girls have their own lives. Their upbringing taught them independence. They don't need me cluttering them up." Elation grew as she asked, "So, will the signora sell to me?"

"Sì, sì. Amelia." Signora Scutari looked carefully at her Australian friend before continuing in English. "You will allow me to help, eh? I know her boys. Andrea, he is greedy. Dario, he is not so bad."

"Shouldn't I get an agent?"

"Non necessario, I am your agent. But you will not pay me." Bria's finger waggled across the desk. "Momento." She was silent, her brow furrowed. "Ahh, first you must have la prova, er, proof, that she owns all the apartment."

"What do you mean, all of the apartment?"

"In Italy, sometimes a place is owned by many. After death. Perhaps, after her husband he died, her sons are owners too."

"Well, if they all want to sell, what would be the problem?"

"Ahh, Amelia, you are not here long enough to understand us Italians." Bria laughed a little. "We love to make things difficult, not only for foreigners, but for us also!"

Amelia blinked back tears as doubts crowded in, again. "Oh God, I don't know." It was all very well living in Italy on a whim, but to commit. Lucy's words came back to her. Too many decisions too soon. Would she even be able to get proper residency?

A bell tinkled and Bria patted Amelia's shoulder as she went out to the reception.

And how much would they want? What a privilege for that concern not to be the first thought. She sighed and stood to look out at the sleepy canal in front of the hotel. Her apartment in Palazzo Ambrosio was on the busier Misericordia. Huh! That would probably put the price up.

But to own a slice of a palace. What fun. And nothing was forever. Why not? While she still could. This was independence. This was carefree. She snorted. "Well, maybe not entirely carefree." Funny. She wasn't asking Leo nearly so much these days. But she hadn't had a full winter in Venice yet. The sky so far was either a brilliant blue or a murky gray. What if she didn't like the damp and fog? She could always head to Sydney if it got too bad. And the acqua alta? Wading along overflowing canals sounded the opposite of fun.

"So?"

Amelia turned at Bria's voice from the door. She smiled and nodded.

"Va bene, I will talk to Beatrice. She can be..." Bria paused, searching for a word, then gave up. "She can be spargere il cervello!" Her violet eyes sparkled as she laughed.

Amelia dug in her handbag for the dictionary. Flipping through pages, she came to it.

"Hah, scatter-brained!"

"Scarta-brain?" Bria asked. "I like. You go now. Tomorrow, the next day, you call me, okay? Don't worry, eh? There is no hurry. We move slow here."

Amelia hugged the straight-backed woman and breathed in the lavender that always surrounded her. She had no idea of Bria's age, or much about her history, but delighted in their growing friendship.

Back on the street, Amelia saw Stefano chatting with his father. She sighed, not wanting to talk to anyone at the moment. That would be difficult. A five-minute walk to the enoteca for a bottle of wine could take fifteen minutes by the time shop-keepers and acquaintances had been greeted. Part of the allure of Venice. She stepped out from behind the urns, each now planted with a small pine decorated with fairy lights ready for Christmas, to be immediately hailed by Stefano and Riccardo.

With a smile, she passed the time of day then headed at a brisk clip along to the little bridge that led to Calle Turlino and straight to one of her favorite places, Dodo Caffè, opposite the

Ghetto. With luck, she would be early enough to get a table outside. Even though a nip chilled the air, people preferred to watch the comings and goings around the square. She remembered the panic that had assailed her first visit when she realized she would not be able to hide behind a printed menu. Her usual fall back as she had played for time, figuring out what everything meant, and how to ask for it. Instead, a blackboard propped by the door listed the day's specialties. She'd been early and the waiter had taken time to listen to her garbled Italian and, even better, had replied in slow Italian. For that alone, the establishment ranked high on her list of to-go places.

"Ciao, Amelia," Matteo said, jutting his chin to an empty table as he slid past with a tray full of beer. "Il tuo soliti?"

Amelia smiled and nodded. With a jolt, she realized that even though she was alone, she wasn't lonely. The way living with Leo had been at times. She wrapped her pashmina a little tighter as a gust channeled along the canal. Would she, after years in the tropics, find it too cold in Venice when winter really hit? Underfloor heating would help. She shivered, not sure if it came from chill or anticipation. Maybe she should call the girls. No. This had to be her decision.

"Ecco qui." Matteo put the glass down on a mat, his usual pell-mell pace paused. "You are happy, I think."

"I am, Matteo." She nodded her thanks for the Campari Spritz, her go-to drink if out at lunch, the bitterness of the Campari tamped by Prosecco and a splash of soda. No more gin and tonics for this girl. She grinned. Who was she calling a girl?

"Ah, è Venezia!"

She raised her glass to him as he bustled away. She'd do it. Own an apartment in a palace. A laugh burbled up with the bubbles from her drink, and she reached for her phone. She'd call, not for advice, but to tell them.

"Lucy?"

"Hey, Mum. You just caught me, I'm heading out the door. What's up?"

Amelia laughed. "Darling, I'm buying the apartment."

"What? Wait a minute."

The sound of voices slithered across the oceans in a hiss.

"Okay, now tell me what's going on?"

"What about your date?"

"Not a date. It's Just Mike. We're meeting up with some uni friends for a drink, only down the road. I'll catch him up."

"Does Mike know you call him 'Just Mike?'"

"Shut up, Mum. You're really buying the apartment. How come?"

Glee, tinged with concern, erupted with each of her daughter's questions and exclamations as Amelia explained and answered, as best she could.

"Lucy," she said, exasperation creeping in, "I don't have all the answers yet, but I'm buying the bloody apartment, okay? Now, go out and enjoy yourself. Say hi to Mike for me. I love you, bye." Amelia clicked the phone off. She imagined her next call to Lucy's sister would be much the same, but that she'd wait until a more reasonable hour.

Amelia pulled out her notebook, scrawled with Italian phrases she'd heard and wanted to remember and, staring at a blank page, wondered where to start. She headed the page *Whys?* and *Why Nots?* and drew a line between, tapped her teeth then wrote in caps, *BECAUSE I WANT TO!* She snapped the notebook shut and grinned as her phone, face down on the table, vibrated.

"Pronto?" Amelia answered, not noticing who was calling.

"Mum, it's me." No evidence of sleep-tinged Moira's voice, despite it being five-thirty in the morning.

"I told Lucy not to call you! It's too early. How are you feeling? Is that little pearl making herself felt?"

"All the time. Don't change the subject. And really, Ma, you expect Lucy to keep that little nugget of news to herself? Wow. We did not see this coming. Are you sure?"

"Yes, at least I think so. It's only just happened. I'm sitting at Dodo's, grinning like an idiot."

"That's probably the Campari!" Moira's laugh trickled through from New York. "Oh, Mum," her voice turned serious, "so many changes in one year. Don't rush into anything."

"What, like not running away to Italy?" Amelia asked.

"This is a bit different. It's a real commitment."

"If it doesn't work, I can always rent the place out from wherever I choose to go next."

"My God, Mum. What happened to you?"

"I'm living my life, darling."

There was quiet and Amelia could almost feel Moira's thoughts turning.

"Well, then, that's great. Just don't get screwed by some smarmy-talking realtor."

"Signora Scutari is helping me. And there won't be any agents."

"A smooth-talking lawyer then," her daughter said. "You are getting a lawyer, aren't you, Mum?"

"Of course I am, Moria. I'm not a fool." Amelia's tone turned sharp.

"I know, I'm sorry. It's just so unlike you. All these big decisions made on a whim."

"Not on a whim, darling. On gut. There's a difference. Now go back to bed for an hour. You need to take care of my granddaughter."

"I think it's a boy," Moira said with a sigh. "Call when you know more. Promise?"

"Of course!" Amelia repeated. "Bye now. I love you." She pressed the red button before Moira could respond.

Chapter 7

On first arriving in Italy, Amelia had obtained her permit of stay and, within the required twenty days, had applied for residency. The process had been an early example of bureaucracy but not one which fazed her unduly, having been through similar hoops in Papua New Guinea and when they had first gone to the United States. There, her indignation had reached boiling point when an officious immigration clerk had intimated she had married an American to gain citizenship. Maybe that was why she never had applied, letting her Green Card lapse after leaving New York.

But at least there had been no language barrier in either of those places. Amelia decided it would be prudent to learn as much as possible about property purchase before any agreement was signed. The moment she closed her eyes at night, acronyms surfaced like alphabetized grains of sand—TASI, TARI, IMU. She needed a mnemonic to help. She sniggered. IMU could be the impostor tax. New words churned—cadastral, another impostor tax that was in effect stamp duty. And others. She thanked the gods daily for Bria Scutari's steadfast and patient help.

The proof of ownership Bria talked about came through faster than expected. Signora Bianchi and her sons were combined owners and, after some deliberations, Dario agreed to his mother and brother's wish to sell the apartment. Signora Bianchi had found a place she wanted in Rome so was keen for the sale to now move quickly. But then things stalled. Due entirely, Bria sniffed, to the avarice of the younger son. Andrea's first price demand sent Amelia's head, and heart, into a spin.

"No, assolutamente no!" Bria's outrage tempered Amelia's shock. Negotiations continued until, with the click of the phone and Bria's triumphant smile across the desk, Amelia realized an agreeable compromise had been reached.

"It is done. The fool boy has agreed to our offer."

"Your offer, Bria! I think I'd have settled days ago."

✝

The only time Amelia demurred with Bria was over a building inspection. Some details were hard to get from Signora Bianchi, and Bria could not understand Amelia's insistence on knowing as much as possible.

"The inspector, he will tell you the palazzo is old. He will tell you it crumbles. He will tell you the magazzino," Bria paused, searching for the word in English, "the underfloor, is damp."

All things with which Amelia agreed but she still wanted an inspection. Her "just in case" clause. She had never been in the apartment above, more an attic than the grander-sounding second reception floor, with smaller windows, usually with a colorful array of laundry flapping between them like prayer flags on a Tibetan mountainside. She'd like some idea of the roof's state and who paid for what. The couple who lived there were in their fifties and appeared friendly enough but reserved. The ground floor, what Bria called the underfloor, was divided into two small apartments with, it seemed, a revolving door of young men and women coming and going. Grids covered their windows and a strange wire mesh Amelia thought far too wide for mosquitoes. Her disgust was palpable when Bria explained it was for i ratti that rose from the sewers with the acqua alta. The thought of a wet, ferrety-looking rat face peering at her through the mesh turned her stomach.

There had been no high water this autumn but Amelia knew it was only a matter of time before she would have to slosh around with the rest of Venice. At least there wouldn't be too many tourists to hear complaining. Why did people travel if they didn't want things to be different from wherever home was?

The inspector, a squat jolly man with pebble glasses, whose dungarees stretched tight over his ample belly, finally showed up and gave his verbal report. As expected, but with a bonus that the electrical system had been upgraded about ten years earlier. A relief as Amelia had heard horror stories of an entire building run on one circuit breaker. He spoke little English, but enough to express his dismay when Amelia asked about building permits for renovations. His anguish evidenced by rapid blinking as he clasped her arm saying, "no, no," then an explanation that it was better to beg forgiveness than ask for permission. At least that's what Amelia thought he meant. He left the apartment with a promise that his written inspection would be stamped and delivered, pronto!

A month later, Amelia began doubting her understanding of the word.

Once the apartment was hers, she'd start working toward her integration agreement quota of thirty points by having formal Italian lessons and learning the history and culture. The latter two were easy, the former not quite so. The thought of being tested filled her with dread. Perhaps she should enroll at the Istituto Venezia for their three-month intensive language course.

"Non ora, quando?" One of Bria Scutari's favorite sayings spun in and Amelia smiled. "What do you think, Leo? If not now, when?"

But for now, she had renovations to plan, if not execute. She spent hours wandering the rooms with a tape measure. She carried a chair with her to get every angle and view. Sitting in the small entrance hall one morning, she decided a mezzanine had to be included. One that could double as a spare bedroom-cum-study. That and the kitchen would be the major jobs. And the floors. The swirling tiles that rose up to her in a mist of gray and brown would have to go. Parquet would be far better. But could she have underfloor heating with that?

Amelia sat cross-legged on the kitchen counter, playing with designs. Her starting point had to be a double door fridge with an icemaker, and a full-size oven. Something she had learned was unusual in Venice. An English woman she'd met at Dodo's told her cooking Christmas lunch was a nightmare, explaining she'd had to ask her local pizzeria if she could borrow their oven.

"What do you think, Leo?" she asked again. "Can I fit both in here? Shit, how am I going to get them up in the lift or up the stairs? Oh well, I'll cross that bridge when I come to it. Part of me wants to go away while the work is being done, but the stronger voice is saying 'stay.' I think there would be the distinct possibility of procrastination if I'm not here to harangue."

The doorbell interrupted her conversation. Not necessarily someone wanting her. The ten-year electrical upgrade had somehow not wired the doorbells separately. Or, if it had, the wires had been crossed somewhere. It was an intermittent problem shared by all the residents of Palazzo Ambrosio.

She jumped down and padded across to the balcony to peer over and see who was waiting at the heavy front door. A group of students jostled at the entrance. Nothing to do with her. Signor Malvestio leaned over his balcony and shrugged.

News had traveled fast that she would buy the Bianchi apartment. News met with, on the whole, delight, although she'd heard a few murmurs from Venetians about keeping La Serenissima for Venetians. Comments her friends told her to ignore. Amelia also got the impression her erstwhile landlady could be a simpering ninny one minute and a harridan the next. She was glad she hadn't had the pleasure of meeting her but grateful for Bria, Riccardo and Stefano's continued guidance on Venetian ways, with supplemental help from Luca at her breakfast haunt, and Matteo, the waiter at Dodo's.

The earlier downpour had eased, although the sky still looked heavy, and Amelia decided to risk a trip along the Grand Canal to her favorite food store. Antica Drogheria Mascari had been in existence since 1948, Luca told her, and was now run by the sons of the original owners.

"You tell Gabriele and Gino that Luca sent you," he'd insisted.

Amelia had not introduced herself until her third or fourth venture to their store but now, with her bone fides assured, a warm greeting always awaited her. It was the kind of shop, she told Leo, where you came out with far more than you went in for. Delicious aromas assailed the senses the minute the door opened. Herbs, jams, pastries. Amelia loved buying the spices stored loose in drawers. Cardamom, mace, garam masala—whatever was needed—would be spooned out and folded onto pieces of paper which were then taped shut.

Remembering her first foray to buy spices when the twisted cones had unraveled into a miasma of colors and smells at the bottom of her carrello, Amelia loaded her cart with care before she started for home, just making it before soft drizzle threatened to mingle her purchases again as water seeped through the fabric.

†

Grateful she could at least live in the apartment, even if formalities of ownership were taking far longer than she wanted, Amelia buried herself in Italian history, determined not to fail any part of the integration test. She had willing helpers.

A slow afternoon at Dodo's had Matteo explaining the history of the Old Ghetto. When words and meanings became confused, they resorted to English.

"You know ghetto, it come from Italian il geto. That mean…" Matteo stopped, stumped.

"Momento," Amelia said, burrowing into her handbag for the dictionary. "Okay, casting," she announced, then showed the waiter the definition. "I suppose a foundry?"

"Ah." He nodded. "Boom, boom." His raised voice startled nearby pigeons who rose en masse before settling back on the uneven cobbles.

"Guns?" Amelia suggested.

"Si, cannoni," he bobbed his head again then continued. "Many Jewish persons live 'ere long time past. Molto difficile. Many lire for Jew to be outside the walls at night. Only open gates after the marangona—you know the bell at St. Mark's Campanile—ring in the morning."

"The Jews seem to have been stymied all over the world," Amelia said, shaking her head.

"Che cosa?"

"Nothing," Amelia said. "So, Ghetto Vecchio is old, and Ghetto Nuovo is new, right?"

"Non proprio," Matteo said, his wide mouth a curved grin that split his face like a "U."

"Not really? But vecchio means old, doesn't it?"

The waiter shrugged and agreed. "But for Jewish persons the Ghetto Nuovo is older."

Amelia shook her head. "I'm never going to pass!"

"Sì, sì, you pass. You pass. Ah, scusi!" Matteo sprang into action as a group of German tourists huddled into chairs under a heater at a nearby table. Confusion gnawed as she made her way back to the palazzo. Amelia frowned. Leo would've told her to let it go. Who cared? But she had always cared about the little inconsistencies. Then had so often ignored nagging suspicions, the big inconsistencies. Not anymore. Big or little. She'd look the words up when she got home.

†

She tossed her things on the countertop and went into the girls' bedroom. Her trunks from Patanga had arrived, too early really. It would've been easier not to have them shoved under the beds and piled against the walls. She at least knew where to find the guide to the island's more than two hundred churches; that had been a purchase since arriving in Italy.

Amelia flipped pages of the guidebook. "Huh. Who knew?" She read aloud. "The word 'ghetto' originates from the Jewish Quarter of Venice, which emerged from the area of the foundry in use in 1516. By 1899, the term had been extended to over-crowded urban areas of other minority groups." She nodded. Made sense.

Next, she opened the larger dictionary. "Oh God, Leo, I'm never going to pass. Why can't a bell just be a bell? No, in Venice it has to be called a carpenter." She sighed. "I'm going to have to get a cat. I can't keep talking to a dead man. Or myself." She snickered then shook her head and sank onto one of the beds and continued to read. "Hah! I was right, though. Marangona is feminine, and a carpenter. That would make her a carpentress?" Amelia giggled. "Oh, okay, that makes sense. 'Rung to mark the beginning and the end of the working day for the carpenters building ships in the Venetian Arsenal.' No cell phones then. You would've liked that, Leo."

His name, spoken out loud, brought Amelia back to those big inconsistencies. The half-truths that had hovered in the air as his fame grew. His throw-away lines about a quick drink on the way back from his studio that turned into a late-night session. Or an invitation to a party folded into a jacket pocket. One she had known nothing about.

She slammed the book shut. Why think about that now? Cell phones. That's why. After a row when she hadn't been able to get hold of him. "For God's sake, Amelia!" Leo's words surged around the little bedroom in Venice. "Five years ago we didn't even have these damn things. Now, if you can't find me, you go into full panic mode."

She'd stormed from the room in tears, shouting. "Yes, when our children need you! I couldn't care less." But she had cared.

Amelia shook her head. He'd never before put a fling before the girls. That was when she'd known his latest woman was serious. Perhaps enough to derail a marriage perceived by some to be unconventional. For her, maybe. Not him.

Then it all changed.

Chapter 8

"You're looking very glamorous this evening, dear one," Leo said. Leaning in to kiss her cheek, he tweaked the vivid green swirl of silk at her neck.

"Have you just got here, too?" Amelia asked, "Your lips are cold!" She drew off her black leather gloves then shrugged out of the new camel-colored cashmere coat and handed it to the hat-check girl with a nod of thanks. Amelia smoothed the navy dress, also silk, over her hips and glanced around. She wondered, in the hubbub of the gallery, which of the many lithe and scented women was Leo's newest fancy.

"Well?" she asked, noting he hadn't changed into his usual opening night garb of black trousers, a brocade frock coat with a cravat knotted lazily at his throat.

"Well, what?" Leo responded. He urged her into the throng, his eyes on the milling crowd sipping champagne, looking at his art.

"Why aren't you dressed? Have you just got here?" Amelia repeated her questions. She noted a weariness around his eyes.

"No time. And, yes. I've been running late all day."

"Where were you?"

"Amelia, I don't need an inquisition here. Anywhere. There's Harvey," he pointed to the portly man studying a nude, paint slathered on with rough abandon—the knife strokes brutal, yet somehow intimate. "I wouldn't be surprised if he bought that. It's good."

"Is it her?" Amelia asked, no longer surprised at Leo's certainty of his own talent. She missed the days of doubt. The days when it was she Leo turned to for reassurance.

"Who?"

"Your latest?"

Leo took her arm, his calloused fingers hard through the silk of her sleeve and propelled her forward to the collector. "Not here, Amelia. We'll talk later. It'll be okay."

Before she could ask what would be okay, Charles Warner, the gallery owner, clinked his champagne flute, shoved his glasses up his pugnacious nose, and welcomed New York's elite. Amelia always thought he looked more like a boxing promoter than one of the city's most respected art historians. She felt Leo's shoulder sag and glanced at him, startled. At this point, he would normally stride to Charlie, the first owner to offer him a show over twenty years earlier, ready to lap up the accolades, throwing a quip back at the audience whenever the occasion allowed. Instead, Leo stayed by her side, his grip no less firm, his smile tight.

"What? No words, Leo?" Charles called across the gallery to general laughter.

"This time not. Just thanks, Charlie. Thanks for the faith the years over. And…" Leo paused… "thanks to my wonderful wife, who always believed in me. Long before any of you."

Amelia struggled to hide her surprise amidst the smattering of laughter and applause.

"Now, have another drink—Charlie's paying—then buy a painting." Leo grabbed a glass from a waiter's tray and gulped the champagne.

"Whoa, slow down, Leo," Amelia said, her voice quiet. "It's a long night ahead. We've got dinner at La Grenouille after this."

"Not tonight. Let's get out of here."

"What?"

"Come on," Leo tugged her arm.

"What's going on, Leo? Have you told Charlie?"

"No. It'll be fine. It's the usual crowd who'll be there."

"But it's rude. They'll be there to speak to you, not Charlie."

"Not tonight, Amelia."

It had taken a while to make their way to the door. Amelia had smiled and made small talk, shooting glances at Leo's rigid back and stilted words. Harvey caught them as Amelia waited for her coat.

"A red dot on the buxom nude, Leo," he said, his chest puffed with pride at the acquisition. "One of your best. You're not leaving yet, are you?"

Leo nodded and helped Amelia into her coat. "A few quiet moments at..." Leo paused, his brow furrowed, "... at the place where I work."

"Oh well, see you both later. I'd like to know more about the filly, eh?" Harvey's laughter followed them into the frigid night.

"That man's a creep. A filly? Really?" Amelia said as Leo hailed a cab. "And what's with 'at the place where I work'? Where are we going?"

"Home."

✝

"Where are the girls?" Leo flicked lights on in the hall and bent to pet Sheba, curling around his legs.

"For God's sake, Leo. Moira is, I presume, in her apartment and Lucy is, again I presume, at college. If you'd been home a bit more recently, you'd know." Amelia threw her coat over the newel post.

"Yes, of course. Sorry. Pour me a drink."

"What, no 'please?'" Amelia frowned. "Champagne or Armagnac?"

"Whatever I had before is fine."

Amelia went to the fridge. Letitia, as always, had left the kitchen gleaming. Only coming twice a week now the girls had left home, Amelia missed the garrulous Mexican's company. Twelve years was a long time to share household duties, and child rearing. Always ready with a pronouncement on anything in the news, the woman had made their family's life significantly less complicated.

Easing the bottle from the cork, Amelia wondered what was going on. Leo in this kind of mood was almost worse than when adrenaline pulsed through him. She poured Moët into two flutes and watched the stream of bubbles rise to a satisfying pop on the surface. Rather than put the bottle back in the fridge, she took out a silver bucket, added ice and, putting everything on a tray, carried it through to the morning room. The place where all family discussions took place. No television to distract anyone.

Leo, still wearing his overcoat, stood looking out at the garden. Sheba, sinewy and black, perched on the table in front of him, purring as he petted her ears. The cat eyed Amelia warily, knowing table hopping was forbidden.

Amelia scooted the cat off, slid the tray onto the table and handing Leo a glass, touched his shoulder, then sat on one of the chairs. "What's going on, darling? Sit down. You're scaring me."

†

Amelia stumbled downstairs to make a cup of tea. The upended bottle in the ice bucket an ugly reminder of the evening. The clock on the cooker blinked 2:34. The order of the time a cruel parody of what was to become of their lives.

Steam rose from the kettle and she switched it off before the whistle could wake Leo.

She jiggled the teabag, a fusion of chamomile and mint drifting up from the cup. Amelia drew her dressing gown around her and leaned against the counter, her bare feet warm on the underfloor heating. Tears leaked down her cheeks.

A creak and the sound of the cat flap swinging told her Sheba had seen the light and come to investigate any late-night happenings in the kitchen. Amelia lifted the cat and buried her face in the sleek fur, roughened by the cold air outside. The cat accepted the indignity for a moment, struggled to get down, then sauntered to the laundry for a snack.

"How did I miss it?" she asked the cat's retreating back.

Leo's stark words came back through a haze of disbelief.

"I have Alzheimer's."

Amelia had looked at him, her glass dribbling champagne to the carpet where she had knocked it. "What? No!" She moved to put her arms around his hunched shoulders but he had tensed.

"No!" He shrugged her off. "Let me get this out."

She sat back, tears coursing down her face as she listened.

"I haven't been having a fling, dear one. Not this time." His smile had been rueful. "I really have been working at the studio—hah, I just remembered what it was called." He stroked her wet cheek. "Haven't you noticed I've been forgetting things? Simple things. Asking the same questions."

"You've been like that for years when preparing for a show. And, frankly, Leo, you haven't been around much lately."

"Touché."

Amelia asked, "This isn't one of your panics about aging, is it? Your mortality? We all forget things, darling."

"Not this time. I haven't had the neurologist's report—that's where I was this afternoon—but Dr. Sheen, and you know how blunt he can be, seems to think it likely."

"Likely is not confirmation, Leo."

"I'd have to be dead for that, Amelia." Leo's smile was sad. "Dr. Sheen gave me the MMSE—don't ask me what it stands for, I can't remember. The test's been around for years. I didn't score well. Thirteen."

"Out of how many?"

"More than twenty-five. I don't know. Can't remember that either."

"Why didn't you take me with you? To the neurologist? This afternoon?"

"What was the point? No need us both crying."

"Oh, darling." She stroked his hand. "What did he do?"

"Redid the MM... whatever it is. Then I had to draw a clock and put the numbers, the hands," Leo corrected himself, "the hands at ten to eleven. Couldn't do it, dear one. Couldn't do it."

"That's it? That's how they can tell? By getting a stupid diagram of a clock wrong!"

"It's a tool, Amelia. There are other things. I couldn't count backward..."

Amelia jumped in. "I can't count backward. Never have been able to. Doesn't mean I've got bloody Alzheimer's."

"Shh, no, of course it doesn't. But that combined with other things in the test, like remembering an address the..." Leo hit his head in frustration. "Shit, this is real. The man, you know, the man in a white coat, gave me at the beginning of the appointment. I couldn't do it, Amelia."

"We'll see another doctor." She gripped his hand. "And another, if necessary."

"No, we won't." Leo pulled his hand back and bent to pick up her glass. Pouring champagne, he raised his glass. "We'll cry tonight, then move on."

"When will we get the results from the neurologist?" Amelia didn't wait for an answer. "There must be medication you can take."

Leo shook his head. "Not really. It might slow the progression. But it can have unpleasant side effects. I don't want that. I must be able to paint."

"Paint! For fuck's sake, Leo. If there's something we can do, we must do it. Forget painting!"

"I can't do that, Amelia. You know that. I have to paint. It's who I am."

"No. You're my husband. The girls' father. That's who you are. Painting doesn't define you."

"Of course it does, dear one." Leo sipped champagne. "I wonder what sense goes first? I'd miss the taste of this." He smiled.

"For God's sake, this is not funny." Amelia hit him. Hard.

"I'm not laughing." He rubbed his arm. "But, Amelia, we are going to have to laugh at the silly things in life, the silly things I might do. And it won't always be funny." Leo stopped, turned his chair to face his wife, and took both her hands. "Amelia, dear one, we both know I haven't always been faithful to the word, even the letter," he lowered his gaze, his voice muffled, "but I have never loved anyone else. Ever. It is a lot, asking you to see me through this. It could take years. But I am asking."

"Oh, darling, I'm not going anywhere." Amelia kissed him, tasting champagne on his lips. They clung together until, her mind replaying his words, she asked, "Leo, what do you mean 'move on'?"

Chapter 9

Amelia looked down at her hands, still holding the book on Venetian churches, surprised to see tears trembling on them before soaking into the paperback. She touched her cheeks. Strange how sometimes she could scream her tears, and other times they trickled, unnoticed.

She stood and smoothed the doona over the bed, a smile tugging her lips. She might not have lived in Australia for over thirty years but you couldn't take the Aussie out of her. She'd make sure her granddaughter knew her heritage. Maybe she'd start with the 'ds'—doona, drongo, and dingo. Lucy could help compile a dictionary. Hell, she could illustrate it too.

Street lights flickered on, throwing elongated shadows of people hurrying home on the walls across the canal. She shivered, Leo's remembered words so vivid she glanced around.

"This is ridiculous," she muttered. "I'm tense, that's all. Worrying about the test." She put a pan of water on to boil for pasta. Pappardelle tonight. The long flat strands with a mushroom sauce. Quick and simple. Amelia glanced down at her stomach. She couldn't believe she wasn't putting on weight, eating pasta pretty much every day. If anything, she'd firmed up.

She wouldn't be eating at home for the rest of the week. The workmen would start in the morning. A Dio piacendo! She smiled. It must be a good sign—thinking in Italian, even if it was only asking for God's help.

The hiss of bubbling water brought her back to the kitchen. "This is your last night!" she said to the fizzing stove top. "And yours, il frigorifero!" She pulled the note taped to the fridge door. One week the carpenter had promised. She hoped his pronto was more reliable than the building inspector's. Amelia had been running perishables down for the last few days and emptied the last of the cream into the pan with the chopped garlic, parsley, and mushrooms. Was it worth opening a bottle of wine? She hesitated. Pulling a pretty glass from the box, the cut glass stem a soft pink below a clear bowl, she uncorked the Soave Classico and sipped. "Never a bad time!" She toasted the kitchen. "Out with the old. Please let the new begin tomorrow. Pronto!"

Cold air hit as she opened the door to the balcony. Tonight might be the last evening she could spend out there before winter really set in. Amelia lit a candle and set a place at the marble-top table. Another market find. "Buonasera, Signor Malvestio," she called along the street.

"Buonasera, Amelia. Domani, eh? Tomorrow they come?"

"Sì, domani, spero! I hope," she added under her breath.

He waved his pipe in her direction and returned to his paper.

The smell of frying mushroom and garlic drew her back to the kitchen. She filled a plate, picked up a pashmina, and returned to the table. A smile hovered as she sat down. "Who'da thought it?" she asked Venice.

Packing the cleaned plate and cutlery away in the one of the boxes stored in the girls' room, Amelia poured another glass of wine then wandered from room to room. In the entrance hall, she gazed up to where the mezzanine would, one day, provide her with a study and daybed. Tiny, but functional she'd told the builder. She knew she should have started with that but the thought of battling with the oven and fridge in the impractical kitchen one more day than necessary had decided her. "Kitchen, mezzanine, floors," she muttered. Putting her glass down, she lifted down Leo's painting of the girls and leaned it, face in, against the wall in the spare room, then closed the doors.

It was going to be messy, but worth it.

☦

"Buongiorno, Signora Amelia." A voice called from the street.

Peering over the balcony, Amelia saw Stefano and the carpenter. On time. Perhaps Riccardo had put the fear of God into him.

"Good morning!" She waved them up. Excitement trickled down her shoulders as she passed the kitchen. "Ciao, Stefano, what are you doing here?"

"Zio Pietro, he is my mother's brother. I help him. His English is not so good."

Amelia patted Stefano's arm with a grin. She and Pietro had managed just fine when they had discussed her plans and his cost. A wink from the thick-set man of about fifty made her smile. She nodded. Both understood Stefano was determined to be in on the transformation of Signora Amelia's apartment.

"You will leave. Is better," Pietro said. It wasn't a suggestion.

She looked at the man and boy, both descendants of old Venetian gondola builders. Amelia hesitated. She hated the thought of not being around to keep an eye on the destruction of her home but she could always pop back at lunchtime. Just to check.

"Is okay, signora," Stefano said. "Is better you not see. My father, he waits for you on the boat. He takes you to Burano. You go. Is okay."

"Murano?" Amelia asked.

"No, no. Burano. He tell. You go now!"

"Okay. Fine. I can tell I'm not wanted. Don't knock my home down, eh, Pietro?" She tried to smile as she picked up her handbag and camera, then shrugged into her coat. "Ciao," she called from the door. About to step into the tiny lift she heard a clatter. Leaning over the balustrade, she saw two men, one hefty, one slender, manhandling a pulley-kind of contraption up the stairs. "Oh, God," she muttered. "They're right. Probably best to go."

"Buongiorno, Amelia." Riccardo hailed her as she stepped over the lintel. "Come va?"

"Tutto a posto. Everything's okay." She spoiled her assertion by adding, "I think."

"Come. Today we go to Burano."

"Don't you have to work?"

"No. Today I play." Riccardo grinned, the spiky ends of his mustache twitching as he helped Amelia into his motoscafo. "You know Burano?"

"Not really. I keep thinking you're saying Murano. Which I don't know either, apart from it being the glass-blowing island. Where's Burano?"

"I take you."

Riccardo urged Amelia back to the small cabin of the boat.

"Can't I sit up here with you?" She asked as Riccardo turned on the engine.

"Certo, sure," he replied with a smile, "but for you is cold. We go north. Maybe four kilometers."

Amelia ducked behind the windscreen and tugged a scarf from her bag. She smiled up at the boatman, then took the lens cap off and took his photo. The girls were right. His hair streaked by both sun and age gave him a rakish air—he was attractive. Quiet, she watched as he navigated the canals, busy despite the off season, then into the wider basin of the Misericordia where he opened up the throttle and set off toward Isola di San Vincenzo, Venice's cemetery, then Burano. "With a 'B,'" Amelia murmured. Riccardo glanced down, a question in his eyes. She shook her head and pointed to her ear—too noisy to talk. And he had been right. Despite the sun, a chill nipped her cheeks and she snuggled deeper into her coat, away from the wind and occasional spritz of salt water.

Riccardo slowed the launch as they approached the island half an hour later. Amelia gasped at the sight of buildings slumped against each other in a panoply of color along the canals— magenta to lime green to orange to red. Barges, motoscarfi, and little putt-putts jostled prow to stern, ropes creaked on the poles holding them in line. Laundry fluttered from upper floor windows, and curtains billowed from windows and doors opening on to the narrow pavements, even in late autumn.

"Oh, Riccardo, this is fabulous," Amelia said, her camera clicking in time to her words. "Tell me about the place. Lacemaking, right?" She'd remembered something from a guidebook she'd read months ago.

"Sì, but by hand, not so much today. It take long time so molto costoso." Riccardo rubbed his thumbs and fingers together in the gesture known around the world.

"Very expensive," Amelia translated. "Always lace?"

"No. The Romans they come in the sixth century. Some say a family called Buriana, another story say because people came from the town Buranello, perhaps eight kilometers south. Burano never have own government, always from Torcello. Not same privilege like Murano."

"So when did the lacemaking begin?" Amelia asked. "And how?"

"You know Cipro?"

Amelia shook her head.

"Cipro, the island, far south."

"Ahh, Cyprus?"

"Sì." Riccardo tried out the word. "Cyprus. Bene. So long time past, sixteenth century, Venice she rule Cipro, Cyprus. They make lace and teach ladies here to make, with needles, for maybe one hundred fifty years. Very important for Burano. But, you know, expensive. Then in," Riccardo paused, searching for the date, "sì, 1872, a school for lace it opens and now still it is here. And a museum."

"Can we visit it?" Amelia asked, watching as Riccardo maneuvered his craft into a small space, nudging the prow of another boat to reach a pole.

"Sure. We go now."

Clambering out, Amelia looked along the picture-postcard canal. "I must bring Lucy here. She'd love this. Can the owners choose any color?"

"No, no. It must be stamped. Here. The palace of Podestà."

Turning a corner, they entered a square, far larger than Amelia had expected, and in front of them stood a bare brick building, windows under Moorish arches rather like those at Palazzo Ambrosio, and a large blue sign with a lace design.

"So," Riccardo continued his lesson, "in 1978 the government in Venice and the Andriana Marcello Foundations they give money to make museum, and to teach to make lace again—the old way." He pushed open the door.

"Ciao, Riccardo." The woman at the ticket desk smiled broadly. "Just one today?" she asked.

"Buongiorno, Maria." He leaned across to kiss her cheeks. "This is my friend, from Australia, Signora Amelia Paignton. Amelia, this is my friend, Signora Maria Volpato. She know my wife since children."

Amelia felt the slender woman's gaze sharpen as they shook hands. Her fingers, adorned with chunky silver jewelry, tightened and her face flushed above the exquisite collar of white lace that softened the severe plum-colored dress.

Riccardo must have felt the frisson too because he rushed to explain that Pietro and Stefano were demolishing the signora's kitchen and needed her out of the way. Maria relaxed and patted his arm.

"Uffa, okay," she said, her smile once again in place. "You will enjoy," she said to Amelia. "Riccardo knows much. He brings many people. Today, he bring a friend. No charge."

"Thank you, signora," Amelia said, trying not to laugh. She had ten years on Riccardo at least. The girls would giggle at the thought of their mother being considered a cougar.

The well laid out museum exhibited the different styles of lace through the centuries. Amelia wondered how human fingers could create patterns of such delicacy. The outside of the museum might have been bare of color but the rooms inside had walls of teal, of lemon, of salmon, each the perfect backdrop for the lengths of rare and precious lace attached.

After the museum they, along with Maria, shared a pizza and jug of vino rosso della casa, the younger woman warming as the meal progressed, to the extent that she leaned in to buss Amelia's cheeks when she left to return to work. Next, Amelia and Riccardo wandered along to the Oratoria di Santa Barbara, more chapel than church-like, but still with the obligatory bell tower. Amelia laughed to see the far grander San Martino Church with its campanile leaning against the simpler structure.

"Not quite as impressive as Pisa's Leaning Tower," Amelia said.

Riccardo shrugged and pointed to the painting of the crucifixion by Tiepolo. "Pisa no have this!"

"Can we just wander for a while, or do you have to get back?" Amelia asked. "I'd like to look in some of the galleries. It really is an artist's colony, isn't it?" Photo opportunities appeared around every corner and Riccardo proved a patient tour guide, happy to chat with people he knew as he waited for Amelia.

On the ride back to Venice, the dipping sun drove Amelia into the cabin. Guilt tugged as she watched Riccardo at the wheel but, when he turned to grin at her, realized he loved being on the open water with the throttle open.

Her mind drifted back to the apartment, not sure if she wanted to see Pietro and Stefano, or just survey the chaos on her own. Either way, she'd have supper at Dodo's. She dozed, to wake to Riccardo's touch on her shoulder.

"Siamo qui," he said, pointing to the landing along from the palazzo.

"It was a perfect day, thank you, Riccardo," Amelia said, kissing his wind-blown cheeks.

"We do again, eh?"

Amelia nodded and waved, eager now to get home.

No sound came from behind her door. She turned the key and, not sure what to expect, pushed the door gingerly then gasped as she put her handbag on the floor. Gone were the two walls that had turned the kitchen into a furnace-cum-sauna, especially when the dryer churned. Gone were the chunky wooden units, gone was the fridge, and gone was the despised stove. The rickety island had also gone and in its place, on the floor, stood a Chianti bottle sprouting purple and pink asters, their centers a smile of sunshine yellow.

"Oh, Leo," Amelia bent to pick up the make-do vase, "such kindness!" She looked around the shell of the apartment. "How the hell did they get everything out so fast?"

An unfamiliar shape caught her eye on the balcony. Closer inspection showed it to be the pulley contraption she had seen the men lug upstairs earlier in the day. "I think," she said as she closed the French doors and visions of swaying appliances being hauled up from the narrow pavement played across her eyes, "that I shall make sure I'm out for that day as well."

She poured a glass of wine, tugged off her boots, flicked a dustcover off one of the armchairs, another find at the Sunday flea market, and sank down. It had been a great day. Fun to meet someone new, even if Maria Volpato's manner had been cool at first. Amelia frowned, then wondered if others thought there was more to her and Riccardo. She hoped not. That could be awkward.

"To hell with them if they do," she said with a sigh. Caffè Dodo could wait. Leaning her head back she spoke to the echoey apartment, "I'm too tired to go out again."

A wave of loneliness engulfed her, catching her by surprise. "What happened to carefree, Amelia?" she asked, then scrolled through her phone and stared at a photograph of Leo, debonair and charming in his opening night attire.

The frock coat and a couple of cravats were stored in one of the boxes under the beds.

Her thoughts trundled back to those early days when, at the end of Leo's Peace Corps contract and after deciding art and not teaching was to be his life, Amelia had been stunned and excited when Leo, by then her husband, had been eager to try Australia.

After six years at boarding school in Sydney, the city had grown on her until she considered herself a native. It had seen her adolescent misdemeanors, her first loves, had eased her into a more cultured life than the one experienced in early childhood on the plantation on New Britain. She had still loved going back to New Guinea for holidays—the freedom of the ocean on her doorstep, then Leo—but at heart she had become a city girl.

The Atherden Gallery, owned by Amelia's old boss and relocated from the top of Argyle Place to The Rocks, was the first to give Leo space to exhibit his wildly colorful canvases, most still abstract expressionism. Paintings Amelia failed to fathom. The Atherden, only ever known as that, had been the first to open in the area after the sometimes violent period that became known as "The Battle for The Rocks" in the early 1970s. His paintings, Leo had said, captured that struggle between high-rise developers and the working-class neighborhood. She, though, had struggled to see the point of hours spent in a studio either throwing paint at the canvas on the floor or daubing it in blocks at the easel.

It all became a moot point as those working-class families died, or were eased out, and the area became a historic tourist attraction. Trendy art galleries. Boutiques selling scented soap and candles. Chi-chi cafés. Amelia gazed into her glass, drawn back to that first opening night—the first of many.

Leo had appeared in the bedroom of their cramped flat, not far from the gallery, dressed in a frock coat of deep damask green, black trousers and a maroon and green cravat.

She'd laughed. "What the hell, Leo? We're in Sydney, not Edwardian London." Once out, the words could not be withdrawn. Defiance, and a mote of embarrassment, had sent him storming from the flat.

He had never liked to be the butt of laughter.

Chapter 10

A sharp barp of a motoscafo horn jarred Amelia back to Italy. She swished her glass, noting the wine change from scarlet to crimson to rose as it caught the light on its journey around the bowl. It reminded her of the ruby-colored caftan she'd worn to that first opening. Embroidered flowers and glimmers of mirror garlanded the neckline, diverting attention from the bulge of her belly. She had been defiant too. Perhaps that had accounted for her unusually sarcastic comment. Still smarting from Leo's indifference to her pregnancy. A family would detract from his image as an American maverick about town. A free-spirited wife was fine, but kids. That was another story. Too pedestrian. Too ordinary. Too dull. Amelia sighed.

"Oh, Leo. I suppose you were right about some things. A frock coat became your trademark. Stood you out in a crowd of long-haired, sandal-wearing artists."

That first frock coat had been bought at a costumer's going out of business. The one folded in tissue paper in the box under the bed in Italy had been custom made in New York. Nothing second hand for Leo Paignton for many years. Amelia didn't think Leo had ever forgiven that laugh. Moira's words replayed in her mind, about her father being Bohemian, but he had never been a natural. Kansas ran deep.

A liminal time. Amelia had thought she'd slot right back into Sydney life. She had accepted she would never be an artist but had wanted to stay in the gallery business, help Leo. But it hadn't been like that. He wanted the art world to himself. And Amelia had gone along with it. Had accepted her role as that of a decorative prop. Until, a smile tugged, she saw her young self throwing out the blister pack of The Pill. "If I'd waited for you, Leo, we would never have had kids." Why was all this resurfacing? Such a long time ago. "But you were smitten, weren't you? The moment you held Moira. Your saving grace? Then it became okay to be seen a family man. Look at me, I'm an artist, I'm hip but I'm also a dad."

Amelia looked back at what had been the kitchen. "You could be such a shit, Leo. Then you'd romance me and I'd fall in love all over again. Or did I fall in line? I don't know now."

Tired, Amelia stripped and had a shower in the girls' bathroom then padded through to her room and collapsed into bed. Two hours later, wide awake still, she got up to make cocoa.

"Or not," she said to the bare walls of her kitchen. The tears came in torrents. "Goddamnit, Leo, I'm happy. Go away." She rubbed her sore eyes. "Did I waste all those years?" What had she said to the girls? About being happy. Well, she had been. Happiness comes in different levels. Different definitions for different times in life. "It's just this mess," Amelia muttered to the shadowy space before stumbling back to bed.

Sleep finally came with the dawn when, it seemed not long after, Amelia was startled awake by the sound of her name.

"Bugger!" She leaped out of bed and shouted over the balustrade to Stefano. "Solo un momento!" She dragged on jeans from the day before, pulled out a clean T-shirt, brushed her teeth and hair, and found Pietro and Stefano outside the front door lounging against the wall.

"Tutto bene, signora?" Pietro asked, his eyes concerned.

Amelia nodded and bade them enter. She listened, through her aching head, as he outlined his plan for the day.

"Signora, I think," he winked and unfolded a simple schematic, next to which lots of numbers made Amelia's head spin. "Is better to go up now, eh?" He pointed to the area above the entrance, then drew her attention to the plan again and showed her where he would build the pillars to support the mezzanine. "È facile!"

"Easier for who?" Amelia asked. She hadn't even decided if it should be Pietro or another contractor she'd approached who got the job. The kitchen was the test. She looked at Pietro's open face, and Stefano's hopeful one. At least she knew him, them. There was a connection. Riccardo would never let his brother-in-law screw her. "Metaphorically," she muttered.

"Prego?" Stefano asked.

She shook her head.

"You think, yes," Pietro said, "no hurry." He ambled through to the kitchen, where he pulled a thermos out of his toolbox.

The numbers scrawled line by line next to words like il legname started to make sense. Her smile was smug. Who knew she knew words like lumber? Perhaps she did know more of the language than she realized. Nails, concrete. "Pietro," she called him over and pointed to a separate set of numbers, "what are these?"

"For to make balcony," he explained. Before she could ask, he pulled a pencil from the bib pocket of his overalls and drew metal work. Nothing intricate, but quirky. Uprights with a few curved bars. She liked it.

"Safe, yes?" she asked. "For bambina?" Nothing on which a toddler could get a foothold. Her granddaughter might not yet be born but Amelia wasn't going to live in a building site twice.

"Certo, signora, certo!" he assured her.

Amelia looked again at the bottom line. Huh. Okay, not so bad. What the hell? She wanted it done. Why not? "What about permission?" she asked.

Pietro's shrug reminded her of the building inspector. "Not necessary."

Amelia doubted that. Was it worth getting on the wrong side of the authorities? What happened if she wanted to sell the place? She walked out to the balcony and gazed along the canal, wondering where Riccardo was today. No Signor Malvestio this morning either. She waved to the boy delivering water next door, his carrello loaded with bottles. She couldn't imagine leaving. Why worry about that now, anyway? Carefree. Remember? She loved it here, hidden away in Cannaregio. Returning to the entrance hall, she looked up, imagining the area above her. She wanted a space to spread out. To be able to set up her computer and leave it up. Maybe buy a separate screen. Space to play with her photography. No, not play. To work at it. She couldn't keep wandering from café to café, from cappuccino to Campari! There had to be a purpose to this new life.

"Righto!" The loudness startled her. "Bene, Pietro. Let's do it!"

Stefano clapped his hands. Pietro winked, again. Amelia wondered whether he really was winking—a bit of a Casanova— or just had a tic. Whatever! She liked him. She rubbed her eyes and remembered one of the girl's warning about not making major decisions for a year after a spouse died. Well, hers would fill a suitcase soon. She needed to stop second guessing. The reason for her sleepless night. Just let life take her along. That's what made the days, like yesterday with Riccardo in Burano, such a joy.

First a bird bath. Much as she loved the claw-foot bath, she didn't want to be lolling in a bath or traipsing from the girls' bathroom to hers with the men around. Huh! Perhaps she could get a shower put in her bathroom. Maybe the bath could be turned around. Or over the bath. Then she'd have the best of both worlds. Her laughter sent a sparrow hopscotching along the balcony, aflutter.

She watched it come to land again and recalled Matteo's indignation when she called them common. He'd told her it was an Italian sparrow, different to the house and Spanish sparrow. Who knew a Spanish sparrow even existed? Amelia eyed the bird now, its head tilted, considering its chances of a crumb. It looked remarkably like an ordinary sparrow to her—chunky and cheeky. She grinned. Matteo had sworn the Italian sparrow sounded different to its Spanish counterpart. Either way, it had been designated the bird of Venice.

†

A wash, and clean clothes, revived her somewhat but as the sound of destruction thudded through from the kitchen, she wondered at her decision. Her head ached. Perhaps she should have waited. At least talked to Bria or the girls about it. She rubbed her eyes then, about to go out to the men, glanced in the mirror and saw she'd smeared mascara.

"Oh, bugger," she told her reflection, "not looking good, Amelia." She wiped her raccoon eyes clean and reapplied the makeup.

"You leave today?" Stefano again suggested when she appeared in what had been the door to the kitchen.

"Is better, yes," Pietro added his tuppence worth.

She nodded. Her pounding head did not need to be compounded by the sound of hammering, or whatever it was they planned to do. Perhaps she'd move out altogether rather than live in chaos for however long it took. First coffee and a cornetto at Luca's then she'd go and see if Bria Scutari had a room available just for a few nights. "Or maybe," Amelia spoke aloud as she went down the stairs, "I should just go away. Go and see Padua!" She snorted. Leo would agree. She could almost hear his voice. "Shakespeare set *The Taming of the Shrew* there. Might rub off on you!" Her laughter bounced back off the marble. He had been funny, if sardonic at times.

Chapter 11

Paintbrush in hand, Amelia stood back in satisfaction. "Yes!" The second attempt had worked. She had replicated the buttermilk color of the kitchen walls in the undercoat of the units, then topped them with teal before distressing them. The first try, fortunately only on a side panel, had looked like chicken scratchings. Her flea market finds displayed on the open shelves would add a quirky interest. About to start the tedious process of washing the brush, she instead tossed it in the black bin bag. "I am done!"

Looking out the kitchen window she saw shadows had moved across the inner courtyard of the palazzo reminding her, along with a grumbling stomach, that she had missed lunch in her determination to finish the job. She washed her hands, scolded Dafne for jumping onto the counter to watch water swirl down the plughole, then picked the kitten up for a snuggle.

"You are so spoiled!" she said, rubbing her face in the fur. Soft now, the kitten was being fed and loved. "And lucky," Amelia added, as the memory of her first acqua alta a few weeks earlier intruded. She had been at Antica Drogheria Mascari restocking her spices for Christmas when she'd heard the long siren warning. Only one sound which, Stefano had told her before, meant a low high water, and she should not be concerned because Cannaregio rarely flooded. If she heard four sounds, it meant a more serious acqua alta. Either way, she hadn't been entirely sure what to expect and, naturally, the Wellington boots she had bought especially for such an event remained safely stored in the new closet by the front door at the palazzo and not on her feet.

Venetians, Amelia learned, took pride in a business-as-usual attitude and traversed the raised walkways, passerelles, with a nonchalance missing from visitors who scurried to buy plastic knee-high shoe covers at tourist kiosks, then dashed to St. Mark's Square in the hopes of seeing the basilica's reflection shimmer in the water covering the piazza.

Amelia felt torn between wanting to see the mirage-like image and getting home before the levels rose too high. Her decision became easier when a pitiful mewling near the moto-scarfi landing at Pescheria stopped her rush. A sopping bundle of bones cowered on a windowsill, huddled against the wire mesh, the dreaded rat deterrent. A token hiss ended in a hesitant purr as she scooped the kitten into her basket and covered it with her scarf.

Crossing the Grand Canal, she felt relieved she could navigate her way home without getting lost. It had only taken six months, she reminded herself with a wry grin as she kicked off her soggy shoes, peeled off her coat and shook the strands of hair plastered across her face. Amelia lifted the saturated scarf draped over the basket to find inquisitive eyes squinting up at her. She gingerly reached in and, after an ineffectual cuff at her hand and another feeble hiss, the kitten allowed herself to be picked up.

A bowl of tuna and some water for the kitten and a glass of Chianti for her had sealed their relationship. Watching the wary bundle explore the chaos of the kitchen and clamber over a stacked pile of lumber, words from *Rebecca* had filled her head. *An empty house can be as lonely as a full hotel.* "You have a home and your name is Daphne, but we'll drop the 'du Maurier,'" she had told the kitten, then, in honor of the city that embraced her, she decided on the Italian spelling, Dafne.

Now, in complete confidence about her place in the world, Dafne draped herself around Amelia's neck as her owner pushed in a Zucchero CD and waited for his gravelly tones singing "Senza una donna" to fill the apartment. Pure happiness accompanied his words as she flopped down on the sofa and Dafne slid down to her lap then kneaded Amelia's thighs, her purrs a warm blanket of contentment.

Her head resting on the sofa, eyes shut, Amelia marveled at her life, so different from the previous year. Guilt still nipped her, usually when sleep would not, but along with her home, she felt herself coming alive. Curiosity had overtaken the apathy she had sometimes experienced as she had waited for Leo to die. A lethargy she had fought but one which nonetheless had swamped her with fear, then a restlessness that had been hard to ignore. It was those times she had dreamed of Venice.

Lucy's ringtone shattered her reverie and, upending Dafne, she lunged for the phone.

"Darling, how lovely," she said. "Wait, what's wrong? It's one in the morning in Sydney."

"Nothing, Mum. Just a heads up. I'll be in Venice next weekend. Thought you'd like to know!" Lucy's laugh gurgled down the phone.

"What? Oh, darling, that's wonderful. Are you coming for Christmas? How exciting!"

"No, Mum, sorry. But we'll be there for four days."

"We? Who's we?"

"Just Mike and I."

Amelia's smile stretched wide. "What?"

"Yeah, we sort of decided we liked each other."

"Oh, Lucy. I could've told you that years ago. I am thrilled. Finally!"

"Well, I guess I had to figure it out for myself, Ma. Anyway, he's got meetings in London and suggested I go with him. I'm between jobs, so it's easy. Then he was the one who suggested we add a few days and drop in and see you!"

"I've always liked that man. Now I love him," Amelia said with a laugh. "You're sure you can't stay for Christmas, Lucy?"

"Really sure, I'm sorry, Mum. He has to get back, and so do I."

"Okay, my darling. I can't wait to see you. Both of you. With a bit of luck, the place will be safe and the railing up around the mezzanine, but I'm learning pronto does not always mean pronto!"

"Can't wait to see it all, Mum. Oh, and I haven't told Moira yet. She'll be pissed off."

"She can't travel anyway, darling. She's about to pop."

There was a brief silence before Lucy spoke again.

"Mum, don't you think you should go to New York? Be with Mo?"

"She doesn't want me there. I did offer, more than once." Amelia reached down to help Dafne, who was hauling herself up Amelia's jeans.

"Are you sure it's not Mo being Mo? You know, stubborn. 'I can manage' sort of thing."

"I did wonder that, darling, but she really does want to do this on her own. Or without me anyway." Amelia sighed. "She did promise me that Cynthia would be with her. Be her birth partner. Moira said she wanted to figure things out before there was someone to watch her screw up."

"Sounds like Mo. Don't think you'll get away with that with me, Mum," Lucy said with a giggle. "They have such crap maternity leave in the US. She should've come to Sydney. It's not brilliant, like in Scandinavia, but it's better."

"I know, Lucy, but your sister's a smart cookie. She knows what she's doing."

"Not always, Mum. Anyway, we can talk about it over the weekend. I can't wait. I'll call you from London. Not sure of times, but we should be with you by Friday afternoon. It's all very sudden."

"Give Mike a hug from me. I'm so delighted for you, darling."

"Me too, see ya. I love you, Mum."

"Back at you, kid!"

"That's what Dad used to say."

"It was, wasn't it? Well, it's true. Night night, darling!" Amelia clicked off, plonked the cat on the floor and went to the fridge. Pulling the door open, she had a moment's pang that her dream fridge with a water dispenser had proved completely impractical. Even getting it up to the apartment, let alone fitting it in. Blithely, she had suggested Pietro haul it up the way he'd hauled some of the building materials on the pulley system still rigged on the balcony.

"Non possible!" He had been aghast. "It fall."

Instead, she had to settle for one that fitted under the counter, along with a separate freezer. The counter along which Dafne now sauntered before being tipped off. Amelia smiled at the cat's indignation, then sighed. She took out a bottle of wine and poured a glass. In reality the fridge was more than adequate. Nonetheless, getting both purchases and the oven up to her apartment been a challenge, but one with which Stefano and the delivery man took much glee. Amelia, drawn to the raised voices, had stood at the top of the stairs watching the charade. The fridge, followed by the freezer, manhandled into the open-grated lift with Stefano sitting on the box as he clanged the iron gates shut and waited as it juddered upwards, passing the delivery man grunting his way up the angled stairs. The operation was repeated with the stove but this time, with no room for a human occupant, and with a yelled instruction to her to push the button, had presaged Stefano's mad dash up to meet the lift's arrival.

Amelia looked up to where the top of the wall dividing the entry hall and the kitchen waited for the railing. How lucky her little piece of palazzo had unusually high ceilings. She loved the idea of her study being open to both the kitchen and living room, and it gave her some natural light.

She ran her hand along the countertop, loving the practicality and feel of the composite stone, small blue flecks lifting the uniformity of the sand color. The scent of summer rose up as she poured a glass of Soave. "God, I love Italy," she said to Dafne, "if not Lorenzo."

The much-awaited trip to Bria's family vineyard had not been a successful weekend. The glorious estate in Veneto, about an hour from Lombardy, did not match the welcome from Bria's brother. Awkward silences, terse responses to questions she had asked had accompanied their first evening. The next night, Bria had opted for dinner in the kitchen with Agnese, the cook and housekeeper, rather than face the rumbling rage of her brother. Divorce, twice over, had made him a bitter man. "How can such a superb wine come from such a miserable git?" Amelia asked the cat.

Sitting back on the sofa, Gorgonzola, crackers, and a sliced apple in front of her, Amelia replayed Lucy's words. Perhaps she should have forced the issue with Moira. Her older daughter had often been the prickly one. Yet Amelia understood her need to find her feet as a new mum without her mother hovering. When Moira had been born, eighteen months after they'd arrived in Sydney, her mum had nearly driven her mad. Suggesting in the kindest, but still insistent, manner that Amelia should do things in a certain way. Too tired to argue, Amelia had gone to bed most nights in tears. Leo, eager to get settled into his artistic life, had been little help, despite loving the baby that before being born had threatened his image of himself. Slowly, slowly Amelia had got to grips with the wriggly infant intent on being awake as much as possible.

No, she'd made the right call. Moira knew her mother would be on the first plane to New York if she was needed. At least Cynthia, the house mate Amelia had never met but had heard lots about, would be there to hold Moira's hand. And Adam, the other person who shared the brownstone. Amelia would have to be content with that.

She looked around the apartment. The hated sixties floor tiles still had to be ripped up but that was a job for the new year. She had five days to get sorted. Most of the boxes stored in the girls' room could now be emptied, the mismatched maiolica plates, and colored glasses—her flea market finds—could be arranged on the open shelves in the kitchen.

Re-upholstering the tub chair she had found in a market the same weekend as the trip to the Scutari Vineyard had been far harder than she expected, but, as she looked at it now, pride squeezed out the memory of aching hands. The navy-blue bouclé fabric looked classic, although it already showed signs of where Dafne had caught her claws, but what the hell. She'd never lived in a show house and she wasn't about to start now.

"Tomorrow. I'll get cracking tomorrow."

With a sigh, Amelia finished her cheese and crackers, rinsed out her glass, and went to ready herself for bed. Dafne took up her usual position on the rim of the bath, fascinated by the bubbles popping as Amelia swished water, glad she'd decided against putting a shower in her bathroom. It would have diminished the grandeur, the sense of decadence the black and white tiled room gave her.

Beds! What about the beds? Amelia's last image before she fell asleep and as she felt Dafne tuck into the crook of her curled knees was of silk rope tied to bedposts. Kinky!

Chapter 12

"What a wonderful, wonderful surprise, my darling." Amelia gathered Lucy in her arms. "And Mike, welcome. It's lovely to see you again."

"You too, Mrs. Paignton." A broad smile disappeared into his beard.

"Amelia, please. You make me feel ancient." Amelia jumped back into the boat.

"Buon pomerrigio!" Riccardo kissed Lucy on both cheeks and helped her down to the motoscarfo, then turned to hold his hand out to Mike. "Welcome to my city, signor."

"Ciao, Riccardo, it's great to be back." Lucy watched the comings and goings along the Fondamenta Nuove.

"Your mother want to send me only because she busy at home, but I say she must come too." His laugh rolled around the little boat and sent his mustache quivering.

Amelia fluttered her hands, and said, "Well, there's a lot to do."

His shrug dismissive, Riccardo agreed. "Much dirt from builder. And preparation for her party."

"I can't wait to see the place. It was your brother-in-law, and Stefano, who did most of the work, wasn't it?" Lucy smiled at Riccardo's nod. "Thank you for making sure she wasn't cheated.

And done on time. That hardly ever happens, anywhere in the world."

"She special lady."

Lucy looked sharply at her mother then the boatman who spun the wheel to avoid another motoscarfo inching into the jetty, or maybe to avoid meeting her eyes.

"You have been to Venice before?" Riccardo asked the languid Australian leaning against the windscreen watching the water traffic.

"No, mate, never. It's beautiful. But no surf!"

"Uffa, for surf you must go Liguria, but best in Sardinia."

"Be a bit colder here than home," Lucy said, and reached up to ruffle Mike's red hair.

Ten minutes later, Riccardo tossed the line over a pole outside the Palazzo Ambrosio. "Eccoci qui! We are here," he said and glanced up to the balcony from where Dafne peered through the balustrade.

"Benvenuti, my darlings!" Amelia said again. "Thanks, Riccardo. See you later, eh? About seven thirty."

"Va bene, ciao!"

"My God, Mum, you sound Italian. Since when did you start adding 'eh' to the end of your sentences?"

"Oh, hush up." Amelia climbed the stairs with Mike, secretly pleased with Lucy's comment. Perhaps she did belong to this floating city. She smiled as she heard the lift groan its way up with Lucy and the luggage. Amelia's early warning signal. Who needed a dog? She hurried to fling open the front door. "Tah dah! Come in, come in. Just ignore the ghastly floor which, now everything is starting to come together, looks even worse than before. It's next on the list." She grinned as she paused to fluff her hair in the mirror, and, as well as a splat of buttermilk paint under her ear from where she'd touched up a wall, saw the living room reflected. Fairy lights twinkled on the little Christmas tree in the corner. Hung with ornaments Moira and Lucy had made as children, and other old favorites that gave meaning to the season each and every year. Until the last Christmas with Leo, decorating the tree had always been something she and Leo had done together. This year, the expected melancholy had not seeped in. Perhaps the excitement of seeing Lucy, perhaps her new surroundings. Whatever the reason, Amelia felt glad.

"Mum, wow, it looks fantastic! So fresh. Sophisticated. And even lighter." Lucy rounded the corner to the kitchen, her voice calling back. "I love this! Your plates look great."

"Thank you, darling. I've had such fun."

"And I see you've got a bed now. She was sleeping on an air bed on the floor last time I was here," Lucy told Mike. "Not what I expected though, Mum."

"Nor me," Amelia responded. "But I wanted to face the French doors—I wonder if they should be called Italian doors here— and I need all the storage I can get. Ergo, Pietro built me a bed."

"It's actually kind of cool. I would never have thought to plonk a bed in the middle of a room, but with that tall head-board-cum-bookshelf, it looks like a wall. Clever. I love it."

"Thank you, again."

Lucy followed Amelia from the bedroom and gazed up. "Is it safe to go up those?" she nodded to the spiral staircase, also missing the banister.

"Sure. Just don't dive off the edge. I can't decide which Italian word is better used to describe the wait for the railings. Presto or pronto! Neither seems to mean much. Mike, put your cases in here." Amelia showed him the bedroom, the beds lashed together with silk curtain cords. "Bathroom's through there.

Be aware there is also a door to the entry hall!" She watched him dump the bags, then stretch.

"This is a special place, Amelia." Mike ambled to the window overlooking the canal. "Lucy described it well, but not the sense of space and warmth."

"Thank you. I love it and have to pinch myself sometimes that it really is mine. Now, I have Prosecco, or would you prefer a beer?" Amelia asked. "Nastro Azzurro or Peroni. The former is, I'm reliably informed, the best-selling Italian beer in the world, and is made from corn exclusive to the soil here. Whatever that means."

"And is it Riccardo who reliably informs you?" Lucy's voice came from the mezzanine.

"No, actually, Pietro! So, Mike, what's it to be?"

"Prosecco, please. We are celebrating, after all."

"Here... you do it." She handed the rangy Australian the bottle, then reached for three flutes, their short blue stems picking up the flecks in the countertop. "Just being here, or something else?" Amelia asked as Lucy appeared.

"I warned you." Lucy kissed Mike's shoulder, a tender gesture that made Amelia smile. "My mother has ESP."

"Come on then," Amelia said.

"Well, I hadn't quite planned it like this, but what the hell? Amelia, I'd like to ask Lucy to marry me. Before she decides she made a mistake about agreeing to see me as more than Just Mike!" His laugh thrummed along the kitchen and back.

"Oh, darlings, that's wonderful." Amelia hugged Lucy, then Mike. "I assume you've asked her," she added with a laugh.

"Tentatively," he replied. "Well?" he asked, reaching for Lucy's hand, his thumb stroking the back of it. "Will you marry me?"

"You know I will, you big galoot!"

Amelia grinned as they kissed. "This is the most perfect Christmas present. To you both, long life, love and happiness with lots of trips to Italy!" Laughter enveloped them as they clinked glasses. "Does Moira know?"

"She knows I'm here, but not about this. Let's call her. What about your dad, hon?" Lucy asked Mike. "Shouldn't we call him, too?"

✝

Lying in the bath an hour later Amelia's face ached from grinning. She sighed. Of course she'd made life harder by preparing everything for the party herself, but she wanted to host the people whose kindness had made her welcome. A sort of thank you, Buon Natale, a housewarming and now an engagement party all rolled into one. The first entertaining she'd done since Leo's funeral.

Dove-gray, fine woolen slacks, topped with a white silk blouse, accentuated Amelia's slender body. Never large, she had noticed over the last few years her muscle tone had stretched, even with swimming at Kimbe, but all the walking, and painting, had firmed up her legs and arms. She felt good. "And now," she muttered as she spritzed J'Adore at her neck, between her breasts and on her wrists, "I smell good!" Eyeliner and mascara, a dab of burgundy lipstick and she was ready. Almost. "There," she told her reflection, as she clipped on a pink seed-pearl necklace and slid on her rings. She looked at her wedding ring then kissed it. She slipped into red flats, spun in front of the mirror to check for a knicker line, then went to put the finishing touches to the cicchetti, the niblets ready to be plated from the fridge.

Sardines marinated in red wine then pureed with tomatoes and spread on crostini, nestled next to miniature pastry cups filled with tuna salad spiced up with garam masala. She'd had a wonderful time at Antica Drogheria Mascari buying different kinds of olives, and fresh almonds. An antipasto platter held different salamis, cheeses, asparagus, and baby tomatoes. A long-used salmon dip recipe had been given an Italian twist with the addition of pesto, made from the basil and parsley she grew on the balcony in summer and on the kitchen sill now it was getting cooler.

Wine and champagne glasses clustered near ice buckets set out on the drop-leaf table. Ivy garlands encircled the ice buckets and candles glimmered in more flea market finds of different height candlesticks, some silver, some crystal. A cut glass trifle bowl on a squat stem, another found treasure, held gold and silver metallic baubles threaded through with a garland of fairy lights that sent shards of light dancing across the green tablecloth.

"Mum, this is gorgeous," Lucy said, hugging her, "absolutely gorgeous! Anyone would think you knew we would get engaged the moment we walked in the door." She waggled her left hand in front of Amelia. "Look! He just gave it to me." An oval black opal, shafts of blue and green glinting within a circlet of diamonds. "Isn't it beautiful? It was his mum's. How special is that?"

"Darling girl," Amelia said, tears glistening on her lashes, "I am so very happy for you, and Just Mike. He's perfect for you. And you him!"

"Do you think Dad would approve?" Lucy asked, the light in her eyes dimming a little.

"Yes, my darling, I know he would. He liked Mike."

"I'm glad they met, even if it was years ago. Before, well you know, before it all went pear-shaped."

"Yes, I know, darling." Amelia stroked her daughter's cheek. "Did you ever meet Mike's mother?"

"A couple of times. Way back, when we were at uni. She was nice." Lucy giggled. "Moira is going to be devo to miss this!"

"Don't tell her!"

"Not a chance," Lucy said. "I hardly ever get one up on her." She popped an olive in her mouth. "Er, Mum, is there anything you want to tell me?"

Amelia looked surprised. "I don't think so."

"About Riccardo?"

"Oh, for God's sake, Lucy, he's a friend. He's been very good to me. He, Pietro, and Stefano. They all have. I can't believe my luck at having fallen in with them, and Bria of course."

"Okay. Just asking! Who else is coming?"

"An English woman I met at language class, Fenella Thompson. She's quite grand but lovely once she relaxes. Tigran, can't pronounce his surname, an Armenian chap from school as well. He's a sweetheart. Very swarthy. We all sort of formed a triumvirate of despair during grammar class. And a young Polish girl, Janina, very clever, also from class, who I think would be perfect for Stefano."

"Really, Mum? You're matchmaking?"

"Of course I am. Stefano's a dear boy who just needs a little direction. His mum dying sent him into a spiral. That's when he started getting all the tats. Riccardo is delighted he's been working with Pietro. Apparently, it's the first time he's shown any inclination to do anything long term."

"I can't remember ever seeing you so relaxed, Mum. Despite all the work that went into this spread." Lucy poured them each a Prosecco. "Here's to the Paignton women. All three of them!"

"Soon to be four," Amelia said, thinking of Moira's baby.

"You're going to be very disappointed if it's a boy," Lucy said, turning to welcome her fiancé, her blue eyes alight with love. "I'm glad Mo didn't want to know the sex."

"It won't be!" Amelia smiled as she moved toward the front door where Riccardo and Stefano were crowding in with Pietro and his wife, Giana, whom she had not met before. She knew Bria would be a bit late. Her hotel had no vacancies and faith in the new night receptionist did not run high.

✝

The tub chair cocooned Amelia. She held a glass of iced water with one hand and tickled Dafne's tummy with the other. Her toes, topped in burgundy to match her now worn-off lipstick, wriggled in delight at their release from the red flats that lay at angles on the floor beside the ottoman.

"That was fun, but I'm exhausted! Thanks for the help in tidying up, both of you."

"Nice bunch," Mike said, Lucy tucked into his shoulder.

"I'm impressed with your Italian, Mum. And you're right, Tigran is a sweetie. They all are. Tonight reminded me of our place in New York. Lots of seemingly disparate people coming together at parties. It was fun. You didn't do that at Patanga, did you?"

"A different time in our lives, Lu."

"Well, I'm just glad you're entertaining—having fun—again. You deserve it, Mum, you really do."

"Thank you, darling, now off you both go. Bed time. We have things to do, places to see, wine to drink tomorrow."

"You're not doing anything else now, are you, Amelia?" Mike asked, pulling Lucy to her feet.

"Not a thing. I'm just going to sit for a moment. Good night, my darlings, and congratulations!"

†

The weekend went in a whirl of everything Amelia had promised.

After breakfast at Luca's on Saturday, they picked up a motoscarfo to the Ponte dell'Accademia, then joined the surge of tourists and Italians making their way north to the Christmas Village, at Campo Santa Stefano. The square, usually a wide expanse of stone paving, now housed stalls—alpine huts with red and yellow striped awnings. And lights. Thousands of lights. Children darted in between browsing adults, and pine, orange, and cinnamon filled the air.

"Riccardo told me last night that Father Christmas, can't remember what he's called in Italian..."

"Babbo Natale," Amelia said.

"That's it," Lucy nodded, "well, Riccardo said he'd be on seven-foot stilts!"

"Really? Why?" Mike asked.

"Didn't get that far," Lucy said, fingering a colorful wool scarf tumbling from a basket of them. "I'm going to get this. It's gorgeous. And I'm cold."

"How about a mulled wine?" Amelia asked, seeing a stall further along selling mugs of the brew.

"That too," Lucy replied. "Oh God, there he is! Santa on stilts."

They watched as Babbo Natale and his helper, dressed in a carnival outfit, handed out caramelle e dolci to eager children. Amelia could only imagine the sugar high that would follow as she clicked away at the excited faces. She glanced up to find Lucy watching her.

"I can hardly remember a time Mum didn't have a camera to hand," Lucy said to Mike. "Are you ever going to do anything with all those pics?"

Amelia snapped a photo of the brew bubbling in a copper pot, then one of the girl with rosy cheeks, in an elf hat, who served them mulled wine. "When I have my mezzanine, yes, I will," she replied. "Not sure what yet, but something."

"Good for you, Mum. This really is your time!"

"You know what, darling, I think it is." Amelia took a sip. "This is yum. Okay, I'm going to wander. Let's meet up by the Campiello dei Golossi—it's at the end of the piazza—in an hour or so. Lunch can be sampling all the different things on offer. Bria translated the name as 'greedy corner' so it must be good."

"Righto, see you in a bit."

Amelia watched them merge, hand in hand, into the throng then turned to a stall selling wooden toys. She was going to have fun spoiling her granddaughter. Next, she doubled back and bought Mike the bauta, the Harlequin carnival mask, he had been admiring. The vendor, a voluble bloke wrapped against the chill in a thick scarf and mittens, went into detail about the arlecchino mask's features but after recognizing the words for savage and peasant, Amelia lost the thread. Something about a beard and a bump and a devil. A knave maybe? Her face must have showed her confusion because, after wrapping the mask, he folded a brief description in English into the bag.

"Grazie mille," she said, and laughed and caught his kiss blown with a breezy "Buon Natale." Carefree. The word bubbled up again. Was every Italian a flirt?

As the weak sun became shrouded in fog that oozed in over the lagoon, they headed home for a cup of tea.

"I want you to go out to dinner on your own this evening," Amelia said, waiting for the kettle to boil. "No," she held up her hand to Lucy's protest, "Venice has got to be one of the most romantic cities in the world. You're in love. Go and enjoy it. And frankly, I'm knackered. Dafne and I are going to curl up with a book and glass of that Refosco you kindly gave me, Mike. I might even have two glasses then an early night."

Her phone pinged and, glancing down, she saw a message from Riccardo.

"Oh, wow, Riccardo is offering to take us to Murano tomorrow to see Natale di Vetro."

"Christmas in Glass?" Lucy asked.

"Yes, I've heard it's wonderful—a twenty-foot-tall glass Christmas tree trimmed with glass baubles and decorations. Not to mention the chance to buy all, or any, manner of glassware. Shall I say yes?"

†

Sunday flew by, and chilled by sea spray and fog that had dropped back over them on their way home from Murano, Amelia sank onto the sofa and lay her head back. Mike and Riccardo puttered in the kitchen, setting out fresh panini and porchetta, the roast pork rolled with rosemary and fennel pollen Riccardo had bought at the market. She could hear Lucy humming in the shower. Tomorrow she'd be sad, but today happiness warmed her.

Chapter 13

Lucy's words played a sonata in Amelia's head as she ambled back to the apartment after waving them off on the water taxi to the airport. "Mum, Riccardo really likes you. What's the harm?" The harm? Amelia snorted, then raised a placatory hand to the startled woman pulling a carrello along the pavement. The harm would be spoiling a friendship. Bringing tension to the little group of people who warmed her. Riccardo and Stefano, Pietro and Giana, Bria, and her classmates. And, really, was she cut out for a dalliance?

Fenella, Tigran, and Amelia had agreed to spend Christmas Day together. Each contributing something to the feast to be prepared in Amelia's kitchen, with its full-size oven. There would be no struggling for words—Tigran's English was fluent—just companionship and fun.

Amelia shrugged. No need to think about it for a few days. Riccardo and Stefano had gone south to Rome to stay with his sister. They'd be back for New Year when, Riccardo had said, he would take her to St. Mark's for the fireworks. "But only in the sky, chum," Amelia muttered.

But Lucy's words would not die down.

Peeling spuds for the classmate's feast the following day, Amelia's mind drifted to the good-looking boatman. Nine years.

Christ, she really would be a cougar. And how would Stefano feel? He was just getting his act together. Deciding he'd like to work for Pietro full time. Maybe take some woodworking courses. A fling with his father could send him looping backward. Amelia couldn't do that. And yet, he'd always seemed delighted when his dad took days off to take Amelia to new places.

"He is attractive, although I'm not sure about the mustache. Riccardo, not Stefano," Amelia assured Dafne. But really, where could it go? She rinsed her hands, then poured a glass of the Refosco, her new favorite red wine. Did it matter? Of course it matters! I'm nearly sixty-three. I'm not going to start leaping into bed with every hunky Italian I fancy. Actually, any hunky Italian. Especially one so much younger. And do I want a casual fling? Do I want anything? I'm perfectly happy the way I am. She rubbed her arms. Am I? If I am, why am I obsessing over this? New motto. "Be pleasant, be firm, be friends!"

Amelia bathed and changed for the Christmas Eve midnight mass at St. Mark's Basilica. Bria had warned her to be early in order to ensure a space on a pew. She had also warned her to wrap up warm.

Incense and flickering candles met their entrance in an ethereal welcome. Punctually—Amelia wondered whether it was pronto or presto—music swelled from the organ to embrace those waiting for benediction in the ornate Byzantine basilica. Surprise made her glance at Bria's serene profile when she realized the service would be conducted in English, French, German and, of course, Italian. She glanced around, trying to gauge how many of each nationality graced the pews or those who stood behind. The basilica was packed. People craning to see the altar from the very back of the nave, babies asleep in their parents' arms, children running up and down the aisles. This was family.

The words of the mass glossed over Amelia but the choir, hidden on either side of the chancel, moved her as they sang in one pure and sweet voice. She clutched Bria's hand, tears in her eyes as Italy's favorite Christmas hymn—"Tu Scendi dalle Stelle"—one she'd heard many times but never like this, soared then settled over the congregation like a celestial blanket. Comforting, hopeful that Christ would indeed descend from the starry skies.

As the service drew to a close and the blessing given, the vaulted ceilings lit up in a shimmering cascade of glorious color, a tribute to God, the saints, the angels, Amelia didn't know who, didn't care. Humbled, she whispered, "Amen" and, probably, for the first time in her life, meant it.

"Grazie mille, Bria," she thanked her friend when they emerged into the foggy night stamping their frozen feet, "è magnifico!" Catching the last vaporetto back to Canareggio together, they bussed each other on the cheek as they separated.

Bria's voice wishing her "Buon Natale," followed Amelia down the street.

Her first Venetian Christmas had started perfectly.

Dafne twined around her legs as Amelia locked the door behind her. "Brr, it's cold out there, kitty-kat!"

She shoved her gloves into her coat pocket and hung it and her scarf in the closet fitted behind the spiral stairs. She glanced upward, wondering when the railings would be in place. No point worrying. Right now, she needed hot chocolate. Something shiny caught her eye, and going over to the tree, she saw a shattered ornament.

"Really, Dafne! It's a good thing it was just a bauble and not something precious!" She lifted the kitten and buried her nose in the warm fur. "Leave the tree alone."

Still without a microwave, Amelia padded through to her bedroom after she put milk on to heat. She snuggled into her new dressing gown, an early Christmas present from Lucy, the soft mauve cashmere instantly warming her. Sports socks spoiled the glamour but served a purpose.

Whisking chocolate into the milk, she added a sugar lump, then took a sip and smiled. Decadence. She turned off the main lights so just the tree twinkled, then curled onto the sofa, Dafne on her lap, and thought about the service.

Her hot chocolate finished, she pulled a chenille throw over her legs and lay back looking at the tree. Christmases past paraded in front of her. Leo. Then Lucy and Mike, and Riccardo. And Moira. One more week and she'd be a grandmother.

✝

An insistent brrt, brrt, brrt, nudged her awake. She groped for the phone, wedged between her hip and the sofa.

"Pronto," she answered, disoriented, the Christmas tree lights still flickering.

"You were right. You have a granddaughter."

Amelia bolted upright, dislodging Dafne. "What?"

"You have a granddaughter, Ma."

Amelia realized she was crying. "Oh, my darling girl! How wonderful! You're early. What happened? Why didn't you let me know?"

"A few questions in there."

"Sorry. Are you okay? Is the baby okay? You sound groggy."

120

"I'm okay. She's okay. All a bit quick. She went into distress and they whipped her out."

"You had a C-section?"

"Yeah. I started okay, then it went tits-up."

"But you're okay now? You're sure? You poor darling."

"I'm a bit spacey, even though they didn't have to knock me out. It felt weird knowing they were slicing my belly open behind the curtain. They wouldn't let Cynthia come in with me. Not family." Before Amelia could respond, Moira continued, her voice suddenly small, "Mum, can you come?"

"Oh, my darling, of course. I'll be on a plane in the morning." She could hear her daughter crying too. "Moira, everything is okay, yes? You're not keeping anything from me?"

"No, Mum, I promise. I just want you. I don't want to be alone. Cynthia and Adam are great but they're not you."

"Then I'll be there. You need to get some sleep now. And I've got things to arrange."

"Thank you, Mum. I'll let Adam know you'll be arriving. He called Cynthia for me then got me here. Thank God I've got such a wonderful tenant." She paused. "She's beautiful, Mum. Don't you want to know her name?" There was a smile in Moira's voice. As if she could relax now she knew her mother was coming.

"Of course I do, darling. I'm sorry. I was just worried about you. And her."

"It has to be 'Natalie,' doesn't it?"

"Yes, I suppose it does. Born on Christmas Day. A very special delivery, my darling girl."

"They're coming in to check on us again. Will you let Lucy know?"

"Of course. Get some sleep now. I'll be there sometime tomorrow. Today. Happy Christmas, darling girl!"

Two hours later, Amelia stretched and yawned. She ticked hours off backward on her fingers. If her flight left at 1:30 p.m., she had to be at the airport at 11:30 a.m. There would be limited vaporetto service on Christmas Day, and Riccardo wasn't around to call on, so she'd need to leave the apartment at 10 a.m. to make sure. Fenella and Tigran would still come and cook in her kitchen, then Fenella would take Dafne home with her. The Englishwoman was proving to be a good friend. She'd keep an eye on the place too. The cat carrier? Amelia went to the closet by the front door and reached up for it. Oh God, her back ached. Pack now, or sleep now? Sleep won. She could grab three hours. Maybe.

Amelia lay down on the bed, her mind scrabbling. Lucy had burst into tears too. Amelia had heard Mike's worried voice, then his bellow of a laugh and a shouted, "Congratulations, Nonna!"

She must remember to send Riccardo a text in the morning. She could do that from the airport. And Bria. Now sleep.

✝

It felt strange to be sitting on a half-empty plane on Christmas Day. She wondered whether the crew would be resentful at ferrying people around the world but, so far, everyone had been more than pleasant.

She finished her Prosecco, tightened her seat belt, and settled back. She should try to get a bit more sleep. Moira had been so grateful when she'd called back before she left the palazzo that she'd burst into tears again. Her tough-talking daughter reduced to a soggy mess in one day of motherhood. Amelia smiled. She could hardly wait to hold her granddaughter.

Natalie. "What would you have said to that, Leo?" Her whispered words bounced back from the window as Marco Polo Airport became swallowed in the winter mist.

The deep sleep Amelia craved did not come even with a movie scrolling in front of her eyes and yet she was too tired to read. She ate lunch, had one more glass of Prosecco, then switched to water, had the afternoon snack then, as her ears popped and she felt the plane begin to descend, her head nodded back.

Eyes red-rimmed and gritty she accepted her passport from the immigration official's terse welcome and pulled her carry-on to the taxi rank. Despite knowing the taxi would take longer and cost considerably more, the thought of battling the E train, then changing twice, was too much for her addled mind.

The cab neared Harlem and, as familiar landmarks appeared, Amelia felt her energy surge. Memories of the children playing and riding their bikes in Riverside Park, of Sunday brunches at outdoor cafés, of the flower shop on Broadway. It had been a good life, for the most part. New York's diversity, Harlem in particular, had given her a sense of freedom she'd found lacking in Sydney. The place she had once considered home but which had not lived up to her expectations after her return from Papua New Guinea. She'd learned that going back anywhere was never easy. Amelia sighed. Home, as a concept, had turned into an elusive ideal. That place that accepted you with no strings. Perhaps it was all just notional, theoretical. Promulgated to keep the masses happy! Perhaps her attitude of home was wherever she happened to be played into that sense. "Whatever, adaptability is no bad thing."

"You say what?" the cabbie glanced at her in the rearview mirror.

"Sorry, talking to myself," Amelia said, fishing for her purse as they pulled up outside a four-story brownstone. It was as big as the one she and Leo had owned eleven years ago. Concern nudged pride. She had no idea the art world, well, the auction-eering world paid so well. But Moira did have a lodger.

The front door opened moments after she rang the bell. "Hi. Adam?"

The tall, stooped, owl-eyed man, his chin strewn with stubble, nodded. "You must be Moira's mom. Come on in."

"Yes, I'm Amelia Paignton. Thank you. And thank you, Adam, for getting her to the hospital." She could feel his pale eyes on her back as she hauled her case up the steps.

"She'd have managed," he replied with a shrug. "She always does."

"Doesn't mean she should have to," Amelia said, resentment building.

"No, 'spose not. But Cynthia met us there. Here you are. The kitchen. I picked up a few supplies for you on my way back from the hospital this morning."

"That's very kind, thank you." Amelia couldn't quite gauge the man. "How is she?"

"Actually," a smile flicked, "she's weepy. Not like her at all."

"A baby will do that." Amelia bristled at Adam's tone. "Espe-cially after a difficult birth."

"I 'spose." He shrugged. "I imagine you'll want to see Moira immediately."

Amelia nodded.

"There's a list of numbers on the board over there. Cabs and so forth. Oh, and I'll show you your room. It's on the next floor up. The baby will be in Cynthia's old room. Up another floor and across from Moira. She, Cynthia, left a month ago."

"Yes, I know. I can find my way around, thank you. Your apartment is on the top floor, right?"

"Yeah. That's the elevator there," he pointed to a door by the kitchen. "Right, I'll leave you. My number's on the list too, if you need anything. Or you can just shout. That's what Moira does."

Amelia watched him pull the elevator door closed then heard it ascend. Strange man, and yet Moira spoke fondly of him. He could've carried her case up. "Not fair, Amelia. He would've if you'd let him show you. Or maybe not." She tried to recall what he did. She knew he was always around. She remembered Moira saying it was very useful having someone to open the door to deliveries. A writer, maybe.

"Righto," Amelia said to the kitchen. "A cup of tea." She filled the kettle, relieved Moira had one. A vision of searching New York City for a kettle when they had first arrived in America thirty years earlier flashed before her eyes. Leo had not understood her frustration, telling her to just use the microwave like everyone else. "Then a nose around. Then a shower. Then Moira. And Natalie!"

Chapter 14

"Tomorrow?" Amelia tried to keep her voice calm, her finger clutched by Natalie's tiny hand.

"Insurance, Mum, don't you remember? Three days tops, unless you're dying!"

"That's outrageous. You've just had a C-section. Your milk's not in yet. You're an old first-time mum."

"Gee, thanks for that!" Moira laughed.

"You know what I mean. I'll speak to someone."

"No, you won't. It'll be fine. And anyway, you're here."

"That's not the point. No one should be shoved out just because of health insurance."

"Welcome to America! You've forgotten a lot in eleven years, haven't you?" Moira looked at her baby. "She is beautiful, isn't she? It's not just me."

"Yes, darling, she is. And nice deflection. But I still think two days is not long enough."

"It'll be fine. I want to get home. Get used to things. It's noisy here."

"Alright. But I want the doctor on speed dial. And the cab service. And anyone else I can think of should we need something."

"The most important person to have on speed dial is Adam. He's a master at getting things done."

"Hmm!" Amelia fitted her granddaughter into the crook of her arm. "I love her dark hair."

"I take it you haven't taken to my lodger."

"He's a bit strange, darling."

"I suppose he is. But once you get used to him, he's a dear. And, Mum, he has been so good to me."

"Well, then, I shall like him. No matter what. Now, if you're leaving hospital tomorrow, I'm going to get going and pick up some groceries and sort out a few things."

"Yeah, I'm sorry. I really didn't expect her to be early. Everyone told me the first was always late. I know I wasn't as organized as I should've been. I just didn't want to miss that auction—the one on the lesser-known Impressionists. To put an Alfred Sisley, and a Gustave Caillebotte, under the hammer was incredible. It was a blast, Mum."

"I'm surprised you could fit behind the lectern!"

"Funny!" Moira looked at her daughter in her mother's arms. "I can't wait to be able to talk to Lucy, properly. You know, not in here. I'm going to ask her to be Natalie's godmother. And Cynthia. Not that she's going to be christened. She can make her own mind up when she's older."

Amelia thought of the lace christening gown she'd bought on her trip to Burano with Riccardo but stopped herself from commenting. That was a battle for another day.

✝

Amelia's initial reaction to Adam did ease as over the next few weeks he more than justified Moira's championing, and the more she realized the man in the attic cared deeply for her daughter. Too deeply. Moira treated him with a teasing respect, a fondness but nothing more.

Careful not to intrude, Adam always took the elevator rather than the stairs that climbed through the old house, but always happened to be around when something was needed. He had been right. Moira rarely phoned him, instead standing at the bottom of the stairs to his apartment and shouting. He was surprisingly adept with the baby, another plus in Amelia's book. More so than Cynthia, although she handled Moira with adroitness.

Her daughter, on New Year's Eve and unused to restricted movement, learned that stitches across the abdomen had a tendency to limit even the most determined. After railing at her inactivity and getting tetchy, Amelia had suggested they take a slow walk along the street, just to the corner and back.

"Only," Amelia warned Moira, "if you walk and don't push the pram. It's a dull day, so not very tempting to go far."

"Fine."

"My God, you sound like a grumpy teenager! Go get my granddaughter ready. Slowly."

Amelia bumped the pram down the porch steps and waited for Moira and Natalie to appear. London plane trees lined the street in military precision, splendid despite their naked limbs, a few rusty leaves loitered at the base of the trunks. Clusters of fuzzy brown seed balls clung to the bare branches. With her camera to her eye, Amelia did not hear the front door opening, only Moira's wail. She spun to see her self-possessed daughter clutching her daughter, tears flowing down both their cheeks.

"She pooped, again!"

"They do that."

"No. You don't understand. I've just changed her. It took forever to get her dressed. I can't do this."

Amelia tugged the pram back up the steps and manhandled it through the front door, then took the crying baby. "Come on, darling, let's not bother today. It's overcast and cold. You put the kettle on. I'll change Natalie and we'll save the walk for a nicer day."

"But I want to go out!"

"Okay, you go. Just be careful of slippery leaves."

"But I wanted to take her."

"Enough now, Moira," Amelia said. "Either go by yourself, or put the kettle on."

Unlayering the baby, Amelia dropped the stained snowsuit and soiled leggings in the bucket by the changing table, grabbed Natalie's waving legs in one hand and a clutch of baby wipes in the other. "You are pretty disgusting, sweetpea. You need to give your mama a break, okay? She's trying her best."

A gurgle escaped around the fist in Natalie's mouth.

"Disgusting but gorgeous!" Amelia amended. "Come on, let's find Mum." The baby tucked into her arm, she held onto the stair rail, terrified she'd lose her footing. She couldn't remember being this cautious with her babies. "You were nearly forty years younger," she said to the wall.

Moira stood, staring out the kitchen window, sobs and hiccups accompanying her heaving shoulders.

"What was I thinking?" she asked, swiping her running nose. "I can't do this. What will I do when you leave?"

"Here, take Natalie while I get us a cup of tea. Or would you like a hot chocolate?"

"I don't want anything. Oh God, why does she always cry when I take her?"

"She doesn't. But right now she is because, my darling, she knows you are her milk machine and crying is the only way she can tell you she's hungry. And, Moira, she can sense your stress. So, for both your sakes, and mine, you need to calm down."

"Mum, what will I do? When you're gone." Fresh tears dribbled down Moira's face.

Amelia reached up and wiped them away. "Well, I'm not going for another few weeks, by which time you will be absolutely fine. Most of the time. Get used to the fact you will have periodic rants and tears, for the next eighteen years at least. And right now, Moira, you are having a fit of the baby blues. It's normal."

"I'm a cow." Moira looked at milk seeping through her jumper. "I'm wearing pads and I'm still leaking."

"Yup. Cow just about describes it. Now, whip 'em out and feed your daughter. Despite what some baby books say, you cannot spoil a baby this young. All she needs is you. It's demanding. It's exhausting. But, and I really mean this, darling, this is the most important job you have at the moment, okay. To feed your baby."

"Did Gran tell you all this?" Moira lifted her sweater and Natalie, her lips searching, latched on. "Ouch!" Moira winced.

"Some of it. She believed more in the schedule-style of parenting. Your dad, though, was wonderful. For someone who had not been thrilled at the prospect of parenthood, you charmed him from the moment he held you."

"That would be nice. Someone to share it with."

"I know, darling. But you've always chosen the tough route and, Moira, you've always succeeded. You'll be fine."

"But you're a world away!"

"Would you really want me on your doorstep?" Amelia whisked milk for hot chocolate.

"Yes, if you looked after everything all the time. Like now."

Moira pushed her breast back into the maternity bra and handed Natalie to her grandmother. "You burp her."

"No, you burp her. Get used to doing things with one hand. It's surprising how adept we become."

✝

Days flowed into calmer days, into calmer weeks until, at the five-week mark, Amelia began to feel it was time to head home. Moira's auction house allowed six weeks' paid maternity leave, unusual in the US, and another six weeks' unpaid leave that she was not sure she should take.

"You're nuts!"

Amelia, cooking supper, could hear Lucy's voice over the speaker-phone in the study, where Moira was catching up on mail, the baby asleep in her bassinet.

"Natalie might be the only child you have, and you want to rush back to work? Enjoy her. What's another six weeks? You can afford it. And, frankly Mo, you need to get used to having a child without Mum around to pick up the pieces."

"Sod you, Lucy!"

"Okay but think about it. Now, you might be a lady of leisure but I have to get to work. It's eight o'clock here, and Mike is dropping me off this morning."

"Lu, I didn't mean that. I'm sorry!"

"I know. It's okay. But think about it, yeah?" Lucy repeated. "Mum's got to get back to Venice, to her life. She deserves it. Take another six weeks, get your chicks in order. You know, with child minding and stuff. Then go back to work."

"When are you coming to meet your niece?"

"When I don't have to change a nappy!"

"Ha, ha! No, really Lu, when?"

"How does Easter sound?"

Amelia grinned as she heard the phone clicking.

✝

As Moira relaxed into motherhood, Amelia gradually lengthened her forays away from the brownstone on 152nd Street, to give her daughter time and space to figure out a routine that would work for her. Considering how many had shown up for Leo's funeral, Amelia only felt drawn to a handful of people from the old days.

Sarah Bailey, of course, from whom she'd learned so much about African American history. Particularly the Geechee culture. Sarah's pride in being able to trace her lineage back to the Gullah barrier island had been what piqued Amelia's interest in understanding more about Australian aboriginal culture, particularly painting. They'd met in a coffee shop in Harlem. Two young women whose glance had connected over a child's bad behavior. Fortunately, neither of Amelia's children. Sarah had been an adjunct professor at City College specializing in Black studies, and their friendship had grown from the occasional coffee, to talks long into the night over a bottle of wine. Sarah had been one of the two people who had known of Leo's dementia in those frightening early days.

And Charlie Warner, now elderly and who had not been able to travel all that distance for the funeral, had been the other. Not only had he been the first in New York to believe in Leo's work, he had also helped Moira with internships as she forged her way in the art world after her return from London. His delight at the news of his second Paignton protégé had been palpable, and Moira had promised she would take Natalie to meet him.

"Amelia, my dear," Charlie said, levering himself up on his cane to greet her as his housekeeper closed the door. "How lovely to see you are still a beautiful woman. I'm not in the least surprised. Your kind of grace ages well."

"And you're still a charmer, Charlie," Amelia said, with a laugh as she kissed his sunken cheeks.

"Sadly, no longer. Come, sit, sit. Mrs. Puddleduck will bring champagne."

"Mrs. Puddleduck, really? And champagne. It's only three."

"Don't be so pedestrian, my dear. Champagne is acceptable at any time of the day, or night, come to that. And her name is Jemima. How could she possibly be anything but Mrs. Puddleduck? Fortunately, she has a sense of humor and doesn't seem to mind! Now, tell me everything!"

Amelia had forgotten how engaging Charlie could be. She laughed at his sometimes pithy wit and piercing observations of both current events and old acquaintances, eyes lively behind bottle-top glasses. His delight in her decision to live in Venice made her realize how much she missed La Serenissima. That it was almost time to go back.

"And what about you, Charlie?" Amelia asked. "It's been all about me, and the girls, and the latest Paignton. How are you? Really? No brush off."

"Oh, my dear, old age is rather tedious. Add gay, and life can be lonely. I should have found a younger lover when I still could, rather than always be the younger in the couple. And of course, so many of my, what I call 'true' friends, died well before their prime. AIDs nearly achieved what the evangelicals still long to do. Kill us off." His chuckle was sad.

Amelia reached for his hand, now wrinkled and dry. His face, despite the boxer's nose, once attractive and tanned, now hatched with lines and age spots.

"You know, my dear, Leo had it right. Leave town before town leaves you. Although going to the Pacific might have been a bit extreme. His talent was prodigious. Right until the end."

"Not the last five years," Amelia corrected. "It seemed to happen overnight. One day he could mix color, and paint, the next he hardly knew which end of a brush to hold. It made him so angry." Tears trembled on her lashes. "Silly, it was years ago."

"Not silly at all, Amelia. I hope Leo knew how lucky he was. Not always the easiest of men! Now, shall we open another bottle?"

✝

Moira stood on the sidewalk, Natalie in her arms, as Adam lifted Amelia's suitcase into the trunk of the cab, the driver comfortable behind the wheel. Adam blushed behind his stubble when she hugged him, his eyes flicking rapidly as he backed away.

Amelia stroked Natalie's dark curls. "Alright, sweetpea, be good for Mummy and I'll see you in Venice in the summer. And you, my darling," she leaned over Natalie to kiss her daughter, "be kind to yourself. Remember you're a good mum and that there are no real rules."

"I'm learning that! Thank you, Mum. I couldn't have got through this without you."

"Of course you would've. You've got it covered, Moira. You just have to figure it out one day at a time. You've got Adam and Cynthia. And Lucy will be here soon. And Just Mike." Amelia blinked hard and swallowed the lump in her throat. "You call me, anytime. Promise?"

"You bet. You'll probably regret that. Now go, before I start crying."

"Me too!"

Settled in her seat and about to turn her phone to airplane mode, Amelia noticed a message from Moira. She laughed as she read.

Thank you, Nonna. I love my Italian christening gown. Now Mummy will have to baptize me. I can't wait to see you in Venice in the summer. With love from Natalie. XXX

Chapter 15

"Ciao, Amelia!"

Waiting in line to climb aboard the vaporetto, Amelia spun to see Riccardo waving from the jetty near Marco Polo Airport. "What are you doing here?"

"Moira, she message me." He grinned as he helped her into the motoscafo and kissed her cheeks. "Long time you gone, Amelia. Benevenuta a casa!" He welcomed her home. "We miss you."

Apart from letting him know she would not be joining him for New Year's Eve, Amelia had not contacted Riccardo, giving herself time to view him from a distance. She and Bria, on the other hand, had emailed a number of times, and Fenella had sent regular Dafne updates. The wind whipped her hair and she fumbled for dark glasses, the glare hitting her eyes as they headed south east to Venice. Excitement rumbled in her stomach. So different to when she first arrived, over a year earlier. Then it had been trepidation. She grinned up at Riccardo. This really did feel like coming home.

"You join me for wine and cicchetti tonight, yes?" he asked as they pulled up outside Palazzo Ambrosio.

"Not tonight, Riccardo. I need to sleep." Disappointment dulled his eyes. "Thank you for meeting me. It was kind. I'll see you tomorrow, eh?" Italian felt rusty on her tongue. She clambered out and pulled her case across the cobbles. About to key in the code, a long-haired young man, an earring glinting, opened the door and lifted her case over the lintel.

"Grazie mille," she said. "Vivi qui?"

"Sì, I think," he replied, his face coloring. "I'm sorry but that's about the extent of my Italian. I think you asked if I lived here. Right?"

"Oh, you're English. I didn't expect that. Sorry. And thanks,"

"Do you want some help?" he nodded to her case.

"No, no. Have wheels will travel. But thanks. See you around."

"Okay. I'm James, James Arnold, by the way."

"Nice to meet you, James. I'm Amelia Paignton. Bye now!" She hurried to the lift and dragged the metal door open, then clanged it shut and waited as it shuddered to a start. Fumbling for her key, she felt an overwhelming sense of belonging. She pushed the front door open and laughed. "Honey, I'm home! Hello, Dafne." She picked up the kitten weaving around her legs, who burrowed into her neck. "I think you remember me. You've grown. That was kind of Fenella to have you here to greet me."

Amelia kicked the door shut, left her case, and carried the cat on a tour of the apartment. Her apartment. Peach-colored roses filled the air with their heady scent. "G'day, Leo," she said to his photograph on the bedside table. Only as she came back into the living room did she realize someone had taken down the Christmas decorations, then, glancing up, saw that railing now graced the mezzanine.

"I am the luckiest woman alive," she said to the kitten. "What kindness."

✝

Jet lag made her sluggish. West to east always hit harder. After cappuccino and a cornetto at Luca's the second morning, Amelia ambled over to see Bria in her little office behind the hotel reception. The tubs at the entrance to the hotel now flourished with forget-me-nots and daffodils. The colors matched laundry hanging from the windows opposite.

They embraced as Bria said, "Ciao, Amelia. I miss you. Riccardo, he missed you. Always he ask of news."

"I missed you too." Amelia groaned. "What am I going to do, Bria? He's a dear man but I'm not looking for a lover. Just friends."

Bria laughed. "Italian men all want to be lovers. You tell 'im. It's okay." She poured coffee, "And I think is better, you know for Stefano. Adesso, now, Pasqua, it is soon, eh?"

Amelia nodded. "Lucy and Mike are going to New York for Easter to meet the baby. It's nice for Moira to have something to look forward to."

"And you? You do not want to be there?"

"You know what, Bria? I don't. Strange, eh? I love that I could go and help Moira. How lucky I can afford to hop on a plane, and that little toot is just gorgeous. But I've had my babies. I'm thrilled to be Nonna but I don't need to be involved all the time. And Moira's got to figure things out for herself. Does that make me a bad mother?"

"In Italy, yes!" Bria's violet eyes twinkled.

"Did you ever want kids?" Silence accompanied Amelia's question and she hoped she hadn't overstepped the mark. She stayed quiet.

"No." Bria sighed. "I don't know. Maybe. Maybe if Giovanni lived. It is expected." The regal woman sipped her coffee.

"And you were never tempted to marry again? He died a long time ago."

"No. But I have some lovers. When I am young."

Amelia spluttered, her coffee spilling onto the saucer. "Maybe you should hook up with Riccardo." Their laughter flowed around the small room as she quoted back one of Bria's favorite sayings, "Non ora, quando?"

"Uffa, you learn too much Italian. If not now, when? I tell you. Never!" The bell on the reception desk tinkled and Bria stood. "I have a question. You wait, eh?"

Muffled voices then the sound of the lift grate closing followed by the office door opening told of new guests. "So," Bria picked up their conversation, "Pasqua, Easter, it is too busy in Venice. Martina needs help, so my niece from Milano, she comes to work here. For experience. I tell you she studies hotel management, yes?"

Amelia nodded as she put away the shopping list she had started to compile. In bold letters, she had written 'desk and rug.' The mezzanine was finished. No excuse not to get started. Ideas for a coffee-table book had bubbled on her walks in New York, and on the plane home. She was ready.

"So..."

Bria's voice broke into her fleeting thoughts.

"... Silvia, my niece from my husband, work and we go to the vineyard. Yes?"

"Thank you, Bria, but I think I need to stay put for a while."

"No, no. Easter is for family. You come."

An image of Lorenzo floated in. Surly and unwelcoming. "Honestly, I don't think your brother would be keen on that."

"Uffa, it is my home too. I am too old for his nonsense. Lorenzo is too old. No, we go!"

And with that, it was settled. They would go to the vineyard on Good Friday and stay four nights. Leaving Bria to her guests, Amelia stopped at the corner shop and loaded up her carrello with groceries and wine. What the hell. Isn't this what she wanted? The freedom not to be tied. "Damn. The cat." Her exclamation alarmed an elderly man walking by. She couldn't keep asking Fenella.

†

"How's Natalie?" Amelia switched the phone off speaker for clearer reception.

"She smiled, Mum. And it's not wind."

"Oh, darling, what fun. You'll start to feel less cow-like now."

"Tell that to my boobs!"

Amelia laughed, delighted Moira's mood was light.

"Is Natalie ready to meet her aunt and Just Mike? They'll be there soon."

"Yeah, we're good. And I forgot to tell you, Mrs. Humphreys, the neighbor you met, the one who used to be a pediatric nurse, remember? She's looked after Natalie a couple of evenings now and is a lovely woman. Really calm and practical. Natalie loves her. And Adam. And Cynthia's getting better, not quite so terrified. My daughter is going to be the most spoiled child in Harlem!"

"She deserves nothing less, darling," Amelia said, thrilled there was someone so close and so reliable to care for her granddaughter.

"And the other bit of news, well, two other bits really, is that I've asked work if I can have an extra three weeks' unpaid leave— until a couple of weeks after Easter. So I can play while Lucy and Mike are here. And they said yes! I'll do a bit of legwork from home for the next auction—another Impressionist one, but not as grand as the one last December. Isn't that great?"

"Good for you, Moira. I know it's hard work sometimes but you'll never regret this time with that little munchkin."

"That's what I thought. And now she's sleeping through most nights, life is altogether different."

Amelia laughed. "You didn't sleep through until you were about eight months. It nearly killed me. Count yourself lucky, kiddo!"

"I think Natalie's got your genes. She's pretty chilled. What are you doing for Easter, Mum?"

Amelia heard the baby gurgle and felt a tug of longing. "I'm going to Bria's vineyard."

"I thought you didn't like her brother. What's his name?"

"Lorenzo. I don't. But Bria promises he's less pissy now—it's been six months since I've seen him, so fingers crossed. Although I still think I got browbeaten."

"What about Dafne?"

"There's a young Englishman living downstairs who's going to come and feed her."

"You sure about that, Mum? What's he like?"

"Long-haired and ear-ringed. Well, one ear."

"Really?"

"He's a good kid. Studying Italian and art. He's looking forward to having a quiet space to get some work done. It seems to be party central in his apartment. And despite his looks, he's really rather serious. It'll be fine."

Amelia picked a black cat hair off her cream sweater. A pointless action as she then gathered Dafne up. There was silence. She looked along the canal as she waited. Moira had said there were two things, but there would be no point prodding her.

"Mum?"

"Still here, darling. What's up?"

"Nothing really."

"You're sure?"

There was a moment's silence, again.

"Natalie's father got in touch."

Amelia frowned. "Oh? How do you feel about that?"

"Weird, actually, Ma!"

"What prompted him? Has he heard about Natalie? You must know some people in common."

"Not really. We were discreet and it didn't last enough to get entangled in each other's lives."

Amelia waited.

"He's left his wife. Again."

"I thought you said they were having another baby."

"They did. But it's not enough to save their marriage."

"Okay." Amelia tipped Dafne onto the floor and went to the kitchen. Her phone back on speaker, she poured a glass of sparkling water and, as she sliced a lemon, heard Moira's voice.

"That's it? Okay?"

"I'm thinking, darling. I don't want to say the wrong thing."

"For God's sake, just say it, Mum!"

Amelia sneezed.

"Sorry. Bubbles up my nose. Okay, Moira. I understood, though didn't altogether agree, about not telling him you were pregnant. But that was over a year ago, and you haven't mentioned him once. Not even when Natalie was first born. Doesn't that tell you something?"

She heard her daughter sigh and waited.

"That's rather what I thought, Mum, but I keep thinking of what you said. You know, about Natalie knowing her father?"

"He's got four other children, darling. How much time will he have for a baby the same age as his last child?"

"But what about down the line? What about when she starts asking about her father? Or health issues?"

"Darling, you have a beautiful, healthy baby. You don't owe this man anything. If, when Natalie is older and wants to meet to him, then fine. In this day and age, it's not hard to find someone. It's clichéd, but let's cross that bridge when we have to. In the meantime, Natalie has Adam, and soon, Just Mike, that's enough men in her life. And who knows what's around the corner? You could be whisked off your feet tomorrow. Baby and all. Okay?"

"Not with leaking boobs!"

Amelia laughed. "Moira, you're gorgeous any which way. And smart. And accomplished. Don't ever forget."

"You're my mum, you have to say that." A wail came from across the ocean. "Thanks, Mum, gotta go. Love you."

"Back at you, kiddo. Bye!"

Her glass of water drained, Amelia tipped the lemon slice into the sink then poured a glass of Custoza, a wine from Veneto she had never heard of until Matteo had introduced her to it at Caffè Dodo. Next, she flipped on Vivaldi's "Four Seasons," tipped olives and feta into a bowl, and took it and her wine and settled into the tub chair.

Her feet on the ottoman, she twisted the glass and watched as light caught the swirling wine in an eddy of cornsilk yellow. She couldn't decide if it was orange blossom or elderflower she could smell. The crisp, slightly bitter aftertaste left a tingle on her lips.

"So, Leo, what do you think of that? I'm still never quite sure with Moira. She's always been so much pricklier than Lucy." Amelia sipped her wine. "I think Natalie's father, whatever his name is, sounds a shit. He walks out again three months after his new baby is born. Both his new babies. I don't care how many times Moira said I'd have liked him." Her feet dropped to the floor and she stood. Gazing along the canal she wondered how she would've felt if one of Leo's affairs had resulted in a baby. Would she have ever known? She sighed. Probably. He would not have been able to keep a secret that big. Perhaps that was why she forgave him his dalliances. Because they were short-lived. Never a real threat. But a baby? No, even for her, that would've been too much.

"Oh, Leo, was I a fool? Naïve? Probably yes, on both counts. But I loved you. With every fiber of my being."

Amelia licked her lips, surprised they were salty. Tears? She hadn't cried for him for months.

Chapter 16

This time, it was Amelia who hired the car for her and Bria to drive to the Scutari Vineyard a few miles west of Soave. Her nerves threatened to get the better of her as she waited for her friend at the Piazzale Roma, the transport hub and only place for cars in Venice.

"It's only ninety kilometers. Straight road. E70 all the way. I can do this."

"Ciao, Amelia. You speak to yourself?" Bria's violet eyes glimmered with amusement as they kissed.

"I'm giving myself a pep talk," Amelia admitted, eyeing the Fiat Panda. Much as she'd liked the idea of zipping around in a Fiat 500, she wanted something larger for her first foray on Italian roads.

"Non c'è bisogno, no need. It is easy. And better I am with you, the first time, eh? Remember, all Italians think they are Enzo Ferrari, or maybe today, Mario Andretti."

"Huh, I thought he was an American racing driver."

"Uffa, born in Italy, so he is Italian. He win Formula One twelve times."

"Bravo for him!" Amelia adjusted the mirrors, hoping she could keep track of vehicles speeding all around her. "Just don't talk until we've left Venice."

Bria laughed as she buckled up. "We stop in Padua for coffee, eh? You have heard of Caffè Pedrocchi?"

Amelia shook her head, her grip tight on the steering wheel. "I'll need more than a bloody coffee after this."

Bria ignored her and continued, "Caffè Pedrocchi—it is special. È sublime!"

Amelia risked a glance at the woman sitting tall next to her. Sublime? "Wow! Why?"

"Padua is famous for many things. Your Shakespeare, eh? Katherina in Taming of the Shrew. The university. The botanical gardens and, of course, Giotto's frescoes." Bria paused. "But also, to us Italians, it is known as 'the city of the three withouts.'"

About to question her understanding of Italian, she was stopped by Bria as she raised her forefinger in the air and began the list.

"One, Prato della Valle. You know the translation in English?" she asked.

Amelia shook her head. She couldn't focus on Italian while driving.

"In ancient times, it is a bog—the meadow without grass—now it is one of the biggest squares in not just Italy, but Europe. Two," another finger went up, "the saint without a name."

"That must be the only saint in Italy without one," Amelia said, thinking of all the saint's days on the calendar.

"He has a name—St. Anthony, but Paduani just refer to the church as 'the Saint.'"

"That's a bit of a stretch then," Amelia said with a laugh. The moment she realized she had relaxed, she tensed again.

"And three," Bria's third finger joined the others in the periphery of Amelia's vision, "Caffè Pedrocchi!"

"What hasn't that got?" Amelia asked,

"It is the café without doors because it has never closed. In nearly two hundred years."

"Okay, I guess we'd better go there then. Is it easy to get to? I don't want to get stuck in traffic."

"Molto facile!"

Driving around central Padua looking for a parking spot did not prove easy, despite Bria's words, and Amelia began to wish for the smaller Fiat 500.

"I hope this coffee is worth it," she said, locking the car and following Bria's straight back through a smattering of people to the main square.

"Eccoci qui," Bria said, heading for the only free table under the portico. She turned to a hovering waiter, "Due Caffè Pedrocchi," she ordered.

Amelia, her shoulders lowering, turned to watch the square, playing her usual game of spot the nationality. The waiter delivered two steaming cups of coffee. Etched with great panache on the white china was the majestic Caffè Pedrocchi gold logo.

"So what's all the fuss about?" she asked, reaching for the spoon.

"No, no." Bria stopped her hand. "You must not stir! Just taste."

A hint of mint rose up through the dusting of cocoa as Amelia lifted the cup.

"Oh, God, that is good," she said to Bria's smug look. "What's in it?"

"One hundred percent Arabica espresso, fresh cream, and mint syrup. If you stir, the unique balance of flavors is changed."

"You win. This is definitely worth the agony of parking."

After their coffee and a brief look around, they continued on to the Scutari Vineyard. Amelia, her confidence growing behind the wheel, enjoyed the undulating countryside, each hillside planted with vines at angles most advantageous to the sun like a giant quilt threaded with large cross stitches. Greens of every hue shaking off the drabness of winter. When they turned off the autostrada, wildflowers filled the verges in an exuberant display of spring.

Amelia noticed a smile tweak Bria's lips as they passed through the newly painted gates of the vineyard and the straightened sign. Orderly lines of vines, in the throes of their bud burst, spread out from either side of the poplar-lined and repaved drive. Shutters had been rehung and painted hunter green, a contrast to the old stone of the villa. The previous air of neglect lifted further as vats of geraniums, a welcome splash of red and purple, delineated the edge of the patio, behind which a table was already set for lunch.

"Bravissimo!" Bria hit the dash in excitement. "He is back. Lorenzo is back! The man you met before, that was not my brother. He just is foolish with the women. Always he choose the wrong one. Come!"

✝

After greeting Agnese, the jovial housekeeper whose bottom lip jiggled as if in a constant state of anticipation, Amelia went to her room to unpack while Bria discussed the feast to be prepared for Easter Sunday. A day, Bria told Amelia, when the vineyard workers and their families came and ate roast lamb with the family out on the patio. If the rain gods planned on performing, the feast would be moved indoors to the formal dining room which ran the width of the villa and was rarely used. But, Bria assured her, it never rained at Easter.

Changing into walking boots, Amelia picked up her camera and made her way downstairs and out to the wisteria-clad pergola running from the villa to the pool, then on to fields of vines. Pea-shaped blooms tumbled around her like a purple waterfall. Breathing in the sweet lilac-like scent, she felt a moment of pure happiness, followed by melancholy. Leo would have stopped, reached for his sketchpad and, a week later, a painting would begin to emerge. Amelia shook her head to dislodge the image, then reached for her camera and ambled along the bee-filled bower.

"Buongiorno, Amelia."

She spun from the macro-shot she was composing. Surprised even more when Lorenzo leaned in to kiss her cheeks, and a dog of indeterminate parentage jumped up at the same time.

"Oh, you startled me. Buongiorno, Lorenzo. Nice to see you. Thank you for having me here, again."

He shrugged, scolded the dog away, then asked in English, "You have seen wisteria like this before?"

"No. It's glorious. It reminds me of the jacaranda trees at home. In Australia, I mean."

"But here only a few short weeks. It is the harbinger of summer."

For a man who barely spoke a word the last time she was here, and never in English, Amelia wasn't quite sure what to make of this Lorenzo. Charm oozed from every pore. Bria must have spoken to him.

"Come, Bria sent me to say lunch is ready."

Franco, the new manager, joined them. Yet another striking Italian, Amelia noted as the lunch slipped into a laughter-filled afternoon, fueled by the delicious and crisp Soave in which the vineyard specialized. Franco, recently returned from a couple of years in America working in the Napa Valley, proved a lively addition. He told Amelia he came from a long line of vintners but that his two elder brothers were in line to inherit the family business.

"If it's a family business, isn't there room for you?" Amelia asked.

"Not if I want to make new wines. Experiment. My father and my brothers are tradition bound."

"Tradition is not always bad, Franco." Lorenzo broke off his quiet discussion with Bria.

"No, but it must not stall progress. Hand in hand, eh, in conjunction with innovation?" Franco replied, his face serious. "And now I must return to work. Ciao." He pushed his chair back, bowed slightly to the ladies, nodded to Lorenzo and left.

Amelia glanced at her host, and could almost sense Bria holding her breath, waiting for an explosion from her brother.

Instead, he asked, "You will allow me to show you the estate, Amelia? We did not have the chance when you were here last. You will see old and new working together."

"Di sicuro, for sure, Lorenzo." Bria winked at Amelia, "You and Franco!"

"My sister, she thinks she is funny, eh, Amelia?" Lorenzo's hands kneaded Bria's shoulders. "So, the estate?" He asked again.

"Sure, sounds great," Amelia agreed. "But not today."

"Or tomorrow," Bria said. "We must prepare for Sunday. That is the only reason I asked Amelia. She is a wonderful cook!"

"Maybe Monday," Amelia said, with a smile. She stood and began to gather plates. "Before we head back to Venice."

"No, no, Amelia. Today you are a guest," Bria said, looking at Lorenzo as he answered the persistent buzzing of his phone with a frown.

"Nonsense, I can at least help clear. Come on."

True to Bria's predictions, Jupiter, the rain god, stayed away and the long refectory table set up on the patio disappeared under a mound of platters tickling Amelia's nose with tempting smells of rosemary, mint, and roast lamb. Vases full of wildflowers and wine glasses added sparkle. Lorenzo presided at one end, Bria at the other, but as the meal wore on and the babble became louder, people swapped places in order to catch up on gossip. Children darted around, one minute on someone's lap, the next playing chase.

Amelia, her mind wandering and her foot nudged, ducked under the table to find a little girl feeding slithers of lamb to one of Lorenzo's dogs, but not the same as the one who had greeted her a couple of days earlier. Of a more salubrious lineage, Stella, a Spinone Italiano, was a beautiful white hunting dog with orange markings. Although a puppy, she already had a thick mustache and eyebrows. Keen to follow her master everywhere, she had been relegated to the kitchen garden for the feast but had obviously escaped.

Amelia remembered Bria telling her another reason Lorenzo had been so despondent and abrupt on her earlier visit was the recent death of his previous dog, also a Spinone Italiano. Not old but afflicted with a neurological disorder that affected its gait and mentality. Why, she wondered, did he get another dog of the same breed?

She was brought back to the chatter with her name being called.

"Amelia," Franco raised his glass from half-way down the table then kissed his fingers, "Bria says you made the pasqualina. Brava!"

"Grazie mille," she replied, looking at the empty pie dishes, delighted her first attempt had passed the Italian taste test, although pasqualina, the Easter speciality seemed remarkably similar to a spinach quiche.

The workers, some of whom had tended the vines at the Scutari Vineyard for generations, and their families started to drift away as the sun dipped and a crispness reminded them it wasn't yet summer. Amelia watched, surprised, when Lorenzo helped clear the table strewn with plates, glasses and crumbs from the Colomba di Pasqua, another new delicacy and which, so Franco told her, translated as Easter dove. Although shaped, she supposed, like a dove, it tasted very like the Christmas panettone.

Lorenzo lit a fire in the informal sitting room, which led through from the kitchen and opened onto the patio and, as the evening deepened, they snacked on cold cuts, cheese, and olives, washed down with Refosco rather than a Scutari Soave. Comfortable silences were occasionally broken by muted voices. Carefree came in different guises. Promising to tour the estate with Lorenzo in the morning, Amelia thanked her hosts and, snuggled into her down coat, she had a quiet walk under the pergola to gaze at the hills bathed in a soft moonlight, before going to bed. An image of Lorenzo's frowning face drifted in from a couple of days before, the one that drove animation and pleasure away as he answered his phone. She wondered who the call had been from.

†

Her eyes felt heavy. Prizing them open, Amelia saw dawn peeking through the shutters. Something had woken her. An insistent thrum. She realized it was her phone.

"Pronto," she muttered, her tongue furry. Too much wine. Her eyes flew open as Lucy's voice came over the line.

"Mum," her daughter's voice sounded raw, "oh, Christ, Ma, something terrible has happened."

Amelia sat up, wide awake. She pushed hair out of her face. "What? What's happened? Is it Mike?"

"No. Oh, Mum, Natalie's dead."

The pillow swathed Amelia's head like a halo as she fell back. "What? What do you mean? Moira?" Her stomach clenched and panic bubbled in her throat. She thought she'd vomit.

"No, she's okay. Well, she's not but you know what I mean."

Lucy's sobs broke Amelia's stasis. She had to get up. She couldn't hear this lying down. "Lucy, calm down. Take a deep breath. Tell me what happened."

"She just died, Mum, just died."

"I don't understand, darling." Amelia gripped the bedpost, her head swirling. "What happened?"

Words tumbled. "Mo went in to wake her for a last feed before she went to bed. Natalie wasn't moving, wasn't breathing. Mo screamed and we raced in. Mike tried to resuscitate her. But she wouldn't breathe. Oh, Mum, it's awful."

Amelia sat back on the edge of the bed. She stood again. She walked to the window and thrust the shutters open. She shook her head. Lucy's sobs accompanied every action. No, this couldn't be. She took a deep breath. She had to know the facts.

"Lucy, where's Moira now?"

"With the medic. Mike's with her. The police are here too. And Adam. Cynthia's on the way."

"Oh, my God, my poor baby." Tears finally came to Amelia's eyes. "I'll come as soon as I can get a flight."

"Mum, after the first shock, Moira hasn't cried. She's really, really calm. Scary calm. She took Natalie from Mike, went to her rocking chair and just held her. Then she told us to get out. She wouldn't let anyone touch her, even when the ambulance arrived. It was Adam who persuaded her to let him take Natalie."

"Did she ask you to call me?"

"No. She's not speaking."

"Okay, it's okay, Lucy. You did the right thing. Are the police being kind?"

"Yeah. There's a woman copper, not in uniform. She's older. The other one, a bloke, spoke to Mike and me separately." Lucy hiccuped. "I told him we've been with Mo all evening, sitting in the kitchen. He asked if we'd been drinking. I said Mike and I had a couple of glasses of wine, but Mo wasn't because she's still feeding Natalie. We'd just said goodnight and were in our bedroom when she screamed. Mum, Mike was so calm. He took over. Adam heard the scream and raced down. He called the ambulance. They called the police. Mum, it's awful. I don't know what to say to Mo."

"There is nothing you can say, my darling. Just be there." Amelia swallowed a sob. "I'll be there, hopefully tomorrow."

"Okay. Shall I tell Mo I called?"

"Of course, and try to get her to call me. I'll use Bria's phone to get my flight sorted, so mine's free. Alright, darling, now go and be with your sister. Once the medics and police finish, don't leave her alone. I don't care what she says. Stay with her."

"Okay. Thanks, Mum. Bye now."

"Bye, darling. I'll talk to you in a little while."

Tears landed on the clothes Amelia threw into her case. She glanced at her watch. Nearly six. A gentle rap on the door followed by Bria's quiet voice told her the household was waking.

"Cara, I can enter? What has happened?"

Bria looked at Amelia's tear-streaked face and took her into her arms. As the words tumbled out in English, Bria drew her to the window seat and listened, their tears intermingling.

"I have to go," Amelia said, as her sobs lessened.

"Di sicuro, do you wish to go home first? We will have coffee then leave."

"I suppose I should. Get a few things. The flights usually leave in the afternoon. May I use your phone? So mine is free if Moira calls."

"Of course, cara, of course. Come. It's in the kitchen."

They walked down the uneven stone stairs, Amelia holding the banister, afraid her legs would buckle. The smell of brewing coffee met them as they entered the kitchen.

"Buongiorno a tutti." Lorenzo turned from the oven. "I heard voices so thought coffee might be needed."

"Grazie, Lorenzo," Bria said, guiding Amelia to a chair then, in quick-fire Italian, explained what had happened.

Amelia heard the word SIDS.

"Mio Dio," Lorenzo said, and pulled her into a hug. "Mi dispiace molto, I am sorry, Amelia, so sorry." Her buzzing phone interrupted his words.

"Moira?" Amelia walked out the kitchen door to the patio. She shivered.

"Yeah, it's me, Mum."

"Oh, my darling, what a terrible thing." She felt a jacket being draped over her shoulders.

"Yup. I can't really talk, Mum." Moira gulped. "Lucy said she'd called and that you are booking a flight." The line went quiet and Amelia waited. She scrubbed her eyes.

"Mum, I don't want you to come. Okay?"

Amelia gasped, tears streaking down her cheeks again. "Moira, please, you can't do this alone."

"I'm not alone. Lucy's going to stay when Mike leaves in a couple of days. And Adam's here. And Cynthia. Please don't race over."

"But why, darling? I could at least take some pressure off you with practicalities. I could hug you."

Silence followed her question, and Amelia managed to stop herself from pleading. A part of her understood. Sometimes managing horror, having to cope, got one through the blackness. She made a mental note to talk to Lucy, to remind her not to harry her sister.

"I'm not sure. But I think you being here would make it too real. Too horrible. For now. Give me a few days to think. Promise?"

"Alright, darling." Amelia's shoulders dropped in resignation. "But you call me, anytime. You promise me that?"

"Okay. I've gotta go."

"I love you, Moira. And, darling, Natalie had a wonderful mother. You must believe that."

A sob met her words, then a click as the phone went dead.

Chapter 17

Bria drove them back to Venice, then escorted Amelia to Palazzo Ambrosio, made her a cup of blackcurrant tea and left her with Dafne snuggled into her shoulder and a promise to return later with supper.

"Stai bene, Amelia?"

"Sì, e grazie, Bria."

"Prego, cara, ciao." Bria patted her friend on the cheek. Amelia heard her voice as the door opened, then an English accent. James. She sighed, not sure if she was up to seeing anyone. But he'd been kind and looked after Dafne.

"It's okay, Bria," she called. "Come in, James."

James didn't say a word. Just sat on the sofa, his long legs stretched in front of him, and waited. Amelia didn't know how long they sat in silence. Fifteen minutes? An hour? Until Dafne jumped from her to James' lap. He glanced across and saw her slight smile.

"Traitor," she said.

He nodded and petted the cat. "Would you like another tea? Anything?"

"Is it too early for a proper drink?"

"We're in Italy. It's never too early. And it's almost lunchtime. What would you like?"

"Campari soda, please?" She stretched her neck. "Will you join me?"

"Sure. I can see the Campari on the trolley. Where's the soda?"

"In the end cupboard."

She heard the clink of ice and the fizz as he popped the can. Then the fridge open and packets being unwrapped.

James put the tray of cheese and crackers down and handed her a drink. "Here you go, saluti!"

"Saluti, and thanks, James."

"I'm not sure what to say, Amelia. Nothing seems right."

"There isn't anything to say. It's life throwing boulders." She sipped her drink. "You know, I don't care what happens to me. But it's not fair. Moira's a good mum. She loved Natalie with all her heart. I mean, what the fuck? How does this happen?"

"I don't know. I don't know much about it."

"Nope, me neither. I didn't know anything about Alzheimer's either, but I learned."

"Your husband?"

"Yep."

"Are you religious?" James stopped, flustered. "Sorry, that's probably impertinent."

"No, it's fine. And no, I'm not. Why?"

"I dunno. I'm not either, but I know people get comfort from their religion."

"I struggle with a god, any god, who deals this sort of shit."

"Me too."

They lapsed into silence again. Companionable. Amelia felt glad James had stayed. She leaned her head back and closed her eyes. She'd wake up and all this would be a dream.

✝

Garlic woke her. The aroma drifting around the darkening room. Then a sizzling as something dropped into hot oil.

Amelia's neck hurt. She sat up and realized someone, James, had put a throw over her.

"Hello?"

"Ciao, cara, you are awake. Supper will be soon. Just simple, eh? Fettuccine and mushrooms."

"Sounds wonderful, thank you." She saw a note on the coffee table.

I had class. Home at about eight. Call if you need anything. Otherwise, I'll leave you in peace. X J

She smiled. How lucky she was with the people around her. As she stood, she heard Bria from the kitchen say, "Sit, sit. I bring you wine in a moment."

"I need to pee," Amelia said, heading for her bathroom.

They ate at the kitchen counter. A bottle of Scutari Soave in the ice bucket next to them.

Amelia, aware of Bria's deep belief in God, appreciated her friend's reticence and care with the words chosen. She didn't think she could bear to hear, 'it is God's will,' no matter who spoke them. Instead, Bria encouraged her to talk about her time in New York, to show her photos of Natalie, despite the fact she had already seen most of them. More tears fell as the realization swamped her afresh that she would never hold the baby again, wouldn't see her toddle her first steps. Just wouldn't see her.

"I don't understand why Moira doesn't want me there," Amelia said, at last, her voice small. "Well, I suppose I do, but it hurts."

"Sometimes," Bria said, pouring more wine for Amelia, "our pain, it is so great we do not want to share. We must hold it close. Keep it for ourselves. It is the only way to move from one day to the other."

"Is that how you felt when Giovanni died?"

"Yes." Bria rose from the barstool and put their plates in the dishwasher. "It took a long time. But we learn to manage our grief. We have to. Now, I will leave. Finish your wine. We will talk tomorrow, eh?" The scent of lavender enveloped Amelia as Bria kissed her cheeks. She picked up her handbag, then said from the door, "Oh, cara, I talk to Fenella. I think maybe you do not wish to say the same thing many times. She will come by. And, James, he is a good boy."

Amelia took her glass and, gathering the woolen throw lying on the sofa, wrapped herself in it before moving out to the cool of the terrace. She sat at the little table, looking along the canal, then up at the clear night sky. She remembered telling the girls when they were little and their beloved dog Sadie died, that she was now a star and could watch over them, always. Tears fell again, and she hoped Natalie was watching over her bereft mother. And grandmother.

Through the fog of sadness, Amelia heard her phone. Her glass shattered as she knocked the table in her rush. Idiot. Shouldn't have left it inside.

"Hello?"

"Hey, Mum." Lucy's voice, less tearful but very subdued, came through as if she were next door. "Are you okay? I know Moira told you not to come. I'm sorry."

"I'm okay. What about you? And Moira? Is she talking?"

"Not really. Just sitting in Natalie's room."

"She's saying goodbye."

"Yeah, I guess. She let me in for a while about an hour ago. I took her a cup of chamomile tea, which she drank. The first thing."

"That's good. What about you?"

"Mike and I, and Cynthia, had a late lunch, and a glass of wine." Lucy sounded guilty.

"Me too. Bria drove me home, then James stayed with me, then Bria cooked supper. She left about an hour ago."

"I'm glad you've got lovely people around you, Mum. You do seem to attract them."

"So do you, darling. You both do."

"But are you okay about not flying over?"

"I am now. And Moira might change her mind. But, if she doesn't, that's fine. It was Bria who helped me understand. She said sometimes sharing the pain is too, well, too painful. So, darling, you mustn't worry if Moira doesn't want to talk. Let her decide. She'll talk when she's ready."

"Yeah, that's pretty much what Mike said."

"He's a wise one, that man of yours," Amelia said.

"Yep. Mum, there's something else."

"Oh shit, what?"

"There has to be an autopsy. Mo nearly collapsed when the policewoman told her."

"That doesn't surprise me, darling."

"I told you the coppers interviewed Mike and me separately, then both of them took Mo out of Natalie's room and talked to her. Then the bloke went back into the nursery alone, took photos and talked to the paramedics. And a coroner came."

Amelia could hear Lucy crying. "I suppose that was good. At least it meant you didn't have to go to the hospital. That would've been so impersonal."

"Yeah." Lucy sniffed. "I got the impression that's unusual. I mean, getting the coroner to the house. Maybe because Natalie was a baby. I don't know. Anyway, everyone has been kind. Cynthia left a while ago. And Adam is wonderful. You know he loves Mo, don't you?"

"Yes, darling. But it's not reciprocated."

"I know. But thank God he's here. Because he seems to know everyone, and who to call."

A bubble threatened to choke Amelia. "Lucy, darling, I'm going to hang up now because I don't want to cry on the phone. Thanks for letting me know what's going on. Try and get Moira to call me tomorrow or send me a text when it's a good time for me to call her. Anytime. Okay?"

"Alright, Mum. try to get some sleep. I love you. What a terrible day."

"Yes, it is. Goodnight, darling."

Taking the dustpan and brush out to the terrace, Amelia swept up the shards of glass, tossed them in the bin then poured another glass of wine and took it into her bathroom. Sinking into the bathtub, she eased her sore neck in the hot bubbly water, sipped, and looked at a painting, one of the last Leo did, of the beach at Patanga from the house. Crotons framed the sea, and at the end of the jetty, a figure could just be made out. It was Amelia.

"It's been a hell of day, Leo," she said. "Our poor baby. She's so like you. Won't talk. Hides away. I do understand, more so now, thanks to Bria, but damn, it's hard. Thank God Lucy is there with her. And Mike. And Adam."

The water cooled and, dripping wet, Amelia caught sight of herself in the mirror. She looked old. When did that happen? Was it just this morning or had it been creeping up? "Who cares?" she muttered as she dried and pulled on her dressing gown and bed socks. She padded out to the kitchen and, knowing she wouldn't sleep after her earlier nap, she poured another glass of wine and took it back out to the terrace along with the throw.

Pipe smoke followed Signor Malvestio's quiet voice. "Buon-asera, signora."

She waved and returned the greeting, then sat back down at the table, each quiet with their thoughts until he called, "Buona notte, Amelia."

Dafne scratched at the door and Amelia rose to let her onto the terrace to sit on the balustrade. The cat enjoyed watching the goings on along the canal and Amelia had given up worrying about her falling. But tonight, Dafne jumped onto her lap and curled there.

"You know, don't you kitty-kat?" she said, stroking the soft fur. They sat outside a long time. Sounds from the canal lessening as vaporetti chugged home, bars closed and tourists wandered back to their hotels.

Eventually the cold air sent them indoors, and huddling under the doona, Dafne tucked in at her side, Amelia watched the light from the canal play across the ceiling of her bedroom.

She turned her head to look at Leo's photo.

"Two days, Leo, two days that will never be the same again. Christmas and Easter."

Chapter 18

The night of Natalie's funeral—at Moira's absolute insistence, only Moira, Lucy, Cynthia, and Adam—Amelia drank a bottle of wine. She didn't set out to do so. She sat first on the terrace, then as the cold drove her in, she ended up on the sofa with Dafne. She woke there in the morning, hung over and sad.

As she came out from a shower in the girls' bathroom, she heard a knocking. Tentative at first, then more insistent. Throwing on her dressing gown, she opened the door to James.

"Oh, thank Christ," he said. "I've been worried."

"Why?"

"I came up last night to check on you. I know yesterday was the funeral. First you wouldn't answer, then you told me to bugger off. Your words, not mine."

"James, I'm so sorry."

"That's okay. Are you okay?"

"I've got a hangover, feel like shit, but I'm okay. Thank you. Come in."

"Right, you get dressed. I'll make coffee. Do you fancy a fry-up?"

"Not really, but it would probably do me good. There are eggs in the basket on the counter."

"I've got everything we need right here," James said, picking up a basket of produce from outside the door. "Go, get dressed. Otherwise, the neighbors will talk."

"What neighbors, you foolish boy?"

✝

Days dragged into more days, then weeks. Each slightly more bearable. Amelia had researched as much as possible about SIDS—Sudden Infant Death Syndrome, an appropriate acronym—but the only help came from the absolute randomness of the tragedy. Natalie had always been put to bed on her back in a cot, empty of toys and wearing a sleeping sack. She did not have a cold. She was breastfeeding, and Moira's breast milk had been normal. She was, as far as Amelia's reading could ascertain, not in the socio-economic group in which many SIDS were recorded. And the kicker. Apparently, boys were at greater risk.

Amelia walked the canals of Venice, her camera always ready. Her focus, rather than buildings and views, became children— at play, on their way to school, chasing pigeons, enjoying a family meal.

Bria and James had been a constant in the first couple of weeks after Natalie's death. Riccardo, too. And her two friends Fenella and Tigran from the Istituto Venezia, her language classes, had also been stalwarts in their support. One bright spot had been the burgeoning romance between her young Polish friend, Janina, and Stefano. They were all becoming a tight-knit group, and now that Riccardo knew there would be no romance, Amelia felt easy once again in his company.

That had been an awkward discussion, and she knew she had hurt him. She remembered her words and his response as they had sat indoors at Dodo's. Amelia had chosen a time she knew Matteo would not be working.

"So, Riccardo, you know I care for you," she stayed his reaching hand and took a deep breath, "but as a friend. Not a lover." She watched his smile disappear and felt rotten. A fleeting thought interrupted her words. When had she become comfortable saying the word 'lover' to a man? Italy was rubbing off on her. "You have been so kind to me, all of you have, but Riccardo, I am not looking for love. Even an affair. You understand?"

"You think you are too old? But you are never too old for love, Amelia. This I know."

Irritated by his assumption, she bristled. "I hope not, Riccardo."

"So, I wait."

His smile and certainty irked her. "No! Not now, not yet. And not you!" Amelia watched his hand turning the glass. He must understand, for God's sake. His wife had died. Swallowing her ill-temper she said, "I'm sorry. Come, Riccardo, let's drink to friendship."

They finished their wine, then with a kiss to his cheek, she went out into the cold and made her way home, hoping their bond had not been destroyed.

✝

Lucy had sent all the photos of Natalie she had on her phone and had persuaded Moira to send some too. Amelia spent hours editing them, some in color, others black and white, then she laid out exactly how she wanted the little book to look and sent it to the printer for three copies to be made. It started with a footprint. The final photograph was not of the tiny coffin with white and pink orchids on top, but a photo Lucy had taken on Good Friday, of Moira sitting on a park bench with Natalie laughing in her arms. It spoke to the love of mother and daughter and made Amelia cry each time she looked at it.

Amelia decided she would not send the book but hand it to Moira, either in New York or Venice.

Once back in Sydney with Mike, Lucy spoke to Moira every day then often relayed their conversation to Amelia. Until Mo told her to stop hovering.

"G'day, Mum," Lucy sounded uncertain.

"Hi, darling. How are you doing? How's Mike?"

"All good."

Amelia imagined the roll of the waves off Sydney's shoreline through the static, then shook herself. Those days were long gone. Voices flitted through the air now. It didn't seem so romantic somehow, but definitely easier. "But?" She waited.

"I dunno, something's up. Mo's being cagey."

"I expect she's anxious about going back to work. It's been nearly six months."

"Yeah, I know. But her MO is to throw herself into what's new, what's out, what's on the way in—particularly if she's not prepping for an auction."

"And she's not?" Amelia asked.

"Nope. She's lost her zing. I might be the actual artist but she's far more knowledgeable about art history than me and finding the next big name. You know that."

Amelia nodded. "Lucy, it's going to take time, then more time, for Moira to get through this. And, in a way, I doubt she'll ever be the same again."

"What do you mean?"

"Darling, we can only imagine what she is going through. And, despite the fact Natalie's death is completely and utterly random, Moira will still, maybe will always, feel an element of guilt."

"I think she should talk to someone. You know? A professional."

"I quite agree, but she has to want to do that. Neither you nor I can force the issue. She is very like your father in that respect. Sometimes the fight is there, but you know the flip side of that, right? The flight."

"Yeah, I know. That's what you and Dad did."

"That's what Dad did, darling. I just went along with it because I loved him."

There was silence until Lucy asked, "Mum, did you ever regret going to Kimbe?"

"Of course. There were days when, if I could've flown on a magic carpet, I would've taken off." Amelia paused, her mind filled with Leo on a good day. "But, Lucy, all things considered they were few, and far apart."

"You know, Mum, I never said, but I really admire what you did for Dad. You were so isolated. Your whole world revolved around him."

"Not at the start. The first few years weren't too bad."

"The last five must've been hell."

"I suppose they were. But hell comes in a lot of guises, darling. And it wasn't all awful. Living on a Pacific island, swimming in water clearer than crystal, would be many people's idea of heaven."

"I don't know if I could do that. For Mike, I mean. If he got Alzheimer's."

"You don't know what you can do, Lucy, until you're faced with something. And that is why I know Moira will get through this. At her own pace."

"I guess. But I still think she's up to something. Okay, I've got to go. Thanks, Mum, you always know what to say. Love you!"

"Not always, darling. Bye now."

✝

Venice in June was one of Amelia's favorite times. The sun shone most days, but it wasn't muggy, and not too many tourists. She returned to her warm-weather routine of breakfast at Luca's and would then sometimes amble up to see Bria for a natter, if the hotelier wasn't too busy.

"Buongiorno, Bria," she called into the office behind reception.

"Ciao." Her friend's usually serene face looked disgruntled.

"Oh dear, what's up?" Amelia asked.

"Lorenzo! He is a fool!"

"What's he done?"

"At Easter..." Bria paused apologetically, as if not wanting to remind Amelia of those dreadful days.

"Bria, the world has not stopped because of Natalie. It's okay. What happened at Easter?"

"Va bene. So maybe you remember Lorenzo received a call that made him angry?"

Amelia thought back. "Yes, I do vaguely remember that. Who was it?"

"His sciattona!"

"His what?"

"Putana!"

Amelia did know that word. "Whoa! Really? His prostitute?"

"Uffa," Bria exclaimed, "his wife. The second one. Idiota!"

"Who, her or him?

"Both!"

"Oh dear, I thought that was all over. Divorced. Finito."

"But now," Bria switched to English, "she think maybe she has been foolish. He is old. She is young. She wants Scutari Vineyards. Greedy—he gives her too much already."

"Ahh. But he seemed so much more relaxed, pleasant, at Easter compared to when I first visited. He can't be thinking of getting back together, can he?"

"He is a man! Vain. He goes to Florence soon to talk. Only talk, he says." Bria's words rattled around the room.

"Okay. Well, maybe that will close the door on her. What's her name?"

"Serafina."

"That's pretty."

"And she know it. But not a beautiful soul."

"Bria, he didn't look like he was pleased to hear from her. You've got to let him sort it out. There's no point getting upset. And the more you say, the more he might do the opposite. Dealing with a man is sometimes like dealing with a child."

Amelia was pleased to make Bria laugh.

"I tell him you say that!"

"I'd rather you didn't. I might never be asked back."

"So, enough about my fool of a brother. You are looking better. That is good."

"I feel better. I don't think I've ever walked so much but it's been good for me. And I can finally navigate a bit more of Venice without getting horribly lost."

"How is James? He is a good boy."

Amelia remembered Bria saying that before. "Yes, he is. He's a good museum companion and he likes antique hunting too. He's got a good eye."

Amelia, determined to give Moira space, rarely called her unless she hadn't heard anything for a few days. From either of her daughters. About to brush her teeth and join Dafne already kneading the bed, her phone rang.

"Hi, Mum," Moira said. "How are you doing? I've not woken you, have I?"

"No, darling, and I'm fine. How was your first day back at work?"

"Strange. I thought I'd like it. I had even started to look forward to it. But once I got there, I felt divorced from the whole place. Everyone. Like everything was surreal."

"It's going to feel odd for a while, I should think, Moira." Amelia padded back out to the sofa. "You've had a terrible thing happen. You can't go back. Life will always be different."

"I know. But I thought work would be a kind of constant. But everyone was too kind, treated me with kid gloves, so it didn't feel like work. I couldn't wait to leave."

"Give it a while, my darling. People will be anxious about saying the wrong thing, upsetting you." She heard Dafne jump down from the bed, no doubt looking for her.

"Yeah, I guess. Dominic took me into his office, gave me coffee, didn't rant and rave, told me I could work on whatever I wanted. That really spooked me out."

"What did you say?"

"After a few minutes, I told him to stop being so bloody kind. And asked him how I was expected to be normal if he wasn't."

"Oh God, Moira, that poor man."

"I know. I feel a bit mean now."

"Darling, difficult as this is for you, if you talk about Natalie, it will ease the way for others to know it's okay to say her name."

"It's so hard, Ma."

"I know, my darling. But, Moira, do you remember, when you were little, seeing funerals in China Town—the clanging cymbals, the incense, the wailing, the paper cars and planes, and God knows what else?"

"Yeah, why?"

"Well, the louder the wailing, the more important or older the person who died. When a baby or child dies, there is no noise, no celebration—if that's the right word—just silence." Her voice broke. "Because the poor little thing didn't have time to live a full life and so therefore is not worthy of being remembered." Amelia could hear Moira crying. "My darling, I'm not trying to make you miserable, and even though Natalie only lived a few months, she brought immense joy to us all. We have to talk about her, to remember her, to honor her life."

"Oh, Mum, I'm just so bloody sad. And guilty."

"I know, my darling. But, please, Moira, the guilt will make you sick. You have nothing to be guilty about. You do know that, don't you? You mustn't become a bitter woman because of this tragedy. It won't help. And I think you will have to accept that a part of you will be sad forever because it's hard not to think of what-might-have-beens." Amelia took a deep breath. "But, darling, treasure the memories you have. Talk about her. Watch the videos. Look at her photos. That doesn't mean building a shrine to her." Amelia felt her throat constrict but she went on, "It means she's real in your heart, in all our hearts."

"Maybe I should go out and get some cymbals." Moira half sobbed, half laughed.

"I'm good with that, darling!"

"Mum, do you remember when Sadie died? Lu and I were heartbroken and you told us she was a star keeping watch over us?"

"I remember." The lump in Amelia's throat grew.

"Well, I look out every starry night and imagine Natalie up there."

"That's lovely, darling. So do I."

The silence over the phone felt comfortable.

"Okay, I've got to go, Mum. But thanks. You know, I'm surprised at how tired I am after one day of work. Or non-work."

"Alright, sleep tight. We'll talk soon."

With the light out in her bedroom, Amelia pulled the curtains open. She liked going to sleep with shadows dancing on the ceiling. She lay awake a long time, thinking. Trying not to worry about Moira. Wondering when she'd see her next, and where. Time. She had to give her time.

"Oh, Leo," she asked the photograph, "what happened to carefree?"

Chapter 19

"Wow, look at you!" Amelia laughed at the young man's bashful grin. "What brought that on?"

James rubbed the nape of his now-naked neck. "It was time for a cut." He paused. "Grow up, I suppose, or at least tidy up." He lifted her carry-on over the high threshold and onto the cobblestones running beside the canal.

"Non ora, quando?" She laughed, using Bria's well-worn phrase, and one James knew too. "Well, from this old broad's viewpoint, you look great."

"Thanks, Amelia. I guess I'm trying to find me. Not who I think I should be."

"Who you think, or who others think?" she asked.

"Now that's the question?" James answered, "but not one before a coffee. Come on, let's get to the station. We can get one there and catch the 09:30 if we get a move on, which will put us in Florence by noon."

Settling into their seats on the train as a whistle announced its imminent departure, Amelia could sense James' unease. "What's up?"

"Look, Amelia," he wouldn't catch her eye, "I'm really not comfortable about you paying for my hotel room."

"Too late now, mate," she said. "James, this is my thank you. For looking after Dafne, hell, for looking after me. Don't forget the place used to be a convent. If it makes you feel any better, you've got a hole-in-the-wall room. Remember the *Da Vinci Code*? You can self-flagellate all you like!"

James spluttered into his paper coffee cup. "Oh, God, Amelia, really!"

She laughed and patted his hand. "Seriously, James, we're only in Florence for a few days and with a list of things we want to do. Let's make the most of them. And, dear boy, that is not to say you are tied to my apron. You do what you want to do, when you want to do it. And you know I'll crater early, so please do not feel you have to dance attendance in the evenings. We'll browse some markets, maybe a museum or two, drink a little wine, and enjoy each other's company—if it suits us both, okay?"

"I've never met anyone quite like you, Amelia."

"What, Australian? A basket case?" She laughed. "About the only thing you can't call me is a cougar! I'm not interested in your body."

James choked on his coffee. "You're mad," he said, wiping his mouth. "Okay. Thank you. And by the way, Mrs. Cougar, I'm gay."

"Yes, dear James, I am well aware of that." She softened her words with a pat on James' hand.

"Really? You knew?"

"Of course, I knew. Who cares? You're kind and great company. Now shut up," Amelia winked at the blushing young man, "I'm going to doze. That's what old women do!"

"Hardly old, Amelia!"

She grinned and closed her eyes.

The hotel on Via di Mezzo lived up to Amelia's expectations, fanned by Bria's enthusiasm and determination she should stay there. Vaulted ceilings in the reception areas added a sense of grandeur, a quiet elegance cocooned guests in comfortable armchairs placed to induce conversation, or contemplation. Her bedroom on the top floor led onto a private balcony overlooking an inner courtyard where a couple of sparrows—Amelia wondered if they were Italian—larked in water splashing from a central fountain.

A rap brought her back into the room. She opened the door to find James grinning broadly.

"Well, compared to this, mine is a hole-in-the-wall," he said, looking around the luxurious furnishings, "but compared to where I could've been staying, it's the lap of divine luxury." He leaned in to give Amelia a peck on the cheek. "Thanks, again!"

"My pleasure. Now come on, we could either give in to an afternoon spent eating truffle sandwiches and drinking and playing the tourist at Procacci or we could explore."

"Either way, playing the tourist!" James said. "Let's just grab a panini and a coffee. I noticed a place just along the street. Save the glamour for the evening."

"Righto! The bar has been there since 1885, so it can wait a bit longer for me." Amelia glanced at her watch, one of the last presents from Leo, a delicate silver filigree band, with tiny diamonds around the face. "This hotel really is ideal for markets, but we're too late for some today. The Sant'Ambrogio, down the road, closes soon. At two, I think." She looked at the young man, his earring glinting in a shaft of light. "Can you hold on a bit for lunch?"

"Sure. What have you in mind?"

"Well, Bria mentioned the central market at San Lorenzo was great for deli foods. I bet we could grab something there."

"Okay." James looked at the map on his phone. "Too far to walk on an empty stomach. Let's get a bus. Huh," he said, reading the screen, "designed by Giuseppe Mengoni and opened 1874."

"Been around a while then," Amelia said, slipping on her shoes.

"Not as long as Covent Garden Market in London. That opened in about 1835, I think."

"Now, how on earth would you know that?"

"I like markets!"

A cornucopia of color met them. The market, like a scented quilt patched together with oranges and plums and peaches interspersed with greens from lettuce and cucumbers and zucchini spread before them. Bursts of purple came from big fat figs.

"You know," Amelia said, gazing upwards, "it does look a bit like Covent Garden. The glass ceilings and lots of arches."

"Says here," James read from a sign, "that next year they'll be reopening the upper floor. Cool, it'll be a dedicated space for regional Italian specialties—you know, cheeses, wines, and so on. Lots of stalls and a large seating area."

"Well, this year, right now, I want to find Perini's. Bria said it's on the Via Ariento side, and where you get the best prosciutto, and homemade chutneys."

Their afternoon disappeared in a plethora of sensory over-load. Laden with bottles of balsamic vinegar and mostarda—not mustard, Amelia found out, but a spicy jam—and cheese, olives, and fresh figs, and, with James clutching a bottle of Chianti, they got a bus back to the hotel.

"Let's meet back here in an hour or so," Amelia said, taking the bag James had carried for her as they reached her room. "We can have a drink and cicchetti on my balcony."

✝

A cool shower revived Amelia's flagging energy and she slipped into a pair of olive green palazzo pants and a cream linen top. She didn't bother with makeup but did spritz her wrists with J'Adore. A shaft of memory pierced her languor. Leo had presented her with a bottle not long after Dior released the perfume. The summer Moira graduated. The summer Leo spent on the Cape, and not with her and the girls. Despite the remorse with which the scent had been given, she'd loved it and had worn nothing else since. It reminded her of balmy days, the underlying tartness of mandarin and plum and something else she'd never been able to put her finger on. An apt metaphor for her conflicted feelings all those years ago.

Shaking her head to dislodge the images, she unwrapped the cheeses. She'd opened the wine earlier. She breathed in the hint of cherry rising from the bottle and licked her lips.

Amelia tipped her toothbrush out of the glass in the bathroom, and took it and another out to the table on the balcony. About to pour, she heard James' quiet knock.

"Oh, good," she said, opening the door. "I was about to start without you."

Always easy company, they toasted Florence and nibbled on cheese and olives, conversation idle between them. Lights began to flicker as the sun dipped behind clay-tiled rooftops, ochre and Terracotta merging in the changing shadows.

Amelia saw James rub his temples. "What's up? Headache?"

"No, just thinking," he said, his voice strained.

178

"Not very happy thoughts, it seems. Anything you want to talk about?"

"Not really."

"Okay, but I'm a good listener."

Silence enveloped them, this time not so comfortable. Amelia sipped and waited, her mind wandering back to her earlier thoughts of Leo.

"My parents don't know," James said at last, looking into his glass.

"Know what?"

"That I'm gay."

"Oh. Are you sure? I mean, not that you're gay but that they don't know. Perhaps they're just waiting." Amelia topped up his glass. "You know, it's not always easy to broach a subject. We worry about upsetting our kids. Or putting voice to our, or their, concerns or fears."

"That wouldn't bother them. It's never stopped them letting me know how disappointed they are in me." Bitterness dripped through his words.

Amelia's head shot up. "Tell me about them. About growing up. You've never said much."

"Can one be a black sheep when one's an only child?"

"A black sheep? I find that hard to believe, you dear boy."

"I've not, and am not, following their prescribed path. You know—doctor, lawyer, accountant."

"Rich man, poor man, beggar man, thief! And I happen to think tinker and tailor are better than soldier or sailor," Amelia said with a slight smile. "And so is artist."

"Not to them." James swirled his wine. "Dad's a barrister. A Queen's Counsel."

"Ahh." Amelia pictured a dour Scot in a gown and wig. "And art doesn't fit their ideal of you?"

"Don't forget being gay. And no, art does not fit one little bit. Which is ironic, as it was Mum who encouraged me to paint when I was little. She's actually quite a good artist. She wanted a well-rounded son."

"Well, she got one," Amelia said.

"Not as far as they're concerned. Art is for dabbling. Not a career."

"Leo would not agree, and neither do I. Look at my girls. Moira an art appraiser and auctioneer, and Lucy a graphic artist. Who, by the way, I think is coming around to pure art. Slowly, slowly."

"But they grew up in a kind of Bohemian environment. I grew up in North London. The right schools. Then blew it by turning down Durham University."

"What about art school? You're good enough, and more."

"That was a non-starter. I didn't even apply."

"Dear James, you know I'm on your side, but that sounds pretty defeatist."

James, fingers fiddling with his shoelaces, wouldn't meet her eyes. "I suppose so. The whole drama choked me."

"Drama?" Amelia looked at the pale young man with alarm.

"No, no, not violence or shouting, just disappointed sighs and silences. And endless tales of their friends' children's stellar options."

"You have stellar options, James. You'll find them. And Italy is a good step." She sipped her Chianti. She thought of the excitement for them all when the girls were at a similar stage in life. She wanted to shake his parents. "So, what did you do?"

"I got a job at a gallery in Mayfair which showcases upcoming artists and, after my first paycheck, I moved out. Lived in a crappy flat with a crazy girl from deepest Somerset. It was great. Both the flat and the job. And her, actually." A smile transformed his face. "And I learned a lot about the business side of things."

"I have to ask, James, and I'm sorry, but how are you affording Italy?"

"Legally, Amelia!" A tight grin creased his face. "My Nana left me some dosh. I loved her." He paused. "She would've liked you."

A thought shot across Amelia's brain. "James, do your parents know where you are?"

There was silence.

"For God sakes, James, they must be out of their minds with worry."

"They know I'm in Italy." His face red, he looked down at his feet.

"What about friends?"

"Joanne, my old flatmate, knows. But I've always been a loner. Apart from when I played cricket. I was rather good at that. They liked that."

"I find it hard to believe your parents would not be proud of what you're doing. Of the young man you are."

"But where's it going to lead?" James said. "That's their constant question."

"You won't know until you follow your dream. Maybe you won't be the next David Hockney or Leo Paignton, but art is what you love. And your knowledge of art history is prodigious—particularly for someone who hasn't been to university or art college. I mean, how many Brits know of Henry Ossawa Tanner? Hell, not many Americans do! Or Albert Namatjira?"

"Well, they were both trail blazers," James explained his knowledge. "Tanner for his deft touch with light, and Namatjira for introducing Indigenous art to the White Australian world."

"Doesn't mean many people know of them. Did you know, by the way, that he was the first Aborigine to be granted Australian citizenship? In the late 1950s, I think. Pretty shameful, eh?"

James nodded. His voice contemplative, he continued, "They might be able to get their head around the art but being gay as well plays into all their preconceived ideas."

"James, my dear," Amelia chose her words with care, "don't you think you should give them the chance? You've been in Italy nearly six months. Your Italian is already better than mine, damn it! You've got a gallery interested. That's a lot to be proud of."

"For you, not for them."

"Give them a chance." She paused, bit into a piece of cheese, then laughed. "I know! When the exhibition is firmed up, why don't you invite them over, for the opening?" Amelia ignored his shaking head. "Staying with you might be a stretch—what with the revolving door of tenants downstairs—but book them in at Bria's. I'll have them over to dinner with Fenella and a few others. We'll wear them down."

"Maybe."

"Now," Amelia said, standing, "if I'm to be in the best haggling form for crafty antique dealers tomorrow, I need my bed. You go out and have some fun."

James got to his feet. "I'm always saying thanks to you, Amelia. And I always mean it."

"It goes both ways, kiddo. Just think about it, okay? Give them a chance," she repeated. "Good night, dear James. I'll see you in the morning."

Sleeping in the middle of the bed had, since Leo's death, been her way not to feel so alone at night. That and Dafne curling around her legs. Amelia spread out in the crisp white sheets as Florence flickered outside the open curtains, the quiet trickle of the fountain occasionally dulled by laughter from hotel guests in the courtyard. She sighed. She still didn't know much about James' parents but maybe that was best. Not too many biased notions. She would convince him to invite them to Venice.

Yawning, she snuggled into the pillows and, as she closed her eyes, Natalie's face drifted in. Perhaps she slept, she wasn't sure. She sat up, confused. Her phone. She grabbed it from the bedside table. The girls?

"Hello?"

"Buonasera, Amelia, sono io, Lorenzo."

"What?" She tried to focus on her watch, the face too small to see in the half-light.

"Mi dispiace," he apologized. "I wake you?"

"You did. I think. What time is it?"

"Er, about ten."

"Then yes, you did wake me!"

"Uffa, this is Italy, Amelia. We do not go out until ten." His voice rumbled with laughter.

"Maybe. But I'm not Italian. And why are you calling? Oh God, is it Bria? Is she okay?"

"Lei sta bene, she's fine. She tells me you are in Florence. I am in Florence. I take you to dinner. Now."

"Now? Not a chance!"

"Che cosa?"

"I am not going out to dinner with you. It's late. I'm tired. And, don't you know it is impolite to ask a woman out this late?

You have obviously been turned down by someone else. Good night, Lorenzo."

She clicked the phone off, shoved it into her handbag by the side of the bed, and rolled over. She felt the vibration of it ringing again and buried her head. "Bloody man!"

Chapter 20

A message pinged. Putting down her eyeliner, Amelia rootled around for her phone and saw it came from James. Good, not Lorenzo.

Found a bar. Late night. Can we meet at the Piazza Amigoni market at one-ish?

She typed back.

Sure!

She applied mascara and, with a swipe of damson-colored lipstick, felt ready to face the day. Coffee. Then the Boboli Gardens. Ever since going there with the girls the year before, she'd wanted to go back and soak up the ordered calm filled with statues and grottos. And take photos in peace.

Amelia dropped her key at the foyer desk then made her way to the hotel entrance. About to push the revolving door, she heard her name called.

"Signora Amelia, buongiorno." A barrel-chested figure in jeans and a blazer rose from one of the chintz-covered armchairs.

"Lorenzo!"

"Mi dispiace, Amelia. I am sorry to wake you last night." He touched his hand to his heart. "My manners, they were not good. You will forgive me?"

"No, they weren't." She tempered her words with a smile, made broader by his discomfort. "And yes, I will. I need coffee. Would you like to join me?"

"Certo, grazie," he said, pushing the door. "We go where?"

"I think there's a café along the street. Let's try that?" Amelia saw a pained expression cross his face. "What's the matter? Che cosa?"

"I know a better place."

"Not smart enough for you?" she teased.

He ignored her question. "My car, it is outside. You will permit me to take you somewhere?"

Amelia nodded. "How on earth did you find a parking space?" She asked. "Ahh, Italian parking!" Amelia answered her own question, then gasped. "Oh, my God, that's it?"

Lorenzo shrugged, nudged aside a group of admiring men, and opened the door to a tomato red classic sports car parked on the pavement.

"How come I haven't seen this at the vineyard?" she asked, sliding past the men and into the low-slung vehicle. "It's gorgeous!"

"Sì, mi piace anche," he agreed. "But she is no good for work." Lorenzo folded in behind the steering wheel.

"Yeah, I can see that. I love classic cars but I don't know them. What is it? I mean," she corrected herself, "I know it's an Alfa Romeo."

"She is GTV6 from 1986. Always she has been mine!" The pride in his voice made Amelia smile. "Before I have a wife, I have this!"

"Probably a good thing," Amelia said with a laugh as they eased forward. "Wives are expensive!"

"Certo!" He overtook a slow-moving Fiat.

Amelia stroked the leather dash. "Where are we going?"

"So," Lorenzo said, flashing a grin, "today is giovedì, er, Thursday. Yes?"

"It is."

"Ecco, we go to Caffè Gilli."

"Oh, I've heard of that. Why does it have to be Thursday?"

Lorenzo looked pleased. "Poi, then, we go to the flower market. It too is on the Piazza della Repubblica. Only Thursdays. Molto bello!"

"Sounds heavenly. Can we park? I thought Florence was strict about that."

"In Italy, always!"

A sugar high from the fruit tart piled with whipped cream, and a caffè corretto, an espresso flavored with a shot of grappa, Amelia felt ready to handle anything. Even Lorenzo's charm offensive.

"I buy for you." He started negotiating with a vendor for a bunch of peonies and roses Amelia had bent to smell from one of the buckets and buckets of flowers lining the deep colonnaded arcade.

"Thank you, Lorenzo, but no." She put her hand on his arm. "I can't carry flowers around all day."

"We go to the hotel first." He turned back to the flower seller.

"No, Lorenzo." She thanked him again. "This is gorgeous—a lovely start to my day, but now I'm off to the Boboli Gardens. Thanks for breakfast. I'll see you soon." She laughed at his surprise. "And I love your car!"

"We do not stay together today?" He asked.

"No. I'm here to go to the antique markets, and wander, and take photos. With James."

"Uffa!"

Amelia reached up to kiss his cheek. "Grazie mille, Lorenzo. I'll see you soon. At Scutari Vineyard. Bria has asked me to join you for the leaf thinning and green harvest—veraison. Yes?" He nodded, then shrugged. "Bene. Ciao, bella." He winked.

✝

Both her breakfast with Lorenzo and her meander through the Boboli Gardens took longer than Amelia expected. Time fled while searching for the goat and tortoise on the façade of the Buontalenti Grotto. "Perhaps a few politicians today should take a slice off your marble, Cosimo," she said to the walls as she translated festina lenta into "hastily slowly," Cosimo Medici's words being, she decided, a convoluted way to caution prudence to be successful in government.

Photographing shadows playing over and through the ancient and knobbly fruit trees, like arthritic hands, in the Lemon House took up more minutes. The scent of citrus accompanying every snap of the shutter.

Hailing a taxi, she crossed back over the River Arno and sent James a message.

Sorry. On my way!

Seconds later, his response came back:

Nessun problema—no problem.

"Ciao!" Amelia tapped James' arm twenty minutes later. "What's that?" She peered over his shoulder at the dog-eared book he'd picked up from the bookseller's table in front of him.

"*Fiabe Italiane*," James replied, showing Amelia the cover. "By Italo Calvino. I don't think my Italian is up to his other works, but this is the Italian equivalent to the Brothers Grimm, so might be a bit easier."

"Never heard of him. Maybe that's what I should be doing. Reading *Corriere della Sera* or *La Gazzetta* is as far as I've got but at least I don't underline quite so many words in the newspaper these days."

"I'm going to get it," James said, closing the book with a snap. "You can read it after me. Quanto?"

Amelia left him to negotiate. That was what she liked about wandering with James. They didn't have to be shoulder to shoulder. He'd catch her up somewhere along the line of stalls at the antique market at Piazza Amigoni. Mainly old furniture. She smiled. Of course, Mercato delle Pulci.

She turned to James. "More flea than antique. I didn't translate the name!"

"It's still fun. Look," he pointed, "clothes."

"I've never really been into wearing other people's clothes," Amelia said, her hand trailing down the sleeve of a long midnight blue velvet coat.

"Why not?"

"Feels a bit creepy. They might be dead."

James' laughter brought the vendor over.

"Bellisimo, no?" she asked, her nose stud sparkling among a welter of wrinkles. "You try."

"No, grazie."

"Go on," James' voice followed her along the rack. "It's your color."

"Oh, you're a fashion expert now, are you?" Her eyes went back to the evening coat, cinched at the waist but with no seams to spoil the line. The shawl collar stood high, elegant. "I'm not at the opera or the ballet every night, you know."

"So? Who says you can't be glam at any time of the day?" James took it off the hanger. "Come on, try it."

"Fine!" Amelia slung her bag off her arm and handed it to him. "You're worse than the girls!"

James laughed again and watched the grinning stall holder slip the coat over Amelia's shoulders where it settled, as if made for her.

"It is nice." She stroked the fabric, watching the nap change.

"Nice? It's gorgeous! Perfect length if you had heels on."

"Perhaps you should go into fashion." Amelia allowed herself to be drawn to the full-length mirror. "I think it goes rather well with flatties and jeans!"

"I know, you can wear it to my opening. It'll be cooler by then."

"That is the lowest form of persuasion." She looked up at James. "I'll get this if you ask your parents."

"Damn! Who's talking coercion?"

Amelia turned back to the mirror. "I could wear my cream silk dress under it," she murmured.

"Venduta! Sold!" James told the woman.

"Hey, what happened to negotiating?" Amelia asked. The haggle ended quickly and, about to walk off with her new old coat, the grinning vendor thrust a silk scarf of violet, green, and blue swirls into her hands. "Now I know I paid too much!"

†

Falling into bed after supper with James the following evening, Amelia called Moira.

"Buonasera, Mamma."

Amelia checked the phone. Must've misconnected. "Moira?"

"Yes, it's me. I'm kicking up my Italian lessons. Need something to focus on."

"That's a good idea. How's it going?"

"Great. It's such a pretty language."

"Have you got to how to say 'no' yet?"

"No!"

Moira's chuckle made Amelia smile. "Well, there are numerous ways to make an error. And I've made most of them. Who knew there were so many connotations to that little word?"

"So, are you in Florence?"

"Yup. Had a lovely day. We have to come back next time you're over."

"Better than Venice?"

"Different. And the traffic is chaotic. Venice has my heart. I like not having cars barping around me, though guess what I drove in this morning?"

"You know I hate guessing, Mum. What?"

"A 1986 Alfa Romeo. Very low key. Bright red."

"Wow! How come?"

"Oh, darling, you know I know people!" It felt good to hear Moira laugh.

"No, really, Mum, whose car?"

"Lorenzo."

"I thought you were in Florence with James, the innocuous English kid."

"Do you know how disparaging that sounds? He's a lovely young man. He's quite good looking in a bookish kind of way. It's as if he's gone from artistic to academic in a haircut."

"I have no idea what you're talking about, Ma—you're obviously going doolally! I'd better come and check on you. And your men. How come you and Lorenzo happened to be driving around Florence in an Alfa Romeo?"

"He's here seeing his ex, and he kindly took me out to breakfast. That's all. And, my darling girl, that is all it is ever going to be! So don't go getting on the phone to Lucy with wild tales." Amelia stopped talking, her mind whirring. "Moira? Did you just say you were coming to Italy?"

"I think I did, Mum."

"Oh, darling, that would be wonderful. When?"

"No idea. I've just this minute decided. Stuff to sort out first. I'll let you know. Are you racing off anywhere else soon?"

"Of course not. I'll be here. That truly is the best news, Moira. I can't wait."

"Yeah, me neither." The line went quiet. "I need to get out of New York. It hurts too much." Moira's laughter had turned to quiet sobs. "I forget for a moment, then guilt whams me in the guts. The 'what should I have dones' haunt me, Mum."

"Then come to Italy, darling. Natalie will never be far from your thoughts but the intervals between the agony will grow longer. I can promise you that."

"Thank God for that, because she is everywhere I look." Moira gasped. "I don't mean I don't want to see her, remember her, but I'll go mad if I can't have some respite."

"I know, my darling. It's okay."

"Thanks, Mum." Amelia heard Moira sniff. "I'm okay. Change of subject, please. What are you doing tomorrow? And with whom?"

"Very funny! James, emphasis on James, and I are going to the Piazza Indipendenza—there's an antique market the third weekend of every month where traders come from all over the country."

"Now that does sound like fun! Maybe I'll time my trip to take that in. Find a long-lost work of art."

"I think that's what James is secretly hoping for," Amelia said with a laugh. "Me, I'm just looking for a desk."

"I thought you took the train down."

"We did. But I can always drive a truck back."

"Or ask Lorenzo to put it in his Alfa Romeo!" The line went dead before Amelia could respond.

✝

Good morning, Velvet-coated lady. Late again. Can we meet at the market at about one?

Amelia smiled. James' texts seemed lighter of heart. As if he'd been lifted. She wondered if he'd met someone.

Sure. I'm off on a photo-taking walk.

She could sense his grin.

All your walks are photo-taking!

She smiled and responded.

True. See you later.

Although later than she'd planned, the light was still soft. Not wanting to waste time, Amelia stood at the counter of a café and gulped down an espresso. She'd hoped that Saturday morning would be less congested than weekday Florence. Pavements less blocked with cars parked haphazardly, and tourists cluttering the alleys. She smiled. When did she stop feeling a visitor in Italy?

Perhaps when she stopped worrying about getting lost. Or panicking when someone spoke to her. She could thank the mob in Venice for that. They had taken her under their collective wing. Helped her fill in paperwork for her residency, tutored her in Italian, and helped her celebrate receipt of her long-awaited residence card, her Carta di Soggiorno.

The counter filled with people eager for their morning coffee. She handed euros to the barista and headed out. Her confidence had grown. For years she had considered herself a fake, but today she carried her camera case with pride. Did that mean she was now a photographer? Maybe not with a capital 'P' but getting there. She grinned. Carefree.

"Ciao, bella," a mustachioed roué called as she stepped into the street.

She laughed. Yes. Carefree.

Hopelessly but happily lost and refusing to consult a map, either on her phone or the one in her bag, Amelia wandered. Cobbled streets led to cobbled alleys where children played while cats looked on, disdain twitching from their whiskers. Delight settled over her shoulders, then thirst and hunger drove her into an enoteca, the shop cum wine bar's cool interior a panacea for sore feet. Reviving with an Aperol Spritz and a slice of mushroom pizza, Amelia sent a text to James.

Running late. Drinking. See you two-ish!

She hit send and smiled. Her turn. They'd still have plenty of time to amble around the market.

The market lived up to their expectations. Stall after stall of furniture, books, paintings, and sculptures. And more clothes. A two-foot-high statuette of St. Francis holding a fawn found its way into her possession. Not particularly old or valuable, she was sure, but she loved it, if not the weight. And she returned the sartorial favor by insisting James buy a leather jacket.

"It's very James Dean," she said, watching him flip up the collar.

"I suppose you think you can flatter me into carrying Frank," he said, taking the statue.

The hoped-for desk did not materialize which, Amelia admitted to James, was probably a good thing. Would she really have been up to driving a truck back to Venice?

They grabbed a pavement table at a café bustling with weary bargain hunters and ordered two glasses of Prosecco to toast another successful day.

"Um, Amelia," James started. He blushed and looked at his glass. "Um, would you mind if I didn't get the train back with you tomorrow?"

She laughed. "Not as long as you carry Frank to the station."

"Oh, of course, of course."

"I'm teasing, you silly boy. Why would you possibly think I'd mind?"

"Well, it's not very chivalrous?"

"James, my dear, you are not my lover." His color deepened. "You do not have to be chivalrous! Can I ask why?"

"I'd just like to spend a bit longer in Florence, that's all."

"Righto!" Amelia itched to grill him but instead sipped her drink and crowd watched.

"That's it?"

"It's none of my business, James. Now, shall we have some nibbles to sop up the alcohol?"

"Thanks. You're an amazing woman, Amelia."

"Rubbish. I've just learned not to question too much. Remember, I have two daughters. One of whom, by the way, is planning a visit." She raised her glass and grinned.

"Moira?"

"Yup. I don't know when but soon, I think."

"That could be difficult."

"I thought about that as I roamed the streets this morning. But actually, I think, even though she knew she was pregnant when she was here last time, it will be a relief to be somewhere different. The hard part will be going back to New York."

"Well, worry about that then."

"For a young man who is a bit daft at times, you can be quite wise."

They finished their drinks and, as James went to the bar to pay, Amelia watched a bright red Alfa Romeo zoom by at the end of the street.

Chapter 21

"Ciao, you are back." Riccardo's voice bounced along the cobblestones. "You have l'aperitivo with me? Soon I finish."

"Ciao, e certo. The usual place? One hour?" Amelia waved to his nod, delighted no resentment lingered with the amiable boatman, and stepped over the threshold into the cool of Palazzo Ambrosio's courtyard. How she loved the space. Plumbago climbed from the pots she'd planted. Flowers stretching around the courtyard columns like purple coronets.

Amelia unlocked the door to find Dafne eyeing her from the back of the sofa before she stalked off. The cat's food and water bowl had both been freshened. Amelia's doubts about James' assurances that his flat mate would be a responsible provider had proved unfounded.

Kicking off her shoes, she padded after Dafne. "Hi," she said to the photo by her bed. "Leo, meet Frank." She rested the statuette on her bed. "Frank, meet Leo, my husband." Amelia laughed then hoisted the saint up, opened the door onto the tiny terrace off her bedroom, and stood him among pots of magenta, lilac and red geraniums. Curious, Dafne came to see what was going on. Amelia scooped the cat up before she could be ignored again, "Let's sit out here for a minute," she said, and put her feet up on the balustrade as she stroked Dafne until a purr signaled the cat's forgiveness. She had time, then a cup of tea and soak in the bath before meeting Riccardo.

†

"So," Riccardo said, holding a chair for her at Caffè Dodo, "you like Firenze more than Venezia?"

"Mai, never! My heart is here." Amelia looked across the canal to the Ghetto.

"With me?"

She frowned. "Riccardo, please, no." The waiter appeared and she smiled. "Buonasera, Matteo, vorrei un negroni, per favore," she ordered, before he could say anything then laughed when he complimented her accent. "I have the best teachers!" Amelia waited until Matteo took Riccardo's order for a dark beer before turning back to her companion.

His mustache tickled when he kissed her hand. "Amelia, I tease, okay? I am Italian. If I do not ask often you will think I no longer want you!"

She laughed. "Riccardo, I don't want you to want me. It's exhausting. I don't want anyone. Okay?"

"Va bene," he shrugged. "Okay, but no Italian woman would ever say such a thing!"

"Not even Bria?" Amelia asked with a smile.

"No. You know she have lovers? Before. Not so much now."

"Good for her. But I don't want one. Finito!"

"But, Amelia, bella, I keep asking."

"You're impossible, Riccardo!" But it was impossible to stay cross and the early evening passed in a mixture of English and Italian as Amelia described her few days in Florence. Although she left out her suspicions about James. And her morning with Lorenzo.

"And," Amelia said, "Moira is coming back."

"Fantastico! It is good for her, and you."

"Yeah, it will be. I'll take her back to Florence."

"Maybe, Amelia," Riccardo said, his voice hesitant, "Moira would like to visit the city alone. Maybe she needs to walk, like you, when unhappy, eh? To think?"

Amelia looked across the table at the attractive man who had shown her so much kindness, who wanted to make love to her, but there was no spark. Even without the age difference. "Maybe you're right, Riccardo. I guess I just have to let things play out. Not be pushy."

She finished her drink, bent to kiss his cheeks, and headed home with a wave to Matteo.

Daylight had faded and activity on the canal eased. Amelia's favorite time of the day. The time she felt a part of Venice. Ensconced in her palazzo, she smelled a hint of rum and vanilla smoke through the open doors. Signor Malvestio. She smiled and wandered through to the fridge and poured a glass of Scutari wine and put together a plate of cheese, crackers, and olives and returned to the balcony.

Although flattered by Riccardo's ongoing overtures, she really did want them to stop. Perhaps it was all a game. One she didn't play well. Leo would've fit right in. Probably a good thing they had never come to Italy together. When they had been younger, she'd watched him charm so many women, some she knew became his lovers. She sighed. The hurt still spiked every now and then. "Why did you do it, Leo?" She sipped her wine. "I know you loved me and the girls. Why did you always need more?"

Perhaps that was the reason she couldn't dally with Riccardo, or anyone. She thought of the red Alfa Romeo she'd seen at the end of the street the night before in Florence and wondered again if it had been Lorenzo.

✝

"Good morning!" Fenella's crisp tones rang up from the street.

"G'day," Amelia called over the balcony. "Are you just saying hi or are you coming up for a coffee?"

"The latter, please, if you're not busy?"

"Not for you!"

They stood in the kitchen chatting as the coffee brewed, then Amelia carried the tray out to the balcony and moved Dafne off the other chair. "So what's up?"

"What do you mean?" Fenella asked.

"You're not usually in this neighborhood this early. Ergo, something must be up."

"Ergo?" Fenella queried with a laugh. "You've been here too long!"

"Oh please, a posh dame like you doesn't drop that into conversation all the time," Amelia said, grinning. "Come on, spill it!"

Fenella blushed.

"Oh, God, you've fallen for someone! Who?" Amelia looked at her friend. "It's Tigran!" She didn't wait for Fenella's nod. "But that's fantastic. Isn't it?"

"Not really, no."

"Why ever not? Doesn't he feel the same way?"

Her friend nodded.

"Then what's the problem?"

"Culture." Fenella looked close to tears. "And I'm not long out of a failed marriage. I've run away to Italy. The only bit of my story that isn't cliché is that he's Armenian and not Italian. I'm a bit old to be taking Latin lovers."

200

"Rubbish. Which, by the way, is essentially what Riccardo said to me last night. We are not too old. And you are fifteen years younger than me. Honestly, Fenella, I don't see the issue here. You're both single. You're both dear people. What could be better?"

"Children!"

Amelia looked up from her coffee, her eyes sharp. "Did Tigran say that?"

"No. But, culturally, children are important to Armenians."

"Fenella, don't you think you might be looking for problems? If he hasn't said anything, why are you? It's not like he's a spring chook either. And he's not a fool—far from it. And he doesn't seem to be scrabbling for a living." Amelia paused. She and Fenella had felt an instant rapport, despite very different backgrounds, but they hadn't known each other that long.

"We come from opposite ends of every spectrum. I'm, as you say, posh English. He's from humble beginnings. It doesn't bother me, but it would my family."

"They're not the ones thinking about sleeping with him!" Amelia was glad to see Fenella smile.

"True. But they're still a specter."

"Do you know what my mother used to say? It doesn't matter a toss what people look like, where they've come from. What matters is integrity." Amelia paused. Perhaps that was why her mother had never warmed to Leo. She shook the thought away. "And intellect," she continued. "And Mum didn't mean book learning."

Amelia's thoughts flew to the husband of their house meri in New Britain. He'd been their boatman and general handyman and she had spent many hours working alongside him in the garden. Every morning Jonas would devour the *Post-Courier* after she finished reading the local paper to Leo, who would nod and gaze vacantly at the ocean beyond the verandah. Jonas, on the other hand, had opinions on most things—from politics to anthropology—his words thoughtful, questioning, provoking. Amelia looked at Fenella. "Are you maybe looking too far ahead?"

"What do you mean?"

"What would be wrong with a fling?"

"A fling?"

"Yeah. You don't have to sign on any dotted line. Just see where it goes?"

"I don't think either Tigran or I are like that."

"Like what?"

"You know? Casual. And," it was Fenella's turn to pause, "I don't think you are either."

"Well, perhaps we bloody well should be! Perhaps Leo had it right all along!" Amelia clamped her hand over her mouth. "Shit! I didn't mean to say that." She reddened, appalled at her disloyalty to a dead man. She felt her eyes water. "I'm sorry. That was crass."

"No, Amelia, that was honest." Fenella leaned across and poured them each another coffee, then looked at the cups, her lips curling up. "Do you have any grappa? Let's have a caffè corretto!"

Amelia rubbed her eyes dry. "I do, and to hell with it. It's Monday!" She went through to the bar trolley and returned with the bottle. She smiled as she added grappa to their coffee. She might not always be serene but this was carefree.

✝

Lying in bed that night, restlessness overtook carefree as her conversation with Fenella played in her head. Had she been completely honest, with either Fenella or herself? Leo was one of two men with whom she'd slept. Amelia sniggered. And the adolescent fumblings that technically took her virginity did not really count. What was his name? "Amelia Paignton, you tart!" Dafne's claws dug in as giggles became laughter. "Sorry, kitty-kat." She smoothed the ruffled fur. "David? Damian? D-something." She laughed again. Then shook her head. No. Casual sex didn't get it. Another face came into view. Not Leo's. Ralph. No chiseled cheekbones. No cleft in his chin. No sexy dimples. Nothing remarkable. But a pleasant face, and brown eyes that lit up whenever she appeared. And beautiful hands. The man who almost. A few lunches. Never dinner. Why not? "Because," Amelia said aloud, "you didn't trust yourself." But that hadn't been casual. If it hadn't been for the girls, teenagers at the time, she might well have. Ralph had filled a void opened by yet another Leo infatuation. Made her feel adored. He'd left New York when it became too difficult to avoid each other. She'd always been grateful for that. Or maybe he just moved somewhere else in the city. She'd never know. "I hope he's happy."

The air was still. Amelia thumped her pillow and flung off the sheet. Hot chocolate! She needed hot chocolate. Ignored by Dafne, she padded naked through to the kitchen, switching on a table lamp as she went. Just enough light to see by. Not enough to disrupt her thoughts. She wanted to think this through. Really think it through. Perhaps for the first time. She leaned against the countertop and waited for the milk to simmer. All part of the ritual. Heating milk in a microwave negated the time for middle-of-the-night contemplation.

"Sugar," she muttered, then plopped a lump into the mug and stirred. Fenella and Tigran are different. No commitments to others. Free. In Venice. It wasn't known as the city of love, but love seemed to show up. Amelia blew on the hot chocolate. Why not? And Tigran cared. That was obvious. She'd been right. It wouldn't be a casual decision for either of them. Still leaning against the counter, she took a sip. And another.

"Desmond! D for Desmond!" Her laughter sent hot chocolate sloshing down over her breasts and onto the floor. "Oh, bugger!" She wiped up the mess and wondered where in the world he was. She rinsed her mug and went back to bed.

"Move over," she shoved Dafne, "I told you hot chocolate always works."

Chapter 22

"Hello, stranger," Amelia greeted James when they bumped into each other in the courtyard of the palazzo. "It seems weeks since I've seen you. Everything okay?" She put the lens cap back on her camera, pleased to have caught the play of early sunlight dancing across the worn tiles.

James looked at his feet.

"Have you been avoiding me?"

"No!" He blushed. "Yes."

"Why?" She swatted his arm. "Not, I hope, because of what we talked about."

"No. Yes," he said. "Look, have you time for a coffee? Let's go to Dodo's."

"Righto!"

They talked of nothing—the weather, the tourists, the pigeons—until Matteo brought them cappuccinos.

"I wish I could drink these all day long," Amelia said with a sigh. "I love the cinnamon."

"That would tell every Italian waiter in Venice you are a tourista idiota," replied James.

He spooned some froth, again not meeting Amelia's eyes.

"So?" she asked, "What's going on?"

"I really have been busy. Painting. And trying not to panic about the exhibition."

"And?"

"And I've asked my parents. They seem pleased."

"Told you! Give me the dates they'll be here, and I'll invite them for supper." Amelia looked over the rim of her cup. "And?"

"And I've met someone."

"I knew it!" she laughed. "I just knew it. Dear James, I'm thrilled. Tell me. Everything." Amelia reddened. "Well, not everything, but you know what I mean."

"Florentine. Dealer. Older."

"Okay," Amelia said, "a few questions spring to mind. Dealer of what? How much older?"

"Really, Amelia?" he laughed. "Art dealer." He grinned as she clapped her hands, sending a brace of pigeons flying. "Quite a bit."

"Quite a bit what?"

"Older."

"How much?"

"Damn, Amelia. What is this? An inquisition?"

"Think of it as coaching before your parents arrive and ask the same things."

"They're not going to meet him." It was James' turn to blush.

"I'll come back to that," Amelia said, squinting at him as she licked her spoon. "How much older?"

"About fifteen years."

Her spoon clattered onto the saucer. "Yes, that qualifies as older. About. You said 'about.' Does that mean more or less?"

"A bit more." James drained his cup and waved Matteo over. "I think I'll have another. Would you like one too?"

"Sure. Because, James, we're not going anywhere until I get the full story. Even," she reached for his hand, "if we're still here for cicchetti!"

"I thought you were off to take photos." He looked at the camera on the table.

"That can wait. How old is he?"

"Forty-seven."

"Shit, James. That is rather more than 'a bit!'"

"Yup." He looked miserable. "That's why my parents can't meet him."

"How old are they?"

"Dad's fifty-one. Mum's younger. Forty-six."

"Oh, God, James. Younger than your lover."

"Thank you, Amelia. I know."

"Sorry. A bit of a shock."

"Yup. But he is wonderful. I've never felt like this."

"James, I'm sorry to be coarse, but has he offered you the world?"

"Amelia!" His eyes sharpened as anger replaced anxiety. "No, he bloody hasn't! The opposite."

"What do you mean?" Amelia gentled her tone.

"He likes my work but won't represent me. Says I must make my own way, otherwise it will mean nothing. Maybe not for us. But to others."

"Well, that's good. Although maybe a bit harsh. Every artist needs a patron. Leo had Charlie Warner."

"Yes, but they weren't lovers!"

"True." Amelia laughed. "You don't make life easy for yourself, do you?" She smiled her thanks as Matteo delivered two more cappuccinos. "Okay. We need a plan of action. Attack."

"Attack?"

"Yes. You should introduce..." She paused again. "You haven't said his name."

"Arturo."

"Okay," Amelia started again, "you should introduce Arturo to your parents. Elephant in the room, and all that." On a roll, she ignored James' shaking head. "Is this serious or not?" He nodded. "Then get it over with. What is the point in waiting? Life is too bloody short for family feuds. The exhibition is the perfect time. No, I know," Amelia grabbed his hand again as he started to wave her off, "I'll ask Arturo to supper as well. We'll make it a party to celebrate your success."

"We don't know if the show will be a success," James said, his voice glum.

"Of course it will be. Don't be silly. I might not be an artist, but I lived with one a very long time. You're an artist, and don't you forget it. I know one when I see one."

"Actually, Amelia," a smile lifted his concern, "*you* are an artist. You're a photographer. And don't you forget it!"

They laughed.

"Righto—we're both artists! Now. I need your mum's email. And their names. Let's ask Fenella and Tigran. She can charm anyone. And Tigran is a smart cookie. You know he was a professor at the university in Yerevan."

"Where?"

"Yeah, I'm afraid I had to ask too. It's the capital of Armenia."

"Why did he leave?"

"Not entirely sure. Funding, maybe. He's also a musician."

"Huh! What's he play?"

"Violin. But I've never heard him. Fenella says he's good." She swatted James' hand. "We're getting sidetracked. When do I get to meet Arturo?"

"Dunno!"

"Not good enough. When is he coming to Venice? Oh God," Amelia laughed at the image of anyone over twenty-five being in the ground-floor apartment, "please tell me he's not going to stay downstairs."

James laughed too. "No, he's not. He has the use of a place not far from the basilica."

"Nice! So, when?"

"Next weekend, actually."

"Great. I'll meet him then."

"God, Amelia. You're like a steamroller."

"Good thing you love me then, isn't it?" Amelia grinned, shrugged and plumped her hair as if a young coquette, her blue eyes shimmering like drops of the Mediterranean. "Funny really, I was far more careful with my girls than I am with you!"

"Lucky them." James softened his words with another smile. "Change of topic. When do you think Moira will be here?"

"Don't know. And no, no change of topic. What do you think about asking Bria for supper too, when your parents are here?" Amelia paused. "They do drink, don't they?"

"Oh, yeah, Dad's a bit of a wine snob."

"That's it then. We'll ask her. And Lorenzo. A serious charm offensive."

"I thought you were ambivalent about her brother."

Amelia felt her color heighten and grateful James ignored it, said, "I am, but for you anything. And you don't get much more knowledgeable about wine than a grower." Relish made her eyes shimmer. "They won't know what's hit them."

"Christ, Amelia, I don't know what's hit me! But I do love you."

"I know, James." She looked across the table at the happy young man. "You look different somehow. Less mangy!"

"Mangy? Really? Mangy?"

"Yes. You used to look a bit downtrodden. Then you got a haircut—that helped. Now you look positively urban. Or do I mean urbane? I don't know. Just different. Great. You look great!"

"I can't keep up with you. Thank you. I think. Right, I've got to go. Coffee's on me," he put some euros on the table and bent to kiss Amelia's cheeks. "Thanks. I really do love you!"

"James," she called him back, "is he good to you?"

"Yes."

"Is he rich?"

"I think probably. I don't really know."

✝

Amelia, her mind on James, his lover and his parents, ambled over the bridge and across the Ghetto square. Only when she reached the vaporetto stop on the Grand Canal did she realize she now criss crossed Cannaregio, her little slice of Venice, without a thought. No wrong turns. Happiness accompanied her as she stepped into the boat and watched Venice pass by. She alighted at the Piazza San Marco and merged with tourists milling around the entrance to the Palazzo Ducale which was, she recalled, where 120 doges, the traditional rulers of Venice, were housed for over a thousand years.

She glanced up at the façade melding Byzantine, Gothic, and Renaissance architecture. "No wonder they've got building sussed," she muttered as she waited to enter the palace, hoping she could leapfrog the guided tours. She'd already seen the paintings by Titian, Veronese and Tintoretto staring down from the walls of the Doge's lavish apartments. She hadn't had the nerve to tell any of her Italian friends that she thought Tintoretto's massive painting 'Paradise' overpowering and overbearing. "What would you say to that, Leo?" She giggled under her breath. The Maggior Consiglio hall, over which the painting glowered, had hosted a thousand people waiting to vote on the future of Serenissima. That did seem pretty impressive.

Although delayed by her coffee with James, her mission remained the same. To see the armory. Swords and suchlike held little appeal and she hurried through the halls and headed for the fourth room where, along with various instruments of torture as well as chastity belts, the devil's chest was housed. The sheer ingenuity fascinated her. A chest that fired not one but four hidden pistols when opened, and a key that, when turned, triggered a poisoned dart. She checked the flash was off then started snapping photos. "Bloodthirsty lot." Her words provoked a glare from a docent. "And vindictive." She took a few photos of the Bocca di Leone, the lion's mouth, carved into a door where Venetians could anonymously report on their fellow citizens—an early day hotline.

Amelia considered tagging onto the end of a tour group heading across the Bridge of Sighs to Casanova's cell, supposedly the only person ever to escape the prison, but the call of an over-priced Negroni from Caffè Florian proved more tempting.

Blinking in the early afternoon brilliance, Amelia fumbled for her sunglasses and looked across the square toward the café and saw a queue of tourists. She shrugged and walked back to the water's edge and watched a small flotilla of boats harassing a cruise liner as it glided past. She didn't blame the demonstrators. The authorities had promised the massive ships would be banned from Venice's historic waterways as soon as an alternative dock could be found. Years later, Venetians continued to wait and argue about the pros and cons of the cruise industry.

Amelia watched the wash from the vessel. It seemed easy to her. Ban the bloody beasts. She shrugged and continued on past the park and opened the nondescript doors that led into the simplicity of a compact 1930s bar. A babel of voices greeted her but she spotted an empty barstool and hopped up.

"Good afternoon, signora, welcome to Harry's Bar," the barman said, his nod curt. "A moment, please."

"Buon pomeriggio." She smirked at his surprise. Hah! She might not look Italian but her accent sounded Venetian, thanks to Bria and the gang!

"Brava, tu parli italiano. Cosa vi porto?" he asked, ignoring the wave of a florid man further along the bar.

"Un Bellini, per favore," Amelia replied, asking for the drink concocted by Giuseppe Cipriani and made famous by Hemingway, Hepburn, and other A-list celebrities after the war.

She watched as the barman skipped past a jug full of puree and pulled two fresh white peaches from a bowl. He caught her raised eyebrow and winked. Next, he removed the pit then muddled the peaches and tipped them into a glass, opened a new bottle of Prosecco DOC and poured, gave a gentle stir then presented the drink with a flourish.

"Per la bella donna," he said, only then turning to the American, still trying to get his attention.

"Grazie mille." She thanked him as the lushness of summer teased her lips. God, she loved Italy. Amelia turned to look at the other patrons. Mainly tourists; so easy to spot. When had she become so disparaging? She grinned. The day she decided to make Venice her home. "That's when." The whispered words prompted the man next to her to speak. She smiled but turned away, her thoughts on James. Perhaps she should have waited to meet Arturo before suggesting he attend the dinner party with his parents. What if he turned out to be awful? If the party was a disaster, James would never forgive her. She groaned. Me and my big mouth. Oh sod it, James isn't a fool. She'd just have to work extra hard to make sure everything went well.

✝

Rather than drag her tired legs up the stairs, Amelia clanged the heavy iron gates on the palazzo lift. Hauling them open on the second floor, she felt her bag vibrate then dropped it in a flurry as she scrabbled for her phone. "Bugger!" Finding it, the phone stopped only to vibrate again as she turned the key to her apartment.

"Pronto," she said.

"Ciao, Mamma." The amusement in Moira's voice made Amelia smile.

"Darling, how lovely. Just a minute. Let me get in the door. Or shall I call you back?"

"No. Where've you been?"

"Harry's Bar!" She put her camera and bag on the table under Leo's painting of the girls. She liked seeing it each time she came home.

"God, Mum, you could write a book about the bars in Venice. You always seem to be in one."

"I do not!" Amelia bent to pet Dafne. "I'll have you know I've been very cultural today. I've been to the Doge's Palace looking at weaponry! Let me put the kettle on, proof I do sometimes drink tea." She put the phone on speaker.

"So, Mum, er, I've got a plan."

"Okay. Do I need to sit down, or something stronger than tea?" Moira's laugh made Amelia's heart sing. It had been months since she'd heard happiness in her daughter.

"I'm coming to Italy!"

"I know, darling. You told me."

"No, I mean I'm coming to live in Italy. No more art. I thought I'd get into wine. They auction that too."

"What?"

"Yup. I need out of New York, Mum."

"I get that, darling, but Italy?"

"Why not? You did it."

"I know, but I'm fortunate not to have to work."

"Don't worry, Mum, I'm not coming to cramp your style!"

"That is not what I meant, Moira, and you know it." Amelia sloshed water over a teabag, then jiggled it.

"I know, I'm joking. But I did think you'd be pleased. At least one daughter near you."

"I am pleased, thrilled, darling girl, just surprised." Amelia moved to the sofa, heeling her shoes off as she sat. "Okay, I'm settled. Tell me what's going on."

Chapter 23

Sleep would not come. Amelia threw herself over, again. Even the usually comforting sound of water lapping the fondamenta, the streets running along a canal, failed to soothe her scrambled thoughts. Each time she felt her eyes close, her brain kicked in again. Overthinking? She rolled her head to look at Leo. "No, guilt." Moira's words hammered in. Amelia sat up, dislodging Dafne, and bashed the pillows into a mound to lean against. The cat crept up to her shoulder, purrs providing a backdrop to her thoughts. "She's right, you know? About cramping my style—not that I have one to cramp, but ..." Amelia shook her head, "... Italy's mine!"

The words reverberated around the room. Mean. Selfish. Tears leaked down her face. She felt old. "Oh God, what a terrible thing to say. I don't mean it, Leo, I really don't. Especially after everything Moira's been through." Amelia nudged the cat down and padded through to the kitchen. Hot chocolate. Again. That and cold showers in the middle of the night got her through the menopause. Perhaps both would help now. She looked at the oven clock. No. Couldn't be bothered with a shower. Dafne snaked around her ankles. "Do you want a treat too?" She tipped a few strands of grated cheese onto the floor. "You are one spoiled cat. But at least I don't feel mad talking to a photo with you here, because you do know I'm actually talking to you, right?"

Her mug held to her chest, Amelia slumped into the tub chair and drew the ottoman under her feet. "What the hell is the matter with me? Who wouldn't want their daughter nearer?" But did she want to feel responsible for her? "Damnit, I've done my daily caring. Just like her father." An image of Patanga surfaced. She had loved the haven they had created in PNG, but it had been lonely and it had certainly been Leo who had driven the return to the South Pacific. Like all decisions, he'd had a knack of presenting the matter as a discussion but really his mind had always been made up, a fait accompli. "The right choices for you, Leo, not always for me."

Until Italy. The kernel of a thought that had hardened as Leo's dementia worsened and cancer ate through his body. Italy, something to hold on to as the miserable days became more frequent. Rage that had flared into violence, instantly forgotten as she had ducked Leo's clenched fists to hold him tight. "At least the anger lessened," Amelia told Dafne, once again curled onto her lap. Leo had though never wandered off. He wasn't searching for anywhere. Perhaps some recess of his poor addled mind felt safe on New Britain, his island escape.

"Well, now, Moira needs to feel safe. Have a new beginning. It's not like she's a clinging vine. She's smart, accomplished, and totally independent." Amelia stroked the cat's soft fur. "Get a grip, Amelia. Tonight, you can be self-centered. Tomorrow, you share Italy."

†

Eyes scratchy and dry, the result of her jangled night, Amelia filled the base of the moka pot with water and put it on the stove. Like so many things Italian, she loved the ritual of making the perfect cup of espresso.

"You know who designed the first percolator?" Arturo's voice brought her back.

"No," she shook her head, "but you're about to tell me. An Italian, I'm guessing!"

Arturo's throaty laugh made her smile. She understood how James had fallen in love with the sometimes-irreverent man. He had the knack of lifting spirits wherever he went. "Certo, of course he is Italian. Like all great engineers!"

"Really? I think there've been a few others."

"Galileo, Agnelli, Ferrari, Marconi..."

"Okay, okay! But only because I'm tired and I haven't had coffee yet!"

"And," Arturo took wooden spoons from the jug by the oven for his drum roll, "Alfonso Bialetti, designer of the moka pot."

"Righto, you win on that one."

Silence filled the kitchen as Amelia took down two dainty espresso cups and saucers—another flea market find.

"Talk to him." Arturo, his arms now crossed, leaned against the cabinet. "Please."

"I'm guessing we are no longer talking about what's-his-name, the moka inventor, but rather James. And why me? Shouldn't that be you?" The words filtered over her shoulder as she watched steam rise from the spout.

"No, Amelia, lovers should not give advice. It never lands well."

She laughed. Arturo's fluent English every now and then lent a surprise. James' almost parental delight when it became obvious his friend and his lover liked what they saw in each other had also made them laugh. The supper at Dodo's six weeks earlier had been a great success, so much so that Arturo invariably spent time with Amelia whenever he was in Venice, while James frantically prepared for his exhibition.

And that was the subject of their current conversation. The pounds had fallen from James' already slender frame. He looked gaunt, his eyes haunted.

"It is not the show alone, eh?"

"No," Amelia handed him an espresso for one hand, a grappa for the other. "No, I'd hazard a guess he's terrified of introducing you to his parents." A pang stabbed her. Perhaps she had bullied him. Argh, no point worrying. Everything was in motion now.

"I think it too," Arturo sighed. "What can I do? He is young. I am old. But this, this is for me, very real."

"And for him." Amelia assured him. "I might not have known James long, and I feel a bit disloyal talking to you about him, but he has, apart from this one little..." she paused at Arturo's guffaw, "... this one little thing, lightened up. He's lost his little boy look. Well, he had. It's coming back again." Amelia laughed. "Did he tell you I called him mangy?"

"He did."

"Well, he was. Like a kicked dog. Now he believes he's an artist. He knows who he really is. That's a pretty cool thing at his age. I sure as hell didn't know."

Arturo poured the grappa into the dregs of his coffee and, his gray eyes smiling, asked, "So, Amelia, when did you know?"

"Oh, that's a long story. For another day."

"Why? We make time now."

"Let's just say, only recently."

"There is something more, eh? Something that troubles you?" Arturo lifted Amelia's chin. "Why did you not sleep?"

She sighed. "My daughter, Moira, is coming to live in Italy."

Amelia felt Arturo's gaze sharpen. "And that is not good?"

"No. Yes."

"Ahh, now you are a true Italian. No. Yes. Maybe. Molto bene, cara!"

"I don't want her to come." The bald statement seemed even worse said aloud.

"Because?" Arturo waited.

"Because," Amelia paused, trying to find the right words, "because I wanted somewhere just for me." She glanced up from the fingernail she was tearing and saw him put down his cup.

"Italy, it is big enough for two Paigntons." Arturo took a step nearer and put his arms around her.

She laughed through her sobs. "I'm being so silly. And selfish. And honestly, Arturo, I don't mean it."

"This I know. So, cara, now the words are said, they are powerless."

"But what mother even thinks them?"

"I imagine many mothers. Now, no more, eh." He hugged her tight. "All will be well. For you, for her, for James."

✝

Amelia put the phone down with a groan, helpless to ease Moira's impatience.

"She's just like you, Leo." She glared at his photo. "Mind made up, let's go! But you always had me to deal with the messier side of moving on. She doesn't." Amelia pushed her hair off her face. It needed a cut. "At least Adam is taking over the renting out of the brownstone. Keep an eye on things. I hope Cynthia does decide to move back in." She went to the kitchen to boil the kettle. "I was wrong about him," she continued her one-sided conversation. "Adam's been incredible. And he loves our daughter. She just doesn't love him—well, she does, just not in the special kind of way."

Mint drifted up on the steam as she added hot water to the teabag. "It didn't stop you, did it, Leo? You didn't have to love any of them. Just sleep with them. Damnit, but you can still piss me off." She sipped the tea. Not soothed. "Did you ever think, really think, what your affairs did to me?" She took her cup out to the balcony. Did Signor Malvestio ever think her mad? Her solo conversations. Her soliloquies. His shy smile would curl around his pipe as he nodded across the gap between balconies before disappearing inside to be chastised again by his wife.

"Maybe that's what I should have done, eh, Leo? Shouted and screamed instead of tears. But I believed you each time you said it meant nothing. It was over. It wouldn't happen again. Who was the idiot?"

Amelia gulped the last of her tea then, thoroughly unsettled, went inside, slamming the door behind her. "Bloody man. I get my head together then you burst in again." Her cup clattered into the sink. "Bugger you, Leo. Music! That's what I need."

Music and books. Her solace through the years. Her knowledge of Italian singers had been limited to Mario Lanza—a throwback to her parents—Pavarotti and Andrea Bocelli but now, her repertoire much enlarged, she had a rack of favorites depending on her mood. She skipped past Bocelli with a silent apology. She didn't want to cry. Yes! Litfiba. 1980s rock. Perfect. The sound of drums filled the apartment and she remembered Stefano explaining how the band's name came from the telex code of where they rehearsed. Something about Florence and the street. Telex. She doubted Stefano even knew what that was. She smiled. "What's in a name, eh?" Shakespeare didn't always get it right. Sometimes there is meaning behind one.

Litfiba cranked up, Amelia shot a glance upwards, relieved the Anellos seemed hard of hearing. Never once had they complained. Not that she did it often, and never late. Moira's words beat a chorus in time to the music as she climbed the stairs to the mezzanine. She flicked on the computer. She really did need to sort her Florentine photos but she couldn't settle. She signed into Facebook and scrolled down, making a comment here and there on friends' posts. Not that many, these days. Her fault. She'd let so many things slide away during Leo's last years but, unlike the tide, friendships didn't always flow back in. She smiled at a photo of Tom Richardson shouting on the sideline of a rugby match. At least they had stayed in touch.

She sighed. About to give up, she saw a promotional notice on the sidebar.

"Huh!" She clicked the link, something she rarely did. "That's what I need. Before James' exhibition. Before Moira gets here."

Chapter 24

"Are you sure about this?" Fenella asked as she watched Amelia zip her case closed.

"Of course, I'm sure. I'm not completely helpless you know." Amelia's smile took the sting from her words.

"I know, I know. I didn't mean that. It's just, oh, I don't know, you seem a bit distracted. And that's not always a good time to go off somewhere alone."

"Actually, I think that's the best time," Amelia replied. "Take my sorry arse away for a few days. Seeing the link about Prosecco decided me." She glanced at her friend. "You look fantastic, by the way. Anything to do with that rather gorgeous Armenian professor?" Amelia laughed at Fenella's blush.

"Maybe." The Englishwoman buried her face in Dafne's fur. "Alright, yes! Tigran is wonderful and, yes, you were right. Satisfied?"

"I am!" Amelia hugged her friend. "I am truly delighted. For you both. You deserve happiness."

"I think it was my puritanical upbringing that made me doubt myself. Then marriage to an army officer. What was I thinking?" Laughter rolled through furniture stacked in the bedroom.

"Well, it's great you've ditched the baggage." Amelia felt Fenella's eyes on her. "What?"

"You do know you've got quite a bit to jettison too, don't you?"

"Perhaps I can toss it in Prosecco!"

"Toss it back more likely. It does sound fun. Days of tasting. Nights of feasting."

Amelia slung her bag over her shoulder, feeling the camera bounce against her hip. She rolled the case to the front door and looked back at the bare room. Pietro and Stefano had promised to have the loathed tiles up and a cement skim down by the time she returned. They would score the cement into two-foot tiles then the floor would be spray painted a dusky cream. A practical solution that would not break the bank. The underfloor heating had proved a step too far. She'd just find more rugs.

Fenella put Dafne in the cat carrier and joined Amelia. "If you want to stay longer, just call. I love having the fluff ball to stay."

"Thanks, Fenella. What would I do without you?"

They bundled into the lift then, standing outside the heavy door, bussed cheeks. Fenella's words followed Amelia along the canal, "Now, go and find, or lose yourself in Prosecco!"

✝

Medieval towns passed in a blur as the train sped north to Susegana. Terracotta roof tiles smudged into splodges of orange scattered across the green hilltops, and undulating hills stretched up and away through regimented rows of vines that reminded Amelia of the cornrows her Harlem friend, Sarah, used to wear.

"Oh God, I haven't told her about Natalie." Amelia's words bounced back from the glass, and she made a note to email when she got back to Venice before another CRAFT moment sent the thought flying.

Guilt twinged as Amelia switched off her phone. Bria had not been happy about her unexplained trip and had thrown up the many pitfalls of not informing people of her whereabouts. Amelia had not realized the dangers and vagaries of Italy loomed quite so large in her friend's mind. Or perhaps Bria's natural desire to ensure Amelia saw only the best of her country had been the driving factor. Whatever it had been, Amelia stood firm, assuring Bria she would check messages every evening. Her daughters had also to be placated with the same promise.

How strange to think that in a relatively short time she had become part of a community. How lucky. Nonetheless, it felt good to be invisible. If only for a few days. Sometimes, just sometimes, being on the right side of sixty-five could be a bonus.

Amelia had toyed with the thought of staying at an inn closer to the vineyard that most interested her—the Bortolomiol—but, scouring the internet, an agriturismo farm and vineyard jumped out and it also offered accommodation. A bit isolated, however walking trails and a natural pool had won her over, and she was more than happy to take a bus to wherever she wanted to go. No restaurant on site but a bar. She had snorted. Was there anywhere in Italy not within easy access to wine? Solitary suppers of cheese and olives from the farm shop would be ideal.

The train whispered to a halt and Amelia stepped onto the platform and looked up at the yellow and white station building, complete with the ubiquitous shutters. This time green. Shutters. Such a sensible solution, but probably didn't do curtain sales much good.

Despite checking a map, she could not get her bearings. A rueful smile tweaked as the thought crossed her mind it wasn't only physical bearings she had been struggling with. She seemed to be going backward. What happened to carefree?

But first a taxi. The only taxi, it seemed. She eyed the VW Passat driven by an elderly man with a cigarette glued to his lips, who nodded her in. After the short, silent, if erratic drive, she understood the dings and dents that marred the cab.

The receptionist at the farmhouse assured her the afternoon tour would not leave for at least an hour. The giant key reminded Amelia of the ones at Bria's hotel. Impossible to lose. This one, with a red tassel, turned the lock to a room in which exposed beams and natural flooring added to the rustic charm. She sighed and left her case by the door. Time enough to change and perhaps put her feet up. "I am on holiday," Amelia muttered as she flung open the shutters then shielded her eyes as sunshine flooded the room, sending motes dancing. The sun seemed brighter than in Venice.

Beyond a low wall and the promised natural pool, grape pickers crept along rows of vines. Amelia leaned on the windowsill watching. "Wonder if guests can have a go." In the distance, on the far hill, the crenellated stone parapets of San Salvatore Castle shimmered like a mirage.

She grimaced, kicked off her shoes and bounced onto the bed. "Mmm," she murmured as her head sank into the pillows. There was no photo of Leo here, or a cat curling around her ankles. "I'm in danger of becoming a mad old woman." No one to whom she could pretend she was talking.

"Signora Paignton?" A tap on the door accompanied the voice. "You are there?"

Amelia blinked, wondering where she was. She heard her name again. "Oh, bugger! Yes," she called. "Coming." So much for a relaxed change. She tugged on a pair of flat boots, grabbed her bag, hat and camera and opened the door. "I'm so sorry. I fell asleep."

"Is no matter, signora. Only one person waits. You are ready?"

"Sure."

A ruddy-faced man with a comb over stood waiting on the terrace. Jeans stretched across an ample bottom and polished tasseled shoes made her wonder if he was up to a guided walk along the vines.

"Buon pomeriggio, signor, mi dispiace," she apologized.

"Hi," the man turned, "I don't speak Italian."

"Righto. Sorry for being late. I fell asleep."

"No problem. This place'll do that to you. I'm Phil. Phil Adams. From Delaware. Here for a week. Always wanted to come to Italy. Never thought I'd do it alone."

Amelia suppressed a smile and shook his limp hand, wondering why Americans felt the need to blurt out a life story within seconds of meeting someone.

"Hi, Phil Adams from Delaware. I'm Amelia Paignton. Come on, our guide awaits."

Amelia listened as the guide, Rosa, the enthusiastic reception-ist now in jeans and boots, talked about the harvest as they walked among the pickers. Each used a small curved blade to cut bunches from the vines then placed them, with gentle hands, in baskets to ensure they did not bruise.

"Prosecco is not an exact region like Champagne." Rosa explained.

"What defines it then?" Phil asked as Amelia took photos of the glistening, plump green orbs, some nestled among the vines, others exposed in baskets.

"The grape." Rosa's arm stretched out to encompass the vines. "To be Prosecco, it must be 85% glera."

"So," Amelia joined the conversation, "that's why you can get Australian Prosecco? Doesn't matter where they're grown?"

"Sì. But in Europe it is law that only here, in this region, we produce Prosecco. Like champagne in France. But yes, it is also called the same in Australia." Rosa looked pained. "Uffa! Even my uncle, he lives in Australia. In Victoria. He grows the glera and makes Prosecco."

"Is it grown in the US?" Phil asked.

"No, mai!" Rosa's firm tone made it obvious Prosecco should never be produced in America, and urged them along the line as she continued her talk. "Some in Slovenia. So, the glera, it has high acidity and many varieties, but three main ones—lungo, tondo, and nostrano. We grow the grapes fifty to five hundred meters above the sea."

"What's that in feet? We don't do metric in America."

Amelia jumped in. "Fifty meters is about a hundred and sixty feet."

Rosa flashed her a grateful look, then added, "Also many flavors. Green apple, melon, pear, peaches. Much depends on the soil."

"Mainly stone fruits," Amelia commented.

"Sì. Even honey."

Glad she remembered to bring a hat, Amelia glanced at Phil, not even a baseball cap to protect him. "You okay?"

"Sure." He mopped sweat dribbling down his face with a red check handkerchief.

Rosa turned around. "It is not so long now. Tomorrow we will go to the mandre, the sheds where we make the buffalo cheese. Come, we will head back."

Back in her room, having extricated herself from Phil's monologue of divorce woes, Amelia tossed her hat on the bed, then opened the shutters. Cooler late afternoon air drifted in suffusing the room with the scent of honeysuckle from the pots below her window. Breathing in, she realized hunger had begun to gnaw. "Shit! Agh! I didn't order a platter for supper." The apple and bottle of Pellegrino at lunchtime seemed ages ago. "I'm staying at a vineyard and don't even have a glass of bloody wine."

She heard footsteps in the corridor and felt a surge of hope. Perhaps Phil had gone to his room. She could nip down and talk to Rosa un-accosted. She'd give him a few minutes to settle.

"Hi, you're back!" Phil's voice greeted her.

"Oh, you're still here." Amelia's shoulders slumped.

"Yeah. Too hot in my room. Do you want to join me?" He nodded to the other linen-covered chair in a shaded nook beside the reception desk.

"No, thanks. Just ordering sup..." Amelia bit the word. "... er, just needed to ask Rosa something." She turned her back. Idiot!

"I saw her head out to the pool," Phil said.

"Righto, thanks." Amelia scurried out with a stifled groan. She had not anticipated having to spend her time hiding. The downside of staying somewhere small and intimate. Note to self. Always ensure there is a set of back stairs to avoid bores. "Oh, honestly," she muttered, "this is ridiculous."

Glad she had not kicked her shoes off, Amelia found Rosa in the garden, ordered a supper platter and a bottle of Prosecco tranquillo, never having tried still Prosecco. Somehow, it didn't sound right, but Rosa assured her the wine had the DOC stamp and she would enjoy the different taste. Not wanting to face Phil again, Amelia perched on the shaded stone wall surrounding the natural pool, determined to out-sit him.

Refreshed after a shower and wearing a long floral jersey shift, Amelia tiptoed downstairs in flat sandals, like a teenager trying to avoid parental censure.

"Signora Paignton, ecco. I will bring your wine. Sit, sit." Rosa indicated a wooden table on the patio, her smile sweet as she saw Amelia's tentative glance at the armchairs. A twisted eye tooth added character to the receptionist's smooth face and lively brown eyes. "Signor Adams, he is to go out this evening. But he is not yet gone. Perhaps it is better if you move to here."

Amelia smiled, a little shamefaced. "I just want quiet," she said, gathering her things as she sat at a larger table, but one hidden from view.

"Capisco, I understand, signora. First, I bring your wine, eh?"

"Lovely, thank you, Rosa. And won't you call me Amelia, please?"

Gentle evening light softened the ragged edges of the stone wall—the one she'd sat on earlier. Amelia rummaged for her camera and, standing on the wall, snapped off a rapid series of photos before the light day disappeared completely, and the world around her changed as lamps strung across the patio snapped on.

Rosa appeared with an ice bucket and the Prosecco tranquillo. The dark-haired woman laughed up at Amelia as she scrabbled down from the wall.

"It is beautiful," she said. "How long have you lived here?"

"All my life. My father, he owns the property."

"Not a bad place to grow up." Amelia watched Rosa open the wine, then sniff the cork. "Would you like to join me? Are you allowed?"

"Certo. It is, how do you call it? Eh, customer relations. I will bring another glass."

Amelia didn't wait for Rosa's return to sip the cold wine, surprised to find it light, floral, delicious, just not fizzy. She heard Rosa speak to someone, then the sound of a car door shut. With luck, Phil from Delaware on his merry way. She shivered. With the sun now gone there was a briskness in the almost autumn air. Amelia pulled out a pashmina, glad she'd tossed it in the straw basket, along with her book. What she hadn't tossed in was her phone. She would check for messages before bed. If she didn't let Bria know all was alright, her friend would probably call out the carabinieri. What would that do to the farm's reputation, having the military and police swarming around looking for a lost Australian? Amelia chuckled. This, this is what she had wanted. A word came floating back with the sound of crickets taking over the orchestra from the daytime cicadas. Carefree.

How had she let the feeling slip away? Not totally, but enough that she'd needed a solitary break from Venice. Perhaps it was island living that gave her a restlessness. Whatever! She knew it would be short-lived. She glimpsed the book she'd brought. Now there was a restless man. Bruce Chatwin. She'd first read his essays, *Anatomy of Restlessness*, when the confines of Patanga threatened to overwhelm her. His poignant argument for a nomadic life had spoken to her, at times, almost visceral desire to run away. She swirled her glass. And yet Italy had been where he most felt at home, where he loved to write, up in the tower at Santa Maddalena in the Tuscan hills.

"You are smiling, signora." Rosa's voice brought Amelia back to the farmhouse.

"How can I not?" She poured wine for her hostess. "And you are quite right, this is delicious. Crisp."

"Of what are you thinking?" Rosa asked.

"About," Amelia pulled out the book, "Bruce Chatwin, and how much he loved Italy."

"I do not know him."

"Me neither. And anyway, he's dead. But his words always make me think. I brought this with me—I don't know how many times I've read his essays—but I always find something new." Amelia looked at the play of light in the wine glass as it reflected back the strung lights. "Now, tell me about you and this magical place."

"You will hear it on the tour tomorrow," Rosa said with a smile.

"Actually, I think I'll give it a miss. I can go to the mandre on my own, yes?"

"Of course. I understand. So, I tell you a little, then I will bring your supper." She took a sip. "You speak Italian, yes?"

"Only a little. Enough to pass my residency test." Amelia gave a rueful smile. "I've got to sign up for more classes in a couple of weeks."

"So, in olden times, farmers kept their cattle up the mountains." Rosa pointed to the hills behind. "But to get to the market in Treviso or Venice, they must rest the animals before crossing the river, il fiume Piave, and that is what mandre means. A place to rest. But the word, it comes from Latin for many cattle."

"And you make buffalo cheese in the mandre cowsheds. Makes sense!"

Rosa nodded. "And also it holds a museum. About country life. Also, for the childrens, we have hens and gooses. And peacocks."

Charmed by Rosa's use of plurals, Amelia told her, "When my daughter, Lucy, was little, she called peacocks, 'teatocks.' We all still call them that!" She smiled at Rosa's laughter.

"How old is your daughter?"

"Lucy is thirty-five, and my other daughter is thirty-eight. How did I get to be so old?"

"You do not look so old," Rosa said. "Now, I get your supper."

Amelia looked down at her hands, always the give-away of age. Her left hand still felt bare. Maybe she'd put her wedding ring back on. She sighed. No. That would be going backward, as far from carefree as she could get.

"Signora Amelia, your tray." Rosa put the meat and cheese platter down, along with a bowl of olives, quartered Roma tomatoes, and thick slabs of homemade bread.

"This looks delicious. Is that honey?"

"Sì. We have also bees."

"Wonderful, thank you, Rosa."

"Prego, I go home now, okay? Please, you will put the tray at reception, eh? Buonaserata, signora."

Amelia, full from eating her way through most of the cheese, poured another glass of wine and wandered to the far side of the pool, away from the lights swinging between the terrace trees, and gazed up at the stars. She clasped the pashmina closer. She loved Venice, but this came a close second. A foot in both camps. Now wouldn't that be wonderful?

Ambling back to the table, she sat down to finish her wine. She'd save the rest for tomorrow night. She grinned in the dark. Who knows? Maybe even at lunchtime! The sound of a chair scraping startled her. Oh, no. Surely that bloody man wasn't back already.

Chapter 25

A soft strike, then a spark from the flare of a match followed by an earthy aroma with a hint of toasted coffee, wafted under the trees toward Amelia. She breathed in, thinking of her father. Funny how smells, and music, transported you to different times and places.

She heard the subtle pop of a cork and the fizz of Prosecco being poured, then a sigh. Oh, for God's sake, she couldn't hide out here all night. She gathered her basket, tilting the remains of the bottle in it, stood and picked up the tray. A polite nod, a good night, and she'd get past Phil. Easy.

A startled gasp met her arrival around the corner. The chair screeched on the Terracotta slabs as the figure stood. Not rotund and definitely taller, even in the gloom.

"Buonasera, signora. Scusa, pensavo di essere solo."

In her surprise, Amelia responded in English. "Oh, no, not alone. Sorry. I'm here."

"But you understand Italian. Hi, sorry to have disturbed your peace with both a cigar, and a human."

Amelia laughed. "Oh, I'm just glad it was you!"

"Me?" The man's look was quizzical. "Have we met?"

"No, no. That was rude. Sorry."

"Look, why don't we stop apologizing to each other? I'm Chad Hungerford." He reached for the tray and put it on the table, then shook her hand. His handshake felt firm. Dry.

"Hi. Amelia Paignton."

"As you have probably guessed, Amelia, I'm staying here as well." He paused, drawing on the cigar. "As a matter of interest, who did you think it was?"

"Oh, that doesn't matter. I'm heading in. Good night." She reached for the tray.

"Could I offer you a glass of this excellent Prosecco before you go?"

"I've probably had enough to drink, thank you."

Chad glanced at the bottle in her basket. "Well, that too was a good choice. What did you think of the tranquillo?"

"Delicious, but I kept thinking it should sparkle."

"Well, then, why not have a glass of spumante now, so your taste buds can rest easy?" A deep laugh accompanied his invitation.

Amelia looked at the man. It was a long time since someone had flirted with her. Riccardo, of course. But someone who made her want to flirt back. And Lorenzo didn't count. He hadn't flirted. Just taken charge.

"What the hell? Sure, thank you. I even bring my own glass," she said, reaching for the one on the tray.

"No, no. Mustn't confuse the flavors. I'll put this behind reception. I happen to know where clean glasses are kept. Give me a minute." He balanced the cigar on the edge of the table. "I'll look for an ashtray while I'm there."

She sat down, nudged her basket by her chair, and wished she'd tossed a lipstick in it.

"Oh, for God's sake, settle down," she muttered to the night sky. "It's a drink."

"Here we are. Glass and a flower pot—that'll do." He poured the Prosecco, then raised his glass to her. "To chance encounters. Now, what brings you to Borgoluce, arguably one of my favorite places in the world?"

They chatted easily. He knew Venice, but Florence and Rome better.

"So, tell me," Amelia said, "Chad is a very American name but your accent is pure English."

His infectious laugh enveloped her, along with the scent of the cigar. "American mum, British diplomat dad, hence the different languages. We moved around a lot."

"Did you live here? In Italy, I mean."

"We did. I went to the American Overseas School in Rome. My mother always wanted me to go to university in the US but after a posting back to London in my teenage years, I decided that was where I wanted to stay. Perhaps that became a contributing factor to the end of their marriage."

"I'm sorry."

"Don't be. It was a long time ago. And anyway, we're done apologizing, remember? Now, what do think of the Prosecco?"

"Delicious."

"I'm sure you can do better than that! Close your eyes and describe it."

Amelia looked at the man sitting opposite. "Don't be so bossy. I'm sure if cigar smoke wasn't swirling around, I could smell the wine better."

"Touché. You're quite right. And I don't usually smoke. But these Toscanos are my downfall whenever I'm in Italy. Now I'm the one apologizing." He began to stub out the cigar.

"Don't do that. I don't mind. It's reminding me of my dad. I just don't like to be told what to do."

"Duly noted, but I'm not sure how I feel about reminding you of your father."

They laughed and sipped their wine. This time Amelia tried to focus on the tastes tingling her mouth. "Honeysuckle! Though I admit to not having tasted the flower itself." She noted Chad's even white smile. That was pure American. "But," she continued, "it's like honeysuckle honey, so I suppose that's what I mean."

"Very good. What else?" Chad grinned. "That sounded patronizing, so I do have to apologize for that."

"Well, hi!" Phil's slurred voice broke through their laughter. "Just got back. These Italians sure take their time over dinner. I only went out for a quick bite." He glanced at them both. "I didn't know you two knew each other." He plonked down in a chair between them.

"Good evening, Phil. Do, please, join us."

Amelia suppressed a smile; the irony lost on the man from Delaware.

"Don't mind if I do. What are we drinking?"

"We are drinking a Valdobbiadene Prosecco Superiore. If you would care for a glass, I believe there are some behind the reception desk."

As the man lumbered to his feet and disappeared inside, Chad asked, "Am I right in assuming that was who you were trying to avoid?"

"Could be," Amelia said.

"Here." Phil put the flute on the table and reached for the bottle, but Chad's hand stopped him.

"Allow me." Chad poured half a glass.

"A proper pour, man," Phil said.

"I think not. This is a wine to be savored, not swilled."

"Wine schnob, that's what you are, Hungerford."

"It is his business," said Amelia.

Phil ignored her. "Is that a Toscana?" He pointed to Chad's cigar.

"It is. Would you care for one?"

"Don't mind if I do. Thanks." He took the tapered cigar and studied it. "Don't know why they call it a Toshcano—that's Tushcany, you know," he looked at Amelia, who nodded. "It's pure Kentucky tobacco, with a Kentucky wrapper, even if they grow it here."

"It's the shape, size, and process," Chad said. "They soak the leaves which, during fermentation, are flame-cured by burning oak and beech woods for a couple of weeks." He topped up Amelia's glass, then his own, and upended the bottle in the ice bucket. "I am a mine of fairly useless information, sorry!"

"And by your argument, Phil," Amelia added, disgruntled at his manner, "you could moot that pizza shouldn't be called pizza anywhere but in Italy, though I suppose that's a bit of a stretch."

Amelia laughed as Chad said, "Everyone knows pizza comes from Chicago!"

She watched him tip back his chair to look at the stars as he finished his cigar. Their eyes caught and they smiled. A silent understanding that their easy conversation was over. She took a final sip and stood, smiling an apology for not finishing her glass. "Time for bed. Thank you, Chad, a lovely end to the day."

"I'm coming too," Phil staggered to his feet. The combination of wine and a cigar too much for him.

"No, no, I'm fine." Amelia said, alarmed she'd have to get away from him at her door.

"Sit down, man. Finish your cigar. If she becomes a damsel in distress, we'll hear from here."

Amelia shot Chad a grateful look. "Well then, gentlemen, buonanotte."

"A domani, Amelia," Chad said.

Sliding between crunchy sheets, Amelia did hope she would see him tomorrow. She turned the bedside light out. Dozing off, she jolted awake. "Shit! Messages." If she didn't check them, and respond, Bria would panic.

Chapter 26

Sweet dreams dissolved as Amelia woke to sun streaming in the open shutters. Swinging out of bed, she arched her back, catlike, and padded to the window. San Salvatore Castle beckoned in the morning haze and she wondered how long it would take to walk.

After a quick shower, she tugged on jeans, a blue camisole, and white blouse that she left unbuttoned and untucked. Her hair scrunched up in a topknot, she again reminded herself she needed a haircut. Since her decision that she had reached the age where long hair was no longer appropriate, and terrified of being deemed mutton dressed as lamb, she remembered why she'd never had it short before. The constant need for a trim. "Sod it! Life's too short to sit in a salon," she told her reflection. "And," she continued, "if I'm going to be a mad old woman who talks to herself, I might as well go all out. Become a real Miss Haversham. At least I don't wear my wedding dress." She laughed. Carefree.

Bracing herself for a morning dose of Phil, she went downstairs. Preferably after a coffee, her most pressing need would be to avoid the man from Delaware. She doubted Chad would be around but a finger of disappointment still crept in as she saw empty tables.

A large bowl of mixed berries, and another of yogurt nestled in a tank of ice next to cereals. A platter of cornetti and hearty breads surrounded by a choice of different kinds of jams proved equally tempting. Freshly squeezed orange juice and a pot of coffee ended the offering that lined the table at the entrance to the patio.

"Buongiorno, Signora Amelia." Rosa's voice came from the door behind the reception.

"You sleep well? You would like cappuccino?"

"Buongiorno, Rosa. I did, and I would. Thank you. But there is coffee here."

"No, no, I make you cappuccino. The machine, it is behind here."

"Okay, thanks." Amelia stood on the threshold with her yogurt and berries, breathing in the air scented with pink and peach peonies in tubs that lined the terrace. No cigar smoke this morning.

"Good morning, good morning," Phil called from the table where she had hidden the previous evening. "I've saved a spot for you."

"Oh, good morning, Phil." Amelia moved with determination to another table and, before sitting, said, "I really do prefer a quiet breakfast, if you don't mind."

"Oh, sure, sure," he replied.

A flicker of guilt dusted over Amelia but, as Rosa produced the frothy coffee then with a flourish said, "E qui una nota," she was relieved she'd held her ground.

"Grazie, Rosa." Amelia continued to eat her breakfast, ignoring the note in unfamiliar handwriting. Well, of course it would be unfamiliar.

"Prego."

Amelia could sense Rosa's curiosity and, avoiding eye contact, blew on her coffee.

"Signor Chad, he give it to me."

Amelia, grateful Rosa spoke in Italian, thanked her again. She had no desire for Phil to know her business.

"You know Signor Chad?" The receptionist tried to draw her.

"We met last night." Amelia replied in Italian, ignoring the note.

"Aah!"

Amelia changed the direction of the conversation. "So, today, I'm going to walk to San Salvatore. Can I get there on the trails?"

"Certo. I will give a map. You do not want to see the cowsheds?"

"I do, but the light is beautiful on the ruins. It might not be tomorrow."

"Va bene." Rosa smiled and moved away, glancing at both the note and across at Phil.

In her haste to open the envelope, Amelia sliced her finger. Why did paper cuts smart so much? She sucked the spot of blood, irritated it had daubed the note.

Good morning, Amelia.
I have a day of meetings but wondered if you would care to join
me for dinner at the Osteria Borgoluce this evening. Say 8 p.m.? I'll
book a table.
If you could leave a message, 0044 782 065137, either way.
Enjoy your day,
Chad

She parsed the note—"either way"—smooth. He'd got her phone number. Amelia gave up the struggle to grin. A lovely morning just became even better. Her cappuccino almost finished, Amelia topped it up with coffee from the pot. Something that would certainly provoke a frown from Bria, who believed in the purity of each cup of Joe.

Amelia was brought back to Villa Borgoluce by Phil standing at the table. She'd missed his first words.

"I'm sorry, Phil, I was miles away."

"I can see that. I asked if you wanna come to the buffalo shed with me. I can't remember what it's called."

"Mandre," Amelia said. "Thank you, Phil, but no. I have other plans today."

"Okay. I just thought us foreigners should stick together."

A flicker of chagrin flared again. Would it really be so bad to tour with him? The answer came promptly. Yes. Amelia smiled her apology and walked into the farmhouse with him, then bid him a happy day.

"See you later, perhaps?" His voice followed her up the stairs.

"Not a chance, chum," she muttered, then felt mean.

✝

A surge of delight carried Amelia through a copse of walnut trees at the edge of the property. She crushed a yellowing leaf, surprised as a tangy citrus aroma rose from her fingers. She snapped close ups of the heavily-ridged, gray-brown bark and a cheeky squirrel—sadly gray, not red—darting along the low branches, hoarding as many nuts as possible before the farmer harvested them. Which, judging by the green split hulls, would be soon. She'd like to see the mechanical shaker go along doing its thing, the sound of walnuts rattling to the ground. No wonder the squirrels had a mission. "I pity the poor sods who have to gather them," Amelia said as she bent to pick up a split shell.

The grove gave way to more vines, which led right up to the castle battlements perched on the mesa. The bell tower stood high above the ruined walls that glowed umber in the startling light. Manicured lawns led to the restored building, where events now took place. Owned by the Collato dynasty, Amelia felt heartened by another vineyard determined to focus on sustainability.

After wandering the grounds, she made her way to the store, paid her fee, and tasted three wines, then dithered over whether to purchase olive oil, grappa, or both. Both won. A thank you for Fenella.

Tired from her walk, Amelia pushed through a beaded curtain into a narrow grocery store and bought a Tuscan loaf and some cheese for lunch. A quiet afternoon by the pool, a rest, then dinner with Chad and her day would be complete.

Climbing into the same dinged taxi—she wondered if the town only had one—with the same surly, cigarette-smoking driver who grudgingly took her back to Borgoluce. Amelia had to stop herself from explaining that she wasn't a tourist. She lived in Italy. Didn't that count for something?

She tried to ignore the insistent vibration of her phone as she ate lunch, washed down by the last of the Prosecco tranquillo, but glanced at it anyway and saw Lucy had called five times. "Oh, God, something's happened." It rang off. She called back and it went to voice mail. She waited, then called again.

"Lucy, it's me, what's happened? You've called five times? And now it's late in Sydney."

"Well, you never picked up, Mum, so I just kept calling on the hour. And nothing's happened. I just need to speak to you."

"Thank God. Righto, you have my undivided attention. What's up?"

"We're getting married."

"I know you're getting married, darling girl." Amelia frowned. "Oh, you mean now?"

"No, not now, Mum. Really? But soon. I mean, why wait? We've known each other years. We know it's right."

"So what's the problem?" Amelia paused. "Are you having a baby?"

"No! We just want to get married. But would it matter if we were?"

"Don't be silly, Lucy. So what's the problem? You know I hate guessing."

"Two things. Moira. And Italy."

"Together, or separately?" Amelia's head began to spin.

"Not sure, really. It seems awful to be so happy when she's had such a shit time but we just don't want to wait."

"I get that and, darling, she will too. You speak to her more than I, so you know she's excited about moving here. A wedding might be just the thing for her to focus on. She's going to stay with me a while, until she's sorted."

"Yeah, I know. Which brings me to the second thing."

"Okay, tell me?"

"Italy. We want to get married in Italy. What do you think?"

"Wow, I didn't see that coming. What about all your friends? It's expensive to get here, accommodation, everything." Amelia's voice trailed off. It seemed Italy really was no longer just her domain.

"That's the thing, Mum. We don't want a big brouhaha. And not just because of Natalie. We want something intimate and romantic. And keeping it simple in Sydney would not be easy."

"What does Mike's dad say?"

"We haven't told him. I wanted to run it by you first. But he'll be cool. He's a lovely man."

"So, when are you thinking?" Amelia's head spun.

"Before the end of the year."

"Bloody hell, darling, that's not much time."

"But doable, yeah?" For the first time, Lucy sounded tentative.

"Everything's doable. How convenient your mother happens to live here."

"It is, rather."

Amelia heard Mike's deep rumble, then his voice. "G'day, Amelia. You okay? What do you think?"

Before she could respond, Lucy came back on the line. "So?"

"Righto, a couple of basic questions. Beach, urban, or country? How many guests?"

"Don't need beach. We see one every day. And don't take this the wrong way, Mum, but not Venice. Is that okay?"

"Darling, of course it's okay. It's not my wedding. And actually, I think you're right." Amelia paused and looked across the valley to San Salvatore and smiled. "Lucy, darling, I think I'm looking at your venue."

"What?"

"How does a castle sound?"

"Bloody marvelous! Mike," Lucy called her fiancé back, "what about a castle?"

Amelia could hear his laughter through the ether and a booming yes.

"Well, that was easy! Go online and have a look at San Salvatore. I spent the morning there, and it's lovely. And I'll be here another few days so I can do some preliminary work, if it's what you decide."

"Mike just pulled it up. Mum, this is fantastic."

"I imagine the photos have all been taken in summer, but even in winter it could be magical. Different." Amelia laughed. "Okay, I'll go back tomorrow and talk to them. And I can always stay an extra day or two, or come back up. It's easy to get here."

"Can people stay there?"

"Not sure. But where I'm staying would work. Borgoluce has two farmhouses on the property. And off season, I'm sure we can find places. How many bodies are you thinking?"

"No more than thirty."

"Email me the configurations."

"What do you mean?"

"Couples, singles, kids, family or friends who might like to stay together—that sort of thing."

"Oh, okay."

"Lucy, my darling, this is so exciting." Amelia could feel her daughter's happiness. "Will you let Moira know? She mustn't feel we're keeping her out of anything. Okay?"

"I know. Mum, do you think she'd be my bridesmaid?"

"Ask her, darling. But be prepared for a no."

"That's what Mike said."

"He's a keeper. I'm so happy for you, Lucy."

"Thanks, Mum." Lucy paused. "Oh, there is one other thing."

"What?"

"Do you remember I submitted a design for the uniform competition, for the Qantas Centenary? Well, I'm short listed!"

"Bravissima, darling. My day couldn't get any better."

Chapter 27

The reflection in the full-length mirror showed a trim woman in gray woolen slacks—her standby—a gray silk blouse, and black pumps. Elegant, understated. "Dull!" The word burst from her lips as she frowned at her image. Couldn't do much about the clothes, but blue ballet flats would be an improvement, and her teatock-blue pashmina. That would have to do. "Settle down, Amelia," she said. But she couldn't. The day with Lorenzo in Florence hadn't been planned, and although they'd eaten together, it couldn't be termed a date. Tonight was a date. She clipped on a gold choker Leo had given her on a trip to India, then took it off. Wouldn't it be a bit odd wearing jewelry from her husband on a date with another man? "Oh, for God's sake!" She put it back on. And her mother's engagement ring, a sapphire surrounded by diamonds. The ring she had been going to give Moira, to one day pass along to Natalie. Tears swelled.

"Not now, not now. Don't need puffy eyes." Amelia focused on San Salvatore aglow with lights in the fading day. Magical had been the right word. It would be the perfect place for the wedding. She calmed down, glad she hadn't yet applied makeup.

"You're too early, you foolish woman." She sat in the armchair by the window. She stood. She sat again, and picked up Chatwin, but gave up when she realized she'd read the same paragraph three times and still couldn't recall the words. She looked at the upended Prosecco bottle in the bin. "Should've saved some for Dutch courage." She could probably get a glass from Rosa downstairs but couldn't face the risk of Phil. She poured a glass of Pellegrino instead. "Much more sensible," she said to the rising bubbles, but not as tasty. "I wonder if 'perlage' refers to all bubbly drinks?"

She checked her watch, again. Rosa had arranged for one of the estate cars to take her to the Osteria Borgoluce. If she timed it right, she could sail downstairs, out the doors and into the car before Phil had a chance to say anything. If indeed he happened to be in his usual armchair spot. She stuffed her phone into a small evening purse, then removed it. She'd have been livid if the girls went out without any means of contacting someone in case of an emergency. "How did we manage before cell phones?"

Her steps faltered on the bottom stair. Still time to bail.

"Signora Amelia, bellissima!" Rosa's kind eyes glowed. "Come, the car is here. Signor Adams is not." She winked. "He rests after a long day at the mandre and much sun and wine. And signora, remember, you do not pay the driver. It is a service."

The car, certainly a better option than the dented taxi, did not take long to get from the Borgoluce estate to the Osteria Borgoluce, but time enough to set the fairies fluttering in Amelia's stomach. "It's just dinner!"

"Prego?" The driver, hair flopping over his questioning eyes, looked in the rear mirror at her.

"Nulla, scusa," Amelia realized she'd spoken aloud. Mad Old Biddy syndrome. She'd earn a gold star in MOB. soon.

"Eccoci qui, we are here," the driver grinned, showing a mouthful of braces.

Before Amelia could open the door, Chad stood ready to hand her out of the car.

"Buonasera, Amelia, you look lovely," he said, leaning in to kiss her cheek.

She felt a blush creep up her neck. Get a grip. Everyone in Italy kisses everyone, all the time. He's not Italian. He might as well be. Amelia felt Chad's quizzical eyes and smiled. "Thank you."

"Come on, let's see where they've put us." He ushered her into the restaurant, his hand a gentle presence on the small of her back, then spoke in rapid Italian to the maître d', way too fast for Amelia to follow.

She looked around at the patrons, a mix of Italians and tourists by the look of the dress. She touched her choker, glad she had dressed up rather than down. The simple decor of black metal tables and chairs, yellow and orange napkins providing a splash of color, glowed under lights that garlanded huge earthenware pots of lemon shrubs. Who had to drag them indoors if a winter frost threatened? Each table had votive candles dotted around low pots of honey-scented alyssum. Magical. She smiled. That word was in danger of being overused.

The maître d', talking all the while, poured them a glass of Prosecco from the bottle chilling in an ice bucket by the table.

As they settled, Chad said, "I'm sorry, Amelia. I haven't eaten here yet on this visit, and Enzo can be voluble. We go back a long way and had some catching up."

"That's okay. Find me an Italian who can't be!"

His chuckle was low. "Do you know, I sometimes feel more Italian than either English or American. That's the trouble with a nomadic upbringing. One tends to feel at home in many places."

"Why is that a problem? I think it's a huge advantage. All the languages learned, cultures discovered. What a privilege!"

"Yes, you're right, of course. But sometimes that realization comes with hindsight."

"Did you struggle? As a kid?"

"No, I didn't, but my sister did."

"I'm sorry. That's hard on all the family."

"She's fine now. After a bumpy time at uni and through her twenties, she's found her place. With a whisky-making Highlander, up in the wilds of Scotland. Hardly ever leaves."

"So you're both into booze!"

"So it would seem. And my son follows. Sort of. He's in the Napa Valley studying viniculture."

"Why is it called both viticulture and viniculture?"

"I could tell you but not sure I want to risk sounding schoolmasterly."

Amelia laughed at his self-deprecation. "For the record, in no way do you resemble any schoolmaster I ever had. Now, go on, tell me!"

"I warned you. Okay, 'viti' refers to the science and production of grapes. 'Vini' does the same but for grapes specifically grown and used for wine."

"Well, now I know, but probably won't remember." She picked up the menu, then closed it. "Would you mind ordering for me, Chad? I'm feeling utterly unable to make a decision. And, just so you don't think I'm a feeble female, I can count on one hand the number of times I've done that. Ask someone to order for me."

"That I don't doubt. Sure. Happy to. Anything you don't like?"

"I eat anything, as long as it's not the innards!"

"You know that's cucina provera? Eating every inch of an

animal."

"If you don't tell me what I'm eating, I'll probably be okay."

"I don't think we'll risk it though," he said, opening the menu.

With his eyes down, Amelia had a chance to study him. Graying hair a little too long—more Italian than American, or English. Unless you counted Hugh Grant in *Four Weddings and a Funeral*! Not much taller than her. Lithe, like a runner but not wiry. Square nails on long fingers. Five o'clock shadow that she found oddly attractive. Wide mouth, slightly hooked nose. Beautiful eyes.

"Is the inventory over?" he asked.

"Hey, I'm a photographer." She excused herself. "I can't help it."

"Tell me about you. We didn't get a chance last night to get past the fact neither of us are married."

"Short story. Widowed, two daughters—one in Sydney, one in New York. Lived in a few places, though not as many as you, moved to Italy when my husband died."

"Why Italy?"

"Why not?"

"No, no cop-out answers allowed."

Amelia remained silent, looking at the flute in her hand, bubbles dancing to the top of the glass, each fizz sending a tiny shaft of light back down to bump into the next one rising.

Chad waited. "I suppose," she started, "I suppose because Leo and I had never been here."

"So you wouldn't have memories? I can understand that."

"No. Not that. I needed to go somewhere to make my own life, out from under his."

"Aah. And are you?"

"Yes, I think I am." She smiled. "Now you."

"Two marriages. One divorce, one pending. Three kids—two daughters, and a son—all from my first marriage. I'm fortunate my wife and I remained on cordial terms, so the children don't seem to have too many hangups. I can't say the same for my second wife. What's the expression?"

"Marry in haste, repent at leisure!"

"That's the one. Okay, enough of that. Let's move on."

"You started it," Amelia reminded him with a smile. The waiter, back with a plate of antipasto, moved the flowers aside and placed it between them. Red peppers jostled salami and prosciutto, black olives nudged bocconcini—miniature balls of fresh mozzarella, that Amelia was willing to bet came from Borgoluce.

"I did. Now I'm stopping it. Come on, lunch seemed a long time ago. Buon appetito!"

Food, always a delight for Amelia, became the focus as she tucked first into the antipasto, then the filet of beef in a Gorgonzola sauce sprinkled with walnuts and served on a bed of spinach. She worried she'd spend the rest of the evening with a sprig of green in her teeth. If she did, hopefully, Chad would be kind enough to tell her.

"Would you like to taste my wild boar—a more typical Tuscan dish but I'm sure they roam these hills too?"

"You don't mind? Leo hated me trying his food."

"If I minded, I wouldn't have asked," Chad said, cutting a small piece of boar, adding a slither of apple and polenta. "It's called cinghiale all mele." He reached across the alyssum and held the fork for Amelia, an intimate gesture.

She couldn't meet his eyes as she took the mouthful, then chewed.

"Oh, yum," she grinned. "Sweet and spicy, and not tough at all."

"That's because it marinates in wine, vinegar, and spices for three days, then cooks on a low, slow heat. The apple is added about half an hour before the end."

"Do you cook?"

"Not very well. More bachelor-style, but I quite enjoy it. Do you?"

"I do. I find it relaxing—most of the time."

"Do you cook when it's just you?"

"Yes. I didn't at first. You know, straight after Leo died. I lived on salads. I ate so much damn lettuce I'm surprised I didn't grow long floppy ears." Chad's chuckle rolled across the table like a caress. "But then I decided I had to be able to enjoy my own company, and that became easier with an interesting meal and a glass of wine. Then I banned a book at the table. And no telly. It's been a learning process. To live alone." She felt Chad's gaze. "Sorry, talking too much."

"Not at all. I should probably be taking notes. I invariably have a book, or some work, but no telly. Can I count that as my saving grace?"

"Just!" Amelia felt light-headed. "Does this Prosecco have a higher alcohol content?"

"No. Do you feel alright?"

"Yes, but a bit tipsy."

"You've only had one glass."

"I know. Strange." Amelia smiled.

"Would you like to leave?"

"Absolutely not. I'm fine. Happy."

Foregoing dessert, conversation easy between them, they finished the bottle. Amelia raised her glass. "Thank you, Chad.

This is the first date I've been on since Leo died. Actually, the first time I've gone out alone to dinner with a man in twelve years. James doesn't count."

"Oh, my God, Amelia. That's terrible. And who is James?"

"No, it wasn't terrible. Just my life."

"And James?"

"My young neighbor. Sorry I mentioned it."

"Don't be. I'm flattered, but I find it hard to believe."

"You haven't lived in Papua New Guinea, have you?" Amelia laughed.

"But you've been in Italy over a year. Italian men must be slipping!"

"Thank you. Now let's change the subject."

Their drive back to the farmhouse was quiet. Helping her from the car, Chad eased her toward him. His lips brushed hers. "It's been a lovely evening, thank you, Amelia." Breathing deeply, she leaned against him for a moment, enjoying the feel of his arms, then moved toward the front door. He caught her hand and swung it, saying, "Borgoluce produce a rather good grappa, would you like a glass? I happen to know where it's kept."

"Do you have the run of the place?" Her laugh sounded nervous to her ears.

"I do, rather. I stay here every year, have done for years. It's an honor system."

"Sure." Amelia swallowed her next words, as Phil's voice came from the terrace.

"Hi, you two. Good dinner?"

"Very, thank you," Amelia said as Chad disappeared into the room behind reception.

"A heavy lunch. I fell asleep, otherwise I could have joined you." He sounded wistful.

"Well, why don't you have a grappa with us?" Guilt made her kinder than she felt. "Chad is getting glasses. Go and get another."

"Coward," Amelia muttered as she pulled out a chair. Wondering, in the car, how the evening would end, how she wanted it to end, had made her stomach start fluttering again.

Chapter 28

After a restless night, sleep promised to come as dawn slid, unwanted, into the room. Amelia stomped to the window and slammed the shutters, thoroughly disgruntled. She burrowed into the pillow, refusing to accept the new day.

A soft rap on the door woke her a few hours later.

"Signora Amelia, buongiorno, tutto bene?"

"Morning, Rosa," she called, rubbing her eyes. "Yes, everything's fine, thank you."

"I leave breakfast at the door."

"You're a sweetheart, thank you."

Amelia pulled on a T-shirt, soft from many launders, brushed her teeth, then propped herself up in the bed with the tray. This time, she recognized the writing on the note. His charm did appeal.

Morning, Amelia,

Thank you for last night—delightful. Would you be free tonight? There's a charity event at San Salvatore. It might be helpful for wedding planning to see the space under lights.

You have my number!

Chad

She smiled. "Don't I just!" She spoke to the room, glad Leo wasn't on the bedside table. "Huh. Nothing to wear." Not even anything to cobble together. Receptions at castles had not come into her packing equation. Neither had dress shopping in Susegana been on her list of things to do, but she could combine it with looking at other hotels. She checked her phone. Good. An email from Lucy with a list of who needed what, room-wise—for the moment. That would help. A message from Fenella, happy to have Dafne for three more nights, and one from Bria brimming with excitement about the wedding. Nothing, though, from Moira. Amelia frowned. She didn't want to interfere. Surely Lucy would have mentioned if there'd been a problem.

The same youth from the previous evening dropped her in Susegana. Tempted to have another coffee before facing shops, Amelia pushed the thought away. Just get it done. A bell tinkled as she entered the first store but one quick glance saw her heading out the door. Too young. She couldn't wrap her head around buying jeans with strategically placed tears. Just wear the bloody things out at the knees naturally. She giggled, remembering her mother's wrath when she'd cut up a pair of jeans in order to make a jean skirt.

The next shop looked more promising. The owner, svelte and nearer her age, proved helpful. Half an hour later and after three try-ons Amelia found the one—a cascade of cool color that accentuated her full bust but hid the slight belly she seemed unable to shed. Her dress wrapped in tissue and in a thin suit carrier draped over her arm, she entered a shoe shop. Neutral court shoes with a reasonable heel would do the trick. And be practical. She tripped out ten minutes later. Shopping, Italian style, wasn't so bad but now she had two packages to manage. Better to go back to the farmhouse and start again. She could do some of the research online, narrow the list down and maybe go out again this afternoon or tomorrow morning. Perhaps she'd wander over to the cowshed instead. Check out the bio-digester that Rosa raved about, pat a buffalo or two in the shed, watch mozzarella production, and be back in time to prepare for the evening.

✝

Air-drying her hair in the late afternoon breeze, Amelia poured tea from the pot Rosa had brought up. Chamomile and mint mingled with the scent of lime from her shampoo.

She knew there would be no opportunity to ask specific questions about the venue but she wrote some down anyway. Clarify things in her mind. Then she stroked a deep coral onto her nails, cursing as she botched one.

Waving her fingers around, she muttered again when the phone rang. "Oh, honestly! Sì, pronto?"

"Well, you sound pissy, Mum."

"Oh, Moira, darling, sorry. I've just painted my nails—something I do about twice a year and the phone rings."

"You could've ignored it."

"You know I'm not very good at that if I can actually hear it ringing. So, what's up?"

"You know damn well what's up, Ma!" Her daughter's laughter trickled into the room. "Isn't it wonderful? Just the added impetus to get myself out of New York."

"Are you having second thoughts, darling?"

"Yup, and third and fourth. I cleared out Natalie's room, finally, a couple of days ago. Cynthia offered to help but I needed to do it on my own." Sobs replaced laughter.

"Oh, darling." Amelia's tears dropped onto her lap as the line went quiet and sadness filled the silence. She heard Moira blow her nose and sniff as she wiped away her own tears.

"Moira, can I make a suggestion? Without you getting mad at me?"

"I know what you're going to say, Mum. You don't think I haven't gone back and forth on this a million times? Poor Adam is sick to death of me."

"Now that I don't believe. Just let me say my bit, Moira, okay?" Amelia could almost feel her daughter's nod. "Don't burn your bridges, darling. Do you remember what you and Lucy said to me when Dad died? No big changes within a year."

"Well, you didn't take any notice."

"Darling, I'd had ten years to think about it! Not quite the same as what you're going through. It's only been six months since Natalie died," Amelia's voice caught in her throat, "and, Moira, in the last eighteen months your hormones have been in overdrive. Give yourself a chance to grieve, to think things through." Silence. "So," Amelia continued, "why not take a leave of absence? I bet if you talked to Dominic, he'd agree. You know he doesn't want to lose you. You're too good at what you do, and darling, there is no formula for grief. No right or wrong thing to do. No magic time when it will go away." Tears slid down Amelia's face. Did the death of a child ever go away? Doesn't it just get locked in some deep recess of the brain and heart? Always there. A dull pain that can change to a stab at a trigger, a recollection, a smell.

"Oh, God, Mum, I don't know."

Amelia's heart contracted as Moira's sobs echoed across the miles. "Oh, my darling girl, I wish I could hug you." She sniffed and pulled another tissue from the box. "Okay, let's be practical for a minute, Moira. You haven't agreed to a long lease on the house yet, right?"

"No."

"Righto, then don't. Short-term lease, or don't even bother renting it out. Why don't you drop everything, get on a plane and come to Italy for four months, six months, it doesn't matter? Don't worry about earning, I can help out."

"Thanks, Mum, but I can pay my own way."

"Whatever, darling, just don't worry. You can spend the time honing your Italian and we can arrange Lucy's wedding together. Then next year, which is only three months away, you can start scouting around to see if there is something you'd like to do, apart from vini or viticulture—whichever it is." Silence on the phone prompted Amelia to continue. "To see if Italy really is what you want, Moira. And you never know, things do have a way of popping up."

The silence continued but this time Amelia stayed quiet, waiting.

"I don't know, Mum," Moira said, her voice sad. "I can't seem to make decisions anymore."

"Which is why you shouldn't make this one so final, just yet."

"I guess."

"I'm not trying to dissuade you from changing careers, darling, but art and auctioneering is what you know. What you're extremely good at. Wine is fascinating, kind of romantic, but don't throw away everything you've worked so hard to achieve. Not yet, anyway, until you are quite certain. If in six months you feel the same way, then go for it."

"It's the brownstone, Mum. Everywhere I look, I see Natalie."

"I can only imagine, my darling girl. Get on a plane. Not tomorrow, but soon. I'll be home in a couple of days. Is Adam in?"

"I think so. Why?"

"Take a bottle of wine up, or get him down to the kitchen, and talk it over with him."

"I don't need to. He's been saying the same thing all along."

"Righto, then." Amelia took back every negative thought she'd had about the upstairs lodger. "Let me know your flight details. I'll be at the airport."

✝

"You are utterly lovely, Amelia!" Chad kissed her hand, then tucked it into the crook of his arm as they walked out to the car. "You're like a waterfall, all blues and greens. And smell like summer."

She glowed. Her nipples strained against the lace of her bra. There was something about silk that made a woman feel sensuous. It had been a long time. Somehow the compliment seemed more genuine from him than the protestations of desire that Riccardo rained down when he had attempted to woo her. And Lorenzo? Well, he was a conundrum for another day.

"You look pretty spiffy yourself, Chad." This evening there was no five o'clock shadow. His dark gray fine wool suit, blue silk tie and blue Paisley handkerchief peeking from the top pocket looked timelessly elegant. Almost as if they'd dressed in concert. A sign, maybe. Or just twee?

Amelia folded her legs into the low-slung car, catching a glimpse of her new shoes. Thoughts of practical, neutral ones had gone out the window when she'd spotted the lapis-colored sling backs, with a far too high silver heel.

She sighed.

"Everything alright?" A hint of sandalwood drifted in with him as he slid behind the wheel.

"Everything is just hunky-dory!"

His laugh rolled over her like a warm wave.

"So, a word of warning, Amelia, I will have to schmooze this evening."

"Well, if I disappear, it'll be because I've thrown myself off the battlements in despair!"

He laughed again, and his blue eyes danced as he swung the car out of the drive and headed to San Salvatore.

Chad tossed the keys to the valet then, taking Amelia's hand, they walked through the high stone gates and along a path lit with flickering lanterns hung from arched stakes.

"I almost expect a wood nymph to peep out from behind the shrubbery," Amelia said in delight. "I keep using the word, but it really is magical."

"Wait till you see inside. I don't know if the princess will make an appearance. She does sometimes at charity events like this."

"Princess?" Amelia laughed. "Now it really is a fairytale."

"Yes, she's a remarkable woman. Restored the castle, and more. I'll try and introduce you, if I can."

"Any more surprises?"

"Not at the moment." Chad winked, then took two glasses of Prosecco from the waiter's tray. "This is the winery's Conegliano. Superb."

"Even my palate is beginning to tell the difference. I think I prefer this to the one at Borgoluce, but don't tell Rosa." Amelia sipped again. "What a life you must have. Tasting wine all day long!"

"I would like to point out, my dear, that there is more to my job than that!"

She thrilled at the endearment. "How much more?" She liked the teasing familiarity of their laughter in a few short days.

Chad eased her toward a group of men and women near the center of the room. "Come on, I'll introduce you to a few people. Be prepared for a few raised eyebrows and ever-so-subtle grilling. The last woman I brought here was my first wife."

Her footsteps slowed. "Do you come to the event every year?"

"Without fail. We are one of the sponsors."

"We?"

"My company."

"Oh." The subdued chatter, mainly in Italian, stopped as Chad shook hands, and kissed cheeks, introducing Amelia as he went around the group. Glad she had splurged on both her dress and shoes, Amelia tried to keep up with the rapid-fire words, as she eyed the jewels dripping from ears, necks, arms, and fingers. She glanced down at her sapphire ring, glad she'd put it on again, and the earrings, a present from Leo after another indiscretion. He'd always had exquisite taste, and extravagant. She remembered gasping when she'd opened the case to see shimmering diamond studs, each with three gossamer thin strands of differing length gold that ended in a smaller diamond. She couldn't remember which painting he'd sold to pay for them.

"So, Amelia," Mia, the woman with jet hair, artfully eased into an ornate plait, drew her into the conversation, "Chad says you speak Italian. Brava! Many foreigners do not make the effort."

"I had to learn, in order to get my residency," Amelia replied. "But I would've taken classes anyway. And Chad is being too kind. I can't keep up in a group like this. Too fast and too much hubbub."

"Hubbub?"

"Noise," Amelia clarified.

"That is a good word. I shall use it on my children."

Hard not to warm to the friendly, inquisitive woman, although Amelia tried to deflect some questions back, asking about her children. Another woman, whose name she could not remember, joined the conversation, and another, until the men and women had subtly separated. She noticed Chad had been drawn into another conversation, then she lost sight of him. Time to explore. She excused herself and, going to the powder room, touched up her lipstick before wandering around. What fun to actually stay in the fortress. A grand staircase enticed her up to the next floor where she marveled at the grandeur of chandeliers and furnishings in the different reception rooms, then the books in the library. She could have spent the rest of the evening curled up in a chair with a book. Making her way downstairs again, she was called by Mia, who linked arms with her and drew her into the room which held the silent auction items. Most were too rich for Amelia's palate or purse, but she bid on a charming watercolor of San Salvatore—a wonderful wedding present for Lucy and Mike, if she won it. Moving back to the main ballroom, they were silenced by the quartet stopping and the stage being taken by Chad.

His brief speech, which Amelia could follow, was gracious as he thanked the roomful of well-heeled Italians and other Europeans for their generosity. He went on to exhort them to bid on items in the silent auction, reminding them that all monies would go to the causes outlined on the back of the invitation—literacy, anti-malarial research, and musical instruments for disadvantaged Italian children.

Amelia applauded along with everyone else in the room and, catching her eye, he raised his glass. A gesture noticed by many. She blushed at the public acknowledgment when a number of eyes swiveled her way.

"I'm sorry the princess didn't make an appearance," Chad said as the crowd thinned a few hours later, sated from the delicious hors d'oeuvres passed all evening along with trays of Prosecco. He took her hand. "I should perhaps have mentioned this before, tesoro, but the top floor of the castle has rooms, rather sumptuous rooms. It's part of the deal we have with the castle." He drew her close and spoke quietly, "Would you like to stay the night?"

Amelia pulled back. Surprised, but not surprised. Not sure how to react. She studied his face, not handsome but striking. Thoughts raced as he watched her. The attraction deep and mutual. But this is fast. Too fast. Oh, really, we're not teenagers. Who knows where it will go? Does it matter? What the hell!

"You do know I can read every thought crossing that brain of yours." He smiled.

She nodded and touched his face. "I've never been very good at poker!"

His laugh, intimate and throaty, sent her butterflies flitting again. "Do you mind if we stay a little longer, we don't have to be the last to leave but close to? The staff always send up a light supper up, so we won't go hungry." He kissed her hand. "You, Amelia, are the most delightful surprise I've had in a very long time. Are you okay on your own for a bit longer? Just a few more handshakes and we can leave." He moved away then turned, "Oh, and I'm delighted you won your bid. It's a lovely piece."

Amelia clapped her hands. "I didn't know I had!"

"No, they're not announced. But a list goes up moments after bidding ends and people are discreetly told they need to cough up before they may collect their item. I think we did rather well this year."

Half an hour later, hand in hand, they walked up the stairs

to the top floor. Chad explained the accommodation could be booked by the wedding party. If Amelia had any doubts about the venue, they disappeared the moment she stepped into the suite. Tasteful opulence swathed her as she went to the window to look out over the ramparts and surrounding countryside.

"This is heavenly," she said, accepting a glass of Prosecco from the man who made her stomach flutter. "Seems crazy, but apart from the glass you gave me when we arrived, I have been drinking Pellegrino. I didn't think getting tipsy would help my Italian. Though everyone spoke slowly and listened patiently, for which I'm most grateful."

"Well, here's a secret too," Chad said, touching her glass to his. "I haven't either. I never do at official functions." He broke off as his phone pinged. He pulled it out, glanced at the face, then put it back in his pocket.

"It's fine, answer it." Amelia said, taking a sip. She moved away but he shook his head and drew her back, putting their glasses on the marble coffee table.

"No, nothing important." He tasted her lips. "Delicious. Apricot with a hint of lemon."

"How strange," she smiled at him, "that's how you taste."

As their kiss deepened, the flutters subsided and a warmth spread through her body as his hands slid down her back easing her closer. "Oh, God, Chad, it's been a long time. I'm out of practice." She murmured into his neck.

"It doesn't feel that way, tesoro." They sank onto the sofa, their lips together until his trailed down her throat to the vee of her neckline. "Your breasts have been tantalizing me all evening," he said. "You do know you are a beautiful woman, don't you, Amelia?"

"It's strange, hearing it at my age." She laughed, then moaned as he stroked her nipples through the flimsy fabric.

"Age is nothing, my dear. It's how we carry it that matters." He kissed her again then pulled away as his phone dinged again. "Goddamnit!"

"Chad, please answer it. It must be important if it keeps ringing. It's okay."

He stood, bent to kiss her again, then moved into the bedroom and closed the door.

Amelia retrieved her drink and returned to the window. "Still time to bail," she muttered to the darkness, the lanterns now extinguished. But she knew she wouldn't. She finished her drink, took a slice of prosciutto wrapped around an asparagus spear, and poured another glass. She glanced at the bedroom door. One of his kids, perhaps. His voice, a faint mumble, did not sound happy. She shivered, a thrill running through her body. She wasn't going anywhere.

Unstrapping her shoes, she sat back down on the sofa, the bubbles in her glass trembling in the dim light as she turned it around and around, waiting. She finally put it on the table beside her.

"Amelia? Amelia?" Chad's quiet voice brought her out of a light doze.

Disappointed he hadn't kissed her awake, she swung her feet down to the floor and sat up. "Everything okay?" she asked his back, as he poured another glass, which he downed immediately. He brought the bottle to the table and poured another

"No. It is as far from okay as possible." His jacket off, his tie askew, he looked very different to the suave man who had collected her earlier.

"Oh, God, what's happened? Your kids?" She reached for his hand but he pulled away.

"No. Or maybe yes. I don't know."

"Chad, start from the beginning. I don't like guessing."

He rubbed his temples, his face drawn. "That was Gail. My wife."

"The first or second?" Her question sounded glib.

"Second." No glimmer of amusement touched his face. "She says she's pregnant."

Amelia sprang to her feet, her eyes welling. "Chad, you told me your divorce was pending."

"It is."

"But you still have conjugal rights. Is that it?" Anger bubbled.

"No. I haven't seen her for three months."

"Three months. Chad, I haven't slept with a man for years, and you say three months as if it's a lifetime." A thought popped in. "Or has it been three days? I'm just a convenient sop while you're in Italy."

"No. Absolutely not. Do you think, Amelia, I'd have invited you tonight if that's how I felt? I meant it when I said I hadn't brought another woman here since my wife."

"I can't keep up with your wives. Not even Gail?"

"No. She had no interest in what I did. And doesn't like Italy."

His words sunk in. Amelia smoothed her dress and pushed a stray strand of hair back into her chignon. She bent to strap on her shoes.

"God," Chad said, "what a mess!"

"That's one word for it. At least we didn't get to the bedroom." Amelia drained her glass. "I'd like you to take me back to the farmhouse, please. Then you should return here."

"Amelia, please. I understand. This is very awkward. But you did ask."

"What the fuck, Chad? Of course I asked. I thought something dreadful had happened."

"It has. Gail and I are incompatible. What I said is true. We are divorcing." He paused. "I don't know. She never wanted kids, and I certainly didn't want more. Mine are grown, why would I want to start again? I'm sixty. This is ridiculous."

"As a matter of interest, how old is Gail?" Amelia shook her head. Who bloody cares?

"Thirty-five."

Amelia snorted. "The perfect age to panic. To feel the clock ticking. Okay, let's go."

"Can I see you tomorrow? I'll cancel everything. We can talk. Really talk."

"Nope. There is nothing to talk about."

"Please, tesoro?"

"You know what, Chad? You do not have the right to call me that. So don't."

Chapter 29

Ducking into the kitchen behind reception, Amelia filled the kettle and, while she waited for it to boil, searched for the thermos Rosa had used before. She longed for, no, needed the soothing taste of chamomile. She picked up a bottle of Pellegrino as well, then hurried upstairs, grateful Phil from Delaware did not seem to be around.

She replaced her first inclination to rip off the dress she had worn with such anticipation, with a careful step out of the flowing silk. Next she unstrapped her sandals, then removed her jewelry. She scrubbed her face free of makeup then, stripping, turned the shower to as hot as she could bear and stood under the water and allowed her angry tears to flow down the drain. Amelia did not let her eyes meet her reflection as she slipped into her worn T-shirt, then made tea and, taking the mug, looked across the valley. Lights shone from the top floor of the castle.

"Damnit! I can't even look out the bloody window and not see him." She slammed the shutters and clambered onto the high bed. Pulling her knees up, she rested her head back, only raising it to sip the tea.

Disappointment and rage switched back and forth, both drowning her in tears. Is this what Leo used to do? Woo, bed, ditch. At least she hadn't bedded. But a close call. She reached across to turn out the bedside lamp, then lay down. "Oh Christ," she sat up and switched it back on. "This must have been how Moira felt. Betrayed. By a man who promised his marriage had ended. Did you ever do that, Leo?"

She'd write to Chad. Tell him what she thought. It would be easy enough to find his address now she knew the name of his company. It had been plastered all over the bid sheets.

"Oh, shit! I don't have my painting." Another flurry of tears ended. No, no letter. And he didn't have her number, only she his. "Idiot. Of course he's got it. On her messages." She'd go up to the castle in the morning. Reserve a date, put a deposit down, and get the hell out of Dodge. It would be easy enough to come back up to Susegana when the danger of bumping into Chad had passed. Rosa might allow her to swap the next couple of nights' reservation for a couple of weeks hence.

Exhausted, her eyes closed. Her last thought was the touch of his lips.

✝

"Ciao, Amelia," Bria's violet eyes sharpened as she took in her friend's pale face. "What has happened?"

Words burbled out in English in the sanctuary of her friend's office. "I feel such a fool. What an idiot! I only knew him a few days and I'm behaving as if the love of my life just dumped me! Pride can be painful."

"No, no, Amelia. Attraction makes us, eh, what is the word, sì, vulnerable. And it is you, my friend, who dumped him." She chuckled.

"I'm too old for this shit, Bria."

"Uffa, cara, we are never too old for love."

"Really?" Amelia looked at her bare fingers. "It is just too bloody exhausting. And, I haven't seen you on the arms of some handsome man."

"True. But who knows, eh?"

"Okay. I'm okay. Just needed to vent. Thank you, Bria. A misstep on my road to serenity, that's all."

"Sì, and we have much to do, eh? For the wedding. Easy to forget men."

"Yup." Amelia nodded, pushing anger aside. "And yes, there is stuff to do although the events woman at the castle is a dynamo. She's excited to be doing a wedding in winter." Amelia looked at the woman who had made her so welcome in Venice and smiled at a sudden idea. "Bria, why don't you come up to Susegana with Moira and me at the end of next week? She gets here on Monday. It would be fun. You're always doing things for me. My treat!"

"The hotel?"

"Can't Silvia manage for a couple of nights? She did a good job when we went to your vineyard. We can go whenever it suits you. Please say yes, Bria."

"Bene, I check with my niece. We stop at the vineyard after, eh? You miss the thinning so we go for harvest."

✝

Far jauntier than when she arrived at Bria's hotel, Amelia's steps took her to Dodo Caffè for lunch. Something about the Jewish Quarter always calmed her. Perhaps it was the space—the narrow-arched bridge leading to the wide piazza with the stone well in the middle. And the autumnal weather had lessened the irritation of the persistent zanzare, the mosquitoes that threatened to carry anyone off. Or perhaps it was the Negroni.

She scrolled through some of the photos she'd taken of San Salvatore, grateful she hadn't snapped any of Chad. A near miss. She shrugged. Not heartbroken, more frustrated. Heartbreak had been Leo. Each transgression a stab.

"Grazie," she thanked Matteo for her drink and swirled the Campari with the swizzle stick. Correction: frustrated, dented pride and exasperation. With herself as much as Chad. The first time she actually considered sex, only to be stymied by a wife. Even a pending ex-wife. Amelia sniggered. A good sign. Definitely not heartbroken. Perhaps time to take note of what she'd always told the girls. "Remember, you don't need a man to make you whole," she murmured the words, savoring them, along with her Negroni.

So much in which to be delighted, including her new floors. Perfect timing. Amelia pulled out her notebook and began a new list: call wedding planner at San S; confirm decor—clear plastic chairs with white sashes and greenery, orchids, if poss; menu tasting—passed apps—no soup; fish, chook, or beef? Who provides cake? She tapped her teeth. Think. Venice. What needs to be done here? "Shit, sofa bed!" Lucy and Mike get the spare room, Moira will have to move to the mezzanine. Or she could sleep with me. No. They'd all need some space. Amelia added *sofa bed* to her list. Dafne! Who'd look after Dafne? James and Arturo would be invited, and Fenella and Tigan. Riccardo. Bria, of course. What about Lorenzo? To the wedding, not for Dafne. She wondered whether Stefano could be trusted. He did seem to have calmed down a bit. The apprenticeship with Pietro had made a difference. That, and dating, Janina. Yes, she'd ask them. They could always stay in the apartment. As long as they cleaned it up and cleared out before Amelia and everyone's return from San Salvatore.

Amelia shivered. The temperature had dropped a few degrees the last couple of days. She wondered if it was too early for the bura, the violent winter wind that blew off the Adriatic. She added a dress to the list. Pity it'd be too cold for the waterfall dress and lapis shoes! She couldn't wait to see what Lucy had designed for her wedding dress. Christmas. And darling Moira. It would be difficult. A year since Natalie's birth. Nine months since her death. Amelia shook her head. What a year.

Chapter 30

"Ciao, Amelia," Lorenzo kissed her cheeks, Bria's, and lastly Moira. "Benvenuta, welcome, Moira. You too are beautiful, like your mother."

Laughter surrounded them as they walked into the cheerful kitchen where Agnese, the housekeeper, also bussed both Bria and Amelia's cheeks. Her dark brown eyes kind, she smiled at Moira, her bottom lip still for a moment, then returned to the pot of soup bubbling on the stovetop. On the counter, a platter of bruschetta waited to be carried into the sitting room.

"Come," Bria said, "I show you to your rooms to freshen, then we will have wine, eh?"

"This is wonderful, Bria," Moira said, her hand trailing the walls dimpled with age as they climbed the uneven stone stairs. "Thank you so much!"

"Non è niente, cara. It is nothing. Now we no longer have to speak of wedding business, we will speak Italian, eh? This is how your mother learn."

"Certo, but be ready for dreadful mistakes."

They paused by Amelia's door. "I do love this room, thanks, Bria."

Her hostess smiled. "And Moira, she is beside you."

"Perfect, we'll be down in a moment."

"No speed. It is just us for supper. Oh, and Franco." She trilled her fingers at them both and carried on along the hallway.

"Who's Franco?" Moira asked, rolling her case to the bottom of the four-poster bed. "This is lovely! Can I just stay in bed for the next couple of days? You can deliver food to my door. And wine."

"Not a chance, darling girl. As the saying goes, you ain't seen nothin' yet." She turned to her room. "Oh, yes, and Franco is the manager."

"I've a picture in my head. Wizened but attractive in an older man kind of way. A bit bent. With a perpetual cigarette." She giggled. "No, scratch that. If he's a vintner, he wouldn't smoke. But then again, if he's old, he might."

"Oh, my God, you've described him to a tee! Down to the cigarette. Right, see you in a few minutes. Do you want me to wait for you?"

"No. I'm going to have a quick shower," Moira said. "I'll find my way down. I'm sure I'll hear you all."

Amelia finger combed her hair before tugging it back into a topknot. She freshened her lipstick, glanced at her suitcase, and decided to unpack later. Hunger gnawed and Agnese's delicious-looking bruschetta called. She hoped Franco would be in the room before Moira appeared. She wanted to see the look on her face. Another thought crossed her mind. Did he know Chad's son? Both had worked on a vineyard in the Napa Valley. That would be a question she would never ask. She frowned. Why did the bloody man keep popping up? "Sod off, Chad!" she said under her breath, conscious Moira might be able to hear from next door.

A fire took the edge of chill off the large room and instinctively Amelia gravitated toward it, though stopped by Franco, also welcoming her with a kiss on each cheek.

"You are like a cat, like your Dafne, cara," Bria said with a laugh, "always you move to be warm."

"Ecco," Lorenzo handed her a glass of Soave, "cin cin!"

Conversation, always relaxed now Lorenzo seemed to have accepted her, or perhaps now that he was over his volatile marriage, flowed back and forth, interrupted only briefly when Moira arrived. Amelia struggled not to laugh at her daughter's raised eyebrows as Franco leaped to his feet.

The Scutari Vineyard manager could not have looked further from Moira's image. Similar in height to her daughter, he exuded outdoor vigor, his rugged, clean-shaven good looks enhanced by brown eyes flecked with gold. Amelia enjoyed Moira's surprise, as much as Franco's delight in her daughter.

"So," he said, his English flawless but still accented, "you have missed most of la vendemmia, the grape harvest, but we still have a few rows to pick. And we encourage the children to take part in the pigiatura—the stomping of the grapes!"

"Oh, what fun," Moira said with a laugh, "I've always wanted to do that."

Lorenzo handed her a glass of wine. "So you join in, eh?"

"What about mothers?" Amelia asked.

"Uffa, mothers too!" Lorenzo winked.

Bria passed around the bruschetta. "That is why supper tonight is simple. This and soup."

"Is Agnese feeding everyone?" Moira asked before biting into the baked bread smeared with tomato, basil, and olive oil.

"No, no. But it is a matter of pride that she produce her best. You remember at Easter, Amelia?" Bria asked. "The wives, they too contribute desserts and breads."

"It is my favorite time," Lorenzo chimed in. "A family event. Everyone helps pick the grapes, so everyone celebrates."

"Do you have kids?" Moira asked him.

"Sì. A boy and girl. Now a man and woman! They will join us in the afternoon."

Amelia listened as the conversation, in a mixture of Italian and English, ebbed and flowed around her, first in the sitting room then at the refectory table in the kitchen. She knew Lorenzo had been disappointed neither of his children had shown any interest in the vineyard, preferring city life much like their mother, but Bria assured her he had resigned himself to the fact. Perhaps the reason Franco had been accepted with such warmth.

"So, Amelia," Lorenzo said, his voice low, "if I come to Venice you will allow me to invite you to dinner, eh? I promise I will not wake you this time!" He laughed at her blush.

"Actually, I wanted to ask you to dinner." She rushed on before he could speak. "My friend James' parents are coming to Italy for his art show, and he is anxious about them meeting his boyfriend."

"Uffa, he is gay?" Lorenzo asked.

"Yes, is that a problem?"

"No, no. But I understand his nerve. It would be difficult. I am glad it is not something I must worry for." He patted her hand. "You are a good friend, Amelia. To everyone! Bria, she cares about you."

"And I her. And, Lorenzo, everyone has been so kind to me since I arrived in Italy."

"That is good to hear. So," he smiled, "I come to your apartment. Then you come to my dinner. It is a deal?"

"Okay. Sounds great. Now," Amelia stood, "if you'll excuse me, I'm heading to bed. It's been a long day and I want to be my stomping best for tomorrow."

Laughter followed her up the stairs and she realized the tension she'd been carrying around since the Chad fiasco had eased.

†

Under Franco's patient guidance, Amelia and Moira joined in the grape picking, learning to handle the curved knife without cutting themselves. Milk-like crates, once filled, had to be emptied into larger containers at the end of the row. As only a few rows remained to be picked, the grapes harvested ended up in the pigiatura vat, all the others having gone to the sheds.

Children danced around in excitement and Amelia rethought her desire to join in the treading. Moira had no such reservations and hauled off her boots and socks, washed her feet, and climbed in, much to the glee of the children.

"Come on, Mum," Moira called, "you've always said we should try something once!"

"I hate it when my kids quote me back at me," she replied.

"So," Lorenzo said, "come, show her." He helped her into the vat, grabbing her hand as she slipped.

"Ugh, it's squelchy! Like mud!"

"Smells a lot better though, Mum!"

Amelia, her hands now being held by a couple of the children, joined in, laughing as grape juice stained her legs and splashed her arms as Bria took photos.

"It is I who is now the photographer," she said.

"Okay. That's enough for me." Amelia clambered out, hosed her legs down and accepted a towel from Franco. She saw his eyes rarely strayed from Moira. "Right, if you'll excuse me, I'm going to clean up and change."

Returning half an hour later, now wearing a long boho-style dress with a pashmina at the ready, Amelia found everyone gathering around the tables set up on the terrace outside the kitchen. Like at Easter, there was an easy camaraderie and warmth between the family and the vineyard workers. Everyone drinking the fruits of their collective labor over the years.

Lorenzo's children arrived and fell into the fold as if they did not spend most of their life away from their father and in the city. Amelia liked them and enjoyed seeing their easy banter with everyone around the table.

"It is nice Marco and Isabella get on so well," she said to Bria. "And with Lorenzo."

Her friend nodded. "Always it has been so with Isabella. Not so much with Marco. My brother, he did not like for many years that his son did not want the family business. But it is better now. Marco is happy. Isabella is happy. Is that not what a parent wants?"

"It sure is," Amelia agreed with a hug. "Agnese," she turned to the housekeeper, finally sitting down, "tutto era delizioso, grazie! This is delicious, please, will you share your recipe for the baked pork?"

Agnese's ears turned even pinker than normal, and her bottom lip danced as she promised to try, explaining it was her grandmother's recipe and had never been written down.

As daylight slipped over the hills, now a muted purple and olive green, Franco lit lanterns around the terrace, then brought out his guitar. Amelia watched Moira watch Franco. "Perhaps Italy really is what she needs," she murmured.

"Prego?" Lorenzo asked.

"Sorry, talking to myself. Again," Amelia replied, holding her glass up for a refill. "To you, Lorenzo and Bria, for including my family in yours."

Chapter 31

"Get off the table!" Amelia lunged for Dafne picking her way among the mismatched crystal glasses, candles as yet unlit, and three vases filled with lavender sprigs and maidenhair ferns. "Really?" She lifted the cat vertically. "You know you are not allowed here, or on the countertops." She straightened the napkins the cat had moved. The table looked sophisticated in an understated way. She loved the variety of shapes and styles of the glasses and plates. The only thing that matched was the silverware.

"You okay, Mum?" Moira's voice came from the guest room. "You're talking to yourself again."

"No, I am not, I'm telling Dafne off!" She stopped nuzzling the cat who slid to the floor where she stalked away. "Are you nearly ready, darling, I could do with a hand?"

"Mascara, then I'm done."

"Oh, Moira, you look lovely." She hugged her daughter, elegant in a deep mint shift and black stilettos. "What a pity Franco won't be here!"

"Ha, ha!" Moira shook out a clean pinnie and tied it on. "Right, what needs doing? I thought we were pretty well organized."

"We are, but you could put the green salad together, please? I've done the zucchini and tomato, just have to add avocado. I think I can pop the quiches in the oven now, don't you? They'll only take about fifteen minutes. So they're ready to have with cocktails. I hate it when they're served too hot. Burns the roof of your mouth before you know it!"

"Sounds good." Moira tipped the bag of washed and chopped lettuce into two bowls. "Mum, settle down. Why are you so nervous? You've done this a million times." She paused. "Oh, my God, is it because Lorenzo's coming?" A burst of laughter followed her question but before Amelia could respond, Moira added, "He's interested, you know?"

"No, it is bloody well not that. And don't be silly. He's a friend. Now. He wasn't. But you're right, I am nervous. Not for me, but for James. And Moira, I might have had dinner parties in the past, but not often since your father and I ran away to Patanga."

"We've never really talked about that, Mum."

"And we're not going to now, darling." Amelia frowned. "I'm more worried about Roger and Sally Arnold. James said they didn't say much but, more importantly, didn't go off the deep end when he told them about Arturo."

"Well, if they're as tony as he's told you, their inherent good manners will ensure they behave," Moira assured her mother. "And they must be proud of him. Not every artist gets a solo show in Venice."

"God, I hope so. Arturo is a delight. And James is so happy. It's just," Amelia pushed hair out of her face with the back of her hand, "that I'm the one who encouraged him to invite them to Venice. And to tell them he's gay."

"You really don't think they knew?"

"I don't know. Parents can be pretty obtuse sometimes."

"Only when you want to be, Mum. You've been awesome!"

"Don't make me cry, Moira, but thanks." Amelia checked the seating plan, then the oven clock. "Okay, last chance to change this. What do you think?"

"Lorenzo will be thrilled to be sitting at the head of the table!" Moira dug her mother in the ribs.

"Because it works in the best way. That's all. Will you have enough room to get out to help me clear? We could swap you and Bria. Yes, that's better. You next to James' dad. Bria next to Arturo. God, what a minefield."

"Relax, Mum, it's going to be great."

✝

The door clicked shut behind Bria and Lorenzo, who were to guide Roger and Sally back to the hotel, worried they would get lost in the maze of Cannaregio. Lorenzo also stayed there whenever he visited Venice if his apartment had tenants. Fenella and Tigran had left a little earlier as he had a job interview in Florence in the morning. Amelia kicked off her shoes and padded back to the kitchen where Moira and James filled the dishwasher and tidied up, while Arturo leaned against the counter chatting.

"Amelia, brava e grazie. A wonderful evening. No blood has been shed, and my young lover has not been disowned."

James flushed at Arturo's words but looked pleased. "Yeah, it's been a great night, Amelia. Thank you so much. You charmed my father down from his perch and, oh, I loved it when Lorenzo disagreed with him about a wine. Dad's so used to arguing and winning in court, he expects to around the dinner table as well."

"He's delightful, James," Amelia said, taking a tea towel from him. "And Sally's lovely. She and Fenella got on well. I heard them talking about a trip to Murano together, as Roger isn't interested."

"Mum, you go and sit down, we'll finish this. As you can see, Arturo is a diligent supervisor!" Moira flicked her apron at the older man.

"No, darling, we are all going to sit down. It's shoes off time— well, mine are already off. Arturo, do something useful and bring another bottle of wine, or would anyone prefer a brandy, or grappa?"

"You will permit me to smoke a cigar on the balcony?" Arturo asked Amelia. "It is a vice I rarely follow but I thought perhaps this evening I might need an excuse to leave the table." He smiled at James. "But I did not, eh?"

"Of course! I'll keep you company. Some fresh air will do me good too."

"Hardly fresh if there's cigar smoke drifting around!" James said, his tone sharp.

"Oh, hush." Amelia pulled a soft blanket from the back of the sofa. "Give the guy a break! He's been on his best behavior. Come on, Arturo, bring your glass. The young ones can moan about us in here."

Amelia watched the Italian unwrap his cigar, then carefully clip the end. She breathed in as he lit it. It smelled like a Toscano. The sort Chad had smoked. She made a face in the dark.

"You would care for one?" Arturo asked, looking up. "I have another. My fall back plan in case Roger also smoked."

"No, thanks, though I used to have the occasional cigar when younger. A misspent middle-age rather than youth."

"You know, Amelia, always you talk about others, help others. What of you?"

"What do you mean? I could never have managed settling here if it hadn't been for people like Bria. And so many others."

"Do you never wonder why people want to help you?" Arturo looked at her through a haze of smoke.

"Because people are kind."

"Only when kindness is returned, cara."

"Don't be silly, you've drunk too much."

"No, that is something I never do, Amelia. For many reasons. So, please, just let me say thank you, eh? For helping James. For being kind." He raised his glass and smiled. "To friendship and caring."

✝

"Morning, Mum," Moira stood at the entrance to Amelia's room holding a tray with a vase of lavender, coffee, and a cornetto.

"Oh, darling, what a lovely surprise. Thank you."

"I thought you needed a bit of coddling after last night and before the next onslaught. You do realize it's only a month until the wedding?"

"Thank you, and there I was feeling rested." Amelia patted the bed. "Good, you brought a cup for you."

"Mum?" Moira started, then looked away.

Amelia waited. How could two daughters be so different? Lucy, the blurter, Moira more reserved, less eager for advice, or help.

"Mum," Moira began again then chewed her bottom lip.

"Still here, darling, spit it out."

"Okay, fine. You know how this wedding keeps growing? People Lu didn't think would come are coming. I know it's adding to the expense."

"Moira, the expense is fine, and let me save you the agony of asking. Of course you can invite Franco!"

"Bloody hell. Lucy's right, you do have ESP."

"Nonsense. I'm just attuned to you and Lucy. And she will be thrilled. And nosey. So be prepared." She broke off a corner of her cornetto and offered it to Moira. "What made you decide?"

"I dunno. Looking around the table last night. Seeing people happy. Even James' parents relaxed enough to laugh, and I actually think they like Arturo."

"Be difficult not to. And it is obvious he adores their son. What could be better than that? The icing on the cake will be on Friday when James' exhibition opens and they see just how talented he is." Amelia nibbled the cornetto.

Moira stared into her coffee. "He might not want to come. Or if Lorenzo is away, maybe he can't leave the vineyard. He probably wouldn't be interested. I have so much baggage I need a bloody truck."

"That's nonsense, darling, and you won't know until you ask him. And Moira, Franco does know about Natalie. I was at Scutari when I heard, so no explanations necessary. Now, go ask him."

Amelia wriggled back down under the doona, Dafne snuggling in too. She looked across at Leo and grinned. "So what do you think about that, eh?" Even a flirtation would do Moira good. Particularly heading into Christmas. Amelia rolled over and closed her eyes for what seemed a moment.

"Mum, Mum, he said yes!"

Amelia sat back up, dislodging the cat. "Of course he said yes. You're really surprised, darling? He can't take his eyes off you."

"And," Moira flopped down on the bed beside Amelia, "he asked if I'd like to go away for a weekend before the wedding."

"Does the man not have to work?" Amelia rolled from the pillow Moira threw. "But that's an excellent idea. Get the messy stuff out of the way."

"Mum, really!"

"Ooh, I have an even better idea. Why don't you and he go up to San Salvatore together next week? He can take my place."

"Don't you want to finalize things?"

"Nope, you do it. Now I'm going to have a long lie in, so go away, and take Dafne."

✝

"He's here." Moira rushed into the sitting room from the balcony. "Are you ready?"

"Honestly, darling, don't be so dramatic. It's only dinner," Amelia called from the bedroom. "We made a deal. He'd come and help deflect tension last night, and I'd have dinner with him tonight."

"Yeah, right! Oh, wow, Mum, you look great!"

"Great? I had aimed for stunning, gorgeous, ravishing. But I guess 'great' will have to do!" Amelia grinned. "Now go and open the door while I open the Prosecco."

"No, you open the door, and let him open the Prosecco. Cat and I have a date in my room."

"Don't be silly, Moira. He knows you're here. I'm too old for games. Open the damn door!" The murmur of voices slid into the kitchen as Lorenzo came in.

"Buonosera, Amelia, sei bellissima!" He kissed her cheeks then took the bottle from her and poured three glasses.

Moira grinned behind his back and mouthed, "Told you!"

Small talk about the previous evening accompanied their drinks, then Lorenzo helped Amelia into her coat and ushered her out.

"Don't forget your curfew, Mum," Moira called. They heard her laughter through the door, and Amelia tapped on the kitchen window and shook her finger.

"Moira, she is lighter, eh?" Lorenzo commented with a smile.

"Yeah, she's getting there. Up and down days."

"Of course. It will always be with her."

Amelia shivered. What a thing to have always in your heart.

"Come, no sadness tonight, eh?"

"You're right. So, where are we going?" she asked.

"It is near to here. We walk. My favorite place in Cannaregio, maybe all of Venice. I hope you, too, will like."

Crossing the little bridge to the canal behind hers, Amelia saw the outdoor tables. "Oh, lovely. I've seen it but never been here."

"So, I ask for a table inside. It is small and becomes crowded, but if you prefer, we can sit here." He nodded to an empty table with a mushroom heater glowing nearby. "If you are not too cold."

Amelia dithered, torn between the lively atmosphere outside but the warmth of inside. "Let's take the reserved table. I hate being cold."

"Bene, come." He pushed the door for her. "Buonosera, signorina," Lorenzo leaned in to kiss the owner, a fresh-faced woman with a dark pixie cut. "All is good? This is my friend, Amelia. Cara, this is Lina, the daughter of an old friend."

Lina smiled then ducked around the closely packed tables to bring an ice bucket as they settled.

"Are we having Scutari wine?" Amelia asked, seeing bottles with the familiar label lining a wall.

"Tonight, we have Vespaiolo. From Breganze. You know?"

Amelia shook her head.

"It too is in Veneto. Very good. Dry with the flavor of pear, citrus, and sometimes a note of honey."

"I love the way wine is described. There's always a note of, a hint of, a palate of." Amelia smiled and took the menu from Lina, who darted around like quicksilver. "So, Lorenzo, what's good?"

"Aah, I surprise you. You think I am only traditional. This place, you know what the name means—Anice Stellato?"

Amelia shook her head again and marveled at the difference in the man whom she had first thought dour and uncompromising. Women did as much damage as men sometimes.

"Star anise. Not so Italian, eh? The food is Venetian but with flavors of Asia. Ginger, hoisin, cilantro. Not so Italian," he repeated.

"I'm astounded you even know what they are," Amelia drank some Pellegrino. "But, Lorenzo, I know you're not a conformist. You would not have Franco working for you, with his less conventional, less tradition-bound ways. It's wonderful."

"I learn this from my son, Marco. When I hope he join me on the farm he tells me I am too old to understand he want a different life." Lorenzo played with his fork. "So, I try."

"And is it working? With the winery, I mean?"

"Sì, it is exciting. Franco is... how do you say it? He makes me love the grape again."

"Have you told him that?"

"No, but he knows."

"It's still nice to be told, Lorenzo."

"Like a woman must be told she is beautiful!"

"Only if it's meant."

"So, Amelia, you are beautiful."

The evening and dinner, a delicious fusion of Italian cuisine with Asian twists, sped by. Amelia hadn't been sure what to expect. Lorenzo proved an amusing companion, and he had chosen well. The osteria had a friendly and lively vibe without being overtly romantic, which conversely made it seem more so.

Tucked in close to Lorenzo's burly warmth, they walked home shrouded by the caligo, the fog, that clothed the canals in an ethereal haze. Amelia invited Lorenzo upstairs for grappa and coffee, but he declined. "Thank you, cara, for a lovely evening." He leaned down to kiss her cheeks.

She smiled and stepped over the high threshold and took the stairs slowly to her apartment, vaguely dissatisfied.

Chapter 32

"There they are!" Moira grabbed Amelia's arm. "Well, some of them."

"I can see Mike." Amelia caught a glimpse of her future son-in-law's tall frame and red head through people milling around the arrivals gate at Marco Polo Airport. "Where's Lucy?"

"Talking probably!" The doors shushed almost close again only to reopen.

"Okay, there's his dad. And I guess the people with him at the carousel are guests. Do you recognize any?" Amelia strained to see her other daughter. "Where the hell is Lucy?"

"Relax, Mum. I don't think Mike would be so calm if he'd lost his fiancée."

"I know, I know. I'm glad everyone is arriving at once. I can be excused for not remembering the names. Apart from the Richardsons, and I know them."

"Mum, for God's sake, chill. It's all fine."

"I know," Amelia repeated. "I just want it all to go smoothly."

"It will. The Paignton girls are on it! It's got to be fun for you too, you know."

Amelia hugged Moira. "Okay, here we go!" They had toyed with the idea of hiring a water bus then transferring to moto-scafi once they got to Venice but in the end decided three motor taxis under Riccardo's diligent guidance would be more efficient. Amelia blessed the day she'd fallen into his boat, an exhausted heap after the mammoth flights from Patanga. The doors opened again and there Lucy stood, a grin breaking out when she spotted her mother and sister. She ran forward to embrace them both at once.

"Can you believe it? We're here? And I'm getting married."

"Really, who to?" Moira said, hugging her sister tight, before turning to Mike. "Are you sure you're up for this?" she asked, grinning wider than Amelia remembered for months.

"Well," his voice a laconic drawl, "I figured you'd had her for thirty-six years, it was probably time someone took her off your hands!"

"No wonder we love you, Mike," Amelia said.

"And are eternally grateful," Moira added.

"You know I don't need this abuse from you, Mo, or you, Mum?" Lucy hugged them again, then turned as Mike's dad appeared behind his trolley. "Thanks, Chris," she said with a nod to the suitcases piled high. "Chris, this is my mum, Amelia, and Moira, my much older sister!"

Shaking hands, Chris Laymon, his smile crinkling his eyes, said, "G'day, good to meet you, Amelia, and you, Moira, although I have a feeling we met, years ago, when those two were at uni."

"Oh, here," Moira began to hand out welcome bags, 'Benvenuti in Italia' printed on one side, and the date of the wedding on the other. Inside she'd stuffed a map and small guide book, rain jackets bought from the kiosks that sprang up at the slightest sign of the acqua alta, a bottle of Scutari wine, and a box of chocolates from the traditional Venetian chocolate factory.

Amelia, swamped by people crowding around them, slipped to the exit doors, trying to tamp down the hiccup caught in her throat. Leo should be here. He might not have been the perfect husband but there had never been any doubt about his love for his daughters.

"Amelia?" Riccardo's worried voice brought her back to Venice. She turned, brushing the stray tear from her cheek. "Amelia, va tutto bene?"

"Yeah, everything's fine, thanks, I just need a moment."

"Sì, lo so, I know. Sometime from nowhere the pain comes again, eh."

Amelia nodded, grateful for his intuition. Coming from him, the words meant something. He really did understand. She smiled. "Sto bene, Riccardo, grazie. I'm fine."

She turned at Lucy's shriek as her daughter rushed to hug the boatman. "Riccardo, you're here?"

"Certo, of course, I would be somewhere different?" He laughed and kissed Lucy. "Come," he said, "we put the cases in Enrico's boat. His English is not so good. See, I have colored ribbon. Red for family, white for hotel, and green for appartamenti. The Italian flag, yes?" He and Mike busied themselves sorting luggage. "No worry, eh, he will deliver."

"Now who goes where?" Lucy asked.

"I take to the appartamenti." Riccardo reached for the toddler intent on escaping his fraught parents to clamber aboard. "And Emilio, he goes to the hotel then to Palazzo Ambrosio."

"Why don't we all get off at the hotel?" Amelia turned to the family. "That way, Emilio won't have to wait around while I introduce everyone to Bria. We can walk home from there."

"Sounds good," Lucy agreed. "I could do with a walk after all that sitting on the plane."

"And it's not even raining," Mike said, winking at his fiancée as he glanced skyward. "The gods are smiling!"

"Shh, don't say that yet," Amelia warned. She turned to Riccardo. "You're good to collect everyone from the apartments in time for dinner at Dodo's, yes? It's too far for them to walk, and they'd probably get lost." She smiled at his nod. "And you'll join us? And Maria?"

"Oh, and Stefano and Janina?" Lucy added.

"Sì, grazie."

"Who's Maria?" Lucy asked as they shuffled further into the cabin.

"A delightful woman who was Riccardo's wife's best friend. She works at the lace museum in Burano. They've started dating. It's wonderful."

✝

Three days later, Mike, Chris, and Amelia shepherded the full Australian contingent into three minivans they had hired from the company near the transportation hub next to the bridge to the mainland. She clutched the wheel tightly, wondering why she'd agreed to drive, and cursing Moira for not getting an international driver's license before she'd arrived.

The Scutaris, Fenella and Tigran, and James and Arturo would arrive under their own steam. Riccardo and Maria would come separately. Amelia had been thrilled about their budding romance. It had coincided with a decline in the needling he enjoyed giving Lorenzo, which had not made for stress-free encounters.

She sat, gathering her nerves, as the men loaded the luggage. She focused on the water in the canal where it idled like a lazy gray ribbon, reflecting the sky laden with glowering mercury-colored clouds. Not now. "Please no rain." She heard Lucy's screech as her wedding dress bag got smushed, then Moira's voice telling her to chill. It seemed to be her daughter's favorite word this week. Well, as long as she applied it to herself as well, Amelia didn't mind.

As the two families of guests, four Richardsons and three Williams, clambered into the van, she listened to their toddler fretting at the seatbelt being fastened. Why do I have the ankle-biter? She glared at Moira's grinning wave as she leaped into the seat next to Chris.

"Okay?" Amelia called. "Everyone ready?"

"You right, Amelia?" Tom Richardson nodded at her white knuckles as he settled in beside her.

"All good," she replied to the man she'd known longer than Leo. "Just don't talk to me unless you're telling me where to go!"

"Now that's an invitation I can't refuse," he said with a grin.

✝

Amelia pushed open the shutters as dawn drizzled in on a slate gray light, her shoulders slumped. Bloody rain. Two days of it. She spun at a quiet knock at the door.

"Signora Amelia," she heard Rosa's quiet voice, "I can enter?"

"Of course." Amelia shrugged on her dressing gown as the receptionist came in carrying a tray with a cappuccino and cornetto. You're a darling, Rosa, grazie mille."

"Prego." She put the tray down by the window. "The rain it goes by lunch."

"You promise?" Amelia asked.

"I promise. Guarda! Look," she pointed to the white orchid on top of a note.

"Oh, not again!" Amelia flushed. "You're always delivering notes to me."

Rosa grinned. "This time different, I think," she said, leaving the room with a chuckle.

Cara, we arrive last night. I take you for early lunch. Bria she goes with Moira to San Salvatore to check all is good. You must relax. 12:30.

Lorenzo

"I can't do that," Amelia spoke aloud. Too many people who might need something.

She tossed the note down and picked up the coffee. She'd call him in a minute. Writing on the back of the paper caught her eye. *Lucy she says that is good!* "Oh honestly, bloody men bossing me around. I'm sick of it!"

"Mum, can I come in?" Moira's voice came through the door. "Yes."

"You're talking to yourself again. What's up?" She saw the note. "Ahh, that."

"Yes, that. When did you cook that up?" Amelia glared at Moira. "I need to go to the castle."

"No, you don't. It's all under control. And you know it. Any driving around for anything last minute and either Bria or Franco can help. Go to lunch! Pack your bags and Lorenzo will drop you at the castle in plenty of time. Doesn't that sound cool? The castle." She laughed.

Amelia waved Lorenzo's note in her daughter's face. "You all have to stop making plans behind my back." She plopped down on the bed.

Moira tore a corner off the cornetto and popped it in her mouth, ignoring her mother's outburst. "After Bria and I've been up to San Salvatore, Lucy and I are having lunch together then we'll go up early this afternoon. Mike and Chris are staying here. Well, actually, they're going on a tour to the sheds? There's a cheese-making demonstration on."

"Really? Shouldn't he be doing something useful?" Amelia asked.

"Like what?"

"Oh, God, I don't know. He's getting married this evening."

"Exactly, Mum. What better way to spend his last day of freedom than with his father? I think the best man is joining them, too."

"I suppose so." Amelia finished her coffee. "I hope they don't drink too much at lunchtime."

"Come on, Mum, you've got to chill."

"Moira, I swear, if you say that one more time, I'll smoosh this cornetto in your face."

"Okay, on that friendly note, I shall leave you." Moira hugged her, grinned, and as the door clicked shut, said, "Have fun with Lorenzo!"

✝

The deep thrum of a sports car drew Amelia to the hotel entrance. She grinned to see the bright red Alfa Romeo pull up, then Lorenzo climb out.

"Ciao, cara. Always you are lovely." He bowed and kissed her hand.

"And always, well, nearly always, you are charming!"

"Uffa. You speak of our first meeting. I was not happy. I am sorry for that."

"I'm teasing, Lorenzo. It's fine. You've more than made up for it." She glanced up at the sky. "Rosa said it would stop raining at lunchtime."

"It would not dare to rain on this parade." He laughed, then looked questioning. "That is the correct wording, yes?"

"It is indeed. Now, come on, where are we going?"

"A small place a few miles from here. Where no one will be able to find you."

"Not too far, Lorenzo. I need to get back."

"All is okay, cara. I use the word Moira likes. Chill." He ducked away from Amelia's swat.

"I strongly suggest you don't. I threatened her with pain if she said it one more time."

The village, only a few miles away, had one shop and one small trattoria. Amelia had given up being surprised to see Scutari wine wherever she went, or that Lorenzo seemed to know people everywhere. The thought crossed her mind that, just maybe, he knew Chad. She flushed.

"Va bene, Amelia?" he asked, pulling a chair out for her.

"All fine. Thank you." She buried her face in her bag, and pulled out her phone. She smiled her apology. "I'm sorry. Just in case."

"We have just a glass of wine, eh? Otherwise, we sleep. It is not so good getting older sometimes."

"Thank you. Yes. And can we just have a plate of antipasto? Nothing too heavy." Amelia watched as Lorenzo ordered, then settled back in his chair and looked at her. "What?" she asked.

"I like to look at you."

Amelia blushed again. This time with pleasure not embarrassment.

"Amelia, cara, you know I like you, eh?"

She nodded. "I like you too, Lorenzo. Most of the time."

"Do not joke me. I am serious." His forefinger running the length of her hand felt deeply intimate.

"I'm sorry. I talk too much sometimes. When I'm nervous."

"I do not want you nervous, Amelia. Ever. You will allow me to make love to you, one day soon, eh?" His smile disappeared into his beard.

She pulled her hand away and reached for her wine. "Really, Lorenzo. Today you ask me that?"

"Why not? It is a good day. A day for love. What better?" He waited. "So?"

She hid behind the napkin as she dabbed her lips. A smiled tugged. "Perché no? Why not?" She laughed at his delight. "Now let's eat. We have a wedding to attend."

✝

"What do you think, Leo?" The mirror reflected a striking-looking woman, silver-blonde hair curling over the high collar, blue eyes dancing. Not sure how she'd feel being in the same room in which she'd nearly flung herself at the Englishman, Amelia felt only delight as she sipped chilled Prosecco. Perhaps her lunch with Lorenzo had something to do with it, too.

"You look stunning!" James watched her come down the marble stairs, which had been draped in gauze and ivy. "I knew that blue would look wonderful on you."

Amelia smoothed the velvet coat with a grin. After wavering around looking for a dress suitable for a daughter's wedding, she had realized the one she'd bought for the reception at San Salvatore with Chad was the perfect choice when paired with her flea market find from Florence. And it didn't matter her lapis shoes had sling backs. She wasn't going outside. "Thank you, you're a darling. Isn't this exciting?" She stopped at the door and smiled at Chris waiting to walk in with her. She patted James' hand then took Chris' arm and looked around the library where Lucy and Mike would exchange their vows.

Everyone was there. Apart from Leo. He would have loved this. But would he have allowed Lucy to be the center of attention all evening? She doubted it. She couldn't wait to see the dresses Lucy had designed, sewn, and kept secret from her. All Moira had said was, "You'll be blown away, Mum."

She blew Mike and Fred, his best man, a kiss then took her place next to Tom Richardson and his wife, smiling at their teenage children, both from his second marriage to the petite woman by his side. Amelia often felt gargantuan next to her. And sometimes old, but not tonight.

"You right, love?" Tom asked, squeezing her hand.

"As rain, Tom, as rain."

"Well, thank God that stopped."

She nodded, tears springing to her eyes as the cellist began to play Bach, and she saw Mike's pride and joy in equal measure flit across his face as his bride appeared. He had waited a long time for her daughter. Amelia turned and gasped. "She's beautiful, Leo," she whispered.

Lucy waited at the library door for the notes from the cello to draw her in.

The elegant simplicity of the soft cream coat with tight sleeves, the cream collar reaching high up her neck then folding down to a deep vee at her waist to flare out into a long train, under which peeped a dress in sheer Burano lace, suited Lucy to perfection. Tiny diamanté swirls shimmered in her hair, piled up in gentle curls to show off both her graceful neck and the collar. She wore Amelia's borrowed diamond earrings and carried a bouquet of cascading orchids, a midnight blue ribbon trailing through the greenery. Lucy, her smile brilliant, winked at her mother.

Behind her, Moira, taller by a head, wore a silk dress, the color of Sahel indigo, with a similar collar but which did not delve quite so deep. Falling to the floor in swaying folds, the sleeves mimicked the long train of Lucy's dress. Moira's dark hair was also piled high but with ringlets escaping in studied abandon.

Amelia felt James' glance and she looked down at her coat and smiled. It was as if her ensemble had been part of the plan. Maybe it had. She remembered she'd shown Moira the coat, but not the dress.

Words drifted over her as the scent of roses wafted around the book-lined room—the perfect place to exchange vows in front of the people who truly cared, including new friends from Italy. Amelia watched Lucy and Mike kiss then turn, hand in hand, to walk to the reception hall as the blended voices of Andrea Bocelli and Ed Sheeran came from hidden speakers and the words of "Perfect" filled the room. Tears again threatened to spill as the couple passed, and she felt Lorenzo, in the row behind, reach for her hand then release it as she and Chris met in the aisle to follow Moira, Fred and the bride and groom.

After canapés and Prosecco, they sat at a long table gleaming with crystal and silver, low bowls of pink and white roses allowing conversation to flow over and around the thirty-five guests. Guided by the chef at the castle, dinner was an Italian wedding feast of fried tortellini with Gorgonzola and walnuts nestled in a spinach and radicchio salad, bathed in a balsamic dressing; followed by an option of pan-seared striped bass with cherry tomatoes and white wine, or the classic chicken marsala, both accompanied by a zucchini, mushroom, and red pepper cacciatore.

Amelia, sitting between Lorenzo and Chris, knew it tasted wonderful from the appreciative murmurs but nerves still niggled. *Oh Leo, now I do want you here. You should be doing this.* She took her speech out of her silver evening purse then, at a sign from the maître d' and Moira, she stood.

"My darling Lucy, and you, dearest Just Mike," she waited for the laughter to subside, "I'm a bit nervous so if I fluff this, blame your father for not being here." The paper shook in her hand so, placing the speech on the table, she spoke from her heart. "This is what I think marriage is all about. It is made up of a million small kindnesses, and not the occasional grand gesture." Amelia paused as an image of Leo falling to his knees in Central Park, his arms full of pink roses, flashed in along with the realization that those grand gestures invariably followed a dalliance. She shook her head and continued, "And marriage, I believe, is also about creating an island, a safe space in which no one else may intrude, a space wherein each other's dreams, no matter how crazy, and fears, no matter how haunting, may be freely expressed. Words spoken on that island are sacrosanct—words that bind you together in the knowledge that the trust you share will never be broken. This is my wish for you."

Amelia picked up her glass and looked around the table. "I can't possibly say 'be upstanding' but on your feet everyone, here's to my beautiful daughter and her wonderful husband. And so, alla goccia, to the last drop. To you both, my darlings!"

As she sat down, the tears came.

Lucy reached across the table for her hand, Lorenzo reached under the table for the other.

"Thank you, Mum, for everything. Please stop crying, you'll make your mascara run. And mine!"

"Yes, get it together, Mum, not only do I have to follow that amazing speech but I have to do it with dry eyes, otherwise how can I deliver my witty take on marriage," Moira smiled, and rose to her feet, drawing on her years as an auctioneer.

Mike's speech followed, then his best man, and as he finished, the band set up in the larger reception hall began to play "Shape of You" by Ed Sheeran. Mike swept his bride onto the dance floor and, before the song finished, everyone had joined them with partners swapping time and again. As the younger guests joined in the chorus, Amelia felt Lorenzo's eyes on her, grinning. So the lyrics were not flowing over him unheard. Relief surged, but only for a moment as the singer moved from new to old and sang "At Last" made famous by Etta James. Would every song have a double entendre?

The night ended after much laughter, some tears, and a crazy moment when the Australian contingent staged an impromptu rendition of "I Come from the Land Downunder." Amelia had glanced at the waitstaff, who appeared to be enjoying it all.

Sling backs and evening coat long abandoned, Amelia trailed barefoot up to the bedrooms of the castle behind Moira and Franco. The bride and groom had retreated to theirs a short while earlier, and as Bria and Lorenzo had kissed her goodnight, his lips lingering a moment on her cheek, before they headed down to the farmhouse, a shaft of loneliness had caught Amelia's breath.

Dropping her shoes on the floor, she flung her coat over a chair and went to the ice bucket chilling a bottle of San Salvatore Prosecco. Apart from the toasts, Amelia, knowing she might dissolve into a puddle, had only drunk Pellegrino. But now, now she'd have a drink.

"What a night. You would have loved it, Leo." Amelia took a sip then held the glass to her forehead. "Well, not for many years. But way back when, you would've loved it. Lucy looked amazing—actually, you know what, Leo, the older she gets the more she looks like your mum, and she was a looker. Moira is more my side of the family." Amelia stretched out on the sofa, her feet up. Where was Dafne when she needed her? "So, Leo, perhaps this isn't the time to tell you, but too bad. I'm tired of you hovering on the fringes of my life. You're always bloody there. I think I'm moving on then up you pop. You've got to bugger off."

Chapter 33

Amelia shivered in the dank air and waved from her balcony as the Richardsons, the last of the wedding guests to leave Venice, clambered into Riccardo's motoscafo ready to take them to the airport. She had enjoyed spending time with them while Moira joined Franco at the Scutari Vineyard, and Mike and Lucy took off to Florence for a couple of days. One night on her own, then they'd all head out to the vineyard for Christmas.

Buildings pierced the low clouds and a gray dampness had settled over the city. A yellow-legged seagull loitered on the bridge at the end of the canal. This was not the Venice of the postcards but Amelia didn't mind, it made her feel she belonged. The good with the bad sort of thing. Carefree.

"I'm sorry, Dafne," she said to the cat tripping her up as she tried to get indoors, "life will calm down again soon. But," a tickle behind the ears produced a deep purr in the growing cat, "you are not exactly hard done by. James spoils you rotten and so does Fenella, by the way. This time you're going to Arturo's apartment where he and James can feed you treats by the open fire. Not a bad life for a Venetian queen!" She giggled, remembering Arturo's roar of laughter when she'd explained the term, then his pronouncement that he would henceforth call himself a Florentine queen.

"How lucky I am, eh?" She refilled Dafne's water bowl, then wandered into her bedroom. The bedside table still looked bare without Leo. He had been moved to the mezzanine to hover above her desk on the filing cabinet. She'd told him his new role would be to encourage her in her quest to get her coffee-table book of New Britain photographs published. "I'm a photographer now, Leo, and don't you forget it!"

✝

"Oh, come on, Mum," Lucy's voice came up from the palazzo entrance where Amelia's carrello stood, stuffed with food, among their suitcases. The rest of her words went unheard as Amelia delved one last time in the fridge for anything forgotten.

"Are you right now, Amelia?" Mike leaned against the kitchen wall, his eyes glittering with amusement. "Ignore my wife, she can be a little impatient."

"She would be the first to moan if a Christmas cake did not appear, complete with Santa on top! Or if pavlova had been left off the menu!"

"Yup!" Mike grinned. "Despite her advanced years, there are some things which are sacrosanct, her idea of Christmas being one of them."

"Well, it'll be a blend of Paignton and Italian this year, so she can settle down! Honestly, she's like a child." Amelia looked up at her son-in-law, filling the kitchen with his bulk. "Sorry. A bit mean talking about your wife like that."

"That's alright, she talks about you!" His laugh was contagious and loud enough to tempt Lucy back upstairs.

"What's going on? Are you ever coming down? I'm growing roots." She looked between her husband and mother. "Are you two talking about me?"

"Yup!" Amelia and Mike answered in unison.

"Ready now, darling." Amelia hugged her. "Come on, both of you! Moira will be wondering where we are."

"No, she won't. She's so tied up with Franco she doesn't know which way is up," Lucy said. "But, you know what, Mum? It's perfect, isn't it?"

"It is, but I'm afraid I keep waiting for it to drop. She's kind of glittery, and I don't think it's just new love. It's a brittle glitter, if you know what I mean."

"Yeah, I know. Mike said the same thing, didn't you, hon?"

He nodded. "But Franco knows all about Natalie. And her father. I mean, I knew he knew, but he told me, almost as a reassurance, that he understood where Moira was coming from. He's a good bloke, you know?"

"Yeah, he is. Okay, let's go get our girl. I think it'll be an up-and-down kind of Christmas." Amelia picked up her handbag, stroked Dafne and shooed them out. "James is coming by later to take her to Arturo's fancy-schmancy apartment off San Marco."

"Is Arturo really rich?" Lucy asked, picking up the Christmas cake.

"I rather think he is, darling. Now, come on, let's go."

"Now she's in a rush!" Lucy handed Mike an Esky full of food as Amelia dashed back into her bedroom. "Now what?"

"I'm coming, I'm coming." Amelia reappeared, tucking some-thing into her brown Fendi tote bag. An extravagant indul-gence that still embarrassed her, at times. "Right I'm ready."

"At last! My waiting hours are over," sang Lucy as she raced downstairs.

"You do know those aren't the right words, don't you?" Amelia called.

"But they work!" Her daughter's laughing reply spiraled up. "Etta James would have a fit!"

✝

"At last," Moira said, hugging her mother.

"Don't you start." Amelia breathed in Coco Mademoiselle, the scent Moira had worn for as long as she could remember. "I've had your sister singing that most of the afternoon." She searched Moira's face.

"I'm okay, Mum, really."

"That's great, my darling. Now where's that man of yours to help Just Mike carry this mountain of stuff?"

"Cara!" Lorenzo's rich tones called from the patio doors. He hurried to meet them, taking Mike's outstretched hand as he reached for Amelia. "You are here!" He kissed her cheeks, then laughed. "You flush!"

"It's been a busy day."

"Oh rubbish, Mum, you're blushing!" Lucy laughed.

"Uffa," Lorenzo waved Moira and Lucy away. "Leave your mother alone!"

"Thank you, but not helpful," Amelia said, as her host took the tote and urged her toward the warmth of the kitchen. "Is Bria here yet?"

"No, a problem at the hotel earlier. But she comes soon."

"Buonasera, Agnese," Amelia smiled at the housekeeper in her usual position at the kitchen table, this time up to her elbows in flour. "Is it alright if I put some things in the fridge and larder, please?" She looked around the now familiar hub of the farmhouse and relaxed. Lucy had been right. Tension slipped from her shoulders as the raspy voice of one of Lorenzo's favorite singers, Vasco Rossi, slipped under the closed door. She stood still and listened for a moment.

There would, of course, be some difficult moments, how could there not be? But at least Moira would not find a memory around every corner. A glimpse of Natalie's face, the smell of a freshly bathed baby, her first smile. She replayed her earlier conversation with Lucy.

"But, Ma," Lucy had reminded her, "we have to talk about her, about Natalie. She'll always be part of the family."

"I know, darling, but I can't bear to think of Moira's happiness last year, and this year it's gone."

"I think we should focus on the positives."

"There aren't any, Lucy. Not a single positive of a healthy baby dying."

"Mum! You know that's not what I mean. Come on, give me a break."

"I'm sorry, darling. Just so worried."

"You know she talks to Franco, a lot? About Natalie, I mean. I think it's because he's not been part of the pain."

Amelia sighed and watched Lucy join her sister outside. Aware of Agnese's concerned glance her way as she pummeled bread, her lip trembling, Amelia smiled. The housekeeper nodded toward the patio where they could hear the girls playing with the dogs. A slight smile played around her wrinkled mouth when Lorenzo came into the room, having helped Mike and Franco with the suitcases.

"So, Amelia. You like my Italian music now, eh?" he asked.

"I always liked it, but it is a bit, I don't know, easy listening-ish, isn't it? You know, Perry Como-ish?"

"And that is bad, cara? Another Italian, eh? His name is Pierino Ronald Como."

"Yes, but born in America."

"He speaks no English until he goes to school."

"Okay, okay! Damn, now I have both Arturo and you extolling the many virtues of Italians." Amelia laughed as Lorenzo stole a warm cookie from the rack, cooling before Agnese iced them.

"Non toccare!" the cook scolded. "You no touch!"

He laughed, hugged the flour-clad woman and said to Amelia, "Come, walk with me?" He held out her coat then opened the door. "The children, mine too, will be fine without us."

Amelia laughed, "Hardly children."

"No, but always our children, eh?"

She nodded. For a moment, carefree.

"Andiamo," she said, then looked at Lorenzo in surprise when he took her hand.

"Is okay?" he asked.

She looked at their joined hands and smiled. "Sì, Lorenzo, is okay."

Whistling Stella, whose bristling orange eyebrows always made Amelia laugh, he led her down to the winery where Lorenzo showed her barrels set aside for special occasions. Stella, her tail wagging, snuffled around kegs. Pointing out the different years, Lorenzo told her how Franco had nudged him into a more international frame of mind with regard to marketing. Deep in the cellars, in the dim lighting, Lorenzo reached for both Amelia's hands and drew her close until they were breathing the same cool air.

"Posso baciarti?" His lips hovered above hers.

Amelia shivered, then with a nod reached up and kissed him.

"Ahh, cara mia, for many months I want to do this. I like you much, Amelia."

"Anche tu mi piaci, Lorenzo. I too." They kissed again before she moved away, just a little. "But this is not the time. You understand, with Moira?"

"Lo so, cara, ma un po' di baci fa bene," he said, pulling her close again.

"Yes, a little kissing is good." She reached up, smiling against his mouth. "Very good!"

Strolling back to the house later, Amelia couldn't remember a time she'd felt so thrilled. So cherished. She grinned. All from a little kissing! They stamped their feet on the patio and Lorenzo pushed open the door. She didn't know if was the crackling fire sending sparks up the chimney that reddened her cheeks or the smiling faces as all eyes turned toward them. Bria, at the head of the farmhouse table, raised her glass of red wine in salute as everyone laughed.

"Well, now you really are flushed," Lucy said with a delighted laugh.

"You all would be too if you'd been outside in the cold instead of coddling yourselves by the fire." Amelia shrugged off her coat and handed it to Lorenzo. "Right, I'm going up to change for dinner. Agnese has prepared the pasta and clams, but she allowed me to do the desserts, even when I told her what I wanted to prepare."

"Why?"

"Because, technically, we are not meant to eat meat or dairy products on Christmas Eve," Amelia replied. "You, Lucy, can count yourself lucky you're getting your pavlova!"

"Not just me, Mum, Moira as well."

"In that case, Moira, can you whip the cream, please? And Lucy, stir your stumps, and hull the strawberries. Very expensive out-of-season strawberries, I might add."

"What happened to Mum doing it all at Christmas?" Moira messed Franco's hair as she stood.

"Those days are long gone, my darlings." She looked at Isabella, Lorenzo's daughter. "And you can help set the table." She laughed at Bria's surprise. "Hey, I'm in full-on Christmas mode. Everyone helps—children-wise! You, Bria, are on holiday, you deserve it!"

"What about the boys?" Lucy grinned at Mike, Franco, and Marco, Lorenzo's son. "Don't they get chores, too?"

Before she could respond, Lorenzo, with a beam, beckoned the men to help him with logs and wine.

"Then we can all enjoy the carol singers when they arrive. Lorenzo just told me about them."

✝

"You harlot, Amelia Paignton." Her reflection grinned back as she wiped off her makeup. "It wasn't that long ago you pined for the Englishman!" She tipped a hefty splurge of lime, basil, and mandarin oil under the running taps and watched steam rise from the roll-top bath. Slipping into the water, she felt a surge of happiness mixed with longing. Just maybe.

Later, light spilled from the kitchen onto the patio to send shadows dancing across the faces of children singing through their carol repertoire. Amelia could feel the solid warmth of Lorenzo standing behind her, and leaned into his hand as it caressed her neck in the dappled gloom. She felt Bria's eyes on her and saw a smile flit across her friend's face. As the children piled into the wagon and moved onto the next farm, they all moved back into the warmth of the winery kitchen.

Supper would be early enough for those who wanted to go to midnight mass in town. Franco, Moira, and Isabella decided to go with Agnese and Bria, while the rest lolled around the table, conversation desultory and relaxed, until each drifted off to bed. Amelia made sure she slipped away before Lorenzo could accompany her. Now was not the time.

The crisp sheets felt welcoming in the cooling air and leaning over to turn the bedside light out, guilt snatched at her happiness to mingle with pain as the thought of Moira and Natalie spun into view. A year ago tonight. She closed her eyes hoping sleep would bring a calm morning.

A creak woke her. Disoriented she struggled to sit. No light snaked through the shutters.

"Mum, it's me," Moira whispered in the dark. "No, don't turn on the light. Can I sleep with you tonight?"

"Oh, my darling girl, of course you can. Come on, hop in. How was Mass?"

"Okay, I guess. I thought it would help but it just made me sad."

"Not surprising, darling. It's a strange night, isn't it?" Amelia pulled Moira close, her hand curled around to stroke the hair at the nape of her daughter's neck, a long-remembered practice from when her firstborn was a child. "Is Franco okay?"

"Yeah, he's great, Mum. I really like him. But I wanted to be with you."

"Lucky me, darling."

They lay, propped up by pillows banked around them and talked quietly. Natalie filled their minds. A wisp of light shone from the hall as the door opened again.

"Mum? I heard you talking. Can I come in, too?"

"Come and join us, darling, there's plenty of room." She and Moira eased across the wide bed.

"Christ, your feet are like ice blocks," Moira said, drawing away from her sister.

"I know. I didn't want to wake Mike, so I slipped out without a dressing gown and slippers. Not that I have either! I don't know why, but I didn't expect it to be so cold." Lucy pulled the covers up to her chin. "Did you walk over from Franco's in your jimmies?" she asked.

"Yeah, but he bundled me in a coat and came with me."

"He's a lovely man, darling." Amelia hugged each of them.

"So's Lorenzo, Mum," Moira said, snuggling closer. "Franco thinks the world of him."

"Let's not talk about men tonight."

"Not even Dad?" Lucy asked.

"No, not even him."

"You were happy though, weren't you, Mum?" Lucy asked. "Ouch! What?" she hissed at Moira. "I'm just asking."

"Well don't?" Moira replied.

"Shh, stop it, both of you!" Amelia giggled. "We're running out of room in the bed if anyone else hears us." She chose her words carefully. "Yes, darling, Dad and I had a happy, if not always straightforward, marriage."

Lucy sighed, "Mum, we do know he played around."

Amelia sat up, her arms dropping from their shoulders. "You did?"

"Of course. But you always seemed to sort it out. Then he got sick and things changed."

"They certainly did. Now enough. No men, remember!"

"That's kind of difficult, seeing as we're all in relationships," Moira said. Her voice soft.

"I'm not," said Amelia.

"No, but you could be," Lucy gave a quiet laugh. "Mum, Lorenzo's besotted. You're not being unfaithful to Dad. He was the Janus. Please be happy. And Bria thinks it's fantastic."

"Oh, my God, you're all discussing this before there's a 'this' to discuss! Please stop."

Quiet trickled around the room.

"Mum?" Moira's voice sounded small.

"Yes, my darling, I'm still awake."

"I'm so damn sad. I'm mostly alright, but tonight is hard."

Amelia felt Moira shudder, then Lucy clambered over their legs to get on the other side of her sister. "Of course it is, darling." Her tears fell onto the doona. "Moira, what you've been through is more than so many of us ever have to deal with. And you've done it alone."

"Not really." A sob caught in her throat. "Lu has been wonderful. And you. And Adam, Cynthia. Everyone. Now Franco."

"It's still your special pain though, darling." Amelia wiped her eyes. "And I don't know if it will ever go away. Or even if you want it to go away."

"I suppose," said Lucy, her voice hoarse, "I suppose the sharpness eventually changes to a dull throb."

Moira put her head on Amelia's shoulder, and held Lucy's hand. "The thing is," she gulped, "I can go hours now, especially when I'm with Franco, without Natalie being front and center and then I feel dreadful. Guilty. I mean, what kind of mother forgets her baby?"

"Oh, Moira, darling, don't ever feel that. Whatever works for you, so that you can lead a good, no, a wonderful life, is more than fine. It's fantastic. You cannot wrap yourself in a shroud and wither away."

"And," Lucy said, "though it pains me to say, you are gorgeous and you do absolutely deserve to be happy." Silence surrounded them again until Lucy broke it. "I know we're not meant to be talking men, but Mo, do you think you and Franco are long term?"

"I don't know." Amelia and Lucy stayed still. "I mean, I really like him. And he likes me. He's talked about me staying here with him. But what if this is a rebound thing?"

Amelia sat up straight. "Now, Moira Paignton, you stop that! You are not some flibberty-gibbet. In case you've forgotten, you are thirty-nine. And I think well past rebound danger."

"Yes, but I get that she's anxious," Lucy said. "So many of our friends are on second marriages. Some third. And it's awful. Talk about blended families. I can't keep track of which child belongs to which parent."

Moira snorted. "Trust you! It's a good thing I love you, Lu." They hushed their giggles.

"Mo," Lucy paused, "do you think you'll have another baby?"

Amelia swallowed her words and waited as the quiet stretched.

"I didn't." A sob stopped Moira. "But Franco's Italian, of course he'd like a family. And he's younger than me. But he says he understands if I don't."

"He's only a couple of years younger, Moira. That's nothing." Amelia stroked her daughter's cheek. "So it is serious. My darling, if you're talking children, you are not on the rebound."

"I suppose not. But it makes me feel horribly disloyal to Natalie."

Amelia hadn't heard her self-assured and successful daughter sound so young for years.

"Darling, what better way to honor Natalie's memory than to have a baby with someone who loves you the way Franco obviously does." Amelia sat back up and, flicking on the bedside light, opened the drawer of the table.

"Mum! Turn it off," Moira said, blinking in the brilliance.

"No. I want to give you something." Amelia pulled out the book she had made, the one she had slipped into her Fendi bag, the one with Natalie's footprint on the first page. "My darling, darling girl, I've never known when was the right time, but now I know. It's right now."

Crying, Moira turned the pages, tracing her daughter's face with a tender finger. Lucy and Amelia watched, holding their breath. On the final page, the photograph of her and Natalie laughing in the park faced her. "Oh, Mum, thank you. It's beautiful. She's beautiful."

"Yes, she is. And she will always be a part of this family, darling, no matter if you have more babies, or no babies."

Chapter 34

"What do you think, Mum?"

Amelia could hear worry lacing Lucy's words as they tumbled in from Sydney. She shoved Dafne along the sofa and plumped down.

"I mean, I know I encouraged her at Christmas. You know, about Franco. But I didn't expect this. So soon. He's not like Mike. Mike grew up with a strong mum. But Franco comes from a very traditional, Catholic family, even though he's lived in the US; mother in the kitchen, kind of thing."

"That was me, Lucy. Well, not the Catholic bit."

"Not the same at all, Mum."

"Not that different. Darling, your sister is a smart, independent woman. She's been through hell—with no partner to share the middle-of-the-night agonies. That is something to which I can relate, not in the same way, but the doubts. The what-ifs and what-I-should've-dones." Amelia rushed on before Lucy could interrupt. "Franco adores our girl, thorns and all. And they want children."

"You think Moira wants to do everything differently this time?"

"Yes, I do."

"But don't you think it's too quick? They haven't even known each other a year."

"Darling, just because it took you over ten years to decide Mike is the right one, doesn't mean everyone needs to take that long!"

"Ouch, Mum, harsh."

"But true. Lucy, we have to trust Moira and Franco. Okay?" She fondled Dafne's ears, which produced a purr she thought would be heard in Australia.

"Yeah, I s'pose. I do like him. I just don't want anything else awful to happen. She's had enough heartbreak. Not just with Natalie. She didn't show it at the time, but she was pretty cut up about 'the married man.' You know when he went back to the wife?"

Amelia felt a snarl roll off her tongue. "Then he had the gall to get in touch again, when the marriage didn't survive another baby. Not bad going though. Two babies born within the space of two months."

"To be fair, Mum, he didn't know about Natalie."

"I don't care. He does not, did not, sound a decent man."

"Put like that, Franco is definitely the better option. I just have to shut up, right?"

"That's about it, darling. She needs our support." Amelia watched Dafne stalk off after a shadow. "By the way, I head from Tom Richardson yesterday. They're coming back for the wedding, even though it's term time for the kids. He said 'Italy is an education in itself!' Sweet man. It's a good thing he's retired and can afford to flit to and fro across the world for the Paigntons. Which, my darling, rather neatly brings me to you and Mike." Amelia paused, trying to think of the right words. Then just came out with it. "Do you need some help with fares?"

"Oh, Mum, really? No, we're fine. But thank you. Remember your spiel about smart independent women? Well, I'm one too, you know?"

Amelia smiled. Pride making her weepy.

✝

"Oh, my God, Leo!" Amelia straightened the painting of the girls. "Two weddings in six months. I feel a bit like Mrs. Bennett marrying off my daughters." She grinned at the image. "You never could understand why I loved Jane Austen. I remember trying to explain, but you switched off. Well, now you can't."

She moved into the kitchen and snipped basil and oregano from the pots lining the windowsill, then pulled out a board and started chopping. "Her take on social commentary, you know, exploring the dependence of women on marriage in order to gain security—not just financial but social—is still relevant for some today. That's the irony. And yet look at our girls. Two strong women, and Leo, that's thanks to both of us, and they have chosen to spend their lives with men who accept—no, more than accept, who revel—in their independence." Amelia sliced a lemon and squeezed it into the herb mixture, then picked out a couple of stray pips.

As she pounded a chicken breast, she continued her conversation. "It's human nature to want to share the highs and lows with someone you love. I'm so grateful they've found the right people with whom to do that." Amelia paused, the mallet in midair as Lucy's words came back to her. "We didn't have that, Leo. Share the highs and lows. Not always." The mallet dropped with a thud as it missed the chicken.

"And that was not entirely your fault. Funny, isn't it? Mum always wanted to know what I was doing. Not for you, or the girls, but for me. And I always brushed her off. More fool me, eh? But you know, Leo, I don't think I ever knew. Knew what I wanted to do. It's almost as if you had to die to let me find myself." Amelia felt a tear emerge then trickle down her cheek. "I always felt the strong one. Putting up with your nonsense. But perhaps I wasn't. Perhaps I hid behind convention." She tipped Dafne off the counter. "Get down!" Amelia wiped her eyes with the back of her hand. "Perhaps, Leo, I was just being righteous."

Smothering the chicken breast in the herb mix, Amelia put it in the oven, then took the uncomfortable thought out to the chair on the Juliet balcony off her bedroom. She looked down at Frank and saw tendrils from the honeysuckle she had started to train up an espalier had woven around his feet. The statuette looked as if it had always been there. She'd often see a sparrow perched on St. Francis' head, attractive to birds even in stone.

"Yuk, righteous is not a good mindset, Leo. Not healthy. I'm sorry." She put her feet up in their usual position on the parapet. "Fault on both sides. How tedious I must have seemed to you, not all the time, but certainly sometimes."

Moira's ringtone interrupted Amelia's introspection. "Hi, darling girl. You've saved me from myself. Thank you!"

"What are you talking about, Mum?"

"Oh, I've been blathering on to your father. Again."

"It is kind of weird. Are you always going to do that?"

"Oh, God, I hope not. People will really think I'm round the twist."

"Shouldn't worry about that, Mum. They already do!"

Amelia smiled to hear laughter in her daughter's voice. How could she have ever been concerned about Moira being in Italy? Being in the same time zone made life that much easier. "Okay, enough about your mad mother. What's up?"

"Two things. Both wonderful. No, actually three!"

"Righto then, spill."

"Both Adam and Cynthia are coming to the wedding. Isn't that fantastic?"

"Yes, it is, Moira, but honestly, not surprising. They love you. A lot of people do. What's the third earth-shattering event?

"You ready for this, Mum?"

"Moira!"

"Sorry, sorry, Ma, couldn't resist. Drumroll, are you ready? Are you rolling your eyes?"

"Yes, I bloody am. What is it?"

"Cynthia is in love. I mean full-blown, capital L love! I'm so over the proverbial moon for her, it hurts."

"And she didn't even have to come to Italy to find it," Amelia said, a laugh following her words. "Who is she?"

"I told you Cynthia changed jobs, right? She's moved to a smaller indie publisher. Less money, but so much more freedom. She loves it. Loves having the time to work with her writers."

"That's a lot of love in a couple of sentences. I imagine she's an excellent editor. I wish she did picture books. I'd like to work with her."

"Perhaps she could point you in the right direction. Put a word in somewhere. You should ask her."

"Maybe. So who's she in love with?"

"Well, the publisher works out of the ground floor of a brownstone—actually not far from mine—very convenient for her now she's back there. You know she's in my room? I just couldn't have anyone in Natalie's, Mum."

"Of course not, my darling." Relief flooded Amelia's heart when she didn't hear a sob from Moira at the mention of her baby.

"Anyway, she met the woman who lives above the publisher, not sure how, but hey presto! Love has blossomed. Isn't that the greatest news? And, another drum roll, please, Cynthia is bringing her to the wedding. Her name is Vivian. She's a management consultant who wants to be a florist. I've known Cyn for twenty years and never heard her so happy."

"How lovely. I really am thrilled for her, darling." She'd always liked the gorgeous Amazon. Stunning as well as an athlete. And clever. Maybe she would ask for an introduction to a coffee-table book publisher. And maybe whether she could take a few photos of her.

"Mum," Moira's voice nudged her back to the now, "what were you talking to Dad about? You sounded a bit down when you picked up the phone."

"Oh, nothing important."

"Don't believe you. Go on, tell me."

Amelia remained quiet. The thought too big to say aloud to anyone, let alone a daughter.

"Are you there? Tell me, Mum."

"Okay." Amelia took a deep breath. "I told him I was sorry for being so damn righteous."

"For God's sake, Mum," Moira's explosion barreled down the phone. "That's ridiculous. He played around. You stood by him. Through hell. That is not righteous, that's love."

"Not always, darling. I have a feeling I sort of fell into the role of understanding wife. Became a bit of a martyr. With him, anyway. Don't ever do that, Moira. It's not healthy."

"Well, I think you're being too hard on yourself. You need to..."

"Don't you dare say 'chill!'" Amelia hiccuped a sob.

"I wasn't!" Laughter followed Moira's indignation. "Or maybe I was. What I mean, Mum, is stop analyzing everything with Dad. Move on. You have a delicious Italian who so wants to be your lover."

"Moira!" Amelia spluttered. "Not what a mother wants to hear from her daughter."

But long after they said goodbye, Moira's words sounded in her head. She took her dinner out onto the balcony with a glass of Refosco. Carefree. Serene. Both states that could only be achieved with forgiveness. Not just Leo, but herself as well. And forgetting.

✝

Pigeons rose in a flutter of pique as Amelia approached the table at Caffè Dodo a couple of mornings later. She glanced down at her phone, surprised to be the first at the informal gathering, then shrugged, surprised at being surprised. Italy did not run to a timetable.

Matteo, his mouth seeming too wide for his thin face, grinned. "Cappuccino?" he asked.

"Veramente? Really?" Amelia questioned, glancing again at her watch. "It's too late for cappuccino, and you know it!" Their laughter kept the birds at bay. "Americano, per favore."

"Uffa, you are true Italiana!"

Amelia delved into her Fendi bag and pulled out a copy of the email asking her to join the initial meeting of those concerned at the exodus of Venetians from their island home. Lack of jobs in anything but the tourist industry, and the cost of living in a place made more expensive by those same tourists, had driven thousands away. Apartments that had been in families for generations being turned into accommodation for those visiting for a few days. The escalating numbers of Venetians leaving diminishing the very soul of the city the tourists came to experience.

Guilt twinged, again. Wasn't Amelia one of those very people? A smile formed as she remembered Bria's dismissal of her concerns. She heard her name and turned.

"Buongiorno, Amelia, come stai? You smile at what?" Riccardo bent to kiss her. His role as secretary of the consortium of motor taxis would bring a realistic, and important, perspective to the conversation. As would Bria, as a hotelier. Both their businesses relying on tourism.

"Buongiorno, Riccardo, molto bene, grazie. I remembered Bria telling me I am more Venetian than some Venetians. That's what made me smile."

"Aah, you worry you should not be here. Talking like this?"

"A little," Amelia agreed, sipping her Americano.

"But it is good to hear from someone who chooses to live here, as an Italian, no?"

"I guess. Anyway, I'm just going to listen. Keep quiet."

"Uffa, what good is that?"

"Well, I probably won't be able to follow it all. And," Amelia hurried on, "I don't want anyone to speak English for my sake, okay?"

"Bene." He nodded his thanks as Matteo put an espresso in front of him. "Later you ask me, if you do not understand. Capisci?" he laughed, his chair tipped back, his grin making the ends of his mustache twitch.

More people arrived. Then more. Another table was dragged over, then another. Bria introduced Amelia to those she did not know. Most of them. She could sense curiosity but not animosity. Perhaps she could contribute something, a different outlook maybe. Whatever it turned into, it was nice to be asked. And her indignation at the huge advertising billboard erected in St. Mark's Square matched any Venetians. A travesty explained away by the mayor's claim it was necessary to pay for the city's upkeep and blaming Prime Minister Berlusconi's government policies.

Amelia felt a hand on her shoulder and turned to see Arturo's grin. A question formed but he shook his head, instead easing a chair in beside her, smiling his apology at her neighbor, then listening intently. The art dealer spent more and more time in Venice, not just for James but because he liked the slower pace and the lack of traffic clogging the streets. Perhaps he felt the same as her. That it would be good to have a chance to give back to the city that had welcomed them.

Her attention wavered as voices grew more voluble and it became harder to follow what was being said. She wondered whether Bria had mentioned her inclusion to Lorenzo. The words Coca-Cola jolted her back, and the shared and palpable sense of dismay at huge amounts of money given to the city by the corporation in exchange for vending machines dotted around the piazzas. At the double standards of those same officials when they sent out decorum patrols to stop picnickers dropping cans in the canals. The irony lost on them.

An hour later, those congregated began to return to their workdays with the promise that the next meeting would produce concrete ideas to go forward. A coffee break well spent. And a determination that Venice would not degenerate into a theme park, like its namesake in Las Vegas.

That night when she and Dafne curled up together, the swirl of words and ideas replayed in Amelia's head. Not exactly carefree, but to be included had given her a true sense of belonging.

She fell asleep to an image of Leo dancing with Moira as a little girl standing on his feet as he waltzed her around the kitchen. Her dreams, all monochromatic, chopped and changed as Leo became Lorenzo, and vice versa.

The morning came too soon. She woke with a throbbing behind her eyes as if she'd been crying, and a longing to hold both her girls close. Orange juice and fresh air cleared her head and with a fresh notebook, she started making plans for another wedding. She laughed. Mrs. Bennett had work to do!

Chapter 35

Franco and Moira kissed, then started their walk down the aisle of the ancient church on the edge of the vineyard. Her dress, designed by Lucy, a soft gray silk that verged on lilac, shimmered under the deeper gray Burano lace, and reminded Amelia of the spotted ray that used to live under the jetty at Patanga. Lucy may not have won the Qantas uniform competition, but Amelia had begun to think her daughter's talents might lie in dress design rather than the pure art Leo had always wanted her to pursue.

Bells heralded the end of the nuptials and a cheer from villagers rose as the couple appeared at the church door. Lucy walked down the aisle beside Marco, Lorenzo's son, both grinning as they followed the bride and groom into the late sunshine, spring giving a warmth to the setting day. Next came Amelia and Lorenzo, then Franco's parents, followed by Mike, who escorted Isabella. A gaggle of family came next, most of whom Amelia had been unable to sort, then friends.

Cynthia and Vivian had flown in with Adam, and the triumvirate stood a little apart, looking dazed at the number of children darting in and around their parents and any adult who happened to be in the way. Their high-pitched and excited voices added to the unreserved chatter and laughter surrounding the newly weds. Amelia had taken an instant liking to Vivian, not quite as tall or as striking as her lover, but as a couple, they garnered attention for their beauty and open affection for each other.

After the photographs, Adam moved to her side with a rueful smile. Amelia took his hand. She knew how much he had hoped to be the one Moira would learn to love.

"She's happy," he said, his eyes damp behind thick lenses, "that's all that matters."

"You're a wonderful friend, Adam. You always will be."

"It would help if I could dislike Franco, but he's a good guy. Darn it!"

"Yeah, he is. It will help you not to have Moira around all the time, bumping into her on the stairs, shouting out from the kitchen. There's someone for you, Adam dear." She patted his boney hand.

"I hope so, Amelia." He stopped, kicked a stone like a toddler about to admit to a misdemeanor. "I wanted to ask you something, but I don't want you to say anything to Moira. Okay?"

"I can't promise that, Adam. Not until you tell me."

"Cynthia said you'd say that." He reddened. "Okay, fair enough." He took a deep breath then let the words tumble. "I know this isn't probably the right time, at their wedding and all, but if we can swing it, the three of us—Cyn, Vivian, and me—would like to pool funds and buy the brownstone." He finally met her eyes. "What do you think?"

"Why are you asking me, Adam? It's up to Moira."

"I know, we know. It's just that we're not sure how she'd feel. You know, about Natalie's room."

"Oh, Adam, you are a dear man." She looked across at her daughter and new son-in-law. Their happiness evident in their smiles and clutched hands. Yet, every now and then, a shadow would flit across Moira's face. "I won't say anything. But don't mention it today."

"No, no, of course not. We thought after the weekend—when things have calmed down a bit." He frowned. "Do you think we should talk to them together? Or just Moira?"

"Together. They're a couple now. But don't expect an instant answer. It's going to be an emotional decision." Amelia saw Lucy and Mike approach, then get waylaid by Tom Richardson. She leaned in close. "For what it's worth, I think it's a brilliant idea. And Adam, I know she's glad you came. We all are. "

"Well, I had to see what Italy was all about! It's very different to New York."

"And?" Lorenzo joined the conversation and slipped his arm around Amelia's waist, pulling her close. "You like?"

"I do. This part anyway."

"Tomorrow you come for lunch. I will show you the vineyard. You would like that?"

"Sure, thank you."

"Bene." Lorenzo turned to clap Franco's father on the shoulder. "Now we are family, eh."

Amelia caught the gist of the rapid conversation, something along the lines of two great vineyards becoming one. She smiled. Not a chance. Neither man would relinquish a single vine.

And, Moira had told her, Franco would never consider rejoining his family's business, not after Lorenzo had shown him such trust. Perhaps that had become clear to Franco's family when he said he wanted his marriage to be at the Scutari Vineyard. Amelia touched Lorenzo's hand and nodded toward the vehicles. She looked around for Bria. They had to get back to help Agnese, who had slipped out of the church once the vows had been taken, not even waiting for the benediction.

Bria, her severe white chignon softened by a single pink rose tucked into the pleat, smiled. "Come, cara. Agnese will be fine, but I would like to make sure all is well. The others will follow." As she drove she said, "Moira will be most happy now, eh?"

"Yes, I think so, too." Amelia sighed. "Who knew all this would happen in such a short time? Two weddings in the space of six months. And both in Italy!"

"It is good that Franco has lived in America. He has, how do you say, eh, a better understanding of strong women?"

"Oh, come on, Bria. Italy has its fair share."

"Sì," she agreed, "but not always do the men like that. Mamma's boys." She laughed. "But Franco, he loves her and knows that to keep her, he must let her be herself. Many Italian men are not so good at that."

"Was your husband?" Amelia asked, always careful not to overstep the line.

"Yes. Our marriage was good."

Amelia felt Bria's eyes glance across. "That's a moving definition, isn't it?" she asked. "I thought I had a good marriage until it ended. Or until Leo got so bad there was no 'us' anymore. But the more time passes, the more I realize it was never a partnership." She paused. "Not entirely Leo's fault."

"You were not the one with others." Bria said.

"No, but perhaps I should've been more assertive. About what I wanted for me. Not just about the girls."

"Ahh, Amelia, we cannot fall backward. Only ahead."

"Yeah, I know. But I'm so glad Moira can continue working, thanks to Arturo introducing her to the art world here. She's excited. And so is Franco." Amelia laughed. "Do you know what he said to her?" She saw Bria shake her head. "He told her their marriage will stay alive because every time Moira goes away, it will be a honeymoon when she returns. How's that for Italian charm?"

"And you, Amelia?" Bria asked. "What of you?"

"Let's focus on today. I'm running out of words of wisdom about marriage. Good thing I don't have any more daughters."

✝

Not a skerrick of air ruffled the canals or the lagoon as Venice sat in a torpid bowl of summer soup. July, the hottest month and most Venetians' least favorite time of the year, had become one of Amelia's best liked. She avoided the crowded hotspots where tourists waved maps and hats to generate brief puffs of air or to slap away mosquitoes. She stayed away from the Lido, despite sometimes longing for a dip in the languorous waters of the lagoon. She even avoided, much to Matteo's chagrin, Caffè Dodo at the Campo Ghetto Nuovo.

The afternoon flew by as Amelia checked and double-checked captions for the galleys of her coffee-table book. Her last chance to make sure it was exactly as she wanted, with input from the editor. He not being familiar with Papua New Guinea, it had been up to Amelia to ensure spelling remained consistent with both names and any Pidgin English. Nerves flipped around in her tummy. What if the book didn't sell? People didn't like her angles, her takes? "I can do this!" She muttered her mantra and shut the book with a sigh.

Leo looked over her shoulder from his perch on the filing cabinet. Hot and sticky, Amelia closed the computer, lifted her hair off her neck and turned to him.

"I've been meaning to talk to you, Leo." She tipped her chair back as her face broke into a broad smile. "I think I'm falling in love. Not something I thought would happen. And, Leo, not something I have chased. But it feels right." She looked down at her bare hands. Even the white band from her wedding ring, worn for so many years, had faded. "It's a different kind of love. Deeper somehow. But perhaps that's because we're older. I mean, it's not like we have years and years stretching ahead of us." Her eyes watered. "And Leo, I do believe he'd be faithful. And that is something I crave. I couldn't handle another us. I'm too old and it hurts too much." She wiped her tears. "The girls like him, Leo. They've encouraged me. They're happy. And although Moira has a sadness that can sink her some-times, Franco adores her and can bring her back. And I've told you about Lucy's baby. I'm so hoping Moira has one soon too." Amelia stood and looked over the mezzanine rail at her apartment. "I've made this place mine, Leo. Your paintings are here, of course, but it's my space. So, my old mucker, my old lover, the time has come for me to stop talking to you. There's someone alive, who I hope is falling in love with me, and there must be room for him. And there can't be with you around." She picked up the photograph, kissed it, and tucked it behind the other photos on the cabinet. With a laugh, she went down the spiral stairs and poured a glass of Pellegrino, tossed a slice of lemon in and went out to the balcony.

The quiet of the early evenings, when day-trippers left Venice for the Venetians, and for her, filled her with delight. With all the windows and doors flung wide, Amelia usually got some through breeze, and the worst of the mozzies, the loathed zanzore that guidebooks didn't mention, didn't bother flying up to her balcony although, just in case, lemon grass flourished in her planters and citronella candles flickered every evening. She sat down and put her feet on the parapet and watched as Dafne cleaned her face with fastidious grace. Further down the canal she saw a woman tend pot plants high up on her altana, the tiny wooden terraces balanced on some of the rooftops of Venice.

This was carefree. A voice at her door brought her back. She dropped her feet and sat up. It sounded like Lorenzo.

"Oh, bloody hell," she muttered, looking down at her paint splattered shorts and torn T-shirt. "What's he doing here?" She tiptoed to her bedroom. Perhaps he'd go away if she didn't answer.

"Ciao, Amelia!" His voice came again.

She waited.

"Cara, I know you are here." She could hear a smile in his voice. "I see James downstairs. He let me in."

"Bugger!" She glanced in the mirror. Not a good look. "Oh well, he might as well see me as I am and not dolled up." She twisted her hair up and clipped it, calling, "Solo un minuto!"

She grimaced at her reflection. "Not quite so witch-like, I suppose."

"Ciao, Lorenzo, I didn't expect you until tomorrow." She laughed at his face. "You see before you the real me!"

"Tu sei perfetto, cara mia. Perfect." He pulled her into a bear hug, then kissed her.

"Well, you're a charmer, that's for sure. Come in. What are you doing here?"

"I do not want to wait one more day. So I arrive early."

"Don't you have a vineyard to run?" She disentangled herself and led him into the kitchen. "It's a good thing I never run out of wine or Prosecco!"

"Give to me, I will open." He took the bottle and eased it from the cork with a satisfying pop. "And no, I am not needed. Franco is most efficient. And today Moira is back so I think I shall leave and come to you."

"Does Bria know you're here?" Amelia asked, reaching for two flutes.

"No. I come to you first."

"Why don't you sit on the balcony, there's a little breeze out there, while I have a quick shower and change."

"I like to see your legs." He nodded to her shorts. "You are painting?"

"No, just lolling about. I got too hot working up in the mezzanine so I took the afternoon off."

"That is good. Now I do not disturb you."

"Darling, you are disturbing me." Amelia laughed at his frown. "I'm hardly dressed to receive visitors. Actually, I'm hardly dressed." She pushed him out the doors.

"I like that too!" His gravelly laugh followed her into her room.

She peeled the tatty clothes off then threw herself under the shower in the guest room. Her hair washed and legs shaved, she realized her dressing gown hung happily on the hook behind her bathroom door. "Damn!" She peeped out the door then, wrapped in a towel, sprinted across to her room. She blow dried most of the water off her hair, then finger combed it, before sliding a cotton caftan over matching lace undies, applied eyeliner and mascara and spritzed J'Adore in the usual places. "That'll have to do!"

"Okay, I'm presentable now," she said as Lorenzo stood. She reached up to kiss him, then pulled away when she saw Signor Malvestio beaming from the next balcony. She blushed and waved.

"We are chatting about the crazy Australian who lives here," Lorenzo said. He nodded to the cigar-smoking Italian who moved inside with a slight smile.

"The poor man. He's probably heard a few dramas." She picked up her glass, condensation making it slippery, and sipped.

"That is good. We Italians love drama!" Lorenzo watched Amelia drink, then grinned. "I see you run, just now. In your towel!"

"Oh God, another indignity to live down," she said. "Come on, let's sit."

"You are happy I come to you?"

"Of course, darling. Just surprised. I'm not exactly a glamour puss in my shorts, though. That's when age catches you unawares. Thirty years ago, I wouldn't have minded. Hell, twenty years ago."

"You are like a young girl, Amelia!"

"Now I know you're full of nonsense, Lorenzo."

"No, cara. It is attitude. That is the word, yes?" He hesitated. She nodded. "I suppose so."

"I like your freedom. You do not worry so much. It is good." He took her hand. "Amelia, you must take a compliment, eh."

"Thank you, then, Lorenzo. Would you like to stay for supper? Or we could go out?"

"I would like to stay here. I can help."

"You mean supervise!"

"No, I too can cook. We work together."

"Okay. Come on then." Amelia slipped a CD into the player and they chatted quietly to the strains of Zucchero singing duets as they prepared pasta cacciatore, then took their plates out to the balcony.

Amelia watched Lorenzo wipe his plate clean with a heel of Tuscan bread, then push his plate away with a satisfied sigh. He poured more wine for them and said, "Delizioso, cara! Grazie!"

"Da prego," Amelia replied, "you helped."

They sat in silence, neither bothered about putting on more music, and watched the sun drift away and lights flicker on along the canal.

"I'll get a candle." Amelia said, rising from her chair.

Lorenzo reached for her, easing her onto his lap. "No, cara mia, this is perfect." He nuzzled her neck as his hand ran down her back. "Amelia, tonight, posso restore? I would like to stay, cara."

The hair rose on her neck and a shiver trilled over her shoulders. It had been so long. She looked into his eyes. Dark and warm now, but she had seen them glitter with anger. Was she ready for this? Commitment? Of course this had been coming but somehow she hadn't expected it now. Why not? Would it be any easier to have a planned date to sleep together?

"Cara?" His voice brought her back.

She touched his lips with her finger, then her lips. She felt his smile under hers.

"Yes, darling, please stay the night."

Chapter 36

Amelia swung the Fiat 500 through the gates of Scutari Vineyard. The drive from Venice had become less terrifying with practice, and she'd had a bit of that lately. She grinned. Stella loped down the lane to meet her and, as Amelia braked, stuck her head in the open window.

"Where's your master, you daft dog?" She petted the white and ginger whiskery face before leaning across, opening the door and allowing Stella to clamber onto the passenger seat, then eased the car forward again. Amelia remembered Lorenzo had said he had a meeting that morning in town, but hoped to be back in time for lunch. She didn't mind if he wasn't there. She'd wander back down the road to photograph the sunflower field she'd passed just before the gates, but first Agnese, and a cup of coffee at the kitchen table.

The smell of lavender greeted Amelia as she entered the kitchen and saw a milk churn filled with the last of the summer blooms on the table, a few fallen petals made a pretty pattern on the aged pine. The housekeeper looked up from the pastry rosettes she was forming with a smile and nodded to the ever-present coffee pot.

"Buongiorno, signora, come stai? Caffè?"

Amelia bussed her cheek as she passed and poured a cup, then pulled out a chair. She wondered if Agnese knew her bottom lip trembled like a conga eel.

"That pie looks good enough to eat. Is it for lunch?"

"Sì, the boss he bring two guest."

"Oh, okay, who?"

Agnese shrugged, and Amelia felt a tug of disappointment at the thought of sharing Lorenzo for lunch as well as dinner, when Franco and Moira would join them. Her fault, she should have planned the week better but she had to get back for the next meeting about keeping Venetians in Venice. The group had welcomed her, thanks to Bria, and Riccardo, and she wanted to show her commitment to the cause and, she had come to realize, her perspective as a foreigner calmed some of the more voluble participants.

"What time are they arriving?" she asked.

"No lo so—lunchtime." Agnese shrugged again.

Amelia recognized this was probably a common occurrence. Sudden visitors, particularly at the veraison and crop thinning. She loved this time of year when the grape berries started to change color. Those clustered at the top of the vines turning first before different shades flowed between the leaves in a fountain of green and yellow orbs.

She drained her coffee, left her case for Lorenzo to take up, still not entirely comfortable in assuming his bedroom was also her bedroom, told Agnese she'd be back in an hour or so and, after telling Stella to stay put, headed out with her camera.

Wandering in a maze of giant sunflowers, bees flitted from face to face in their bid to store as much nectar as possible in their honey stomach before heading home to their hives. Amelia took photo after photo. The ease of the digital world.

If she had film in the camera, she would not have been so snap happy. "Not snaps," she muttered, remembering James' words. "I am a photographer!" she laughed. "And in love. Oh hell, and late."

She regretted not taking some water after her hasty return and slowed as she neared the villa. Her cheeks would be beyond flushed and really she should change her blouse before meeting Lorenzo's business colleagues. Not a good first impression. She wondered if she could sneak in and tidy up, then remembered her suitcase in the kitchen.

Hearing voices on the patio, she pushed her sunglasses up, puffed her hair, and rounded the corner to greet everyone.

"Amore," Lorenzo leaped up to kiss her. "You are here. That is good."

"Sorry, I'm late, darling," Amelia said, "I got lost in the sunflowers. And then I rushed. I must look a mess."

"Never, cara, and it is no matter. Come," he took her hand and, as he turned, unblocked her view, "let me introduce you to an old friend, and his wife—a new friend." He smiled.

Amelia, glad she could put her flushed face down to her rush, felt her stomach flip.

"Good God!" The words exploded from Chad's mouth.

"Hello, Chad," Amelia managed to get the words out as she put her hand out, "how nice to see you again."

"How is this possible?" Lorenzo asked, delight wreathed his face.

Before Chad could say anything, Amelia jumped in. "Isn't it a small world? Although I suppose not so small if you consider you're both in viniculture and both in Italy. Especially this part of the country." She knew she was babbling.

"We met at Borgoluce—you know I always stay there, Lorenzo?" Chad interrupted Amelia's flow as he leaned in to kiss her cheeks. "Oh, about a year ago, I think it was. How lovely to see you again, Amelia. How are you?"

"All good, thanks, Chad." She felt Lorenzo's stare and forced a smile. "There was a dreadful man staying at the hotel, too. We met trying to avoid him." She heard the words as they came out of her mouth and knew it sounded cockeyed.

"I wonder what happened to him?" Chad helped out.

"Back in Wyoming, or Delaware, or wherever he came from, I hope."

"Aren't you going to introduce me?" A svelte woman stood. Her off-white linen trousers and sage T-shirt made Amelia feel disheveled, old, and discombobulated.

"Yes, of course, sorry, darling. Amelia, this is my wife, Gail."

"How do you do?"

"A pleasure," Amelia replied, her voice taut. "Would you all mind if I disappeared for a moment and tidied up? I'm sure I have sunflower seeds in my hair. Back in a moment."

"Your case is upstairs and your wine will be here," Lorenzo called after her scurried departure.

Glaring at herself in the bathroom mirror, Amelia asked, "How can that woman have had a baby in the last few months and look like that?" She washed her face and reapplied makeup. "And," she continued, "where the hell is the baby?"

Even Agnese's delicious sciachiatta, the Sicilian meat pie she had been making when Amelia arrived, could do little to ease her tension. Instead of the usual leisurely pace of lunch on the patio, the lingering over a final glass of wine or coffee as laughter danced across the table, the air fizzed between the women.

Chad attempted to lighten the atmosphere, relating stories of how wine had come to take over his life. As Amelia listened, instead of being charmed as she had been at Borgoluce, she found him glib. Self-satisfied. How had she been so wrong? She glanced at Lorenzo. So wrong about both men? The boar had turned into the charmer, and vice versa. She looked at Gail, obviously bored by the conversation and the company. No mention of a baby. Amelia felt Lorenzo's puzzled eyes as she questioned Chad and Gail about their child.

"Oh, Mason's in London, with the nanny," came her airy response.

"Yes, Gail needed a break," Chad said. "And, as she's never been to Italy with me, it seemed the perfect opportunity." He raised his glass to his wife.

Gail's face darkened. "How could you possibly know about him?"

"Chad mentioned it," Amelia replied.

"He didn't know last time he came to Italy."

"Well, he must have, otherwise how would I know?"

"That is what I wondered."

"Gail, darling," Chad broke in, "it must have been after the reception at San Salvatore. That's where I was when you told me. Remember?"

"Whatever!" Gail shrugged, then sighed. "No one told me babies are so exhausting."

Gail's bid for sympathy thudded across the table as Amelia thought of Natalie. Her fingers gripped the wineglass and she felt Lorenzo's touch on the clenched hand in her lap. She sent him a grateful look as he stood, bringing the meal to a close.

"Va bene allora, Chad, we will meet tomorrow for coffee to finalize shipping details, eh? Gail, I hope you will enjoy the rest of your stay. Come, I shall walk you to the car."

"Lovely to see you again, Amelia." Chad's easy smile, the one that had flipped her stomach a year ago, this time curdled it. She stood to receive his kiss, forced a smile for Gail, and began to gather plates.

✝

Amelia loaded the dishwasher, insisting Agnese sit down with coffee and rest. She knew the housekeeper would be making something special for dinner later.

"You are okay?" She asked Amelia.

"Of course. Lunch was delicious. Thank you. Will you show me how to prepare sciachiatta? The pastry tastes like something between a pizza and calzone."

"Ma certo, signora."

Amelia thanked her again and turned as Lorenzo returned.

"Come, Amelia, let's walk." He looked quizzical. "So," he said, as they walked under the wisteria, the blooms long gone, "I think lunch was difficult. For us all." He took her hand. "You did not mention you knew Chad."

"Why would I mention someone I didn't know you knew?"

He shrugged. "There was tension? I understand your feelings about their attitude to the child, but it was strained before that."

"I didn't like her."

Lorenzo nodded. "She is young, and perhaps silly. Like my second wife." They walked in silence, heading toward where workers thinned the crop. He stopped and turned Amelia to him. "You had an affair?"

"No!"

"But you wanted to?"

"My God, Lorenzo. Have I ever questioned you about your wives, note, I say plural? Or your mistresses or girlfriends? Plural again!"

"That is different." He stalked ahead. Stella, her tail between her legs, looked from her master to Amelia.

She flushed and refused to follow. "Why? Why is that different?" She glared after him. "Because you're a man. Get into the real world, Lorenzo," she shouted. Heads popped up, then dropped back to work as the vignaiolo stormed between the vines.

"Sod this! I'm going home." Amelia stomped back to the house, past Agnese in the kitchen and up to the bedroom.

"Hah, glad I didn't unpack." She threw her makeup bag in the case, snapped it shut, then dropped it by the door. She went to the window, taking deep breaths as angry tears dried, knowing she couldn't drive in this state. Images flashed behind closed lids. Of Leo, which became superimposed by Lorenzo. "Goddamnhim!"

"Who?" Lorenzo's tentative voice came from the door. "I can enter?"

"It's your room, Lorenzo." She nodded, but refused to turn around.

"No, cara, I want this to be our room." He touched her shoulders. "Amelia," his thumbs brushed her neck, "we are new together. We have much to learn. About each other, eh?"

She leaned back into his chest, then jerked upright.

"Who do you damn, cara?" He asked again, drawing her back.

"You," she paused. "And Leo."

"Aah, not Chad?"

"Nope. I have to care to damn someone."

"So, that is good, no," he turned her to face him. "We are good, eh? Our first fight." He kissed her, tenderness in his lips as she relaxed. "You know what we do now, cara mia?" His hands slid down her back. "In Italy, it is customary to make love after we argue." His beard tickled her breasts.

"I think," Amelia said, nuzzling his neck, "you will find that is not just an Italian affair."

✝

Hurrying across the boards, water sluicing their feet, as the acqua alta continued to rise, the October air heavy with moisture even though the rain had stopped, Amelia felt Lorenzo's hand tug her under the shelter of a portico.

"What?" she asked, her laughter carefree as she looked out at the sky heavy with full clouds waiting to burst again. "Come on, let's get back before the next downpour."

"Uffa!" Lorenzo stamped his feet, droplets arcing off his shoes. "Since 2003 we wait for the MOSE. Next year, then next year, then another year. Venice will sink before the barriers to stop flooding are finished." He scowled.

"What happened to your famous Italian engineers?" Amelia teased her lover.

"Seventy-eight metal barriers as tall as our tallest palazzo raised by air being pumped into them. That is engineering!"

Amelia smoothed Lorenzo's wet hair back from his forehead. "I read that the gates will only be triggered when water levels reach 110 cm, so they still won't save St. Mark's Piazza."

He nodded. "Certo, but this," he kicked the water, "most of Venice will not have this!" He shook his head. "Politicians, bah, now they say maybe 2023. Corruption. Scandal. The Italian way!" Lorenzo pulled Amelia close and wiped water from her face. "Amore mio, Venezia, it is too much. Come to the vineyard."

"The forecast is good for the weekend, darling. This is the last day you'll get soaked, I promise. And Bria's coming for supper tomorrow. And I think Arturo is in town as well, so he and James might join us."

"No, cara mia. Come and live with me. We can marry, eh? No more running back and forth. Here sometimes, there sometimes. Let us always be together." He kissed her lips, parted in surprise. "Lo sai che ti amo, you know I love you, eh?"

"Oh, Lorenzo, anch'io ti amo." Amelia smiled up into his deep brown eyes, delighting in his love. "But," she took his hand, "but I came to Venice to find myself, I'm not ready to let that go. I don't know if I ever will be."

"We do not have to marry, Amelia. I wish it. But I understand if you do not. I like to be married."

"I know you do, darling! I'd be Signora Scutari, the third!"

"Do not laugh, Amelia. I am serious. Please, amore, ti amo."

"Oh, darling," she stroked his cheek then kissed him, "it's a great honor, thank you. Please, you know I love you, but I am finally doing something with my life that is all mine. My book is coming out in January. I love my palazzo apartment." She paused. "I was going to tell you tonight. Lorenzo, the publisher likes my take, my perspective, a bit different to other picture books."

Rain blew in again and he kissed her wet face. "Amelia, that is wonderful."

She nodded. "I've been asked to do a similar one for Sydney. Maybe other places, if they sell well."

"You would leave Italy?" He frowned.

"No, darling, I'm not leaving. I'd go for a couple of months. Be there for Lucy when she has the baby, then come home. You could join me for a few weeks. Mike knows a lot of people in the wine industry in the Hunter Valley, and in South Australia. I don't know the areas. We could explore them together. Lorenzo, my darling, Venice is home. I'll come back."

"It will always be this, amore mio?"

"I don't know, Lorenzo. But for now, yes."

He looked down at their joined hands, leaned in and kissed her again. "Then that is what it is. You must find your serenissima."

Acknowledgements

Finding Serenissima is my first foray into contemporary fiction and, in my naivety, I thought it would take much less research than my more usual genre of historical fiction. How wrong I was!

Readers with an eagle eye pounce on the novelist with comments like "planes, when coming from the United States, always arrive in Europe in the morning, not the evening," sort of thing. They keep writers on their collective toes.

It is for this reason that Beta readers are so vital to a writer. They catch those inconsistencies, those blips that just don't make sense. And so I thank my wonderful first readers: Kay Chapman, Sandy Lease, Val Miller, Emy Thomas, and my Australian specialist, Mary Cadell. This time, I also called on Julie Blais for help with my dodgy Italian and assure you that all linguistic errors are mine entirely.

The novel might come from the author's imagination, but it takes many people, apart from those important first readers, to get a book into the reader's hands. I am fortunate to be published by Vine Leaves Press (long may that last), however, the manuscript still must go through an acquisitions editor, so I thank Alana King for giving the story a thumbs up. Next comes the developmental editor, who for this book is Ann S. Epstein.

It is she who caught further irregularities in plot, flow, character, and so on. *Finding Serenissima* is infinitely more readable because of her care and attention to detail. Nick Taylor, renamed the Comma King, then polished my words before the manuscript moved through to setting and proof editing, which come under the guardianship of Amie McCracken. The final touch, a vital touch, comes with the magic produced by the cover designer, Jessica Bell.

In this digital age, it is easy to assume readers rely solely on the internet for purchases. Thankfully, there are many readers who still love the intimacy of a bookshop, so I thank booksellers in all the countries in which my books are sold for taking a gamble on me.

My family and friends all now recognize when I am in "writing" mode. They leave me alone, and I thank them for not taking umbrage when I don't reply to either phone calls or emails in a timely manner.

And, as always, my husband John exhibits endless patience. The characters in my head, their words and actions, take over my thoughts, and I have been known to sit with them rather than him. Nonetheless, coffee, tea, and wine appear at my elbow at requisite times, along with encouragement and love. Thank you!

Glossary

a Dio piacendo – God willing

acqua alta – high water (flood)

alla goccia – good luck lit. to the last drop

assolutamente – absolutely

benvenuta – welcome

cadastral – stamp duty

calli – alleys

castellana – chatelaine / hotelier

che cosa? – why not? / what's the matter?

cliente abituale – a regular

CRAFT – Can't Remember a Flipping Thing

Doolally – mad (Deolali, a transit camp in India for British
   army troops)

doona – duvet (Australian)

drongo – a bird, and a simpleton, first used by the RAAF to
   describe a new recruit (Australian)

eccoci qui – we are here

enoteca – small shop, sometimes with a bar

il tuo soliti? – you are alone?

la bella vita – the good life

le mie figlie – my daughters

meri – housegirl (Pidgin English)

miei cari – my darlings

molto facile – very easy

motoscafo – motorboat (motoscafi pl.)

non ora, quando – if not now, when

pedalo – pedal boat

piacere di conoscerti – pleased to meet you

sciattona – whore

senza una donna – without a woman

stai bene? – are you well? / are you okay?

vaporetto – water taxi (vaporetti pl.)

vorrei – I'd like

Vine Leaves Press

Enjoyed this book?
Go to *vineleavespress.com* to find more.
Subscribe to our newsletter:

BV - #0080 - 060225 - C0 - 216/138/20 - PB - 9783988321350 - Matt Lamination